"What was [...]

DJ began brushing the snow off [...]. "A kiss. Apparently it's been a while for you, as well," Beau said. He began helping her brush off the snow.

"I can do it myself," she snapped. She wanted to tell him that she'd only kissed him back because he'd taken her by surprise. But he didn't give her a chance to lie.

"Don't look so shocked. It was just a kiss, right? It wasn't like either of us felt anything."

"I was asking why you thought you could get away with kissing me like that. Or was that part of the bargain you made with my father?" She hoped he caught the sarcasm.

"I was merely doing my job protecting you. Since the one thing your father didn't make clear is who I'm protecting you from. As for the kiss, it just seemed like a good idea. It won't happen again."

"You're right about that, because I don't need your so-called protection."

CARDWELL CHRISTMAS CRIME SCENE

BY
B. J. DANIELS

First Published in Great Britain 2016
By Mills & Boon, an imprint of HarperCollins*Publishers*
1 London Bridge Street, London, SE1 9GF

© 2016 Barbara Heinlein

ISBN: 978-0-263-91924-0

46-1216

Our policy is to use papers that are natural, renewable and recyclable products and made from wood grown in sustainable forests. The logging and manufacturing processes conform to the legal environmental regulations of the country of origin.

Printed and bound in Spain
by CPI, Barcelona

B. J. Daniels is a *New York Times* and *USA TODAY* bestselling author. She wrote her first book after a career as an award-winning newspaper journalist and author of thirty-seven published short stories. She lives in Montana with her husband, Parker, and three springer spaniels. When not writing, she quilts, boats and plays tennis. Contact her at www.bjdaniels.com, on Facebook or on Twitter, @bjdanielsauthor.

With utmost appreciation I dedicate this Cardwell book to Kimberly Rocha, the craziest, most loving, generous, truly beautiful fan I've yet to meet.

Chapter One

DJ Justice opened the door to her apartment and froze. Nothing looked out of place and yet she took a step back. Her gaze went to the lock. There were scratches around the keyhole. The lock set was one of the first things she'd replaced when she'd rented the apartment.

She eased her hand into the large leather hobo bag that she always carried. Her palm fit smoothly around the grip of the weapon, loaded and ready to fire, as she slowly pushed open the door.

The apartment was small and sparsely furnished. She never stayed anywhere long, so she collected nothing of value that couldn't fit into one suitcase. Spending years on the run as a child, she'd had to leave places in the middle of the night with only minutes to pack.

But that had changed over the past few years. She'd just begun to feel…safe. She liked her job, felt content here. She should have known it couldn't last.

The door creaked open wider at the touch of her finger, and she quickly scanned the living area. Moving deeper into the apartment, she stepped to the open bathroom door and glanced in. Nothing amiss. At a glance she could see the bathtub, sink and toilet as well as the mirror on the medicine cabinet. The shower door was clear glass. Nothing behind it.

That left just the bedroom. As she stepped soundlessly toward it, she wanted to be wrong. And yet she knew someone had been here. But why break in unless he or she planned to take something?

Or leave something?

Like the time she'd found the bloody hatchet on the fire escape right outside her window when she was eleven. That message had been for her father, the blood from a chicken, he'd told her. Or maybe it hadn't even been blood, he'd said. As if she hadn't seen his fear. As if they hadn't thrown everything they owned into suitcases and escaped in the middle of the night.

She moved to the open bedroom door. The room was small enough that there was sufficient room only for a bed and a simple nightstand with one shelf. The book she'd been reading the night before was on the nightstand, nothing else.

The double bed was made—just as she'd left it.

She started to turn away when she caught a glimmer of something out of the corner of her eye. Ice ran down her spine as she dropped the gun back into her shoulder bag and stepped closer. Something had been tucked between the pillows and duvet. Gingerly picking up the edge of the duvet, she peeled it back an inch at a time. DJ braced herself for something bloody and dismembered, her mind a hamster on a wheel, spinning wildly.

But what she found was more disturbing than blood and guts. As she uncovered part of it, she saw familiar blank eyes staring up at her. Her breath caught in her throat as tears stung her eyes.

"Trixie?" she whispered, voice breaking, as she stared at the small rag doll's familiar face.

On the run with her father, she'd had little more than the clothes on her back except for the rag doll that had been her only companion since early childhood.

"We should throw this old thing away," her father had said after a dog tore the doll from her hands once and he'd had to chase it down to retrieve what was left because she'd been so hysterical. "I'll buy you another doll. A pretty one, not some stuffed fabric one," he'd pleaded.

She'd been so upset that he'd relented and let her keep the doll she'd always known as Trixie. But she could tell that he would have been happier to get rid of the thing. She wondered if it brought him bad memories, since it was clear that the doll was handmade. Even the clothing. She liked to pretend that her mother had made it for her. If her mother hadn't died in childbirth.

Was that why her father wished she didn't care so much for the doll? Because it brought back the grief, the loss? That might explain why he had seemed to want nothing to do with anything from the past, including her doll. Not that she'd ever understood her father.

Life with him had been sparse and sporadic. He had somehow kept her fed and clothed and managed to get her into school—at least for a while until they were uprooted again. But the incident with the doll now made her wonder.

From as far back as she could remember, she'd believed that the doll with the sewn face and the dull, dark stitched eyes needed her as much as she needed it.

Now she half feared all she would find was Trixie's dismembered head. But as she drew back the covers, she saw that the body was still intact. Someone had left it for her tucked under the covers almost…tenderly. With trembling fingers, she picked up the treasured rag doll, afraid something awful had been done to her that would spoil one of the few good memories she had of her childhood.

Cupping the precious doll in her hands, DJ began to cry—for herself and for Trixie. The doll was in incredible shape for how old she was, not to mention what she must have been through over the years. DJ thought of her being lost, someone discarding her in a trash can as nothing more than junk and that awful feeling she'd had that she would never see her again.

So how had Trixie miraculously turned up again?

Heart in her throat, she looked closer at the doll.

Something was wrong.

The doll looked exactly like Trixie, but… She studied the handmade clothing. It looked as pristine as the doll. Maybe whoever had found it had washed it, taken care of it all these years…

For what possible purpose?

As happy as she'd been to see the doll again, now she realized how unlikely that was. Why would anyone care about some silly rag doll? And how could someone possibly know she was the one who'd lost it all those years ago?

After being her constant companion from as far back as she could remember, Trixie had been the worse for wear before DJ had misplaced her. The doll had spent too many years tucked under one of DJ's chubby arms. So how—

With a jolt, she recalled the accident she'd had with the doll and the dog that had taken off with it all those years ago. The dog had ripped off one of Trixie's legs. With DJ screaming for help, her father had chased down the dog, retrieved the leg and later, at her pleading, painstakingly sewn it back on with the only thread he could find, black.

Her fingers trembling, she lifted the dress hem and peered under the only slightly faded red pantaloons. With both shock and regret, she saw that there was no black thread. No seam where the leg had been re-attached.

This wasn't her doll.

It surprised her that at thirty-five, she could feel such loss for something she'd been missing for so many years.

She stared at the rag doll, now more confused than ever. Why would people break into her apartment to leave it for her? They had to have known that she'd owned one exactly like it. Wouldn't they realize that she'd know the difference between hers and this one? Or was that the point?

DJ studied the doll more closely. She was right. This one and Trixie were almost *identical*, which meant that whoever had made them had made *two*. Why?

She'd never questioned before where her doll had come from. Trixie was in what few photographs she'd seen of her childhood, her doll locked under her arm almost like an extension of herself.

Like hers, this one looked more than thirty years old. The clothing was a little faded, the face even blanker than it had been all those years ago, but not worn and faded like Trixie had been when DJ had lost her.

DJ felt a chill. So who had left this for her?

Someone who'd had this doll—a doll that was identical to hers before Trixie's accident. Someone who'd known there had been two identical dolls. Someone who knew this doll would be meaningful to her.

But why break in to leave it for her tucked under the covers? And why give it to her now? A life on the run had taught her one thing. The people who had left this wanted something from her. They could have mailed it with a note. Unless they had some reason to fear it could be traced back to them?

Regrettably, there was only one person she could ask, someone she hadn't spoken to in seven years. Her father.

She took a couple of deep breaths as she walked back into the living room. She'd left the door open in case she had needed to get out fast, but now she moved to close and lock it.

With her back against the door, she stared at the apartment she'd come to love. She'd made a life for herself here, and just the thought of being forced to give it up—

She was considering what her intruder might want from her when she felt a prick and dropped the doll. Sucking on her bleeding finger, she stared down at the rag doll. The dress had gaped open in the back to expose a straight pin—and what looked like the corner of a photograph.

Carefully picking up the doll so it didn't stick her again, she unpinned the photo and pulled it out. There were three people in the snapshot. A man and two women, one young, one older, all dark-haired. The young woman, the only one smiling, was holding a baby.

She flipped the photo over. Written in a hurried hand were the words: *Your family.*

What? She quickly turned the photograph back over and stared at the people pictured there.

She'd never seen any of them before, but there was something familiar about the smiling woman holding the baby. DJ realized with a start that the woman looked like her. But how was this possible if her mother had died in childbirth?

If it was true and these people were family...was it possible she was the baby in the photo? Why would her father have lied if that were the case? He knew how much she would have loved having family. He'd always said it was just the two of them. But what if that wasn't true?

Still, she thought as she studied the photo, if it was true, wouldn't they have contacted her? Then she realized they *were* contacting her now. But why wait all these years, and why do it like this?

The reason hit her hard. No one had wanted her to know the truth.

But someone had decided to tell her.

Or *warn* her, she thought with a shiver.

Chapter Two

"Are you sure it's the same doll? I thought you lost it years ago."

DJ gripped the utilitarian standard black phone tighter as she looked through the thick Plexiglas in the prison visiting room at her father.

Walter Justice had been a big, handsome man who'd charmed his way out of trouble all his life—until it caught up with him one night when he'd gotten involved in a robbery that went badly and he ended up doing time for second-degree murder. He had aged well even in prison, and that charm was still there in the twinkle of his blue eyes, in his crooked-toothed smile, in the soft reassuring sound of his voice.

She hadn't been able to wait until visiting day, so this was the best that could be done on short notice with the prison warden. But as surprised and pleased as her father had been to see her, he'd given the doll only a cursory look.

"It's the same doll," she said impatiently into the phone. "It's just not *mine*. Apparently someone made two of these dolls. The clothes are handmade—just like my doll. Everything is identical except the doll isn't mine," she explained impatiently. "So whose is it?"

"How should *I* know?"

"You have to know where *my* doll came from," she argued.

"DJ, you don't really expect me to remember where we picked up a rag doll all those years ago, do you?"

"Yes, I do." She frowned, remembering a photo she'd seen of when she was a baby. Trixie had been lying next to her. "I had it from as far back as I can remember. You should remember if someone gave it to me when I was a baby."

He glanced away for a moment. "Look, if you think it is some kind of threat, then maybe you should disappear for a while."

She hadn't said she thought it was a threat. Her eyes widened in both alarm and anger. What wasn't he telling her?

"That is all you have to say? *Run?* Your answer to everything." She thought of the cheap motels, the carryout food, the constantly looking over her shoulder, afraid someone would either kill her father or take him from her. First sign of trouble—and there was always trouble when your father is a con man—and off they would go, usually in the middle of the night. She'd spent too many years on the run with him as a child. This time she wasn't running.

"No," she said, gripping the phone until her fingers ached. "This time I want answers. If you don't tell me, I'll get them on my own."

"I only want you to be…safe."

"*Safe?* So this doll *is* a threat." She cursed under her breath. For years she'd had to deal with people her father had swindled or old partners he'd shortchanged or screwed over. Half the time she didn't know who was after them or why they had to keep moving, always on the run from something. She'd felt as if she'd had a target on her back all her life because of this man. "What have you gotten me into now?"

"You can't believe this doll is my doing."

Why had she thought that her father, a man who lied for living, would be honest with her? Coming here had been a mistake, but then again, she'd had no one else to ask about the doll—or the photo.

She reached into her pocket. She'd come too far to turn around and leave without at least trying to get the truth out of him. "Who are these people in this photograph, and why would someone want me to have it?" she demanded as she pressed the crinkled photo against the Plexiglas between them.

DJ watched all the color drain from his face. Growing up, she'd learned to tell when he was lying. But what she saw now on his face was pain and fear.

His gaze darting away from the photo as he lowered his voice. "I don't know what this is about, but what would it hurt if you just got out of town for a while?"

She shook her head. "Stop lying to me. You recognize these people. Tell me the truth. Is this my mother? Don't you think I noticed that she looks like me? Am I that baby?"

"DJ, how is that possible? I told you, your mother died in childbirth."

"Then this woman isn't my mother?"

"On my life, you aren't the baby in that photo." He crisscrossed his heart. "And those people are not your family."

She'd been so hopeful. She felt like crying as she peeled the photo off the grimy glass and dropped it back into her bag along with the doll. She'd had to leave her gun in her car and felt naked without it. "But you did recognize the people in the photo."

He said nothing, which came as little surprise.

"I have no idea why I came here." She met his gaze. "I knew you'd lie."

"DJ, whatever you think of me, listen to me now," he pleaded.

DJ. That had been his nickname for her, and it had stuck. But hearing him say it had her fighting tears. She'd once thought her father was the most amazing man in the world. That had been a very long time ago.

She got to her feet, shaking her head at her own naïveté as she started to put the phone back. She'd fallen for his promises too many times in her life. She'd made a clean break when he'd gone to prison, telling him she never wanted to see him again.

Drawing the phone to her ear, she said, "It is clear to me that you've lied to me my whole life. What I don't know is why. But I'm going to find out."

"I did the best I could, just the two of us," her father said, his voice breaking. "I know I could have done better, but, DJ—"

She'd heard this before and couldn't bear to hear it again. "If I have family—" Growing up, she'd often dreamed of a big, boisterous family. Now, with Christmas coming, she felt nostalgic. If she had family, if that's why they'd left this for her now…

She'd seen an ad in a magazine of a family around a beautifully decorated tree on Christmas morning. That night she'd prayed to the starlit night that she could be that little girl in the ad.

But her prayer hadn't been answered, and now she

no longer believed in fairy tales. If anything, life had taught her that there were no happy endings.

"DJ, you have to listen to me." He'd raised his voice. The guard was making his way down the line of booths toward him. "You don't know how dangerous—"

"Dangerous?" she echoed.

The guard tapped him on the shoulder. "Time to go."

"DJ—"

"Just tell me the truth." She hated how vulnerable she sounded. She'd seen his face when he'd looked at the people in the photograph. He *had* recognized them. But if they were her family, then why had he looked so…hurt, and yet so frightened? Because he'd been caught in a lie? Or because she had something to fear from them?

She'd had to become strong and trust her own instincts for so long… Growing up on the run with her father had taught her how to survive.

That was, until she'd found the doll and the photo of three people she didn't know, one of them holding a baby who, no matter what he said, was probably her. But what about that would put her in danger?

"Last chance," she said into the phone.

The guard barked another *"Time to go."*

Her father's gaze locked with hers. She saw pleading in his eyes as he quickly said into the phone, "There's a reason I lied all these years, but the truth is…you will be hearing from my family in Montana soon. Go to them until you hear from me." The guard grabbed the phone from her father's hand and slammed it down.

DJ stood staring at him, his words rooting her to the floor. Her father had family in Montana? *She* had family? A family that would be contacting her? If this was another lie…

Slowly she hung up her phone as she watched Walter Justice being led away. Frowning, she pulled out the photo. He's sworn these people weren't her family. Then who were they? Her mother's family? A cold dread filled her at the memory of her father's reaction to the photo.

The doll and the photo proved that they knew about her. That at least someone in that family wanted her to know about them. And now she was going to find them. That she was on her own was nothing new.

And yet the fear she'd seen in her father's eyes almost burned through her resolve.

In Big Sky, Montana, Dana Cardwell Savage braced herself as she pushed open the door to her best friend Hilde's sewing shop. Christmas music played softly among the rows and rows of rich bolts of fabric. For a moment she slowed to admire the Christmas decorations that Hilde had sewn for the occasion, wishing she had time to sew. She missed quilting and the time she used to spend with Hilde back when they were partners in Needles and Pins.

Seeing her friend at the back, she moved on reluctantly. She needed to tell Hilde the news in person. Her only fear was how her friend was going to respond. Their relationship had taken a beating three years ago. Hilde had only begun to trust her again. And now this.

"Dana!" Hilde saw her and smiled, clearly pleased to see her. Raising four children, Dana rarely got down to the shop that she and Hilde had started together. Hilde had bought her out long since then, but Dana still loved coming down here, where it was so peaceful and quiet.

She moved to the stools by the cash register and pulled one up to sit down. There were several people in the shop, but fortunately, Hilde's assistant, Veronica "Ronnie" Tate, was helping them.

"Where are the kids?" Hilde asked.

"With Stacy." She loved that her older sister was so good about taking all of the children to give Dana a break. Stacy's daughter, Ella, was almost five now. Dana's twins were four, Mary was eight and her oldest, Hank, was nine. Where had those years gone?

"So, you're out on the town?" Hilde asked and then seemed to notice how nervous Dana was. "What is it? What's happened?"

"My cousin Dee Anna Justice, the *real* one. Except apparently she goes by DJ. I talked to my uncle, Walter, whom I was led to believe was dead." She didn't want to bias Hilde against the real Dee Anna Justice any more than she might already be, given the past. But she also couldn't keep anything from her. "Walter called from prison."

"Prison?"

Dana nodded. "He assured me that his daughter is nothing like him. In fact, she hadn't talked to him in years until recently. She doesn't know she has family, he said. She was never told about us. My uncle was hoping that I would contact her and invite her to come to Montana for the holidays so she can get to know her family."

Paling, Hilde's hand went to her protruding stomach and the baby inside her. Three years ago, a young woman claiming to be Dee Anna had come to the ranch. Dana, who had so desperately wanted to connect with a part of her family she hadn't known even existed, had fallen for the psychopathic, manipulative woman's lies, and they had all almost paid with their lives.

But Hilde had suffered the most. Dana still couldn't believe that she'd trusted the woman she thought was her cousin over her best friend. She would never forgive herself. The fake Dee Anna, it turned out, had been the roommate of the real Dee Anna Justice for a short period of time. The roommate had opened a piece of her mail and, since they resembled each other, had pretended to be Dee Anna. Dana had believed that the woman was the real Dee Anna Justice and almost lost everything because of it.

"Why would he keep something like that from her?" Hilde finally asked.

"Because his family had disowned him when he married a woman they didn't approve of. He thought his family would turn both him and his daughter away, apparently."

"But now?"

"Now, he said with Christmas coming, he hoped I would reach out to her and not turn her away as his family had done. She doesn't have any other family, he said." She saw Hilde weaken.

"I told my uncle about the woman who pretended to be Dee Anna. He was so sorry about what happened," Dana said quickly. "He said he'd never met DJ's former roommate, but that he was shocked, and his daughter would be, too, to learn that the woman was capable of the horrible things she did."

Hilde nodded. "So, you've contacted her?"

"No, I wouldn't do that without talking to you first."

Her friend took a breath and let it out. "It's all right."

"I won't if it upsets you too much," Dana said, reaching for Hilde's hand.

"You're sure this time she's the real Dee Anna Justice?"

"Hud ran both her and her father through the system. She has been working as a travel writer, going all over the world to exotic places and writing about them under the pen name DJ Price." One of the perks of being married to the local marshal was that he wouldn't let anyone else come to visit without first finding out his or her true identity.

"So Colt knows that the real Dee Anna has turned up?"

The only good thing that had come out of that horrible time three years ago was Deputy Marshal Colt Lawson. He had believed what Hilde was saying about the fake Dee and had ended up saving her life as well as Dana's and the kids'. Now the two were married, and Dana had never seen Hilde looking happier, especially since she was pregnant with their first child.

"I talked to Colt *first*. He said it was up to you, but none of us wants to take any chances with this baby or your health."

Hilde smiled. "I'm as healthy as a horse and the baby is fine. As long as we're sure this woman is the real Dee Anna and not a murdering psychopath."

The other Dee, the fake Dee Anna Justice, had set her sights on Dana's husband, Marshal Hud Savage, planning to replace Dana. So Dana and her children had to go, and Hilde, the interfering friend in the woman's mentally disturbed mind, along with them. Dana shivered at the memory.

She had nightmares sometimes, thinking they were all still locked in that burning barn. "*That* Dee Anna is dead and gone."

Hilde nodded. "But not forgotten."

"No, not forgotten. It was a lesson I will never forget, and neither will Hud." She smiled and squeezed her friend's hand. "I'm just glad you and I are okay."

"We're more than okay. I know how much family means to you. Contact your cousin and tell her she's welcome. I would never stand in the way of you finding more of your relatives on your mother's side."

"I want you to meet her. If for any reason you suspect anything strange about her—"

Hilde laughed. "I'll let you know if she tries to kill me."

Chapter Three

Beau Tanner had always known the debt would come due, and probably at the worst possible time. He'd dreaded this day since he was ten. Over the years he'd waited, knowing there was no way he could deny whatever request was put to him.

The sins of the father, he thought as he stared at the envelope he'd found in his mailbox this morning. The return address was for an attorney in San Diego, California. But the letter inside was from a California state correction facility prisoner by the name of Walter Justice.

He wondered only idly how the man had found him after all these years, forgetting for a moment the kind of people he was dealing with. Beau could have ended up anywhere in the world. Instead, he'd settled in the Gallatin Canyon, where they'd first met. He suspected Walter had kept track of him, knowing that one day he would demand payment for the debt.

The letter had been sent to his home address here on the ranch—instead of his office. So he knew before he opened it that it would be personal.

Telling himself just to get it over with, Beau studied the contents of the envelope. There were two sheets of paper inside. One appeared to be a travel article about Eleuthera, an island in the Bahamas. The other was a plain sheet of paper with a printed note:

Take care of my daughter, DJ. Flight 1129 from LA arriving in Bozeman, Montana, Thursday at 2:45 p.m. Dana Cardwell Savage will be picking her up and taking her to Cardwell Ranch. I highly advise you not to let her know that you're watching out for her—and most especially that it was at my request.

It was signed W. Justice.

Under that he'd written, "Cell phone number for emergencies only."

Today was Thursday. DJ's flight would be coming in *this* afternoon. Walter had called it awfully close. What if Beau had been out of town? If he'd questioned whether Walter had kept track of him, he didn't anymore.

He read the letter again and swore. He had no idea what this was about. Apparently Walter's daughter needed protection? A small clue would have been helpful. And protection from what? Or was it from whom?

Also, he was surprised Walt's daughter would be coming to Montana. That was where their paths had crossed all those years ago. He thought of the dark-haired five-year-old girl with the huge brown expressive eyes and the skinny ten-year-old kid he'd been.

He remembered the way she'd looked up at him, how he'd melted into those eyes, how he'd foolishly wanted to rescue her. What a joke. He hadn't even been able to rescue himself. Like him, she'd been trapped in a life that wasn't her doing.

"Any mail for me?" asked a sleepy-sounding female voice from behind him.

He folded the letter and article and shoved them into his jean jacket pocket before turning to look at the slim, beautiful blonde leaning against his kitchen counter. "Nope. Look, Leah—"

"I really appreciate you letting me stay here, Beau," she said, cutting him off. "If this package I have coming wasn't so important and I wasn't between places right now…"

Beau nodded, mentally kicking himself for getting involved when she'd shown up on his doorstep. "Leah, I wish you hadn't put me in the middle of whatever this is."

"Please, no lectures," she said, raising a hand. "Especially before I've had my coffee. You did make coffee, didn't you? I remember that you always made better coffee than Charlie." Her voice broke at Charlie's name. She turned away from him, but not before he'd seen the tears.

She pulled down a clean cup and poured herself a cup of coffee before turning to him again. He studied her in the steam that rose from the dark liquid. He'd met Leah Barnhart at college when his best friend and roommate, Charlie Mack, had been dating her. The three of them had become good friends. Leah and Charlie had later married and both taken jobs abroad. Over the years, they'd kept in touch for a while, then just an occasional Christmas card. The past few years there hadn't even been a Christmas card.

No wonder he'd been so surprised and caught off guard to find her standing on his doorstep last night.

"And you're not in the middle of anything," she said after taking a long drink of her coffee.

"Why *are* you here?"

"I told you. I'm expecting an important package. I happened to be in Montana and thought about our college days…" She met his gaze and shrugged.

He didn't believe any of it. "Where's Charlie? You said he's still in Europe. I need his number."

She looked away with a sigh. "I don't have it."

He glanced at her bare left-hand ring finger. "Are you *divorced*?"

"No, of course not." She let out a nervous laugh. "We're just— It's a long story, and really not one I'm ready to get into this early in the morning. Can we talk about this later?"

He agreed, since he needed to get to work. DJ Justice would be flying into Montana in a few hours. He had to be ready. He had no idea what was required to keep her safe. It might come down to some extreme measures. Since he didn't know why she even needed protection—or from whom—now was definitely not the time to have a houseguest, especially one who knew nothing about his life before college. He wanted to keep it that way.

"You don't decorate for Christmas?" Leah asked as she looked around the large log home he'd built back in a small valley in the mountains not far from Big Sky. He'd bought enough land that he could have horses—and privacy. That was another reason he'd been surprised to find her on his doorstep. His place wasn't that easy to find.

He raked a hand through his thick, unruly mop of blond hair. "I've never been one for holidays."

She nodded. "I thought you'd at least have had a tree and some lights."

He glanced at his watch. "If you need anything, call my office and talk to Marge."

Leah made a face. "I called your office on my way here. Marge scares me."

He doubted that. He'd known Leah a lifetime ago. Was this woman standing in his kitchen the same Leah he'd toasted when she and Charlie had married? "Marge is a little protective."

"I should say. So you really are a private investigator?"

"That's what my license says."

She studied him with narrowed eyes. "Why do I get the feeling there is more to it?"

"I have no idea," he said. "Are you sure you'll be all right here by yourself?"

"I'll be fine." She smiled. "I won't steal your silverware, if that's what you're worried about."

"I wasn't. Anyway, it's cheap flatware."

She sobered. "I've missed you, Beau. Charlie and I both have. But I honestly do have a package coming here, and it's important or I wouldn't have done it without checking with you first."

"Then we'll talk later," he said and left. It made him nervous, not knowing what was going to be required of him over the next few days or possibly longer—and having Leah here was a complication.

Turning his thoughts again to DJ Justice, he realized he was excited to see the grown-up DJ. He'd thought about her over the years and had hoped her life had turned out all right. But if she was in trouble and needed his help, then there was no way of knowing what her life had been like the past thirty years. He hated to think what kind of trouble she had gotten into that required his help.

Since her father was calling in a promise… Beau was betting it was the dangerous kind.

ANDREI LOOKED AT the coin in his hand for a long moment. His hand shook a little as he tossed the coin and watched it spin before he snatched it from the air and slapped it down on his thick wrist.

He hesitated, mentally arguing with himself. He had a bad feeling this time. But the money was good, and he'd always gone by the flip of a coin.

Superstition dictated that he went through the same steps each time. Otherwise…

He knew too well the *otherwise* as he slowly lifted his palm to expose the coin. Heads, he went ahead with this hit. Tails…

Heads. A strange sense of both worry and disappointment filled him. But the coin toss was sacred to him, so he assured himself he should proceed as he pocketed the coin.

Stepping to the table, he picked up the information he'd been given on the woman he was to kill.

He noticed that a prison snitch had provided her whereabouts. He snorted, shaking his head and trying to ignore that little voice in his head that was telling him this one was a mistake. But he'd worked with the man who'd hired him before, so he pushed aside his doubts and picked up the photo of Dee Anna Justice, or DJ as she was apparently called.

Pretty. He wondered idly what she had done to warrant her death—but didn't let himself stay on that thought long. It had never mattered. It especially couldn't matter this time—his last time.

Maybe that was what had him on edge. He'd decided that this one would be it. With the money added to what he'd saved from the other hits, he could retire at forty-five. That had always been his goal. Another reason he'd taken this job. It would be over quickly. By his birthday he would be home free. He saw that as a sign, since this would be his last job.

Encouraged, he took the data over to the fireplace and lit it with a match. He would already be in Montana, waiting for a sign, by the time Dee Anna Justice arrived.

DJ LEANED BACK into the first-class seat, wishing she could sleep on the airplane. Her mind had been reeling since finding the doll and the photograph. But now, to discover after all these years that she had family, a cousin...

She'd been shocked and wary when she'd gotten the message on her voice mail. *"Hi, my name's Dana Cardwell Savage. I'm your cousin. I live in Montana, where your father was born. I'd really love to talk to you. In fact, I want to invite you to the Cardwell Ranch here at Big Sky for the holidays."*

Instantly she'd known this call had been her father's doing. But how had he gotten her cell phone number? She mentally smacked herself on the forehead as she recalled the guard at the prison searching her purse. The only thing he'd taken was her cell phone, saying she could pick it up on the way out. She should have known her father had friends in prison.

She'd thought about ignoring the message. What if this was just some made-up relative? She wouldn't have put it past her father.

But the voice had sounded…sincere. If this Dana Cardwell Savage really was her cousin…would she be able to fill in the gaps about her father's family? What about her mother's family? Wasn't there a chance she might know something about the doll and photograph?

She'd always had the feeling there was some secret her father had been keeping from her. If Dana Savage had the answer…

After doing some checking, first to verify that Walter William Justice had been born in Montana near Big Sky and then to see if there really was a Cardwell Ranch and a Dana Cardwell Savage, DJ had finally called her back.

A few minutes on the phone and she'd agreed to fly out. "I can't stay for the holidays, but thank you for asking. I would like to meet you, though. I have to ask. What makes you so sure we're cousins?"

Dana explained about discovering an uncle she hadn't known existed until she'd found some old letters from him to her grandparents on her mother's side. "There'd been a falling-out. I hate to say this, but they'd disowned him. That's why I'd never heard of your father until a few years ago, when I found the letters."

His family had disowned him? Was it that simple, why she'd never known about them? "Do you still have those letters?"

"I do."

She had felt her heart soar. Something of substance she could use to find out the truth. She wanted answers so badly. "I've never known anything about my father's family—or my mother's, for that matter, so I'd love to learn more."

"Family is so important. I'm delighted that your father called. I'd heard he had died. I'm so glad that wasn't true."

Little involving her father was the truth, DJ thought. But if his family had disowned him, then maybe that explained why he'd kept them from her. She had a cousin. How many more relatives did she have that he hadn't told her about?

She tried to relax. Her cousin was picking her up at the airport and taking her to the family ranch where her father had been born. These people were his family, *her family*, people she'd never known had existed until recently. She wanted to pinch herself.

Pulling her purse from under the seat in front of her, she peered in at the rag doll. If only it could talk. Still, looking into its sweet face made her smile in spite of herself. It wasn't hers, but it was so much like hers...

She thought of Trixie and remembered leaving a motel room in the middle of the night and not realizing until later that the doll wasn't with her.

"You must have dropped her," her father had said as they sped out of town.

"We have to go back," she'd cried. "We can't leave her."

He'd looked over at her. "We can't, sweetie. If I go back there... We can't. I'll get you another doll."

She hadn't wanted another doll and had cried herself to sleep night after night until she had no more tears.

"It was just a stupid doll," her father had finally snapped.

"It was all I ever had that was mine."

Now, as she looked at the doll resting in her shoulder bag, she wondered where it had been. Had another girl had this doll as she suspected? But how would that girl know about DJ and Trixie? Trixie was lost, while this doll had been well cared for all these years. Why part with it now?

Her head ached with all the questions and a nagging sense of dread that she wasn't going to like what she found out.

It made no sense that people had given her this doll and the photograph unless they wanted her to find out the truth. But the way they'd left it, breaking into her apartment...

She had tucked the photo into a side pocket of her purse and now withdrew it to study the two women, the one man and the baby in the shot. The man and women were looking at the camera, standing next to a stroller. There was nothing in the background other than an unfamiliar stone wall to give her any idea of where it had been shot—or when.

With a start, she saw something in the photo that she hadn't noticed before. She'd always looked at the people in the photo, especially the woman holding the baby.

But now she saw something in the stroller that made her heart pound. A doll. The doll she now had tucked in her purse. Her father hadn't lied. She *wasn't* this baby, because it wasn't her doll in the stroller. But who was the baby, if not her?

Chapter Four

It had snowed last night, dumping another six inches. Fortunately Highway 191 through the Gallatin Canyon had already been plowed by the time Beau dug himself out and drove to his office on the second floor of an old brick building in downtown Bozeman.

"Good morning, boss," Marge said from behind her desk as he came in. Pushing sixty, solid as a brick wall and just as stout, Marge Cooke was as much a part of Tanner Investigations as the furniture.

"I'm on my way to the airport soon," he said, taking the mail and messages she handed him. "I'll probably be out of contact for a few days," he said over his shoulder as he headed for his office. He heard her get up and follow him.

As he sat down behind his desk, he looked up to find her framed in the doorway. She lifted one dark penciled-in eyebrow and asked, "Since you never take any time off and I know you aren't busy decorating for Christmas, I'll assume you're working. You want me to start a client file?"

"No, this is…personal."

Just when he thought her eyebrow couldn't shoot any higher, it arched toward the ceiling.

"It's not personal like *that*," he said, giving her a shake of his head.

"I have no idea what you're talking about."

He laughed. "I'll be checking in, but I know you can handle things until I get back."

"Whatever you say, boss. Far be it from me to suggest that you haven't been on a date since a Bush was in office."

"Clearly you forgot about that brunette a few months ago."

"That wasn't a date," she said as she turned to leave. "And she made such an impression that you don't even remember her name."

He sat for a moment, trying to remember the brunette's name. Sandy? Susie? Sherry? Not that it mattered, he told himself as he sorted through his mail and messages. He wouldn't be seeing her again.

There wasn't anything in the mail or messages that couldn't keep.

Taking out the letter and the article Walter Justice had sent him, he read them again, then flattened out the article, wondering why it had been included until he saw the travel writer's byline: DJ Price.

So was he to assume that DJ Justice's pseudonym was Price? He typed DJ Price into his computer's search engine. More articles came up, but no photo of the author. From the dates on the articles it would appear she was still employed as a freelance writer for a variety of publications. If DJ Price was DJ Justice.

He returned the article and letter to the envelope, folded them into his pocket and shut off his computer. As he walked out of his office past Marge's desk, she said, "Shelly," without looking up as he passed.

"Wouldn't want you straining your brain trying to re-member the woman's name all the way to the airport."

Beau chuckled to himself as he made the drive out into the valley. He couldn't help feeling anxious, since he had no idea what he was getting himself into. Nor did he know what to expect when it came to DJ Justice.

At the airport, he waited on the ground floor by the baggage claim area. There were a half-dozen peo-ple standing around holding signs. Dana Savage was one of them. The sign she held up read, CARDWELL RANCH. DJ.

He hung back as the arrivals began coming down from upstairs. On the drive here, he'd told himself there was no way he would be able to recognize DJ. She'd just been a kid of five all those years ago. He'd been a skinny but worn ten.

But the moment he laid eyes on the dark-haired woman at the top of the escalator, he recognized her. Dee Anna Justice. That brown-eyed girl had grown into a striking woman. Her hair was long, pulled back in a loose bun at the nape of her neck. Burnished strands had come loose and hung around her temples.

Silver flashed at her ears and her wrists and throat. She was wearing jeans, winter leather boots that came up to her knees and a teal blue sweater. She had a leather coat draped over one arm, and there was a carry-on in her hand.

She looked up in his direction as if sensing him staring at her. He quickly looked away. This was not what he expected. DJ didn't look like a woman on the run. She looked like a woman completely in control of the world around her.

So what was he doing here?

DJ HAD STILL been upset as the flight attendant announced they would be landing soon. She'd stuffed her purse back under the seat. Out the window, she'd seen nothing but white. Snow blanketed everything. She'd realized with a start that she'd never felt snow. Or had she?

Now she surveyed the small crowd of people waiting on the level below as she rode the escalator down. She knew she was being watched, could feel an intense stare. But when she looked in the direction it came from, she was surprised to see a cowboy.

He stood leaning against the stone wall next to the baggage claim area. He was dressed in jeans, boots and a red-and-black-plaid wool jacket. His dark Stetson was pulled low, his blond hair curling at the neck of his jacket.

As he tilted his head back, she saw the pale blue familiar eyes and felt a shock before he quickly looked away. There had been a moment of...*recognition*. Or had she just imagined that she knew him? She tried to get a better look at him. Why had she thought she recognized him?

She had no idea.

He was no longer paying any attention to her. She studied his profile. It was strong, very masculine. He held himself in a way that told her he was his own man. He was no urban cowboy. He was the real thing.

She scoffed at the idea that she knew him. She would have remembered a man like that. Still, she couldn't take her eyes off him and was startled when she reached the end of the escalator.

Turning toward the exit, she spotted a woman about

her own age holding a sign that said CARDWELL RANCH on it, and in smaller letters, DJ.

The moment her cousin saw her, she beamed with a huge smile. DJ was surprised how that smile affected her. Tears burned her eyes as she was suddenly filled with emotion. She had the crazy feeling that she'd finally come home. Which was ridiculous, since she'd never had a real home life and, as far as she knew, had never been to Montana.

She swallowed the sudden lump in her throat as she wound her way through the small crowd to the young woman. "Dana?"

"DJ?"

At her nod, Dana gave her a quick hug. "Welcome to Montana." She stepped back to stare at DJ. "You don't look anything like the last Dee Anna Justice."

DJ heard relief in her cousin's voice.

"I'm sorry. I shouldn't have said that," Dana said, then must have noticed that DJ didn't know what she was talking about. "Your father did tell you about your former roommate pretending to be you."

"No, I guess he failed to mention that."

"Well, it's water under the bridge… I'm just glad you're here and I finally get to meet you."

"Me, too," DJ said, feeling that well of emotion again.

"We'll get your luggage—"

"This is all I have." Traveling light wasn't the only habit she'd picked up from her father. She had stopped by the bank before she'd left San Diego. She took cash from her safe-deposit box, just in case she might have reason not to use her credit card. But that would mean that she was on the run and needed to hide.

Dana glanced at the overnight bag. "That's it? Not to worry. We have anything you might need. Ready to see the ranch?"

She was. "I'm looking forward to it." Again she felt someone watching her and quickly scanned the area. It was an old habit from the years when her father used her as a decoy or a lookout.

"Always watch for anyone who seems a little too interested in you—or the ones who are trying hard not to pay you any mind," he used to say.

She spotted the cowboy. He had moved from his spot against the wall and now stood as if waiting for his baggage to arrive. Except he hadn't been on the flight.

"Do you need anything else before we head out?" Dana asked, drawing her attention again.

"No, I'm good," DJ said and followed Dana toward the exit. She didn't have to look back to know that the cowboy was watching her. But he wasn't the only one.

BEAU WATCHED DJ LEAVE, curious if anyone else was watching her. Through the large window, he could see Dana's SUV parked outside. DJ was standing next to it, the two seeming to hit it off.

No one seemed to pay her any attention that he could tell. A few people were by the window, several taking photographs. In the distance, the mountains that surrounded the valley were snowcapped against a robin's-egg-blue sky.

He watched DJ climb into the SUV. As it pulled away, there was the clank of the baggage carousel. The people who'd been standing at the window all turned, pocketing their phones. One man took a moment to send a text before moving to the baggage claim area. Everyone looked suspicious, and no one did.

Beau realized he was flying blind. He had to know why Walter Justice had hired him. He had to know what kind of trouble DJ was in.

Pulling out his phone, he stepped outside into the cold December afternoon. The air smelled of snow. Even with the winter sun shining against the stone wall of the airport, it was still chilly outside.

Beau was glad when the emergency number he'd called was answered. It took a few minutes for Walter to come on the line. He wondered what kind of deal the inmate had made that allowed him such service. Con men always found a way, he thought, remembering his own father.

"Have you seen her?" Walter asked at once.

"I have. But you might recall, I've seen her before."

"She was just a child then."

"She's not now," he said, thinking of the striking woman who'd come down those stairs. "That's just one reason I need to tell her the truth."

"No. That would be a mistake. You don't know her—she doesn't trust anyone."

"Whose fault is that?" Beau asked. "If you want me to get close to her, you have to let me do it my way. Tell me what kind of danger she's in."

"That's just it. I don't know."

Beau swore under his breath. "You expect me to believe that? I have to know what I'm up against." Walter knew enough that he'd "hired" Beau.

Silence filled the line for so long, he feared the inmate had hung up. "It could have something to do with her mother."

"DJ's *mother*?"

"Sorry, not DJ's mother. Carlotta is dead. Her grandmother Marietta is still alive. Marietta might have found DJ."

"Found her?"

"It's complicated."

"I'm sure it is. But if you expect me to keep your daughter safe, you'd better tell me."

There was a sound of clanging doors. Then Walter said, "I have to go. Call me tomorrow." And the man was gone.

Pocketing his phone with a curse, Beau headed for his pickup. He couldn't wait until tomorrow. He would have to do this his way—no matter what Walter Justice had said. He thought of the woman he'd seen. Years ago he'd yearned to save that brown-eyed girl. He was getting a second chance, but he feared he wasn't going to have any more luck than he'd had at ten.

What the hell had he gotten involved in?

DANA CARDWELL SAVAGE was a pleasant surprise. DJ saw at once the family resemblance in this cheerful young woman with the dark hair and eyes. She was so sweet that DJ felt herself relax a little.

"We are so happy to have you here," her cousin was saying. "Your father said that he's been wanting to get us together for years, but with your busy schedule…" Dana glanced over at her and smiled. "I'm glad you finally got the chance. This is the perfect time of year to visit Cardwell Ranch. We had a snow last night. Everything is pretty right now. Do you ski?"

DJ shook her head.

"That's all right. If you want to take a lesson, we

can certainly make that happen. But you ride, your father said."

"Ride?"

"Horses. It might be too cold for you, but it's always an option."

The SUV slipped through an opening between the mountains, and DJ was suddenly in a wonderland of white. Massive pine branches bowed under the weight of the fresh white snow. Next to the highway, the river was a ribbon of frozen green.

DJ had never seen anything like it. Or had she? At the back of her mind, she thought she remembered snow. The cold, soft flakes melting in her child-sized hand. That sense of wonder.

Dana was telling her about the Gallatin Canyon and some of its history. "I'm sorry," she said after a few minutes. "I talk too much when I'm excited."

"No," DJ said quickly. "I'm interested."

Dana smiled at her. "You are so different from the last Dee Anna Justice who visited us. Sorry. You said you hadn't heard about it."

"What happened?"

DJ listened and shuddered to think that she'd lived in the same apartment with someone like that. "I'm so sorry. I didn't really know her. We shared an apartment, but since my job is traveling, I was hardly there."

Her cousin waved that off. "Not your fault. That's why we're excited finally to meet the real you."

The real you? DJ almost laughed. She hadn't gone by her real name in years. She wasn't sure she even knew the real her.

Chapter Five

Jimmy Ryan could hardly hold still, he was so excited. He couldn't believe his luck as he saw the man come into the bar.

"You bring the up-front money?" he asked the moment the man took the stool next to him at the bar. The dive was almost completely empty this time of day. Still, he kept his voice down. This was serious business.

When the man had told him he was looking for someone with Jimmy's…talents, he'd never dreamed how perfect he was for the job.

"Montana? Hell, I used to live up there, you know, near Big Sky," Jimmy had bragged. He hadn't been there since he'd flunked out of high school after knocking up his girlfriend and being forced into a shotgun marriage, but that was beside the point.

"I remember you mentioning that. That's why I thought of you. So maybe you know the area?" the man had said.

"Like the back of my hand. I might even know the target."

"Ever heard of the Cardwell Ranch?"

Jimmy had felt a chill as if someone had walked

over his grave. This *was* too good to be true. "Are you kidding? I used to...date Stacy Cardwell."

"Well, maybe you won't want this one."

As desperate as he was for money, he would have killed anyone they asked, even Stacy herself, though not before he'd spent some quality time with her for old times' sake.

He'd thought it was fate when the man told him the hit was on a woman named DJ Justice, a cousin of the Cardwells. "Don't know her. Don't care even if I did. Just get me some...traveling money and then let me know how you want it handled."

The man had said he'd get back to him, but it had to be done soon. Jimmy had started making plans with what he would do with all that money.

Now, though, he felt his heart drop as he saw the man's expression. "I'm sorry. The client has decided to go with someone else."

"Someone else?" Jimmy cried loud enough that the bartender sent him a look. "Come on," he said, dropping his voice. "I thought I had it? I'm perfect for the job. Shouldn't it be a case of who gets her first? If it's the money—"

"They went with a pro, all right?"

"Excuse me?" Jimmy demanded, mad at the thought of losing the money and taking it as an insult. "I grew up in Montana. Do you have any idea how many deer I killed? You ever kill a deer?"

"A deer is a lot different than killing a woman." The man threw down some bills on the bar. "For your time." He slid off his stool and started to step away.

"You think that bothers me?" Jimmy had known

some women he would have loved to have put a bullet in. He wouldn't even have flinched.

As the man started through the empty bar toward the back door, Jimmy went after him, trotting along beside him, determined not to let him leave without getting the job.

"I'll do it for less than your...pro."

"I don't think money is the issue," the man said without looking at him. "She just wants it done fast."

She? He was thinking jealousy, revenge, a catfight over some man. "So what did this DJ Justice do? Steal some broad's old man?"

The man stopped at the door. Jimmy could tell that he was regretting giving him the details. "Look, forget this one, and maybe the next time I have something..." The man pushed open the door.

"You want to see a pro? I'll show you a pro. I got this one," he called after him. "I'll find her first and I'll be back for the rest of the money."

STACY CARDWELL WIPED her eyes as the movie ended. She couldn't help blubbering, not at the end of a touching love story. Maybe she was a sucker for a happy ending. Not that she expected one for herself. She'd picked the wrong man too many times.

But she was just happy to have her daughter, Ella, who was almost five years old. Ella had the biggest green eyes she'd ever seen and had stolen her heart even before she was born. Sure, Stacy got lonely sometimes, but she had her sister, Dana, and brothers, Jordan and Clay. Jordan just lived up the road. Clay was still in California but visited a couple times a year.

Years ago they'd had a falling-out over the ranch.

Stacy still regretted it. But Dana had forgiven her, and now they were closer than ever.

"Hello?"

She quickly turned off the television as Burt Olsen, the local mailman, stuck his head in the front door of the main ranch house, where Stacy was curled up watching movies.

"Got a package for Dana," he said. "Need a signature."

Stacy waved him on into the house, smiling as he stomped snow off his boots on the porch before entering. Burt was always so polite. Dana was convinced that Burt had a crush on Stacy, but he was just too shy to ask her out. She was glad Dana wasn't here to tease her about him.

"How's your day going?" Burt asked, then quickly lowered his voice. "The kids asleep?"

She laughed and shook her head. "That would be some trick, to get them all to take naps at their ages. No, their grandpa took them sledding. I'm just holding down the fort until my sister gets back."

"Saw your car out front," Burt said. "Figured you might be sitting the kids. What'd ya think of that snow last night? Really came down. I've already been stuck a couple of times today. Glad I have chains on my rig."

She nodded as she signed for the package. "Can I fill up your thermos with coffee? I have a pot going."

"That would be right nice of you," Burt said, blushing a little. He was a big man with a round red face and brown eyes that disappeared in his face when he laughed. He wasn't handsome by anyone's standards, but there was a warmth and a sincerity about him.

"He will make some woman a fine husband," Dana

had said more than once. "A smart woman would snatch him up."

Stacy had never been smart when it came to men, and her sister knew it. But she liked Burt. If she had been looking for a husband... But she wasn't.

When he returned from his truck with the thermos, she took it into the big farmhouse kitchen and proceeded to fill it with hot strong coffee. Burt had followed her only as far as the kitchen doorway.

"Having electrical problems?" Burt asked.

She turned to frown. "No, why?"

"I saw some feller up a pole not far from the house."

Stacy shrugged. "Here, I made sugar cookies. I'll put a couple of them in a bag for you."

"Oh, you don't have to..."

"Dana would insist if she was here," Stacy said.

"Well, thank you." He took the thermos and the plastic bag. "Shaped like Christmas trees," he said, holding up the bag to see the cookies. "You did a real nice job on them."

She felt her cheeks heat. Burt was so appreciative of even the smallest kind gesture a person did for him. "Thank you."

"Well, I'll be getting along, then." He nodded, not quite looking at her. "Might want to dig out some candles in case that lineman turns off your power. You have a nice day now."

"I'm going to try." She watched him drive away, wondering when Burt was going to get around to asking her out and how she was going to let him down easy.

In the kitchen, she got herself some cookies and milk. Going back to the television, she found another

Christmas love story and hoped Burt was wrong about the power man cutting off her television. She didn't get that much time alone to watch.

But this show didn't hold her attention. She wondered when Dana would be back with their cousin Dee Anna Justice and what surprises this cousin might bring to the ranch.

As BEAU CLIMBED into his SUV and began the drive out of the airport on the newly constructed roads, his cell phone rang. The roads were new because Gallatin Field was now the busiest airport in the state. "Beau Tanner."

"What is your hourly rate?"

He recognized Leah's voice and imagined her standing in his living room. "You can't afford me. Seriously, what is this about?"

"I lied to you. Charlie and I...we're in trouble."

Beau wasn't surprised. "So, there isn't an important package?"

"There is, kind of. I hate involving you in this."

"I can't wait to hear what this is exactly, but can we talk about it when I get home?"

"Yes. But I insist on hiring you. I have money, if that's what you're worried about."

"That isn't it. I have something right now that is going to take all of my attention."

He got off the call, cursing under his breath. If this was about marital problems between her and Charlie...

He really couldn't deal with this right now. Ahead he could see Dana Cardwell's black Suburban heading toward Big Sky. Beau followed, worried about Leah and Charlie, even more worried about DJ Justice.

What kind of trouble was DJ in? Her father thought it might have something to do with her grandmother? That her grandmother had *found* her? He cursed Walter. Who knew how many skeletons the man had in his closet?

But what did that have to do with his daughter?

If Beau had to lay money down on it, he would have bet there was a man in DJ Justice's story. A man with a jealous wife or girlfriend? Or had DJ chosen a life of crime like her father? At least Beau's father had reformed somewhat after that night here in the canyon when Beau had made the deal with Walter Justice.

Since becoming a private investigator, he'd thought he'd heard every story there was. Where it got dangerous was when the spouse or lover would do anything to cover up an affair—or even a score. Usually money was involved. And passion.

So what was DJ's story?

MARIETTA PISANI STOOD at her mirror, considering the almost eighty-year-old woman she saw reflected there. *Merda!* She looked as cranky as she felt, which almost made her smile. When had she gotten so old? She didn't feel all that different than she had in her twenties, except now her long, beautiful, raven-black hair was gray. Her once-smooth porcelain skin was wrinkled.

She knew what had aged her more than the years— her only child, Carlotta. That girl had seemed determined to drive her crazy. It had been one thing after another from an early age. She shook her head, remembering the hell Carlotta had put her through, and then softened her thoughts as she was reminded that her beautiful, foolish daughter was in her grave.

Not that she hadn't left a storm in her wake. And now Marietta had to clean it up.

"Can I get you anything else, Mrs. Pisani?" asked a deep, elderly voice behind her.

She glanced past her reflection in the mirror to Ester, who'd been with her for almost fifty years. Ester had grayed since she'd begun working here as a teen. Sometimes Marietta mixed her up with her mother, Inez, who'd been her first housekeeper right after her marriage.

"No, Ester, I don't need anything."

"What about you, Mr. Douglas?" Ester asked Marietta's solicitor.

Roger shook his head. "I'll be leaving shortly."

"You can turn in," Marietta told the housekeeper.

"Just ring." The sixty-seven-year-old woman turned to leave. "Sleep well." She'd said the same thing every night for the past fifty years.

As Ester closed the door behind her, Marietta focused again on her own reflection. Nothing had changed except now her brows were knit into a deep frown. Ester hadn't been herself lately.

The thought caused Marietta a moment of alarm. Was the woman sick? Marietta was too old to train another housekeeper. Not that Ester kept house anymore. A housecleaning crew came in once a week, and she employed a full-time cook, as well. Ester's only job now was to see to her mistress.

Of course, Ester didn't see it that way. She resented the housekeeping crew and the cook and often sent the cook home early so she could take over the kitchen. She would then make Marietta's favorite meals, just as her mother had done.

The thought that Ester might leave her for any reason was more than she could stand. Ester was the only person in the world Marietta trusted—other than her granddaughter Bianca. She tried to put her worries aside, assuring herself that she'd be dead before Ester went anywhere.

Still, it nagged at her. Not that Ester had said anything. It was more of a...feeling that something was wrong. Unfortunately she knew nothing about the woman's personal life—or if she even had one. Ester had married some worthless man years ago, but she'd had the good sense to get rid of him early on. Since then, as far as Marietta knew, there was no one else in her life. Ester had doted on her and Carlotta and thought that the sun rose and set with Bianca.

When Carlotta had died a few months ago, Ester had taken it harder than Marietta. The housekeeper had loved that child as if she were her own. She'd helped raise her and was the first to make excuses when Carlotta got into trouble, which was often.

But the one Ester loved even more than life itself was Bianca.

It was her thirty-four-year-old granddaughter Marietta worried about now because of Carlotta's deathbed confession.

She clenched her gnarled hands into fists at the memory. The stupid, stupid girl. The secret she'd kept from them all could destroy the legacy Marietta had preserved for so many years—not to mention what it could do to the family fortune.

That was why the mess her daughter had left behind had to be cleaned up. For the family's sake. For Bianca's sake and the generations to come.

"I should go," Roger said.

She'd forgotten he was even still in the room. A slight man with an unmemorable face, he practically disappeared into the wallpaper. "You're sure you can handle this properly?" she asked as she looked past her own image to his.

He sighed. "Yes."

"I don't want Bianca ever to know. If that means paying this woman to keep quiet—"

"I told you I would take care of it. But it is going to cost you. Your daughter left us little choice unless you want to see your family's reputation destroyed by a complete stranger."

A complete stranger. That was what Dee Anna Justice was to her. Marietta had never laid eyes on this... granddaughter, hadn't even known she existed until her daughter's deathbed confession. "Just see that it's done and spare me the sordid details."

"Don't I always?" As he started to leave, she heard a rustling sound and looked up in time to see Ester skittering away.

DANA WAS TELLING her about the "canyon," as the locals called the Gallatin Canyon. It ran from just south of Gallatin Gateway almost to West Yellowstone, some fifty miles of twisting road that cut through the mountains. Sheer rock cliffs overlooked the highway and the Gallatin River.

The drive was breathtaking, especially for DJ, who'd never been in the mountains before—let alone in winter. The winding highway followed the river, a blue-ribbon trout stream, up over the Continental Divide.

"There used to be just a few places in the canyon, mostly ranches or dude ranches, a few summer cabins, but that was before Big Sky," Dana was saying.

DJ could see that luxury houses had sprouted up along the highway as they got closer to the ski resort and community that had grown around it.

"Our ranch was one of the first," her cousin said with obvious pride. "It is home. The only one I've known. And I have no intention of ever leaving it."

DJ couldn't imagine what it must have been like living her whole life in one place.

Dana slowed and turned not far past the sign for Big Sky Resort. Across the river and a half mile back up a wide valley, the Cardwell Ranch house sat against a backdrop of granite cliffs, towering snow-filled pines and bare-limbed aspens. The house was a big, two-story rambling affair with a wide front porch and a brick red metal roof. Behind it stood a huge new barn and some older outbuildings and corrals.

"Hud, my husband, keeps saying we need to build a bigger house, since we have four children now. But… well…"

"It's wonderful," DJ said and tried to imagine herself growing up here.

"You'll be staying in one of our guest cabins," her cousin said and pointed to some log buildings up on the side of the mountain. "I think you'll be comfortable there, and you'll have your privacy."

DJ was overwhelmed by all of it, so much so that she couldn't speak. As Dana parked, a dark-haired woman came out on the porch to greet them.

"Stacy," Dana called. "Come meet our cousin."

Chapter Six

DJ thought Stacy looked like an older version of her sister. She'd been prettier at one time, but her face told of a harder life than Dana had lived. Seeing how much she resembled both of her cousins gave DJ a strange feeling. For once, her father had told the truth. These people were her *family*.

Dana introduced them and then asked her sister, "How were the kids?"

"Dad came by and took them sledding," Stacy said. "He called just before you drove up to say he's decided to take them to Texas Boys Barbecue, since they say they're too starved to wait for supper. The café is owned by our cousins from Texas," she said to DJ. Turning back to her sister, she said, "I'm working this afternoon at the sewing shop, so I'd better get going, since I need to pick up a few things before then."

"Go, and thanks."

Stacy looked to DJ, who'd been taking in the ranch in a kind of awe. "It was great to meet you. I'll see you later?"

"You'll see her. DJ's staying for a while," Dana declared and climbed the porch steps to open the door and usher DJ in.

She stepped into the house and stopped. The decor was very Western, from the huge rock fireplace to the antler lamps and the Native American rugs on the hardwood floors. Even the Christmas decorations looked as if they'd been in the family for years.

There was also a feeling of déjà vu as if she'd been here before. Crazy, she thought, hurriedly wiping at her eyes.

"It's so…beautiful," DJ said, her voice breaking.

Dana laughed. "*My Christmas tree? I* know it's hard to put into words," she said, considering the misshaped evergreen in the corner, decorated with ornaments obviously made by children. "But I've always been a sucker for trees that would never have gotten to be Christmas trees if it wasn't for me."

DJ managed to laugh around the lump in her throat. "I meant your house," she said, smiling at the sight of the ungainly tree, "but your Christmas tree is…lovely. An orphan tree that you brought home. It's charming."

Her cousin smiled at her. "Let's have a late lunch, since I know you couldn't have gotten much on the plane, and we can visit."

She followed Dana into the large, cheery kitchen, wondering if she hadn't been here before. It felt strangely…familiar. Had her father brought her here at some point? Why else was she feeling so emotional about this large, rambling old house?

"I can't tell you how surprised I was when I found some letters from your father and realized that my mother had a brother I'd never known existed," Dana said as she opened the refrigerator and pulled out a large bowl. "I hope you like shrimp macaroni salad." DJ nodded and Dana continued. "It wasn't like my mother, Mary Justice, to keep a secret like that. Then to find out that he hadn't actually died…" Her cousin put the bowl on the table and got out plates, forks and what looked like homemade rolls. "Coffee, tea, milk?"

"Milk." She couldn't remember the last time she'd had milk, but it sounded so good, and it felt right in this kitchen. Everywhere she looked she saw family history in this house. One wall was covered with photos of the children, most atop horses.

"Sit, please." Dana waved her into one of the mismatched multicolored wooden chairs in front of the long, scarred table.

"I didn't know about you, either," DJ said as she pulled out the chair and sat. Dana joined her after filling two plates with pasta salad. DJ took a bite. "This is delicious."

They ate in a companionable silence for a while. The house was warm and comfortable. From the window over the sink, DJ could see snow-laden pines and granite cliffs. It was all so beautiful, exactly how she had pictured Montana in December. She hadn't thought she was hungry, but the salad and the warm homemade roll dripping with butter quickly disappeared. This felt so right, being here, that she'd forgotten for a while why she'd accepted the invitation.

DJ was running her finger along one of the scars on the table when Dana said, "I can't understand why my grandparents would disown their son the way they did. They were a lot older when they had your father. Maybe it was that generation…but not to tell us…"

DJ took a sip of cold milk before she asked, "Who told you he was dead?"

"I didn't speak to your mother personally, but her assistant—"

"My *mother's assistant*?" DJ asked, abruptly putting down her milk glass. "When was this?"

Her cousin thought for a moment. "That would have been in the spring three years ago. Her assistant, at least, that's who she said she was, told me that your mother couldn't come to the phone."

"I was always told that my mother's been dead since I was born," DJ said. "It's what I've believed all my life, so I don't understand this."

"I don't understand it, either. Then whose assistant did I speak with, if not Marietta Pisani's?"

"She told you my mother's name was Marietta?" She shook her head. "Where did you get the number to call her?"

"From…from the woman who'd pretended to be you, Camilla Northland. After she was caught, I asked her where the real Dee Anna Justice was. I thought she was telling me the truth." Dana put a hand over her mouth. "Why did I believe anything that woman told me? I feel like such a fool."

"No, please don't. So my roommate gave you the number?"

Dana nodded. "She said a woman had called the apartment asking for you before she left to come out here to Montana to pretend to be you. When your roommate asked who was calling, she said her name was Marietta."

"That's my grandmother's name, but she is also deceased. At least, that's what my father told me. But since he kept all of you from me…" Her life felt like one big, long lie. "My father told me that my mother's name was Carlotta."

Her cousin looked flummoxed. "Camilla seemed to think Marietta was your mother. Either she lied, or—"

"Or the person who called lied."

Dana nodded thoughtfully. "I believed Camilla, since she also told me that the reason my uncle had been disinherited was that he'd married a foreigner. The woman who said she was Marietta's assistant had an Italian accent. I asked about her daughter. I'm not even sure I called you by name. She said you were in Italy—or was it Spain?—visiting friends. Is any of this true?"

DJ shook her head. "I've been in San Diego all this time except when I was traveling for work. I have no idea where my former roommate could have gotten her information, but that she knew my grandmother's name… I don't think she was lying about the phone call. Do you still have that number?"

Dana shook her head. "I'm sorry."

"I was hoping you could help me piece together more of my family history. My father told me that he and I were the only two left. Until he told me that you might be calling, I had no idea that wasn't true."

"Well, you have me and Stacy, plus my brothers, Jordan and Clay, as cousins, plus our cousins from Texas. You'll meet Jordan tonight. Clay lives in California, not that far from where you live now. So, you never met anyone on your mother's side of the family?"

"No. All I knew was that my mother's name was Carlotta and my grandmother's was Marietta. My father's never been very…forthcoming with information. He let me believe I didn't have *any* family."

"Oh, DJ, I'm so sorry," Dana said, reaching across the table to take her hand. "Family is…my heart. My father and uncle, my father-in-law, are often…trying," she said and smiled. "I've fought tooth and nail with my siblings, lost them for a few years, but finally have them back. I can't imagine not having any of them in my life. I'm so glad that now you have all of us."

DJ's eyes burned as she squeezed her cousin's hand.

"All of us *and* Cardwell Ranch," Dana added and let go of her hand.

DJ picked at her lunch for a moment. Was it possible that her grandmother Marietta was still alive? Then wasn't it also possible that her mother, Carlotta, was alive, as well? She could see why her father might have kept her from his family, since they had disinherited him, but why had he kept her from her mother's family?

DJ remembered the night she'd finally badgered her father into telling her about her mother. He'd had too much to drink. Otherwise all he'd ever said was that her mother had died and it was too painful to talk about. That night, though, he told her that Carlotta had been a beautiful princess and the love of his life.

"She was too beautiful," he'd said. "Too spoiled, too rich, too much of everything. Her family didn't think I was good enough for her. They were right, of course." He'd let out a bitter laugh. "It cost me my family as well, but I will never regret loving her." He'd blinked back tears as he looked at DJ. "And I got you. I'm a lucky man."

She'd been full of questions. How could he have lost Carlotta and his family, too?

"Do you understand now why I don't want to talk

about your mother? So, no more," he'd said with a wave of his hand. "I can't bear it." His gaze softened as it fell on her. "Let's just be grateful that we have each other, because it's just you and me, kid."

Even now, she couldn't be sure any of his story was true. Her heritage was a puzzle with most of the pieces missing. "I'm surprised that you'd never heard of my father before you found the letters," she said.

"I was shocked. Like I said, I still can't believe my mother would have kept something like that a secret."

"You said you still have those letters?"

"I can dig them out, along with that number—" At the sound of a vehicle, followed by the eruption of children's voices, Dana added, "After I corral the kids."

DJ cleaned up the dishes while Dana went to greet the children. She could hear laughter and shrieks of playfulness outside. She couldn't help but smile to herself.

Drying her hands, she pulled out the photo and studied it in the light from the kitchen window. With her cousin's help, she was going to find the family she'd been denied.

She gazed at the photo of the baby—and the doll in the stroller. If she wasn't the baby the smiling woman was holding, then who was, and why had someone wanted her to believe they were family?

Whoever had left her the doll and the photo knew the truth—and wanted her to know it. But what was the truth? And what was the motive? To help her? Or to warn her?

She felt a sudden chill. She would find out, but at what cost?

On the way to the small resort town of Big Sky, Stacy couldn't get DJ off her mind. There was a distinct family resemblance because of the dark hair and eyes, but still…she had the feeling that she'd met her when they were kids.

At the drugstore, she got out and was about to lock her car when she heard the sound of footfalls in the new snow behind her.

"Stacy?"

She started at the familiar male voice directly behind her. Turning, she came face-to-face with her old boyfriend from high school. *"Jimmy?"*

He grinned. "I go by James now. I'm surprised you remember me."

How could she not remember Jimmy Ryan? He'd dumped her right before her junior prom to go back to his old girlfriend, Melody Harper. He'd been the first in a long line to break her heart.

"Are you here for the holidays?" He and Melody had gotten married right after high school. Melody, it turned out, had been pregnant. He'd taken a job with Melody's uncle in California, and that was the last Stacy had heard or seen of him.

He was looking at her the way he used to, unnerving her. "I wondered if you were still around."

"I left for a while. How is Melody?"

"Wouldn't know. We're divorced. How about you?"

For a moment she couldn't find her voice. "Divorced." More times than she wanted to admit. "I have a daughter, Ella."

"Lucky you. It turned out that I couldn't have children."

She blurted out in surprise, "But I thought Melody was pregnant."

"Turns out she wasn't," he said bitterly. "She told me that she'd miscarried, so we spent a lot of years trying before the truth came out."

"I'm sorry."

His gaze met and held hers. He was still the most handsome man she'd ever known. His dark hair was salted with gray at the temples, which only seemed to make his gray eyes more intense. "Could I buy you a cup of coffee?"

Stacy felt that old ache. Had she ever gotten over Jimmy? Wasn't he why she'd jumped into one relationship, one marriage after another? "I have to get back to the ranch soon."

"Just a quick cup of coffee. I've thought about you so often over the years and regretted letting you down the way I did."

How many times had she dreamed that he would say those words—or at least words much like them?

She glanced at her watch. "I suppose a cup of coffee wouldn't hurt."

"YOU'RE TIRED FROM your long trip," Dana said after introducing DJ to all the children and her father, Angus Cardwell. "Dad, if you don't mind staying around for a few minutes, I'm going to take DJ to her cabin so she can get some rest."

"You're in good hands," Angus said. "Trust me."

DJ couldn't help but smile. Trust wasn't something that came easy for her. But Dana and this family inspired trust.

"The kids want to go see a movie in Bozeman,"

Angus said. "Maybe we'll do that and really make a day of it."

There were cheers from the five children. Dana laughed. "You haven't had enough of them? Fine. But we're all going to The Corral tonight. Stacy has agreed to babysit."

As they stepped outside, DJ on impulse turned to her cousin and hugged her. "Thank you for everything."

"I haven't done anything yet," Dana said. "But I am so glad you're here. Families need to stick together."

With that, her cousin walked her up to her cabin on the mountainside.

DJ couldn't believe the cabin as her cousin opened the door and ushered her in. Someone had started a fire for her. It blazed bright in a fireplace on the other side of a seating area. There was a small kitchen that she knew would be stocked with anything she might need even before Dana opened the refrigerator door to show her.

But it was the bedroom that stole her heart. "Oh, that bed." It was huge, the frame made of logs, the mattress deep in pillows and quilts. "I won't want to get out of it."

Her cousin smiled and pulled out a step. "This is how you get on the bed. I told them it was too high, but my brother Jordan made the beds, and so far everyone loves them."

"I can see why," DJ said, laughing. "This is amazing. Really, thank you so much."

"It's my pleasure. You'll get to meet Jordan and his wife, Liza. Clay, your other cousin, as I told you, lives in California. He'll be flying up for Christmas. But we'll get to all of that." She smiled. "I'm just happy you're here now. We can talk about Christmas later."

"I can only stay for a few days. With the holidays coming, I don't want to be in the way."

"In the way?" Dana exclaimed. "You're family. You'll make this Christmas even more special."

DJ couldn't help being touched.

"Get settled in and rest. We have something special planned for tonight. The Corral has the best burgers you've ever tasted, and the band playing tonight? It's my uncle and father's band—more relatives of yours I thought you'd enjoy meeting in a more casual atmosphere."

Dana was so thoughtful that DJ couldn't say no.

"I'll drop by some clothing and Western boots that should fit you before we go."

DJ started to tell her that this was all too much, but Dana cut her off. "You have to experience Montana and canyon life. I promise that you'll have a good time."

There was nothing more DJ could say, since she didn't want to disappoint her cousin. Dana had been so welcoming, much more than she should have been for a relative she'd never met before.

She watched Dana walk back down to the main house. Something in the distance flashed, the winter sun glinting off metal. She could see a repairman hanging from a power pole in the distance.

Emotional exhaustion pulled at her. The past few days had been such a roller-coaster ride. She closed the door and locked it. For the first time, she felt…safe.

The cabin was so warm and welcoming, she thought as she walked into the bedroom. The bed beckoned to her. Smiling, DJ pulled back the homemade quilt, kicked off her shoes and crawled up under the covers. She was asleep almost at once.

MARIETTA KNEW SHE wouldn't be able to sleep. She kept thinking about this granddaughter. She realized she knew nothing about her other than what Roger had told her. A father in prison. The young woman writing stories for travel magazines.

"Not married?" she'd asked.

"No. Lives alone. Stays to herself."

She tried to imagine the girl. Did she look like Carlotta or that horrible father of hers? What if she looked like Bianca?

Reaching over, she rang the bell for Ester. It was late, but she knew she'd never get to sleep without some warm milk.

"Is something wrong?" Ester asked moments later from her doorway.

"I can't sleep."

"I'm not surprised."

She stared at her housekeeper. "I beg your pardon?"

Ester shook her head. "I'll heat some milk. Would you like anything else?"

Marietta gritted her teeth as she shook her head. It wasn't her imagination. Ester was acting oddly.

When she returned with a glass of warm milk and a biscuit with butter and honey, Marietta asked, "Roger hasn't called, has he?"

"I'm sure you would have heard the phone if he had, but no."

"You don't like him." She realized she'd given voice to something she'd known for a long time. Not that she normally cared if her housekeeper liked her attorney or not. But tonight, it struck her as odd. Almost as odd as the way Ester was behaving.

"No, I don't like him. Nor do I trust him. You shouldn't, either." Ester started to leave.

"Why would you say that?" she demanded of the housekeeper's retreating back.

Ester stopped and turned slowly. "Because he's been stealing from you for years." With that, she left the room.

Marietta stared after her, dumbstruck. Was Ester losing her mind? It was the only thing that made sense. The woman had never talked to her like this. She would never have dared. And to say something so…outrageous.

She took a sip of the milk, followed by a bite of the biscuit, until both were gone. Neither was going to help her sleep tonight.

Chapter Seven

The Corral turned out to be an old-fashioned bar and restaurant that looked as if it had been there for years. DJ liked the idea of a place having a rich history—just like the ranch Dana had grown up on. She couldn't imagine having that kind of roots. Nor could she imagine knowing the same people for years like Dana did—which quickly became obvious as they climbed out of the large SUV.

The parking lot was full of pickups and a few SUVs. Several trucks drove up at the same time they did. The occupants called to Dana and were so friendly that DJ felt a stab of envy.

"Do you know everyone in the canyon?" she asked.

Her cousin laughed. "Hardly. I did once upon a time. But that was before Big Sky Resort."

The moment they walked through The Corral door, the bartender said hello to Dana, who quickly set them both up with light beers. "You're in Montana now," she said, clinking her beer bottle against DJ's. The band broke into an old country song, the lead guitarist nodding to them as he began to sing.

"You already met my father, Angus Cardwell, on lead guitar," Dana said as she led her to the only empty table, one with a reserved sign on it that read Cardwell Ranch. "And my uncle Harlan is on bass tonight. They switch off. They've been playing music together for years. They've had other names, but they call themselves the Canyon Cowboys now, I think." She laughed. "They're hard to keep track of."

They'd barely sat down and had a drink of their beers when Dana's brother Jordan came in with his wife, Liza, a local deputy still in her uniform. Jordan was dark and good-looking and clearly in love with his wife, who was pregnant.

"We came by to say hello, but can't stay long," Jordan said. "I'm sure we'll get to see you again while you're here, though."

"Is your husband coming?" DJ asked after Jordan and Liza had left.

"Hud's working tonight. But you'll get to meet him." Dana ordered loaded burgers as the band kicked into another song. "Oh, there's Hilde." Her cousin rose to greet her very pregnant friend. They spoke for a moment before Dana drew her over to the table.

Hilde looked reluctant to meet her. But DJ couldn't blame her after everything she'd heard about the pretend Dee Anna Justice.

"I'm so sorry about my former roommate," DJ said. "I had no idea until Dana told me."

Hilde shook her head. "It's just nice that we finally get to meet you. How do you like the ranch?"

"I love it, especially that four-poster log bed I took a nap in earlier."

Hilde laughed as she sat. Her husband came in then, still wearing his marshal's office uniform, and went to the bar to get them drinks.

A shadow fell across the table. When DJ looked up, she was surprised to see the cowboy from the airport standing over her.

"Care to dance?" he asked over the music.

DJ was so startled to see him here that for a moment she couldn't speak.

"Go ahead," Dana said, giving her a friendly push. "Beau Tanner is a great dancer."

Beau Tanner. DJ didn't believe this was a coincidence. "Did you have something to do with this?" she whispered to her cousin.

"Me?" Dana tried to look shocked before she whispered, "Apparently he saw you at the airport and wanted to meet you."

So that was it. DJ pushed back her chair and stood. Maybe his interest in her was innocent. Or not. She was about to find out either way.

He took her hand and pulled her out onto the dance floor and into his arms for a slow dance. He was strong and sure, moving with ease, and definitely in control.

"Dana told me you would be here tonight," he said. "I was hoping you would dance with me."

"Why is that?" she asked, locking her gaze on his.

His pale blue eyes were the color of worn denim, his lashes dark. Looking into those eyes, she felt a small jolt. Why did she get the feeling that she'd looked into those eyes before?

"I saw you at the airport. When I heard that you were Dana's cousin, I was curious." He shrugged.

"Really? You just happened to hear that."

"News travels fast in the canyon."

"What were you doing at the airport? I know you

weren't on my flight. I also know you weren't picking anyone up."

He laughed. "Are you always this suspicious?"

"Always."

She lost herself in those eyes.

"You want to know why I was at the airport? Okay." He looked away for a moment before his gaze locked with hers. "Because of you."

"So much for your story that you just happened to see me at the airport and were curious."

"I don't like lying. That's just one reason we need to talk," he said as he pulled her close and whispered into her ear. "Today at the airport wasn't the first time I'd seen you. We've met before."

She drew back to look into his face. "If this is some kind of pickup line…" Even as she said it, she remembered thinking at the airport that he looked familiar. But she was always thinking people looked like someone from her past. That was normal when you had a past like hers.

"It was years ago, so I'm not surprised that you don't remember," he said as the song ended. He clasped her hand, not letting her get away as another song began.

"Years ago?" she asked as he pulled her close.

"You were five," he said next to her ear. "I was ten. It was only a few miles from here in this canyon."

She drew back to look at him. "That isn't possible. I've never been here before." But hadn't she felt as if she had? "Why would I believe you?"

He looked her in the eye. "Because a part of you knows I'm telling the truth. It's the reason you and I need to talk." Without warning, he drew her off the dance floor, toward the front door.

She could have dug her heels in, pulled away, stopped this, but something in his tone made her follow him out the door and into the winter night. He directed her over to the side of the building where snow had been plowed up into a small mountain. "Okay, what is this about?" she demanded, breaking loose from his hold to cross her arms over her chest. "It's freezing out here, so make it fast."

He seemed to be deciding what to tell her. She noticed that he was watching the darkness as if he expected something out there to concern him. "All those years ago, your father did me a favor," he said.

She laughed, chilled by the night and this man and what he was saying. "Now I know you're lying. My father didn't do favors for anyone, especially for ten-year-olds."

"Not without a cost," he agreed.

She felt her heart bump in her chest and hugged herself tighter to ward off the cold—and what else this man might tell her.

"Your father and mine were…business partners."

"So this is about my father." She started to turn away.

"No, it's about you, DJ, and what your father has asked me to do."

She stared at him. She'd come here wanting answers. Did this man have them? If he was telling the truth, she'd been to Montana with her father years ago. It would explain why some things and some people seemed familiar—including him.

She could see the pale green frozen river across the

highway, the mountains a deep purple backdrop behind it. Everything was covered with snow and ice, including the highway in front of the bar.

"If our fathers were business partners, then I don't want anything to do with you."

"I wouldn't blame you, but my father got out of the...business after the night we met. I'm assuming yours didn't, given that he is now in prison."

She flinched. "How do you know that?"

"I told you. He did me a favor—for a price. He contacted me. It's a long story, but the night we met, your father and I made a deal of sorts. He helped me with the understanding that if he ever needed my help..."

"You said he did a favor for you? My father made a deal with a ten-year-old?"

"I promised to do whatever he wanted if he let my father go."

DJ felt a hard knot form in her chest. "I don't understand." But she feared she did.

"My father had double-crossed yours. Your father was holding a gun to his head."

"And you threw yourself on the sword, so to speak, by promising my father what, exactly?" What could her father have extracted from a boy of ten?

"He asked me to make sure that nothing happens to you."

She laughed, but it fell short. "That's ridiculous. Why would he think *you* could keep me safe?"

"I'm a private investigator. I have an office forty miles away in Bozeman. I'm good at what I do."

"And humble." She rubbed her arms through the flannel shirt her cousin had given her to wear. But it wasn't her body that was chilled as much as her soul.

Her father, the manipulator. He'd gotten her here. Now he was forcing this cowboy to protect her? She shook her head and started to step away again. "I can take care of my—"

A vehicle came roaring into the parking lot. As the headlights swept over them, Beau grabbed her and took her down in the snowbank next to them, landing squarely on top of her.

JIMMY RYAN RUBBED his cold hands together. He'd already spent several hours of his life sitting outside a bar, hoping to get a shot at DJ Justice. Finding out where DJ would be tonight had been child's play. Over coffee with Stacy he'd listened distractedly as she'd told him what she'd been up to since high school.

"So you're living at the ranch?" he'd asked. "How's that working out with family?"

"Fine. Another cousin has turned up. They seem to be coming out of the woodwork," she'd said with a laugh. "First my five male cousins from Texas. They opened Texas Boys Barbecue here in Big Sky. Have you been there yet?"

"Not yet. But you said another cousin has turned up?"

"Dee Anna Justice. DJ. I haven't gotten to spend much time around her and won't tonight. I'm babysitting the kids so Dana can take her out."

"Oh, yeah? Your sister taking her to someplace fancy?"

"The Corral. My father and uncle are playing there. You remember that they have a band, right?"

The Corral. "Sure, I remember. So what does this cousin look like?"

She'd described DJ. Sounded like he couldn't miss her, so to speak.

He'd glanced at his watch. "I'm going to have to cut this short. Maybe we can see each other again." If things went right tonight, that wouldn't be happening. But he hadn't minded giving Stacy false hope. And who knew, he'd thought, maybe they could hook up before he left. She was still pretty foxy, and he could tell she still wanted him.

Now, sitting across the highway in his rented SUV, his rifle lying across his lap, he just hoped he got another chance at DJ. Earlier she'd come out of the bar. But she'd been with some man.

He'd still been tempted to take the shot, but the man had stayed in front of her. When a car had come racing into the parking lot, the cowboy had thrown them both in a snowbank. What was that about?

"WHAT IN THE—" DJ's words were cut off by the sound of laughter as several people tumbled from the vehicle.

"Shh," Beau said, pulling back to look at her. She saw a change in his expression. Still, the kiss took her by more than surprise. She pushed against his hard chest, but his arms were like steel bands around her.

Worse, she felt herself melting into him, into the kiss, into the warmth of his mouth and the taste of beer on his lips. She was vaguely aware of music and laughter and the sound of people as they entered the establishment before he let her go.

She was shaken by the kiss and everything he'd told her as he rose and pulled her to her feet. "What was that?" she demanded as she began to brush cold snow off her backside.

"A kiss. Apparently it's been a while for you, as well," he said with a cockiness that was downright aggravating. He began to help her with the snow, his big hand brushing over the Western shirt, vest and jeans she wore.

"I can do it myself," she snapped and took a step away from him. She wanted to tell him that she'd only kissed him back because he'd taken her by surprise. But he didn't give her a chance to lie.

"Don't look so shocked. It was just a kiss, right?" His blue eyes gleamed in the light from the neon sign over their heads. "It wasn't like you felt anything. Like either of us felt anything."

The man was exasperating. She hadn't come looking for any of this. "I was asking why you thought you could get away with kissing me like that. Or was that part of the bargain you made with my father?" she asked, hoping he caught the sarcasm.

"I wasn't sure who was driving up just then. I was merely doing my job. Protecting you, since the one thing your father didn't make clear is whom I'm protecting you from. As for the kiss, it just seemed like a good idea. It won't happen again."

"You're right about that, because I don't need your so-called protection." With that, she pushed past him and started for the bar as Dana opened the door and called, "DJ, your burger's ready."

JIMMY RYAN WASN'T the only one watching some distance from The Corral. Andrei had learned to be patient, studying his mark, waiting for a sign that the situation was perfect.

He would get only one chance to pull the trigger.

Rushing it would put the mark on alert and make his job next to impossible. That's if he didn't get caught trying to get away after blowing it.

He'd seen Dee Anna Justice, or DJ, as she was called, go into the bar with her cousin. He wasn't even tempted to take the shot. Later everyone would have been drinking and that would add to the confusion about where the shot had come from.

He'd been surprised when DJ had come back out so soon—and with a man. They seemed to be in an intense conversation.

Who was this cowboy?

What happened next turned Andrei's blood to ice. A vehicle came roaring into the bar's parking area. The cowboy with Dee Anna threw her into the snowbank next to where they had been talking.

Andrei sat up straighter, tightening his grip on the binoculars. Why was the cowboy so jumpy? It made no sense.

He swore. Had there been another contract out on her—one that had failed? How else could he explain why the man with her had reacted like that?

What had he gotten himself into?

BEAU STOOD NEXT to the snowbank, cussing under his breath. Walter had warned him not to tell her. Now he understood why. The woman was stubborn as a danged mule.

He touched his tongue to his lower lip and tasted her, smiling as he thought of the kiss. No matter what she'd said, he'd felt her kissing him back.

Another vehicle pulled into the parking lot, dragging him back to the problem at hand. DJ Justice. How was he going to keep her safe? And safe from what? Or whom? He cursed Walter Justice. Tomorrow he would call him back, but in the meantime, all he could do was keep an eye on the man's daughter.

Good luck with that, he told himself as he went back into the bar. She was sitting again with her cousin. He went to the bar, taking a stool where he could watch her in the mirror behind the counter. She looked up and their gazes met for a moment.

She touched her tongue to the corner of her mouth and licked away a dollop of ketchup. Then she smiled as if she knew exactly what that had done to him. It was clear that she understood how their kiss had affected him. Because it had affected her, as well? Not likely.

He pulled his gaze away to nurse his beer. This woman was going to be the death of him.

Chapter Eight

Jimmy cursed and told himself to stay calm. He was going to get his shot. He'd been ready, but the damned man kept blocking his shot. He'd decided to try to take them both out when he got his chance.

He put the crosshairs on her head. His finger teased the trigger. He took a breath. He couldn't blow this.

A semi roared past between him and the bar, kicking up a cloud of snow. When he looked through the scope again, the woman had pulled away from the man and gone back into the bar, the man right behind her. Who was this guy, anyway?

Jimmy swore, hauled his rifle back in and closed his window. He tried not to be discouraged. He had Stacy, which meant he had a standing invitation to Cardwell Ranch. Why rush it? What was another day?

He was getting cold and tired by the time the door of the bar opened again. He put his window down, lifted the rifle and looked through the scope. Two women. He recognized Stacy's sister, Dana, leading the way. Right behind her was…DJ Justice.

His heart began to pound. His finger on the trigger began to shake. Before he could get the crosshairs on her, the door of the Suburban opened and she was gone.

He beat the steering wheel with his fist, then whirred up the window. He'd get his chance. He had to. A thought struck him. He'd find out where DJ was staying on the ranch and take her out quietly, he thought as he tested the blade with his thumb. A bead of blood appeared on his skin at the mere touch.

The idea of cutting her throat appealed to him. He was good with a knife. It would be better this way. Better chance of killing her and then making a clean getaway before anyone was the wiser.

He just had to make sure that the pro didn't get to her first. Maybe their paths would cross. He sheathed the knife, smiling at the prospect of surprising the pro.

DJ WATCHED THE winter landscape sweep past under a full moon. "I really like your friend Hilde."

Dana smiled as she drove them toward the ranch. "I'm so glad. Hilde liked you, too. So, what did you think of Beau Tanner?"

She shot a look at her cousin. "How long have you known him?" she asked, avoiding the question.

"Not all that long. His family is from the canyon, but he returned only about five years ago. You two seemed pretty close when you were dancing."

DJ smiled. "You aren't playing matchmaker, are you? You know I'm going to be in town only a few days."

"You'll be here a lot longer than that if I have my way," Dana said and laughed.

When they reached the house, the porch light was on, but everyone appeared to have gone to bed hours ago.

"I should probably go on up to my cabin," DJ said, getting out of the Suburban.

"I saw that my sister made sugar cookies. I'm thinking cookies and hot cocoa. Interested? It's not that late."

DJ couldn't resist. "If you're sure we won't wake everyone up."

"The kitchen is a long way from the upstairs bedrooms. Come on," she said, leading DJ inside.

A few minutes later, nibbling a sugar cookie, DJ watched her cousin make hot cocoa. Her mind kept returning to Beau Tanner and what he'd told her earlier, not to mention the kiss. That she'd felt something—not just something, but *something*—made her angry with herself. Worse, he'd known she felt it.

But she suspected he had, too. She smiled to herself as she recalled his expression as he'd watched her lick the dab of ketchup from the corner of her mouth.

"DJ?"

She realized she hadn't been listening. "I'm sorry?"

"Do you want me to get out the letters or is it too late?" Dana asked.

"No, I would love it, if you can find them."

"I found them earlier and put them in the desk down here," she said. "I know you're anxious to learn everything you can about your family. Me, too. Pour us each a cup and I'll get them."

DJ filled two mugs with hot cocoa and, with a plate of cookies, sat down at the table. Dana returned, sat down next to her and pushed a bundle of letters toward her.

The envelopes were yellowed with age and tied together with a thin red ribbon. DJ looked at her cousin as she picked them up with trembling fingers. "They must have meant something to your grandmother for her to keep them like this."

Dana nodded. "I thought the same thing. I can't imagine turning my back on my children, no matter what they did."

"You haven't met my father," she said with a sad smile. "I'm sure he sounded charming on the phone. But he was a born con man. He never did an honest day's work in his life. That's how he ended up in prison."

"My grandparents were hardworking ranchers, up before dawn, so they must have been horribly disappointed that their only son wasn't interested in staying on the ranch," Dana said with such diplomacy that DJ loved her all the more for it.

"You don't mind if I open these and read them?" she asked.

"Of course not. They're from your father. If they can help, please. I just don't want them to upset you."

DJ laughed, thinking of all the things she'd been through tonight, Beau being one of them. "I was raised by my father. Nothing about him would surprise me." She knew that wasn't quite true. When he'd mentioned Montana, what she'd heard in his voice—longing, regret, love—*that* had surprised her.

She opened the first letter. Something about her father's precise handwriting made her ache inside. It was clear even before she read the first few words that he was trying hard to make amends. He wanted his parents to get to know his wife.

DJ put that letter away and picked up another. This one was along the same lines as the first. He talked about wanting to return to the ranch, to raise a family there.

The next letter was even more heartbreaking. He was pleading with his parents to forgive him. She saw that the letters had been written only weeks apart.

DJ wasn't sure she could read the last letter. The writing was so neat, so purposeful, so pleading. In this letter, he said that he desperately wanted his family to meet his baby girl, DJ.

> Don't punish her for my mistakes. Please don't deny your grandchild because of mistakes I've made. I will do anything you ask of me. I'll do it for my child... I'd do anything for DJ. All she has is me.

As she read the last lines, her eyes burned with tears, the words blurring before her. She quickly closed the letter and put it back into the envelope. He had pleaded for their forgiveness and asked if he and his baby could come home. Clearly they hadn't forgiven him, since her cousin had never met him.

But she and her father must have come to Montana later, when she was five. How else could she have met ten-year-old Beau Tanner? How else could her father have forced such a promise out of him?

He'd tried to give her family. She didn't think his words could break her heart any further and yet they had. He'd poured his heart out to his parents and yet they hadn't budged. No wonder he'd never told her about his family. But what had he done to make them so cold to him?

"He must have done something they felt was unforgivable. I can't believe it was simply for marrying a woman of Italian descent," she said and looked at her cousin.

"I don't know. I never really knew my grandparents. I was young when they died, but they were very strict, from what my mother told me. However, I'm with you. I don't think it was the marriage. I think something else happened. Maybe if you asked your father—"

"He isn't apt to tell me, unfortunately, since I knew nothing about any of this," she said quickly and got to her feet. "There is something I'd like to show you." She picked up her bag from the chair where she'd dropped it. "Do you recognize this?" she asked as she held out the doll to her cousin.

Dana took the rag doll so carefully, holding it gingerly as she looked into its innocent face. "It's old, isn't it? Was it yours when you were a child?" she asked as she studied the construction and clothing.

"You've never seen it before?"

"No, I'm sorry. I can tell that it is handmade." She pointed to the small embroidered red heart, almost like a birthmark, on the doll's chest, under the collar of her dress. "Did someone make the doll for you?"

"That's what's so…frustrating. I had an identical doll, but I lost it years ago. When I first saw this one, I thought it was mine. It's not, though. Mine had an accident with a dog."

"How odd. So, how did you come to have this one?" Dana asked.

"I recently found it in my bed in my apartment."

Her cousin quickly rubbed her arms as if chilled. "That is spooky. And you have no idea who could have left it for you?"

She shook her head. "None. But this was pinned to the rag doll's body, under her dress." She took out the photo and handed it to her cousin. "What about the people in this photograph? Do you recognize them?" DJ asked hopefully.

Dana studied the old photograph for a long moment before shaking her head. "I'm sorry, but I've never seen them before."

Taking the photo back, she felt a deep sense of disappointment. She'd hoped that her cousin would have the answers she desperately needed.

On the table was one of the first letters she'd opened. "Did you see this part?" she asked her cousin. "There was another woman my father had been in love with that summer. Apparently it was someone his parents adored. If he broke that woman's heart…" She looked back through the letter. "He mentions a Zinnie." Glancing up at Dana, she asked, "Do you know anyone by that name?"

Her cousin thought for a moment. "Could be Zinnia Jameson. Well, at least, that's her name now. She married a local rancher. She would be about the right age. They live about ten miles up the canyon. It's too late to ask her tonight."

"But we could go tomorrow?"

Dana smiled and rose. "Tomorrow, though if your father broke her heart, she might not want to talk about it."

"It was more than thirty-five years ago."

"As if that makes a difference when it comes to a broken heart," her cousin said. "Maybe Zinnia is why Walter's parents couldn't forgive him."

Roger Douglas had just poured himself a drink when his phone rang. He couldn't help being nervous. If he didn't get rid of Dee Anna Justice… Paying her off wasn't an option. That would mean opening up the financials. He couldn't let that happen. All he needed was a little more time to win the money back. There was a poker game tomorrow night. High stakes. With a little luck…

The phone rang again. He pulled it out of his pocket, expecting it would be Marietta. He really wasn't in the mood to talk to her tonight.

With surprise, he saw that it was the man he'd hired to find him a killer. Was he calling to say the deed was done? His heart soared. With Dee Anna Justice dead, he would have the time he desperately needed to cover his tracks.

"Tell me you have good news," he said into the phone without preamble.

"We have a problem."

"I don't want to hear—"

"He thinks you put an earlier hit out on her."

"What? That's ridiculous."

"Well, something's wrong. He says there's this cowboy dogging her like he thinks someone is going to try to kill her."

"I have no idea what that's about, let alone who this cowboy might be. You said that other man you talked to about this…contract could be a problem."

"It's not him."

"You sure about that?"

"Look, I'll talk Andrei down. He's a pro. He'll complete the contract."

"What about the other guy?"

"Jimmy? Who knows? He might get lucky and take her out. He's cheaper, and with the pro getting cold feet, this could work out better for both of us."

"It had better."

"Easy, Roger. The only reason you and I are pals is that you owe my boss a potful of money. So remember who you're talking to." He hung up.

Roger downed his drink and poured himself another. If this blew up in his face…

BEAU WOULDN'T HAVE been surprised to find his house empty when he finally got home. Leah had shown up like a ghost out of the past. He half expected her to vanish the same way.

The house was dark as he entered. As he turned on the light, he was startled for a moment to see a shadowy figure sitting by the window.

"You could have turned on a light," he said, annoyed with her for showing up, for only hinting at whatever was wrong and now for startling him.

"I like the dark," she said, turning to look at him. "Also, you can't see the northern lights with a lamp on. Didn't you notice them?"

He hadn't. He'd had too much on his mind.

"Rough night?" she asked as he hung up his Stetson and coat.

"You could say that. Look, I'm not staying, so now probably isn't the best time for you to tell me what's going on with you and Charlie."

She nodded, making him wonder if she was ever going to tell him. "Is everything all right?"

"Just work."

Leah nodded as if to say she knew he was putting

her off and it was okay. She got up and followed him into the kitchen. In the overhead light, he could see that she'd been crying.

"Once I finish this job—"

"It's all right. But I do appreciate you letting me stay here."

He nodded as he made himself two sandwiches and bagged them with a couple of colas. "I'm going to grab a quick shower."

"I was just headed for bed. I didn't realize how late it was. Beau, if there is anything I can do—"

"No. Thanks for cleaning up after yourself."

She laughed. "I didn't mean in the house. I have some experience with undercover operations."

He stared at her. "As what?"

"An operative. But we can talk about that when this job of yours is over."

An operative? He realized how little he knew about her and Charlie as he watched her head for the guest bedroom. He'd thought that she and his former best friend were having marital problems. Now he didn't know what to think.

He didn't have time to speculate. Right now, his number one problem was DJ Justice.

Chapter Nine

It was after midnight. The snow-covered mountain-side shone like day in the light of the huge white moon hanging overhead.

"Let me walk you to your cabin," Dana said as DJ started to leave.

"No, it's late and I can get there just fine on my own." She smiled at her cousin and gave her a hug. "But thank you. For everything."

"I'm sorry I wasn't more help with the doll and photo. Tomorrow, though, we'll pay Zinnia a visit."

"We'll get it figured out," DJ said, hoping it was true. At least she knew more now than she had before coming here. Her father's letters still broke her heart. What had he done?

"So you liked Beau?" Dana asked almost shyly.

DJ chuckled and shook her head. "The truth is, my father asked him to look after me while I'm out here."

"Really? What did he think might happen to you? Or," she said, smiling, "was he trying to throw the two of you together?" From the glint in her cousin's eyes, it was clear that she thought Walter was also playing matchmaker.

DJ shrugged. She really had no idea. If she hadn't

seen her father's fear… "Again, thank you for everything. See you in the morning." As DJ stepped out on the porch, closing the door behind her, she caught movement out of the corner of her eye. For a startled moment, her hand went to her bag. Unfortunately she'd had to leave her gun behind in California.

Beau Tanner rose from the chair he'd been sprawled in, his boots scraping the wood porch as he tipped his Stetson. "Didn't mean to scare you."

"What are you doing here?" He *had* scared her, but she was trying hard not to show it.

"My job. I told you. Your father—"

"And I told you. I can take care of myself. I release you from any promise you made when you were ten." She started off the porch but heard his boots right behind her. She spun on him. "What are you planning to do? Follow me everywhere?"

"If that's what it takes to make sure you're safe."

She thrust her hands on her hips. "This is crazy. Look, I'm fine. There is nothing to protect me from."

"You sure about that? Well, I'm not. And until I am…"

"Fine. Follow me if it makes you happy." She started up the mountainside, breathing hard from her anger and just seeing him again. The last thing she needed right now was some man who…who irritated her. Her heart was beating faster at just the sound of his long strides as he easily caught up to her.

"Let's just keep to the shadows of the pines," he said, pulling her out of the moonlight.

She indulged him and his paranoia, filling her lungs with the cold night air as she tried to ignore him. The cowboy wasn't the kind who was easily ignored. She caught a whiff of his scent, a mixture of the great out-doors, fragrant soap and a powerful maleness.

DJ hated the effect it had on her as her body be-trayed her. She felt an ache inside her like something she'd never felt before. Maybe it was from years of not feeling safe, but she wanted to be in his arms again. She wanted to feel again like she had that moment in the snowbank when his mouth was on hers. She wanted to feel…protected, and she had in his arms.

Which was why she couldn't let herself give in. She would be here only a few days, and then she would be returning to California and her life there.

"This is where we part company," she said as she climbed the steps to her cabin and started to open the door.

He'd taken the steps in long strides, and now his large hand closed over hers. "Not until I make sure the cabin is secure."

She opened the door, turning on the light as she stepped inside, Beau right behind her. She couldn't be-lieve how far he was taking this. "It's late and I need to get some rest."

He didn't seem to be paying any attention to what she was saying. She hadn't wanted him in her cabin. Earlier the place had felt spacious, but it didn't now. "This is silly. You can see that there is no one in here."

He turned to look at her. "I think you have some idea who might want to harm you. That's information I need. Tonight. Before this goes any further."

She heard the determination in his voice and sighed inwardly. *Let him have his say and then send him on his way*, she thought. "Fine."

It had been a long day, but after the nap earlier and

everything that had happened, she felt more wired than tired, in truth. She moved to the small kitchen and opened the refrigerator, remembering the variety of beverages and snacks her cousin had shown her.

"Wine or beer?" she asked, knowing the only reason she was asking was that she needed the distraction.

"Beer." He had moved to the small breakfast bar and taken a seat on one of the stools. She handed him a bottle of beer and took one for herself. Twisting off the top, she took a drink. It was icy cold and tasted good.

Leaning against the kitchen counter, she studied the handsome cowboy. It was his eyes, she thought. She had remembered them because they were so unusual. Worn denim. Maybe also because there was kindness in those eyes that she would have recognized even as a child of five.

"I'm sorry you got involved in this," she said as she picked at the label on her bottle for a moment. When she looked up, she realized he'd been studying *her*.

"Why does your father think you need protecting?" Beau asked and watched her take another drink of her beer as if stalling. He understood she was holding out on him. He'd been in this business long enough to know the signs. DJ was running scared, but she was trying damned hard not to show it.

"You say you met me years ago?" she finally asked. "Did you know anything about my family before that? Or after that?"

He had removed his Stetson and tossed it on one of the other stools. Now he shrugged out of his coat, the same one he'd worn to the airport. He could see that this was going to take a while.

"Are you going somewhere with these questions? Or just avoiding mine?" he asked after draping his coat over a stool. He locked gazes with her. "I have to wonder why you aren't being straight with me. I hate getting myself killed without knowing why."

She looked chagrined as she put down her beer and turned to him. "I'm not sure what this has to do with anything, but before I left California, my apartment was broken into. The intruder left something for me."

He held his breath as he waited, imagining all kinds of nasty things.

"It was a doll with a photo pinned to it." She nodded as if she could tell that wasn't what he'd expected. "I used to have a rag doll identical to it. It wasn't a commercial doll. Someone had made it. Made two, apparently. Because as it turns out, this one wasn't mine. But it is so much like mine…"

"…that you wondered whose it had been."

She smiled. "Glad you're following along."

"And the photo?"

She reached into her shoulder bag and took out the doll and photo. She handed him the photo. "I don't recognize any of them or have any idea who they might be. I asked my father, but…"

"He said he didn't know them."

"But from his expression when he saw the photo, he knows who they are. He suggested I get out of town."

Beau studied the photo. "You think you might be this baby?"

"My father swore I wasn't."

"But you don't believe him."

She sighed. "I don't know what to believe. For years he told me I had no family. A couple of days ago I find out about the Cardwells—and the Justices. My father was born here, apparently. His family disowned him after he married my mother. He wrote a few letters trying to get back into their good graces. He must even have come here if you and I met all those years ago."

"You think he was here trying to make amends?"

"It doesn't sound like making amends was the only reason my father came here. Otherwise I doubt we would have met."

Beau nodded as he picked up the doll she'd set on the breakfast bar. "I called your father after I saw you at the airport today."

That surprised her. She took a drink of her beer and seemed to be waiting for what was coming.

"I told him that in order to protect you, I needed to know what I was protecting you from," he said. "Your father swore that he didn't know, but when I pressed him, he said it might have something to do with your mother's family. He said they might have...found you."

She shuddered. *"Found me?"*

"That's what *I* said. Unfortunately he had to go before he could tell me anything further. I thought you might know why he would say that."

DJ stepped past him to move to the window that looked out over the ranch. As she drew back the curtain, he said, "I wish you wouldn't do that."

She let the curtain fall into place and turned to look at him. "You think this has something to do with my *mother's* family? Why would they leave me the doll and the photo if they didn't want me to know about them?"

"Maybe they didn't leave them. Maybe some well-meaning person did." He shrugged. "I got the impression that your father thought you had something to fear from them."

She took another sip of her beer. "Well, that's interesting, given that all my life he's told me I didn't have any family. Not just that," she said as she walked back to the counter where she'd been leaning earlier. "I always felt growing up that we were running from something, someone. A few times it was one of my father's...associates. But other times..."

"You think it might have been your mother's family?"

She shrugged and toyed with the label on her beer again. He saw her eyes fill with tears. "That would be something, if the people I have to fear are...family."

"We don't know that." He got up, moved to her and took the nearly full bottle of beer from her. He set it aside. "You should get some rest."

He expected her to put up a fight, but instead she merely nodded. "It has been a long day." Her gaze met his. He did his best not to look at her full mouth.

Stepping away from her, he reached for his coat and hat.

"As it turns out, my father had a girlfriend before he married my mother," she said behind him. "Dana and I are going to visit a woman named Zinnia in the morning. I have a bad feeling he broke her heart. Still, I'm hoping she might be able to help me put another piece into the puzzle that is my father."

"I'm going, too, then."

"I told you. I release you from any promise you made my father years ago."

He nodded as he shrugged into his coat. "Just the same, I can go with you or follow you. Your choice."

Beau snugged his Stetson down over his blond hair. His boots echoed on the hardwood floor as he walked to the door, opened it and turned. "I'll be right outside if you need me." He tipped his hat to her.

She opened her mouth, no doubt to argue the point, but he was out the door before she could speak. As he settled into the swing on the porch, he listened to her moving around inside the cabin and tried not to think of her in that big log bed he'd seen through the open bedroom doorway.

"STACY? DID I wake you?" Jimmy knocked over the bottle of whiskey, swore and grabbed it before most of it ended up in the motel carpet. "You still there?"

"Jimmy?" she said sleepily.

"James. I told you, I go by James now." He took a drink and pushed aside his irritation at her. Tonight hadn't gone as he'd planned, and he felt the clock ticking. Who knew what the pro was doing tonight, but getting into the ranch wouldn't be easy for him—especially at night. There were hired hands, ranch dogs, lots of people living there. Unless they knew you... He told himself he still had the upper hand.

"What do you want?" Stacy asked, sounding irritated with him now.

He quieted his voice. "I was thinking about you. Thinking about old times. You and me." He could almost feel her soften at his words. Whatever he had back then, he still had it—at least where Stacy was concerned.

"So you decided to call me in the middle of the night?" She didn't sound irritated anymore. Maybe she was a little touched by the gesture.

"Yeah, sorry about that. I just couldn't get you off my mind. I wanted to hear your voice."

"You didn't say what you were doing in town. Are you living here now?"

He'd been vague, letting her think he was looking for a job, a place to live, letting her think he might be staying. "We can talk about that sometime, but right now I want to talk about you."

"What about me?"

"I still remember the way you felt in my arms."

"You do?"

"Uh-huh. Do you remember…me?"

She made an affirming sound.

He could imagine her lying in bed. He wondered what she had on. Probably a flannel nightgown, but he could get that off her quick enough.

"You are the sexiest woman I've ever known," he said and took another sip of the whiskey. "You said you live on the ranch now. In one of those cabins on the mountainside that I can see from the road?"

"Jim—James."

"I was thinking maybe—"

"My daughter. Ella, I told you about her. She's here in the cabin with me."

"I would be quiet as a mouse." There was just enough hesitation that it gave him hope, but she quickly drowned that idea.

"No. If that's all you wanted, I really need to get some sleep."

He realized that he'd come on too strong. He cursed under his breath. "No, that's not all I want. I shouldn't have called tonight. But after seeing you… I want to take you out to a nice dinner. That is, if you're free."

Silence, then, "When?"

"Tomorrow night. I figure you'll know a good place to go. Nothing cheap. I want to make up for this call."

"Okay."

He shot a fist into the air. "Great. I'll pick you up. What time? And hey, I want to meet your daughter." He'd almost forgotten about the kid again.

"Sure," she said, sounding pleased. "Tomorrow, say, six? My sister will babysit Ella."

"See if she'll take her for the night, because I want to get you on a dance floor after dinner. I can't wait to get you in my arms again."

Stacy laughed. "I've missed you."

He smiled to himself as he hung up and picked up the hunting knife from the bed. "Tomorrow night." He would mix a little pleasure with business.

Chapter Ten

The next morning, just after sunrise, Dana found Beau on DJ's porch. She handed him a mug of coffee and a key. "Go over to the cabin next door. I can stand guard if you think it's necessary."

He smiled at her, glad to have Dana for a friend. "I don't think you need to stand guard." He figured DJ should be safe in broad daylight with so many people on the ranch. And he didn't plan on being gone long.

"Thanks for the coffee—and the key. But I think I'll run home and get a shower and a change of clothing. DJ said the two of you are going to visit Zinnia Jameson. I'd like to come along."

"Fine with me. I'm glad you're looking after her." Her smile seemed to hold a tiny surprise. "She's special, don't you think?"

He laughed. "You're barking up the wrong tree. It isn't like that." He thought about the kiss and quickly shoved the memory away.

"That's what they all say—until love hits them like a ton of bricks."

Beau left, chuckling to himself. He'd heard that Dana Savage was one great matchmaker. She'd helped all five of her cousins find the loves of their lives. But she'd apparently failed with her older sister, Stacy, he thought.

And she would fail with him.

On the way home, Beau put in another call to the number Walter Justice had given him. A male voice answered just as before. He asked for Walter Justice.

A moment later another male voice came on the line. The gravelly voice informed him that Walter couldn't come to the phone.

"I need to talk to him."

"Not sure if that is ever going to happen. He got shanked last night. They've taken him to the hospital."

"Is he going to be all right?"

"Don't know." The line went dead.

Beau held his phone for a few moments, listening to the silence on the other end. DJ's father was in the hospital, possibly dying? There might never be any answers coming from that end.

He pocketed his phone, telling himself that he needed to let DJ know. She said she didn't care about her father, but having been through this with his own, he knew it wasn't true. When the man was your father, no matter how much he screwed up, his loss...well, it hurt. He remembered feeling racked with guilt because he hadn't kept in touch with his father. For years he'd wanted nothing to do with him.

Ultimately it all came down to blood and a built-in love that came with it.

Reaching his house, he climbed out of his pickup, thinking about the Walter Justice he'd known years ago. He wondered how he'd aged since he'd been in prison. He doubted he'd changed, which could explain why he was in the hospital now.

Beau swore under his breath. He didn't know what to do. He had to keep DJ safe. It was a debt that he wouldn't renege on—even if Walter didn't survive. He wasn't the kind of man who went back on his word. But he also knew there was more to it. He kept thinking about that brown-eyed little girl and the woman she'd become.

He would tell her about her father. But not until after their visit to Zinnia Jameson's house. He wasn't sure how she would take the news. Maybe there was no connection between what had happened to her father and whatever Walter feared might happen to his daughter.

Either way, Beau was even more concerned for her safety.

ANDREI SNIFFED THE WIND, waiting for a sign. He clung to the utility pole, careful not to attract any undue attention.

This job had turned out to be harder than he'd thought. For some reason Dee Anna had picked up an overprotective cowboy. Because of that, he was having trouble getting the right shot.

That alone should have made him quit the job.

But his birthday was coming, and he'd planned this for too long. His last hit. He would feel incomplete if he didn't finish. Also, he never quit a job once he'd flipped the coin and it had come up heads. It felt like a bad idea to do it now. He never liked to test luck.

So he would finish it and celebrate his birthday as he hung up his gun.

All he had to do was kill Dee Anna Justice. But not today, he thought as he sniffed the wind again.

She and the cowboy had to feel safe. Then they would make the mistake of letting him get a clean shot. He would bide his time.

"THIS COULDN'T WAIT until a decent time of the day?" attorney Roger Douglas demanded as he joined Marietta in the library. He stepped to the table where Ester had put out coffee and mini citrus muffins. He poured himself a cup and took two muffins on a small plate before sitting down.

"I wanted an update on the…situation," Marietta said. She felt calm and in control, more than she had in the few months since Carlotta had confessed.

"It's a little early to—"

"I assumed you would be handling this yourself and yet here you sit."

He picked up one of the muffins. She noticed that his hand shook as he popped it into his mouth. Clearly he was stalling for time.

"Have you even found her?" she demanded.

"Yes, of course. She's at a place called the Cardwell Ranch near Big Sky, Montana. She's staying with a cousin on her father's side of the family. I've had her apartment bugged for several months—ever since you asked me to find her."

"But you haven't gotten around to offering her money?"

"What is this really about?" Roger asked patiently, as if she was a child he had to humor.

"Have you offered Dee Anna Justice the money or not?"

He studied her for a moment before dragging his

gaze away. "Maybe we should discuss this when you are more yourself."

"Actually, I am, and for the first time in a long time. I am going to want to see all the financials on the trust funds." He paled, confirming what she'd feared. Her nosy housekeeper knew more than she did about what was right in front of her eyes. "But on this other matter…"

Roger rose. "I don't know what's gotten into you, but I told you I would handle it."

"How much are you planning to offer her?" She saw something in his eyes that made her heart drop. How much money had he stolen from her? Was this why he was dragging his feet? Because there wasn't enough money left to bribe Dee Anna Justice?

"What did you do?" she demanded.

He began to pace the room. "You're not thinking clearly, so I had to take things into my own hands. Trying to buy off this woman is the wrong approach. She would eventually bleed you dry. You know what kind of woman she is given that her father is Walter Justice. I told you I'm taking care of it and I have. I've hired someone to make sure she is no longer a problem."

For a moment Marietta couldn't catch her breath. "You did what?"

He dropped down into a chair next to her and took one of her hands. "It is the only way. I've kept you out of it. I—"

She jerked her hand free. "You stupid fool." Her mind raced. "Is it done already?"

"No, but I should be hearing from him—"

"Stop him!" She shoved to her feet. She was breathing hard, her heart thumping crazily in her chest. She

tried to calm down. If she had a heart attack now...
"You stop him or I will call the police."

Roger looked too shocked to speak. "You wouldn't do that."

"Try me. Call him now!"

"My job is to protect you."

She shook her head. "Protect me? Give me your phone. I will stop the man myself." She held out her hand.

"You can't do that, Marietta." He sounded scared. "You don't know what this man is capable of doing if he feels you're jerking him around."

"You think he is more dangerous than me?" She let out a chuckle, feeling stronger than she had in years. "Roger, get your affairs in order. You're done, and if I find out what I suspect, that you've been stealing from me, prepare for spending the rest of your life in prison. You're fired, and if you try to run, I'll send this man after you."

All the color had drained from his face. "You don't know what you're saying."

"I do, for the first time in a long time. I've depended on you to make decisions for me because you made me question myself. But I'm clearheaded now, Roger." He started to argue, but she cut him off. "Make the call."

She watched, shaking inside. But whoever he was phoning didn't answer. She listened to him leave a message calling off the hit.

"This is a mistake," Roger said as he pocketed his phone. "I've been with you for years. I've—"

"Get out." She pointed toward the door. "Don't make me call the police to have you thrown out. And you'd better pray that the man you hired gets the message."

As he left, Marietta heard a floorboard creak. Ester. The nosy damned woman. She thought about firing her as well, but she was too upset to deal with another traitor in her midst right now.

THE WOMAN WHO answered the door later that morning at the Jameson house was tiny, with a halo of white-blond hair that framed a gentle face. Bright blue eyes peered out at them from behind wire-rimmed glasses. "Yes?" she asked, looking from DJ to Beau and finally to Dana. She brightened when she recognized her.

"Sorry to drop by without calling," Dana said.

"No, I'm delighted." She stepped back to let them enter.

"This is my cousin DJ."

"Dee Anna Justice," DJ added, watching the woman for a reaction to the last name. She didn't have to wait long.

Zinnia froze for a moment before her gaze shot to DJ, her blue eyes widening. "Wally's daughter?"

DJ nodded. She'd never heard anyone call her father Wally.

"And you know Beau Tanner," Dana said.

"Yes," Zinnia said. An awkward silence fell between them, but she quickly filled it. "I was just going to put on a pot of coffee. Come into the kitchen, where we can visit while I make it." Her eyes hadn't left DJ's face.

They followed her into the kitchen. DJ had been so nervous all morning, afraid that this might be another dead end. But now, from Zinnia's reaction to her, she had little doubt this woman had been the one her father's parents had hoped he would marry.

"Dana is helping me piece together my past—and my father's," DJ said, unable to wait a moment longer. "You were a part of the past, if I'm not wrong."

Zinnia had her back to them. She stopped pouring coffee grounds into a white paper filter for a moment. "Yes." She finished putting the coffee on and turned. "Please sit."

DJ pulled out a chair at the table. Her cousin did the same across from her. Beau stood by the window.

Zinnia came around the kitchen island to pull up a chair at the head of the table. When she looked at DJ, her expression softened. "I loved your father. Is that what you wanted to hear?"

"And he loved you."

The woman nodded, a faraway look in those blue eyes. "We'd been in love since grade school." She chuckled. "I know that sounds silly, but it's true. We were inseparable. We even attended Montana State University in Bozeman together. Everyone just assumed we would get married after college."

"Especially my father's parents," DJ said.

"Yes. I had a very good relationship with them. I was like another daughter to them, they said." She smiled in memory.

"What happened?" DJ asked, even though she suspected she already knew.

Zinnia straightened in her chair as if bracing herself. "Wally got a job as a wrangler taking people into Yellowstone Park. His parents were upset with him because they needed him on the ranch, but Wally was restless. He'd already confessed to me that he didn't want to take over the ranch when his parents retired. He wanted to travel. He wanted…" She hesitated. "That's just it. He didn't know what he wanted. He just…*wanted*." Her gaze locked on DJ's. "Then he met your mother. She and some friends were touring the park." Zinnia shrugged, but her voice cracked when she added, "Apparently it was love at first sight."

The coffeemaker let out a sigh, and the woman got up.

DJ rose, too. "May I help?"

Zinnia seemed surprised. "Why, thank you. There are cups in that cabinet."

She took out four cups and watched as Zinnia filled each. DJ carried two over, giving one to Dana and the other to Beau as he finally took a seat at the table. She'd expected to see him on her front porch when she got up this morning, but to her surprise, he'd come driving up, all showered and shaved and ready to go wherever she was going.

He'd been so somber, she wondered if he wasn't having second thoughts about getting involved with her father—and her. She couldn't blame him. It seemed ridiculous for him to tag along, since she seemed to be in no danger. Maybe her father had overreacted.

She'd said as much to Beau, but he'd insisted that he had nothing else planned that day except spend it with her.

Because of some promise he'd made a con man when he was ten? What kind of man would honor that?

Beau Tanner, she thought, turning her attention back to Zinnia.

"My grandparents must have been horribly disappointed," DJ said after taking the cup of coffee the woman handed her and sitting back down.

Zinnia sat, cradling her cup in her two small hands. "They were as brokenhearted as I was," she said with a nod and then took a sip of her coffee, her eyes misty.

DJ wanted to tell her that she'd dodged a bullet by not ending up with her father. But even as she thought it, she wondered what kind of man her father might have been if he'd married Zinnia and gotten over his wanderlust.

"I had no idea that my mother had a brother," Dana said into the awkward silence. "Then I found some old letters. That's how we found you."

Zinnia nodded. "Wally's parents did everything they could to get him not to marry that girl, to come back to the ranch, to help them, since they were getting up in age. Mostly they wanted him to marry me." She smiled sadly. "But in the end…" Her voice broke. "Sadly, I heard the marriage didn't last long." Her gaze was on DJ again.

"My mother died in childbirth."

The older woman seemed startled to hear that.

DJ stared at her. "That is what happened, right?"

"I only know what Wally's parents told me."

"It would help if you could tell us what you do know," Dana said.

Zinnia hesitated for a moment and then spoke quietly. "As you might have guessed, I stayed friends with Wally's parents. They were such sweet people. They were devastated when Wally didn't come back." She took a sip of her coffee as if gathering her thoughts. "Wally called at one point, asking for money. I guess he thought they would give him what he felt was his share of the ranch." She scoffed at that. "He always made things worse."

Seeming to realize that she was talking about DJ's father, Zinnia quickly added, "Forgive me for talking about him like that."

"There isn't anything you can say that I haven't said myself. I know my father. He didn't get better after he left Montana."

"Well," the older woman continued. "When he called for money, he told them that Carlotta—" the name seemed to cause her pain even after all these years "—had left him to go spend time with an aunt in Italy."

DJ reached into her shoulder bag and took out the photo. As she passed it over to Zinnia, she asked, "Do you recognize any of these people?"

Zinnia studied the photo for only a moment before she put it down. "The young woman holding the baby is Carlotta Pisani Justice. Or at least, that had been her name. I saw her only once, but that's definitely her. You can see why Wally fell for her."

Picking up the photograph, DJ stared at the young woman holding the baby. This was her *mother*. "My father swears that the baby she's holding isn't me."

Zinnia looked at her with sympathy. "We heard that her wealthy family had gotten the marriage annulled somehow and threatened that if she didn't go to Italy, they would cut off her money. It seems she met someone her family liked better in Italy, quickly remarried and had a child with him."

"So this child would be my half brother or sister," DJ said more to herself. When she looked up, she saw Zinnia's expression.

The older woman was frowning. "But if her family had the marriage annulled... Why would they have done that after your mother and father had a child together?"

DJ felt an odd buzzing in her ears. She thought about what Beau had told her. Her father feared that her mother's family had "found" her.

"Is it possible they didn't know about me?" DJ asked, finding herself close to tears. Her gaze went to Beau's. She saw sympathy in his gaze but not surprise. All those years on the run. Had they been running to keep the truth from her mother's family?

The doll and the photo meant *someone* knew about her. Not only that, they also wanted her to know about them.

BEAU DROVE DJ and Dana back to the ranch after their visit with Zinnia. Both were quiet on the short drive. The sun had come out, making the snowy landscape sparkle like diamonds. As he drove, he chewed on what they'd learned from Zinnia. He felt for DJ. Apparently her mother had walked away not only from her father but also from her.

But what part had her father played? He could only guess.

He hated that the news he had to give her would only make her feel worse. But he had no choice. He couldn't keep something like this from her. She had to know.

As he pulled into the Cardwell Ranch and parked, Dana's children all came running out. They were begging to go see Santa at the mall in Bozeman.

Stacy was with them. "I didn't put it in their heads," she said quickly.

Dana laughed. "Looks like I'm going to the mall," she said as she started toward the kids. "DJ, you're welcome to come along. You, too, Beau."

Beau shook his head. "Thanks, but DJ and I have some things we need to iron out."

Dana shot her cousin a mischievous look.

"Tell Santa hello for me," DJ said.

Beau said to Dana, "Mind if we take a couple of horses for a ride?"

Dana grinned. "Please. I'll call down to the stables. DJ, you can wear what you wore last night. You'll find a warmer coat just inside the door of the house."

"You do ride, don't you?" he asked her.

"I've been on a horse, if that's what you mean. But whatever you have to tell me, you don't have to take me for a ride to do it."

A man came out of the house just then, wearing a marshal's uniform. Dana introduced them. DJ could tell that something was worrying him and feared it might have to do with her.

"Have you had any trouble with the electricity?" he asked Dana.

"No, why?"

"Burt came by with the mail and told me he'd seen a lineman on one of our poles. By the time I got here, he was gone. Just thought I'd ask. Burt's pretty protective, but still, it did seem odd. Maybe I'll give the power company a call."

As Hud drove away, followed by Stacy and Dana and the kids, DJ turned to Beau. "Seriously, we can't talk here?"

He smiled and shook his head. "Let's get saddled up. We can talk about who's taking whom for a ride once we're on horseback and high in the mountains."

"I'm not going to like whatever it is you need to tell me, am I?"

He shook his head. "No, you're not, but you need to hear it."

WHEN HE'D SEEN Dee Anna and her cowboy saddling up horses, Andrei had known this was the day. Several things had happened that he'd taken as signs. He would have good luck today.

He'd made arrangements the night before to procure a snowmobile. He'd been stealing since he was a boy and still got a thrill out of it. He'd always liked the danger—and the reward. His father had taught him how to get away with it. He smiled to himself at the memory. He missed his father and hoped that he would make him proud today.

Andrei felt good. He was going to get his chance to finish this. He didn't plan to kill the cowboy, too, but he would if he had to. He could tell that the two felt safe here on the ranch. As they rode toward the mountains behind the ranch house, he smiled to himself.

Today would definitely be the day. Last night after stealing the snowmobile, he'd traversed the logging roads behind the ranch. He would be waiting for them on the mountain. He had an idea where they would be riding to. He'd seen horse tracks at a spot where there was a view of the tiny resort town of Big Sky.

He would be waiting for them. One shot. That's all he needed. He would be ahead of schedule. Still, he wanted to get this over with. He knew that feeling wasn't conducive to the type of work that he did. But he couldn't help the way he felt. He was anxious. Once he finished this, he couldn't wait for the future he'd planned since his first job when he was fourteen.

His cell phone rang. He ignored it. He could almost taste success on the wind as he climbed on the snowmobile and headed up one of the logging roads toward the top of the mountain behind Cardwell Ranch.

FROM THE WINDOW Marietta watched her granddaughter come up the circular drive and park the little red sports car that had been her present for her thirtieth birthday.

"She can buy her own car," Ester had said with disapproval. "She has a job. It would be good for her and mean more to her."

Marietta had scoffed at that. "I have no one else to spoil." Which was true—at least, she'd believed that Bianca was her only granddaughter at the time. "She is my blood." Blood meant everything in her family. It was where lines were drawn. It was what made Bianca so precious. She was her daughter's child with a nice Italian man whose life, like her daughter's, had been cut short.

At least, that's what she'd told herself, the thing about blood being thicker than water and all that. But that was before she'd found out her daughter had conceived a child with…with that man.

Bianca got out of her car and glanced up as if she knew her grandmother would be watching. Her raven hair glistened in the sunlight as her gaze found Marietta at her window. Usually this was where her granddaughter smiled and waved and then hurried inside.

Today she stood there staring up, her face expressionless, her manner reserved. After a few moments, she looked toward the front door, brightened, then rushed in that direction.

Marietta knew then that Ester must have opened the door. Bianca loved the housekeeper. Maybe even more than she loved her grandmother.

That thought left a bitter taste in her mouth. She turned away from the window. Out of stubbornness, she thought about staying where she was and letting Bianca come to her.

But after a few minutes had passed, she couldn't stand it any longer and headed downstairs.

She found Ester and Bianca with their heads together, as she often did. The sight instantly annoyed her. But also worried her.

"I thought you would come upstairs," she said, unable to hide her displeasure.

Both women turned toward her but said nothing. Marietta looked from Ester to Bianca and felt her heart drop.

"What's wrong?" she demanded. "Has something happened?"

"I know, Grandmother. *How could you?*"

Chapter Eleven

DJ rode alongside Beau through the snow-covered pines until behind them the house could no longer be seen. The world became a wonderland of snow and evergreen below a sky so blue it hurt to look at it.

She didn't think she'd ever breathed such cold air. It felt good. It helped clear her head.

The cowboy riding beside her seemed to be lost in the beauty of the country around them, as well. What was it about him? She felt drawn to him and his cowboy code of honor. Yet all her instincts told her to be careful. He was the kind of man a woman could fall for, and she would never be the same after.

She'd spent her life never getting attached to anything. This man, this place, this Cardwell family all made her want to plant roots, and that terrified her. For so long she'd believed that was a life she could never have. But maybe, if the doll and photo were her mother's family reaching out to her and not a threat…wasn't it possible that she could finally live a normal life?

They rode up a trail until the trees parted and they got their first good view of Lone Peak across the valley and river. This late morning it was breathtaking.

The stark peak gleamed against the deep blue of the big sky. No wonder this area had been named Big Sky.

"It's incredible, isn't it?" Beau said as he stopped to look.

DJ reined in beside him to stare out at the view. The vastness of it made her feel inconsequential. It wasn't a bad feeling. It certainly made her problems seem small.

"Beautiful," she said on a frosty breath.

"Yes, beautiful."

She felt his gaze on her. Turning in the saddle, she looked into his handsome face. He looked so earnest… "Okay, you got me out here. Why?"

"I thought you'd like the view."

She shook her head. "If you're trying to find a way to tell me that you're stepping away from this—"

"I don't break my promises." He pushed back his Stetson and settled those wonderful blue eyes on her. His look was so intense, she felt a shudder in her chest. "We need to talk about what Zinnia told you. But first I've got some bad news. I called your father this morning." She braced herself. "He was attacked at the prison. He's in the hospital."

DJ wasn't sure what she'd been expecting. Not this.

The news was a blow. For years she'd told herself that she hated him, that she never wanted to see him. She blamed him for her childhood. She blamed him for keeping her family from her. She bit her lip to keep from crying. "Is he—"

"It sounds serious."

DJ nodded, surprised how much her chest ached with unshed tears. "You think his attack…" She didn't need to finish her sentence. She saw that he thought whatever she had to fear, he suspected it was connected to her father's attack. "Why?"

"I don't know yet. But I will find out."

He sounded so sure of himself that she wanted to believe him capable of anything. Wasn't that why her father had cashed in on the promise? He must have believed that if anyone could keep her safe, it would be Beau Tanner.

"You think I'm in danger?"

"I do. We need to find out what is going on. We need to find your mother's family."

"But nothing's happened. Yes, I was left a doll and photo of people I didn't know at the time..."

"They broke into your house to leave it."

"But what if it's my mother's family trying to let me know about them?"

He shook his head. "DJ, if that was the case, then why wouldn't they have simply picked up the phone or mailed the doll and the photo with a letter?"

"You see the doll and photo as a threat?" Hadn't she at first, too?

"I agree, someone wants you to know. The question is, why? Given what we learned from Zinnia Jameson..."

She saw where he was going with this. "It could explain a lot about my childhood. I always felt as if we were running from something. What if my father was trying to keep my mother's family from finding us? You don't think he might have...kidnapped me, do you?"

STACY WASN'T SURPRISED when Jimmy showed up at her part-time job at Needles and Pins, the shop that her sister's best friend, Hilde, owned. He pushed open the door, stepped in and stopped dead.

He was taking in all the bolts of fabric as if realizing he was completely out of his element. Stacy watched him, amused. James Ryan afraid of coming into a quilt shop. It endeared him to her more than she would have liked.

"Jimmy?" she said as if surprised to see him. Actually she wasn't. After she'd run into him yesterday, it had been clear he was hoping to see her again. That he had tracked her down… Well, it did make her heart beat a little faster. She'd always thought of him as the love of her life.

He came in, moving to the counter where Stacy was cutting fabric for a kit she was putting together. "James."

"Right. Sorry. Old habits… Do you like the colors?" she asked as she finished cutting and folded the half yard neatly. "Tangerine, turquoise, yellow and brown."

"Beautiful," James said without looking at the fabric. "So, this is where you work?"

"Part-time. I help Dana with the kids and work some on the ranch."

"Busy lady," James said. "I just wanted to make sure we were on for tonight."

She felt her heart do that little hop she'd missed for a long time. "Tonight. Right." She hesitated, torn. Then heard herself say, "Sure, why not?" even though a few not so good memories had surfaced since his call last night.

"Good. I can't wait." He sounded hopeful, and the look in his eyes transported her straight back to high school, when he used to look at her like that.

Stacy felt a lump in her throat. Was it possible they were being given a second chance at love? It seemed too good to be true. "I never thought I'd see you again."

He grinned, that way too familiar grin that had made her lose her virginity to him all those years ago. "Neither did I. Life is just full of surprises. Great surprises. So, I'll pick you up on the ranch. Which cabin did you say was yours?"

"The one farthest to the right on the side of the mountain. You remember how to get to the ranch?"

He laughed. "Like it was yesterday."

MARIETTA HAD TO sit down. She moved to a chair and dropped into it. Her heart pounded in her ears and she feared it would give out on her. She'd feared something like this might happen and had told Roger as much.

"Maybe the best thing would be to tell Bianca," she'd said.

"Have you lost your mind? Once you do that, you're basically admitting that this…woman has a right to part of your estate," Roger had said. "No, there is a better way to handle this, and Bianca never has to know."

Why had she listened to that man?

Bianca brushed back her long, dark hair and glared at her grandmother. "What have you done?"

Marietta's gaze shifted to Ester. She'd never seen such determination in the woman's expression before. Her lips were clamped tightly together and her eyes were just as dark and angry as Bianca's.

"What have you *done?"* she wanted to demand of her housekeeper. Yes, Ester was nosy. And yes, she'd been acting odd lately. But Marietta had never

dreamed that she would go to Bianca. She'd trusted the woman. A mistake, she saw now.

Bianca crossed her arms over her chest. "Isn't there something you want to tell me, Grandmama?"

Use of that pet name was almost Marietta's undoing. She lived only for Bianca. Everything she'd done was for this precious granddaughter.

"Tell you?" she echoed, stalling for time.

"Tell me the truth," Bianca demanded, raising her voice. "Do I have a sister?"

Marietta had known when her dying daughter had confessed she'd conceived a child with Walter that this day might come.

Now she realized how foolish she'd been to think she could keep something like this a secret. Although her daughter and Walter had certainly managed. It was clear that Ester had known about the other child, probably from the beginning. That realization hurt more than she wanted to admit.

It would be just like Carlotta to have shared this information all those years ago with the woman who'd practically raised her. Suddenly she recalled Ester at the sewing machine in her tiny room. She'd been startled and tried to hide what she was doing. Marietta had thought she was trying to disguise the fact that she wasn't working like she was supposed to be.

But now she remembered what the housekeeper had been working on. Dolls. There'd been two identical dolls! Two rag dolls, and yet Bianca had always had only the one.

Betrayal left a nasty taste in her mouth. Her gaze darted to Ester. "I want you out of my house!"

"No!" her granddaughter cried, stepping in front of

the housekeeper as if to shield her. "Do not blame Ester for this. If you fire her, you'll never see me again." The ultimatum only made the betrayal more bitter. "If it wasn't for Ester, I might never have known that I have a sister you've kept from me all these years."

"I wasn't the one who kept it from you all these years. That was your mother—and Ester." She could see now that Ester had been collaborating with Carlotta for years. Had she been stronger, she would have strangled the woman with her bare hands. "It's Ester who has known for so long, not me. Your mother didn't bother to tell me until she was near death. If you want to blame someone—"

"I'm not here to place blame. My mother had her reasons for keeping it from me. I suspect those reasons had something to do with you. But I won't blame you, either." Bianca stepped toward her. "I just want to know about my sister."

"She isn't your *sister*. She's only half—"

Her granddaughter waved a hand through the air. "She's my *blood*."

That it could hurt even worse came as a surprise. "Your *blood*?" she demanded. "Watered down with the likes of a man…" She sputtered. Her contempt for Walter Justice knew no words.

Bianca dropped to her knees before her grandmother and took both of Marietta's hands in hers. "I want to know about her. I want to know all of it. No more secrets. Grandmama, if you have done something to hurt my sister…" She let go of Marietta's hands. The gesture alone was like a stab in her old heart.

"Get me the phone!" she ordered Ester. She called

Roger's number. It went directly to voice mail. She left a message. "Fix this or else."

BEAU COULDN'T HELP but laugh. "Kidnapped you?" He shook his head as he and DJ dismounted and walked their horses to the edge of the mountainside to look out at the view. "I think anything's possible. But I got the impression from your father that somehow your mother's family didn't know about you. And now they do."

"And that puts me in danger?"

He turned to gaze into her big, beautiful brown eyes, wanting to take away the pain he saw there. He'd been trying to save this woman in his dreams for years. Now here she was, all grown up, and he still felt helpless.

"DJ." His hand cupped the back of her neck. He drew her closer, not sure what he planned to do. Hold her? Kiss her? Whatever it was, he didn't get the chance.

The sound of the bullet whizzing past just inches from her head made him freeze for an instant, and then he grabbed and threw her to the snowy ground as he tried to tell from which direction the shot had come.

"Stay down! Don't give the shooter a target," he ordered as he drew his weapon from beneath his coat. Nothing moved in the dark woods behind them. Only silence filled the cold winter air for long moments.

"The shooter?" she repeated, sounding breathless.

In an explosion of wings, a hawk came flying out of the pines, startling him an instant before he heard the roar of a snowmobile.

"Stay here!" he ordered DJ as he swung up into the saddle.

"Wait. Don't…"

But he was already riding after the snowmobiler. He crested a ridge and drew up short. The smell of fuel permeated the air. Below him on the mountain, the snowmobile zoomed through the pines and disappeared over a rise. There was no way he could catch the man. Nor had he gotten a good look at him.

He swore under his breath as he quickly reined his horse around and headed back to where he'd left DJ.

She'd gotten to her feet but was smart enough to keep the horse between her and the mountainside.

"Are you all right?" he asked. He'd been sure the bullet had missed her. But he'd thrown her down to the ground hard enough to knock the air out of her.

Clearly she was shaken. She hadn't wanted to believe she was in any kind of danger. Until now. "Did you see who it was?" she asked.

"No, he got away. But I'll find him or die trying."

ANDREI COULDN'T BELIEVE he'd missed. It was the cowboy's fault. If he hadn't reached for her right at that moment… But he knew he had only himself to blame. He'd been watching the two through his rifle scope, mesmerized by what he saw. They were in love.

He'd found something touching about that. He'd been in love once, so long ago now that he hardly remembered. But as he watched these two through the scope, he'd recognized it and felt an old pang he'd thought long forgotten.

Fool! Andrei was shaking so hard he had trouble starting the snowmobile. He'd never really considered that he might get caught. As long as the coin toss came up heads, he'd known his luck would hold.

Now, though, he feared his luck had run out. He ripped off his glove and tried the key again. The snowmobile engine sputtered. He should have stolen a new one instead of one that had some miles on it.

He tried the key again. The engine turned over. He let out the breath he hadn't even realized he'd been holding and hit the throttle. He could outrun a horse.

As he raced through the trees, he felt as if his whole life was passing before his eyes. All his instincts told him to run, put this one behind him, forget about Dee Anna Justice.

But even as he thought it, he knew it couldn't end this way. It would ruin his luck, ruin everything. He would make this right because his entire future depended on it.

He was almost back where he'd started a few miles from the main house on Cardwell Ranch when he lost control of the snowmobile and crashed into a tree.

Chapter Twelve

DJ couldn't quit trembling. It had happened so fast that at first she'd been calm. She'd gotten up from the ground, staying behind her horse as she watched the woods for Beau. Had someone really taken a shot at them? Not them. *Her.*

She'd never been so relieved to see anyone as Beau came riding out of the pines toward her and dismounted. He'd given chase but must have realized there was no way he could catch the man. She'd heard the snowmobile engine start up, the sound fading off into the mountains.

Still, she didn't feel safe. "You're sure he's gone?" she asked now as she looked toward those dark woods.

"He's gone. We need to get back to the ranch and call the marshal. I can't get any cell phone coverage up here."

Her legs felt like water. "If you hadn't tried to kiss me again…"

He grinned. "Maybe next time… That's right. I told you there wouldn't be a next time. I'm usually a man of my word."

She could tell he was trying to take her mind off

what had just happened. "I guess you have a kiss coming."

"Glad you see it that way." He looked worried, as if what had almost happened hadn't really hit her yet. Did he expect her to fall apart? She was determined not to—especially in front of him.

She could tell he was shaken, as well—and worried. His gaze was on the trees—just as it had been earlier.

"Why would someone try to kill me?" she demanded. This made no sense. Nor could the same person who'd sent her the doll and the photograph be behind it. That had to be from someone in her family who'd wanted her to know about them.

But she remembered her father's fear when he'd seen the photo. Who was he so afraid of?

"All this can't be about something my father did over thirty years ago," she said, and yet it always had something to do with him. She thought about what Zinnia had told them. "Apparently this person really carries a grudge." She could see that Beau wasn't amused.

"We're going to have to find your grandmother."

"Marietta Pisani. You think she's hired someone to shoot me? Why now?"

"I wish I knew. But maybe it's what your father said. They didn't know about you and now they do."

She shook her head. "They don't even know me. Why would they want to kill me?"

He shook his head. "From what Zinnia said, it could involve money."

"If that's true, no wonder my father told me my mother died in childbirth. He was actually trying to spare me. How do you like that?" She let out another bitter laugh as she turned to look at the cowboy. "So now they want me dead."

"If your mother died a few months ago, maybe that was when the rest of the family found out about you. It must have come as a shock."

"My mother chose her family and their money over me."

"I'm sure it wasn't an easy choice."

She hated the tears that burned her eyes. "I am their flesh and blood. Wouldn't they want to meet me before they had me killed?"

He reached for her, drawing her into his strong chest. She buried her face in his winter coat. "Let's not jump to conclusions until we know what's going on, okay?"

She nodded against his chest. "Why didn't my father tell me the truth when I showed him the photo?" she asked, drawing back.

"I'm sure he regrets it. He swears that when you came to him, he didn't know what was going on."

She pulled away. "My father lies."

BEAU STARED AT her slim back as she swung up onto her horse. She was reasonably hurt by what she'd learned from Zinnia, but she was trying so hard not to show it. "I don't think he's lying about this."

"Someone else knew about me." She turned to look at him. "That person sent me the doll and the photo."

He hated to tell her that maybe the doll and the photo might merely have been a way of verifying that she was indeed Walter Justice's daughter. When she'd received the items, she headed straight for the

prison—and her father, whom she hadn't acknowl-
edged in years.

"But now they're afraid I'll go after the money."
She shook her head. "After years of believing I had
no family other than my father, now I have so much
that some of them have put a price on my head. I don't
know what to say."

Beau didn't, either. "You could contact them, possibly make a deal—"

"I don't want their money!" She spurred her horse.

He had to swing up into the saddle and go after her.
The woman could handle a horse. He rode after her,
sensing that she needed this release. Her horse kicked
up a cloud of snow that hung in the air as he caught up
and raced like the wind alongside her.

Her cheeks were flushed and there was a steely
glint in her eyes that told him of a new determination.

"You'll help me find out who is behind this?" she
asked as they reined in at the barn.

"You know I will. But first we have to report this."
Swinging down from the saddle, he called the marshal's office. Hud told them to stay there. Good to his
word, he was there before the horses were unsaddled
and put away in the pasture.

Hud sent several deputies up into the woods to the
spot Beau told him about. They'd be able to find it easily enough by following the tracks.

Once inside, he steered them both into the kitchen.
"Here," Hud said, shoving a glass of water into DJ's
trembling hands. "I have something stronger if that
would help."

She shook her head and raised the glass to her lips,
surprised she was still trembling. She'd believed she

could take care of herself. Now she was just thankful that Beau had been there. What if it had been she and Dana who'd ridden up into the mountains?

"I'll take that something stronger," Beau said to Hud, and he poured him a little whiskey in a glass. Beau downed it in one gulp but declined more.

"This doesn't make any sense," DJ heard herself saying. "It had to have been an accident." She wanted the men to agree with her. But neither did. She could tell that Beau was convinced this was what her father had feared.

She listened while Beau told Hud in detail what he knew. Then she said, "If I brought whatever this is—"

"We'll get to the bottom of this," Hud said. "I'll tell you what Dana would. You're with family. We aren't going to let anything happen to you."

But even as he said it, DJ could see that he was worried. The last Dee Anna Justice had come here and brought trouble. The real Dee Anna promised herself that wouldn't be the case this time. She had hoped she'd find the answers she needed in Montana. Now she worried that she was endangering the family she'd just found.

She would leave as soon as she could get a flight out.

But even as she thought it, she had a feeling she wouldn't be leaving alone—if Beau had anything to do with it.

A<small>NDREI</small> <small>GRIMACED IN</small> pain as he finished bandaging his leg in his motel room. The snowmobile accident was just another bad sign, he told himself. And yet he had survived it with minimal damage.

He'd managed to push the wrecked snowmobile off into a gully where it wouldn't be found—along with some of the debris that had been knocked off it when he'd hit the tree. He'd gotten away. That alone should have been cause for celebration, since it was the closest he'd come to being caught.

Had he not missed, the cowboy would have been trying to save his beloved instead of racing on horseback in an attempt to catch her would-be killer.

He stood now to test his leg and, groaning in pain, sat back down. He wouldn't be climbing any more power poles, that was for sure. But he wasn't going to let this mishap change anything. He'd be fine by tomorrow, he assured himself.

The problem was that now DJ and her protective cowboy would know he was out here. They would be even more careful than they had been at first. He would have to wait—and watch. In good time, he told himself. And he still had time. He could complete this before his birthday, and he would.

He checked his phone. There were two messages from the man who'd hired him. Andrei didn't bother to listen to them. Whatever the man wanted, it didn't matter. This had become personal. Nothing could stop him now.

MARSHAL HUD SAVAGE leaned back in his chair in his den on the ranch to look at Beau. Dana, Stacy and the kids had returned. Not wanting to upset them, he'd suggested the two of them talk in his den. They'd known each other for years—just not well. Their cases had never overlapped until now.

"So, Dee Anna's father hired you?" Hud asked.

Beau liked to keep things simple. He'd learned that years ago when dealing with his father—and the law. He nodded. "He asked me to watch over his daughter."

"He wasn't more specific than that?"

"No."

"And how exactly did he know about you?"

"I guess he could have looked in the phone book under private investigators," he said, dodging the truth.

Hud nodded. "Seems odd, though, asking you to keep an eye on her while she's here where her cousin's husband is the marshal."

"Not really." He softened his words with a wry smile. "Walter Justice is in prison. It could be he doesn't trust law enforcement."

The marshal chuckled at that. "Point well-taken, given what we know about Walter." He studied Beau openly for a moment. "You had taken DJ for a horse-back ride."

"To talk. DJ's trying to find out more about her family."

"Dana said the three of you went to visit Walter's high school girlfriend, Zinnia Jameson?"

Beau nodded. "DJ knows nothing about her father's past. We were hoping Zinnia could provide some answers."

"That's what you had to talk to DJ about?"

He could tell that Hud was suspicious, since it had been Beau who'd taken her to a spot where a shooter had almost killed her.

"We needed to talk about what we'd learned, but also, I had to give her some bad news. Her father was shanked in prison."

"I'm sorry to hear that. I get the impression from Dana that DJ and her father aren't close."

"No, but he's still her father."

Hud sighed. "There's something about your story... Tell me again what the two of you were doing right before you heard the shot and felt the bullet whiz past."

Beau laughed. He had great respect for the marshal. The man had sensed he hadn't told him everything. "I was about to kiss her. I'd pulled her closer..."

The marshal nodded smiling. "You were trying to kiss her?"

He grinned. "Unfortunately the shooter took a pot-shot at us before that could happen."

"So, this is more than a job for you?"

Beau didn't want to get into the whole story of the first time he saw DJ and how he'd never forgotten her. "There's been some attraction from the start."

"I can understand that. It's those Justice women." He turned serious again. "You didn't get a good look at him?"

"No. Nor the snowmobile. Earlier I thought I heard one in the distance, but I didn't think anything about it. It's December. Everybody and his brother have one of the damned things, and the mountains around here are riddled with old logging roads."

"But you're convinced the bullet was for DJ?"

"Depends on how well the man shoots. If he was aiming for me, he can't hit the side of a barn. But if he was aiming for DJ, he's good. Really good. If I hadn't drawn her toward me when I did..."

"You're thinking a professional?"

"I am."

"You have any idea why someone would want Dee Anna Justice dead?"

Beau hesitated. He understood why Hud had wanted to talk to him alone. DJ was Dana's family. Hud would have done anything for his wife.

"It might have something to do with her mother's family," Beau said after a moment. "I'm going to shadow her until we find out what's going on. I don't have much to go on." He told the marshal the names of both mother and grandmother.

Hud wrote them down. Marietta and Carlotta Pisani. "Why would her own flesh and blood want to harm her?"

Beau shook his head, thinking of Cain and Abel. He couldn't help but wonder about DJ's half sister. "There might be money involved."

"GRANDMAMA, YOU'RE SCARING ME. Tell me what you've done," Bianca demanded as her grandmother hung up the phone. "I'm assuming that was Roger you called. He hired someone to find my sister and then what?" She shook her head as if too disappointed in her grandmother to talk for a moment.

Ester had dropped into a chair across from them.

Marietta looked at her precious granddaughter. Her heart was in her throat. What if the man Roger had hired had already accomplished what he'd paid him to do? Now she realized that she could lose the one person who mattered to her.

"Do you have any idea how much I love you, how much I have tried to protect you—"

Bianca's look stopped her cold. "What have you done?"

"It might not be too late."

"Too late for what?"

Marietta waved that off and tried to rope in her thoughts. Roger would already have called if it was done. Of course he'd stopped it. Roger was too smart to go against her wishes on this. She reminded herself he was so smart that apparently he'd been stealing from her for years. She was the matriarch of this family, but Roger was a man she'd leaned on since her husband had died all those years ago.

"Listen to me. I'm trying to make this right." Her fear of losing Bianca's love, though, was a knife lodged in her chest.

"Tell me everything you know about her," Bianca said, sitting down next to her.

There was no keeping it from her now. "I don't know very much, just what your mother told me. Her name is Dee Anna Justice."

"So after Mother told you, did you try to reach her? You just said it might be too late."

So Ester *hadn't* told her everything. Marietta thought she still might stand a chance of regaining Bianca's love, her trust. "You have to understand. Your mother was very young. She fell in love with this man from Montana who was all wrong for her. Fortunately she realized her mistake…" She almost said, *"before it was too late,"* but that had been what she'd thought at the time.

Now she knew that it *had* been too late. Carlotta had given birth to Walter Justice's child—and kept the truth from nearly everyone.

ON HER DEATHBED, Carlotta had cried, saying it was Marietta's fault that she'd had to keep Dee Anna a secret all these years.

"I wanted my child with me. I needed my child with me. But you had made it clear that if I didn't come home, forget about Walter and go to Italy to stay with my aunt…"

"You are going to blame me for this?" she'd demanded.

"I had to give up my child because of you."

No, Marietta had argued. "You gave up your child for *money*. You knew I would cut off your allowance if you stayed with that man. It was your choice."

Had her daughter thought that one day she could just come home with the child and all would be forgiven? Or had she given up on that foolish idea when she'd met the nice Italian man she'd married and become pregnant with *his* child?

"Surely Walter Justice would have gladly given up the child had you demanded it," she had pointed out to her daughter.

"You're wrong. He loved me. He loved Dee Anna. He would never have let you get near her, knowing how you felt about him. But, Mother, now you can make up for the past. Now you have a chance to know your *first* granddaughter."

Carlotta must have seen her expression, because her own hardened. "Or not. Whatever happens, it's on your head now, Mother."

MARIETTA REALIZED BIANCA had asked her a question.

"Why did you hate my sister's father so much?" Bianca asked again, accusation in her tone.

"He was a crook. All he was interested in was our money."

"*Money.* Why does it always come back to that with you?"

"He's serving time in prison. I think that tells you what kind of man he is." She hated that her voice rose, that she sounded like a woman who'd lost control of her life. A woman who was no longer sure of the stand she'd taken. A woman who would die drowning in regret.

Bianca rose. "I want to meet my sister."

"Stop calling her that!" Marietta snapped irritably. "She is merely your mother's mistake."

Her granddaughter looked horrified at her words.

She regretted them instantly. "You don't understand," she pleaded. "This woman isn't one of us. If she is anything like her father, she'll demand part of your inheritance. I know you think you don't care about the money, about the family legacy—"

"It is the family *curse*," Bianca said. "That's what mother called it. She used to wish her family was dirt-poor."

Marietta wanted to laugh. Her extravagant daughter would not have liked being poor, let alone dirt-poor.

Bianca's eyes narrowed. "So this is about money. You're afraid she will want money."

"No, I was willing to give her money. It's about you, Bianca. I don't want you to be hurt. Contacting this woman can only—"

"Tell me how I can find her," Bianca said, cutting her off.

She swallowed and looked to Ester. "Why don't you ask *her*?" she said, pointing to her housekeeper. "She seems to be well-informed."

Ester's gaze met hers, unspoken secrets between them. The housekeeper hadn't told Bianca about the hit man. But she'd hinted at it. Did Marietta really want her to tell everything she knew?

"I'm asking *you*," her granddaughter said.

Marietta sighed. She knew when she'd lost. Wasn't it possible that Dee Anna Justice could already be dead? If so, Bianca would never forgive her. And the family legacy could already be gone, thanks to Roger. She had only herself to blame for all of this. But to lose both Bianca and her fortune would be unendurable.

"She's at the Cardwell Ranch near Big Sky, Montana, but—"

"I'm going to find her," Bianca said with more determination than Marietta had ever seen in her.

As she started to leave, Ester said, "I'd like to go with you."

Bianca shot a look at her grandmother and seemed to hesitate. "Can you manage alone with your bad heart?"

"I've been on my own before," Marietta snapped, wondering how she *would* manage. "Don't worry about me."

"I'll call when I find her," Bianca said.

Everything she cared about was walking out that door. She didn't think her heart could break further. She was wrong, she realized as she saw Ester's suitcase by the door and knew that she might not see either of them again.

"WE HAVE TO find out who's behind this," Beau told DJ before they left Cardwell Ranch. "I thought we'd go by my office in Bozeman. I should warn you about my assistant. She's... Well, you'll see soon enough."

He wasn't surprised when Marge did one of her eyebrow lifts as they walked in. What did surprise him was how quickly she took to DJ.

Like a mother hen, she scurried around, getting coffee, offering to run down to the cupcake shop for treats.

"We're fine. We won't be here long," he told her with an amused and slightly irritated shake of his head. He ushered DJ into the office, saying, "I'll be right back," and closed the door behind her.

Turning to Marge, he said, "What is going on with you?"

"Me?" She gave him her innocent look.

"This isn't a *date*. DJ is a *client*, of sorts. This one is...off the record, but it is still work. Nothing more."

"DJ, huh?"

He shook his head. "Why do you take so much interest in my love life?"

"*What* love life?" she said, fiddling with some papers on her desk.

Beau ignored that jab. "Are you hoping to get me married off?"

"I never said a word."

"You don't have to." He started for his office, but something was bothering him. Turning back to her, he said, "I have to know. DJ walks in and you instantly like her. You've never liked any of the women I've dated, and you've never done more than share a few words with them on the phone. What is different about this one?" he demanded, trying to keep his voice down.

Marge smiled. "You'll remember this one's name."

Chapter Thirteen

DJ pulled up a chair next to Beau as he turned on the computer and began his search. She felt surprisingly nervous sitting this close to him. It brought back the memory of being in his arms, of his mouth on hers. There was something so masculine about him.

"You all right?" he asked as she moved her chair back a little. "Can you see okay?"

She nodded and tried to breathe. "How long has Marge been with you?"

"Since I started. She's like a mother hen." He shook his head. "But I couldn't run this office without her." She heard true admiration and caring in his voice. She also sensed a strong loyalty in him. Look how he'd agreed to protect her based on a promise he'd made so many years ago.

"I like her."

He glanced over at her. "And she likes you. Believe me, it's a first." Their gazes locked for a moment. She could feel the heat of his look and remembered how he'd almost kissed her up on the mountain.

At the sound of his assistant on the other side of the door, he turned quickly back to the computer. "Okay, let's see what we can find out about your grandmother. Marietta Pisani. There can't be that many, right?"

DJ thought about how this had started with the doll and the photo. Her father's letters had led them to Zinnia, who'd told her more about her father—and mother—than she'd ever known. Leave it to her father to tell Beau that the doll and photo might have something to do with her mother's family. Why couldn't he have told her that?

Because he'd been lying to her since birth, she reminded herself. She felt a stab of guilt. He was in the hospital, badly injured. She'd called but hadn't been able to learn much—just that he was in stable but serious condition. She told herself he was tough. He'd pull through. She hoped it was true.

"Your father told you that your mother was dead, but that your grandmother Marietta is still alive, right?" Beau was saying. "Marietta Pisani. Is there any chance she's related to the noble Pisani family of Malta? Descendants of Giovanni Pisani, the patrician of Venice?"

"I have no idea," DJ said.

"Maybe you'll get a chance to ask her," he said and motioned to the screen. "I found only one in the right age group. A Marietta Pisani of Palm Desert, California."

DJ swallowed the lump in her throat. This was the woman who'd had her daughter's marriage to Walter Justice annulled. "What do we do now? You can't think that my grandmother…" Her words faltered. She could see from his expression that he could think exactly that.

Her father had also thought it. Why else would he

have asked Beau to protect her? But surely she didn't need protecting from her own grandmother?

"We call her," Beau said and reached for the phone.

It took Marietta a while to calm down after Bianca and Ester left. At first she was just scared. Scared that she'd lost everything. Then she was furious with Ester for butting into her family business. She'd tried to reach Roger but suspected he was not picking up. The coward.

At some point, she'd have to find out if there was any money left. But right now, it was her least concern. Her daughter would have thought that funny, she realized. The joke was on her, she realized. Roger had stolen her money. All that worry about the family legacy and now she realized that if she lost Bianca, nothing mattered.

When a middle-aged woman arrived with a suitcase in hand claiming to be Ester's younger sister, May, she almost turned her away.

"I'm not like Ester. I'll see to you, but don't think you can browbeat me the way you do her."

Marietta was offended. "I don't browbeat anyone."

May huffed and slipped past her. "Just tell me where my room is. Then I'll see about getting you fed. I cook whatever I can find to cook and you eat it. That's the deal."

With that, the woman had sashayed off in the direction Marietta had pointed.

This was what her life had come to? She almost wished that she'd died this morning before she'd seen that little red sports car drive up.

But then she wouldn't have seen her precious granddaughter. Not that their visit had gone well.

She tried Roger's number again. Again it went to voice mail. It was in God's hands, she told herself. God's and Bianca's and Ester's and whomever Roger had hired.

She prayed that Dee Anna Justice was still alive. She just didn't want Bianca hurt. But who knew what this Dee Anna Justice was like? She couldn't bear the thought of Dee Anna rejecting Bianca. If there was any money left, she knew her granddaughter would gladly share it with her...sister.

Marietta made the call. She had to take control of her life again, one step at a time, until her old heart gave out.

As STACY DRESSED for her date, she felt torn between excitement and worry. Did she really believe that she and James could start over again after all these years? Maybe she was hanging on to a first-love fantasy James, one who had never existed.

"What has he done for a living since high school?" Dana had asked. She didn't know. "What does he do now?"

"I think he said real estate."

Her sister got that look Stacy knew only too well.

"You remember him," Stacy said. "You liked him in high school, didn't you?"

"I didn't know him," Dana said. "But I do remember that he broke your heart."

"It wasn't his fault. He thought his ex-girlfriend was pregnant..." She stopped when she saw Dana's expression. "He did the right thing by her. He married her."

"I suppose so," her sister said. "Just…be careful. It's not only you now. You have to think of Ella."

She'd thought only of Ella since her daughter's birth. There hadn't been any men, not even one date. But now she could admit that she felt ready. She wanted a husband and a father for Ella and said as much to Dana.

"There is nothing wrong with that," her sister said, giving her a hug. "Maybe James is that man. Maybe he's not. Give it time. Don't let him rush you into anything."

She knew what Dana was getting at. James had rushed her into sex in high school. She hadn't been ready, but she'd feared that she would lose him if she didn't give in to him.

As she finished dressing, Stacy told herself she wasn't that young, naive girl anymore. If James thought she was, then he was in for a surprise.

ROGER SWORE WHEN he saw how many times Marietta had called. He didn't even bother to check the voice mails. He knew she'd be demanding to know what was going on. He'd called the man who'd hired the hit man and had finally heard back.

"He rushed the job and missed," the man told him. "Now he has to fix it. So back off. These things take time. Worse, now she knows someone is trying to kill her. Also, the marshal is involved."

Roger felt sick to his stomach. "You told me that he would make it look like a shooting accident. This isn't what my boss wanted at all. Call him off."

"I'll do what I can. He isn't answering his phone." Could this get any worse?

"He's going to want the rest of the money. You'd best have it ready for him," the man warned.

"Of course." Roger hung up, sweating. His phone rang again. He saw that this time it was the accountant he'd been working with. Marietta. She was checking the trust funds. He was dead meat, he thought as he let her call go to voice mail.

He decided he'd better listen to Marietta's message. What he heard turned his blood to ice.

"Bianca knows! She and Ester are headed for Cardwell Ranch in Montana. If anything happens to them, I'll have you killed in prison, and you know I can do it. I might not have as much money as I once did, but I still have power."

He disconnected, not doubting it for a moment. He looked around the room. He couldn't wait any longer. She knew that he'd been embezzling money for years from the family trust funds. He'd hoped that he could win it back, but his gambling debts were eating him alive. If the thugs he owed didn't kill him, then Marietta would.

His cell phone rang again almost instantly. He put it on mute, telling himself he would throw it in the ocean the first chance he got and buy a new one. Then he stepped to the suitcase. His passport and the plane tickets were on the table by the door. He picked them up, took one last look at the house he had mortgaged to the hilt and, suitcase in hand, walked out.

MARIETTA LET OUT a scream of pain when she heard an estimate of how much money was missing from the trust funds.

May rushed into the room. "If you're not bleeding, this had better be a heart attack or a killer snake in the room."

"I want to die."

May shook her head. "Let me get a knife."

"I've made a horrible mess of things."

"Haven't we all? If you don't want your supper burned, die quietly while I get back to the kitchen."

Marietta could hear her heart pounding and welcomed death. What had she done? Her mind wouldn't stop racing. All she could think about were the mistakes she'd made. She had another granddaughter. Bianca would have loved having a sister. She used to ask for one all the time. It broke Marietta's heart.

The irony was that Carlotta's second husband hadn't been much of a step up from Walter. Gianni had some shady dealings before his death. But at least he'd come from a good Italian family with money.

She had wanted so much for her daughter.

And yet Carlotta still hadn't married well.

"Playing God wearing you out?" May asked as she brought in her dinner tray.

"Do you always say whatever you think without regard to whether or not it is proper?" Marietta demanded.

May smiled. "Not much different from you, huh?"

"I'm not hungry," she said, trying to push the tray away.

"Too bad. I'm going to sit right here until you eat. Ester said all I had to do was keep you alive. I figure you're too mean to die, but just in case…" May pushed the tray back at her and sat down, crossing her arms.

Marietta glared at her for a moment before picking

up her fork. If she had to eat to get the woman out of her room, she would.

"You know nothing about any of this," she said.

May chuckled.

"If I thought Ester was talking behind my back—"

"What would you have done? Fired her?" May shook her head. "Ester didn't have to tell me anything about you. I saw it in the sadness in her eyes. She's been loyal to you, just as our mother was. You don't realize how lucky you are that she put up with you all these years. Anyone else would have put a pillow over your face years ago."

"I feel so much better knowing you'll be staying with me until Ester comes back," she said sarcastically.

"You think Ester is coming back?"

Marietta stopped, the fork halfway to her mouth. She didn't want to acknowledge her fear that Ester was gone for good. "She won't leave me alone. Not after all these years."

"Because of your sweet disposition? Or because you pay her so much?"

She felt her face heat but said nothing as she concentrated on her food again. This was what her life had come to, she told herself. She was an old woman alone with an ingrate who had nothing but contempt for her. She half hoped the woman had poisoned her food.

Chapter Fourteen

The phone rang. Marietta snatched it up, hoping it was Bianca calling. Maybe she'd changed her mind about going to Montana, about meeting her half sister, about…everything.

"Hello?"

"Is this Marietta Pisani?"

"Yes." Her heart pounded.

"My name is Beau Tanner. I'm a private investigator in Montana. I'm calling about your granddaughter."

"Bianca?" Montana? Was it possible Bianca and Ester had gotten a flight out so soon and were now in Montana?

"No, Dee Anna Justice."

She gripped the phone so hard that it made her hand ache. She held her breath. Hadn't he said he was a private investigator? Shouldn't it be the police calling if Dee Anna Justice was dead?

"What about her?" she asked, her voice breaking.

"You recognize the name?"

"Yes. She's my granddaughter. What is this about?"

"I was hoping you would tell her," the private eye said. "I'm putting her on the phone."

"Hello?"

Marietta heard the voice of her first granddaughter and felt the rest of her world drop away.

"Hello?" the voice said again.

Marietta began to cry uncontrollably.

May came in, saw what was happening and took the phone. "I'm sorry. She can't talk right now." She hung up the phone. Turning, she demanded, "Where do you think you're going?"

Marietta had shoved away the food tray, gotten to her feet and gone to her closet. Pulling out her empty suitcase, she laid it on the bed and began to throw random clothing into it. "I'm flying to Montana."

May took in the suitcase the older woman had tossed on the bed. "Do you really think that's a good idea given your...condition? Let alone the fact that you might be arrested when you land."

So Ester had shared information with her sister. Marietta knew she shouldn't have been surprised. "You've been in on all this?"

May smiled. "It was my son who left the doll and a photo of her mother, grandmother and Carlotta's second husband for DJ." She sounded proud of what she'd done. "Ester was afraid of how far you would go. She said DJ couldn't be brought off. She wouldn't have wanted a cent of your money. So all of this was a huge waste on your part."

Marietta finished throwing a few items in, slammed her suitcase and zipped it closed. She'd been surrounded by traitors. "You couldn't possibly understand why I've done what I have."

"Why you used money to keep your daughter away

from a child that she loved?" May demanded. "Did Carlotta tell you how she cried herself to sleep over that baby you forced her to give up?"

"Forced her? It was her choice. Just like it was her choice to marry the man. So easy to blame me, isn't it?"

May put one hand on her bony hip. "What would your daughter think now if she knew that you were trying to kill that child?"

Marietta swallowed. She wanted to argue that it was all Roger's doing. But she'd trusted him to handle it. Her mistake. All she'd thought about was erasing the existence of Dee Anna Justice to save the family.

"Help me with my suitcase."

May didn't move.

"I'm going to save the woman. Does that make you happy?" she barked.

"*The woman?* She's your grandchild. She's your blood. She's Bianca's sister."

"I don't have time to argue with you." She shook her head. "None of you know this Dee Anna Justice. What if she wants nothing to do with our family? What if she rejects Bianca? What then?"

"Bianca is a strong woman. She will survive. I think you might underestimate the connection they have," May said. "Ester kept in touch over the years with Dee Anna's father. She saw the girl grow up."

"My suitcase."

May stepped forward, slid the suitcase from the bed and began to wheel it toward the front door. "You best hope that you're not too late."

It was already too late in so many ways.

"SOME WOMAN TOOK the phone and said she couldn't talk. Before that it sounded like she was…crying," DJ said as she saw Beau's anxious expression.

He took the office phone and replaced it in its cradle. "At least now we know that she's the right one."

"I guess. She was definitely upset. But upset to hear from me or to hear that I'm still alive?" She could see he was even more convinced that her grandmother was behind what had happened earlier today on the mountain.

"What now?" As if she had to ask. "The would-be assassin will try again, won't he?" She didn't give him time to answer. "I can't stay at Cardwell Ranch," she said as she pushed to her feet. "I can't endanger my cousin and her family—"

"That's why I want you to move in with me."

She blinked. "No, I couldn't."

"If it makes you feel any better, I have a…friend staying with me. Leah."

"I see." A friend, huh? Was that what he called it? She realized how little she knew about this man.

"I can protect you better on my home ground."

"I think everyone would be better off if I just left Montana."

"You're wrong. But if you leave, I'm going with you. Sorry, but you're stuck with me until this is over."

She stared at him even though she'd expected this. "You can't be serious, and for how long?"

"As long as it takes. But if you could just give me a few days and not leave, it would be better. If whoever shot at you is still here, it will give me the chance to catch him."

She didn't like the sound of this. She'd come to care

about this man. She didn't want to see him get killed protecting her and said as much.

"Have more faith in me," he said with a grin. "Let's go get your things." They drove in silence to the Cardwell Ranch.

Dana put up a fight when Beau told her his plan.

"Christmas is only a few days away," she argued. "DJ is family. She should be here with us."

"With luck, this will be over by Christmas," he told her. "Hud thinks it is best, too."

"Hud." With that one word, Dana looked resigned.

DJ hugged her. "I'm so sorry. I would never have come here if I thought it might be dangerous for your family."

"You have nothing to be sorry for," Dana said. "You take care of her," she said to Beau. "I'm depending on you."

"I hate this," DJ said as he drove them off the ranch. "I hate that I involved them and, worse, you. You're only doing this because of some stupid promise you made when you were a boy to a man who had no right to ask anything of you."

Beau was quiet for a long moment as he drove. It almost surprised her when he finally spoke. "The first time we met, I wished that I could help you," he said without looking at her. "I've regretted it ever since."

She spoke around the lump that had formed in her throat. "I don't want you to get killed because of me."

"I don't want that, either," he said with a chuckle. "But I'm not that ten-year-old anymore." He finally glanced over at her. "I can help you. I know what I'm doing."

She looked away, fighting back tears. All this was

because of her father falling in love with the wrong woman? Now he was in the hospital possibly dying and she was... She was in Montana with a cowboy who was determined to save her.

They hadn't gone far when Beau turned off the highway and crossed a narrow bridge that spanned the Gallatin River before driving back into the canyon. At the heart of the valley was a large log house. Behind it was a red barn and some outbuildings. A half-dozen paint horses raced around in a large pasture nearby.

"This is where you live?" she asked, a little awed by the beauty of the scene.

"Do you like?" he asked and glanced over at her.

"I love it." She felt a lump form in her throat. She could see Beau here. "You're a real cowboy."

He laughed. "You're just now realizing that?"

She turned to look at him. She was just now realizing a lot of things, she thought as she stared at his handsome profile in the last light of the day.

JIMMY WAS LATE picking her up, making Stacy have even more second thoughts. But he seemed so glad to see her that she pushed them aside and tried to have a nice time.

He took her to one of the local restaurants, ordered them both a cocktail and drained half his glass before letting out a sigh. He actually looked nervous, which made her laugh and forget her own nervousness.

"So tell me about this cousin staying on the ranch," he said.

"Dee Anna Justice. She's the daughter of my mother's brother, whom we didn't know anything about." She really didn't want to talk about DJ, though. "So, what did you say you're doing in Big Sky again?"

"Working. A brother no one had ever heard of?"

"Working at what?" she asked, wondering why he was so interested in the Justice side of the family.

"This and that." He drained his glass. The waiter came over and before Stacy could look at her menu, James ordered for both of them, including more drinks. "You don't mind, do you?" he asked after the waiter had already left.

She shook her head, although she did mind. "How long did you say you've been back?"

"Did I say? A few weeks. Actually, I'm looking for a job. Anything opening up on Cardwell Ranch?"

She couldn't help but laugh. "What do you know about working on a ranch? As I recall, you hated helping on your uncle's."

"I forgot what a good memory you have." That didn't sound like a compliment. The waiter came with their drinks and he downed his quickly.

"Jimmy—"

"But you can't seem to remember that I go by James now." He was clearly irritated and not trying to hide it.

"Sorry. Why did you ask me to dinner tonight?"

He leaned back, giving her a what-do-you-think look. "I thought for old times' sake..." He shrugged. "You dating someone?"

Fortunately their meals came. They talked little. Jimmy ate as if he hadn't had a meal in days. He devoured his steak and then asked her if she was going to finish hers. She'd lost her appetite early on in the date, so she gladly slid her plate over and let him clean it.

What had she been thinking? Her sister was right.

The Jimmy Ryan she'd been in love with all those years ago wasn't the man sitting across from her.

"Ready?" he asked as he signaled the waiter for his bill.

Turning, she spotted Burt Olsen, their mailman. He nodded and smiled at her. He appeared to be picking up something to go.

Stacy just wanted this date to be over. When Jimmy saw her looking at Burt, he threw an arm around her waist and propelled her toward the door.

"Maybe I should drive," she said as they started toward his truck.

"I don't think you should think." He still had hold of her as they neared the pickup. He opened the driver's-side door and practically shoved her in, pushing her over to get behind the wheel.

"Jimmy—James."

"I remember you being a lot more fun," he said, gritting his teeth.

And vice versa, but she said nothing as she saw Burt getting into his vehicle. He'd been watching the two of them. And she knew that if she said anything to Jimmy, it would turn into a fight. Burt was the last person she wanted seeing her and Jimmy fighting. She told herself that Jimmy hadn't had that much to drink—and it was only a short drive to the ranch.

Neither of them spoke during the drive. As they crossed the bridge, he glanced over at her. "You hear me?"

She hadn't realized he'd said anything. "I'm sorry?"

"I'm sure you are." He drove on into the ranch and pulled up in front of her cabin. "So which one is this cousin of yours staying in?"

She pointed to the last one at the other end of the row. She knew what was coming, but Jimmy was out of luck if he thought she was going to invite him in.

"Thanks for dinner," she said as he shut off the engine. She reached for her door handle. But before she could get it open, he leaned over and grabbed her hand to stop her.

"I'm sorry about tonight. It wasn't you. I got some bad news right before I picked you up. I should have canceled." He drew back his hand.

"What kind of bad news?" she asked out of politeness.

"An investment. It fell through. I was counting on it."

She hoped he didn't ask her for money. "I'm sure you'll be able to get a job."

"A *job*." He said the last word like it tasted nasty in his mouth. "Just not on your ranch, huh? You don't even know what I do for a living."

"A little of this and that is all you told me." She reached for the door handle again.

This time his hand came around the back of her neck. He clamped down hard enough to take her breath away. "You're kind of a smart mouth. I do remember that about you."

Stacy tried to wriggle out of his grasp. "Stop!" she said as he pulled her toward him as if to kiss her. "I said *stop*!" That feeling of déjà vu hit her hard. This was what had happened in high school, only then she'd thought that he was so crazy about her he just couldn't help himself. She knew better now.

Chapter Fifteen

Leah looked up expectantly as Beau entered the kitchen. She smiled quickly as if covering her disappointment. Who had she expected? Her husband? Or someone else?

Her gaze went to DJ, her expression one of surprise and something else. Jealousy?

"This is DJ. She's going to be staying with us. DJ, Leah."

"No last names?" Leah asked, pretending to be amused.

He walked to the stove. "You cooked?"

"Don't sound so surprised. I'm a woman of many talents."

Beau could believe that somehow, even though he hadn't been around Leah in years. She'd always seemed...capable.

"Looks like you made enough for three," he said, lifting the lid on one of the pots and glancing into the oven, where what looked like a Mexican casserole bubbled. Looking up, he said, "You must have been expecting company."

She shook her head, but not before he'd seen that

moment of hesitation. Her laugh wasn't quite authentic, either. But he wasn't about to get into it with her now.

He turned to DJ. "Let me show you to a room."

"It was nice meeting you," Leah called after them.

"You, too," DJ said over her shoulder, and then added only for his ears as they climbed the stairs and rounded a corner, "She doesn't want me here. Wouldn't it be better if I—"

"She isn't my *girlfriend*. She's the wife of my former best friend. I have no idea what she's doing here, so what she wants is really of no interest to me."

DJ WAS SURPRISED at his words. He'd been so protective of her, and yet he seemed angry at the woman they'd left downstairs.

He saw her surprise as they reached the end of the hall, and he started to open a door but stopped. "I don't mean to seem cold, but it's what she's not telling me about her and her husband that has me worried."

"It's none of my business."

He studied her openly. "Come on, let's hear it. I can tell there is something on your mind."

"Did the two of you ever—"

"No. She was always Charlie's girl, and before you ask, no, I was never interested in her."

"It's odd, then, because she seems very possessive of you."

He shrugged and pushed open the door to a beautiful room done in pastels.

"What a pretty room."

He didn't seem to hear her. "I'm right next door if you need me. Leah is downstairs in the guest room."

"Who's room is this?" She realized her mistake at once. "I shouldn't have asked."

"I was engaged to a woman with a young daughter. This was going to be her room, but it didn't work out."

"I'm sorry."

He shook his head. "Looking back, I loved the thought of having a child more than I loved having her mother as my wife." He took a step toward the door. "Get unpacked if you like, then come downstairs. Let's find out if Leah really can cook or not."

After he left, DJ looked around the beautiful room. He'd made it so pretty for the little girl. There was such love in the room. She felt sad for him. How lucky that child would have been in so many ways.

She took her time unpacking what little she'd brought, giving Beau time with Leah. Whatever was going on between them, she didn't want to be in the middle of it. She had enough troubles of her own.

Taking out her phone, she put in a call to the prison. Her father was still in serious condition at the hospital.

She withdrew the photo of her mother from her purse and sat down in the white wooden rocker to study it. This woman had been her mother. She hadn't died in childbirth. No, instead, she'd apparently given up her first child to make her family happy, then married another man and had another child.

But what, if anything, did this have to do with the man who'd shot at her? According to what Beau had been able to find out, her mother really had died recently. So who wanted her dead? The grandmother who'd refused to talk to her? Zinnia had said that her mother's family had money. Surely it couldn't be that simple.

But her father had known the moment he looked at the photo. Her mother's family had found her, and that had terrified him enough that he'd pressured Beau Tanner to protect her.

But what about the other daughter? The one who'd had the doll? What about her half sister?

As JIMMY GRABBED at her, Stacy swung her fist and caught him under the left eye. He let out a curse. His grip loosened and she shoved open the door, only to have him drag her back. He thrust his hand down the front of the dress she'd bought for the date. She heard the fabric tear as he groped for her breasts.

With his free hand, he grabbed her flailing wrists and dragged her hard against him. "You like it rough? You'll get it rough," he said, squeezing her right breast until she cried out.

Stacy hardly heard the driver's-side door open. Jimmy had been leaning against it and almost fell out as the door was jerked open.

"She said stop," a familiar male voice said.

Jimmy let go of her, pulling his hand from inside her dress to turn angrily toward the open door—and the intruder. All he got out was "What the he—" when a fist hit him between the eyes.

Stacy saw it only out of the corner of her eye. The moment Jimmy let go of her, she slid across the seat and climbed out of the pickup. That was when she saw who her savior was. Mailman Burt Olsen's face was set, his voice dangerously calm. "You go on inside now, Ms. Cardwell. I'll take care of this."

She hesitated only a moment before scurrying up the steps. Once on the porch, she turned back. Just as she'd feared, Jimmy was out of the truck and looking for a fight. He took a swing, but Burt easily ducked it and caught Jimmy in the jaw with a left hook. He toppled back toward the open truck door. Burt doubled him over as he fell, shoved him back into the truck and closed the door.

"He won't be bothering you anymore tonight," the mailman called over to her. "But if you need me to stay…"

She almost couldn't find the words, she was so surprised. "No, I'm fine now. But thank you, Burt."

He tipped his baseball cap. Past him, she could see where he'd parked his car and walked up the mountainside. He'd come to her rescue after seeing what had been going on at the restaurant, and all she could think was that he'd let his supper get cold to do it.

Inside the cabin, she locked her door just in case Jimmy—*excuse me*—James, didn't get the hint. The man was a fool, but he wasn't stupid, she told herself. Glancing out the window, she saw that Burt was waiting for Jimmy to leave. She was relieved when a few minutes later she heard his truck start up and drive away.

In the bedroom, she saw that her dress was ruined. She tossed it into the trash. Thinking about Burt Olsen, she had to smile. She'd never seen this side of him before.

JIMMY HAD NEVER been so furious. Who the devil had that man been? Stacy's sweetheart? Nice of her to mention, if that was the case. But he'd called her Ms. Cardwell. Must have been a hired man.

Not that it mattered. He'd sat for a moment, stunned

and bleeding and planning his revenge. The lights went out in Stacy's cabin. He considered breaking down the door but realized he wasn't up to it. There was always another day. The woman would pay.

As he started the truck's engine to drive out of the ranch, he thought about the dude who'd hit him. If he ever saw him again…

He hadn't gone far when his headlights flashed over someone in the shadows of one of the outbuildings. For a moment he thought it was the man who'd attacked him. He slowed and saw his mistake. This man, who ducked behind the barn, was much larger, dressed in all black. He was carrying something. The moonlight had caught on the barrel of a rifle.

Jimmy sped on by, pretending not to have noticed. As he drove down the road to where it dropped over a rise, he realized he'd seen the man before. It was the lineman he'd seen on one of the power poles when he'd driven in earlier.

"Lineman, my ass," he said to himself as he quickly pulled over and cut the engine. He pulled his hunting knife from under the seat.

It was time to take care of the competition. He quietly opened his door and stepped out into the winter night. He could see his breath as he started back toward the barn. The pro must be waiting for DJ Justice to return. Stacy had said earlier that she thought DJ had left with some neighboring cowboy.

Well, Jimmy had a surprise for the man, he thought with a grin. He'd take care of the pro, and then maybe he'd double back for Stacy. He was feeling much better suddenly. And if the bitch thought she would get rid of him that easily, she was sadly mistaken.

BEAU FOUND LEAH setting the table for three. "So, what's going on?"

She looked up as if she'd been lost in thought and he'd startled her. "Supper is almost ready. I made a casserole. I'm not much of a cook, but—"

"I'm not talking about food. What are you really cooking up?"

Leah gave him a blank look. "I told you—"

"You were expecting a package, but…" She started to interrupt. He stopped her with an angry slash of his hand through the air. "What are you really doing here? Earlier you told me that you and Charlie were in trouble and you needed my help."

"I was wrong. This is something that will have to work itself out on its own. I can't involve you."

"You've already involved me. I'm tired of whatever game this is that you're playing. Tell me what the hell is going on."

She slowly put down the plate she'd been holding, straightened the napkin and silverware and then finally looked up at him. "There is a lot I can't tell you. Charlie and I…we've become involved in some…covert work. Our latest…assignment didn't go so well. I got out. Charlie…" Her voice broke. "We made a pact years ago that if we ever got separated, we would meet here." Her eyes glistened. "Because you were always our one harbor even in college."

"Why didn't you tell me that right away?" he asked quietly as he considered what she'd told him.

"Because I didn't come here to involve you in anything. You and your friend aren't in any danger. Charlie's and my work is done far from here. No one knows

I'm here except Charlie. I made sure that I wasn't followed."

He had a million questions, which he suspected she wasn't going to answer anyway, but the creak of the stairs told him that their conversation was over. At least for now.

He'd never been a trusting man—thanks to his father. He hated the way his mind worked. He questioned what most people told him. Leah was at the top of the list right now.

The knock at the door made them both jump. Beau had taken off his shoulder holster and hung it by the door. He stepped to it now and motioned for Leah to go into the den. DJ had stopped on the stairs. One look at him and she'd frozen in midstep.

Another knock, this one harder. Beau strode to the door and pulled his weapon. Stepping to the side, he opened the door, the weapon ready.

He felt a moment of shock when he looked at the rugged, clearly exhausted man standing there. *"Charlie?"*

Chapter Sixteen

Andrei heard the car engine as someone left the ranch. He frowned as he waited for the sound of the vehicle crossing the bridge and didn't hear it. He listened. A chill moved up his spine. He had been watching the house from his hiding spot. But now he stopped at the edge of the barn and sniffed the air.

The vehicle had definitely not crossed the bridge. Nor had it turned back. He would have heard it. That meant that it had stopped. The winter night was so quiet he could hear the ice crack on the edge of the river. He heard the soft click of a car door being closed and readied himself.

The driver had seen him. That rattled him enough. But the driver was also trying to sneak up on him. That meant the person would be armed with some kind of weapon.

All Andrei had was a rifle. But he didn't want to shoot and call attention to himself. So he would wait until the man reached the corner of the barn and then he would jump him. He was ready.

He pressed his back against the side of the barn at the corner and waited. This would complicate things, he thought, on a job that was already complicated as it was. But since his accident, he'd been frustrated. Maybe this was exactly what he needed to let out some of that anxiety.

It had always been more satisfying to kill someone with his bare hands than shoot them from a distance. Given that his leg still hurt like hell, he probably should have walked away. But it was too late now. A twig under the snow snapped close by. No time to make a run for it even if he could have run. This could end only one way. One of them was about to die.

The man came around the corner of the barn. The large knife blade in his hand caught the winter light.

"I'M AFRAID WE won't be joining you for dinner," Charlie said after he and Beau had hugged like the old friends they were. His gaze met his wife's. She stood a few feet away, tears in her eyes and relief etched on her face. She hadn't moved since Beau had opened the door, as if to give the two men some time.

"We need to get going, but it is great seeing you," Charlie said.

"That's it?" Beau demanded as Leah scurried down the hall to the guest room, returning moments later with her overnight bag. She stepped to her husband's side and pressed her face into his neck for a moment, his arm coming around her. The hug was hard and filled with emotion. Clearly this was the package she'd been waiting for.

Charlie had always been good-looking. Now, even though he appeared a little haggard, his smile was infectious. "It is so good to see you. One of these days, we'll be back permanently. I hope we can get together then, have a couple of beers and talk. But right now…"

Beau shook his head. He'd been angry at Leah for not telling him what was really going on. But he couldn't be angry with Charlie, his old friend. "Just be careful." He shook Charlie's hand and watched as the two disappeared down the road. Beau saw car lights flash on and heard the sound of an engine, and then they were gone as if they'd never been there.

He turned to look at DJ.

"Are you all right?" she asked.

He gave her a quick nod. "I hope you're hungry. We have a lot of casserole to eat."

She moved toward the kitchen. "I'd better take the casserole out of the oven, then."

"Maybe we could just sit in front of the fire and have a drink while it cools down a little. I could use one." He moved into the living room and stepped to the bar.

"Wine for me," she said when he offered her a bourbon like the one he'd poured for himself. "You don't have to say anything."

He ran a hand over his face and let out a bitter laugh as they sat in front of the fire. "I didn't trust her. Leah was one of my best friends years ago, and when she showed up..." He met DJ's gaze. "I hate how suspicious I am of people. I question everything."

DJ WAS SILENT for a moment before she said, "Your father was a con man, right?" He nodded, making her smile. "And you expect us to be trusting?" She laughed at that. "We grew up with no stability, no security, no feeling that everything was going to be all right. How did you expect us to turn out?"

"You might be the only person who understands. But you seem to have it all together."

"I *do*?" She laughed again. "It's just an act." The wood popped and sparked in the fireplace. Golden warm light flickered over them. She took a drink of her wine and felt heat rush through her.

"You think we will ever be like other people?" he asked.

"Probably not. But maybe at some point we won't have so much to fear."

"I remember the first time I saw you. Those big brown eyes of yours really got to me. I wanted to save you. I told myself that if I ever got the chance, I would do anything to help you."

She met his gaze and felt a start at what she saw in those blue eyes. Thinking of how it had felt to be in his arms, she yearned for him to hold her. It wouldn't change anything. There was still someone out there who wanted to kill her, but for a while...

Except she knew that just being held wasn't enough. He made her feel things she'd never felt with another man. She would want his mouth on hers, his body—

"We should probably eat some of that casserole," she said, getting to her feet. She no longer wanted temporary relief from her life. Could no longer afford it. Tomorrow morning would be too hard on her. Too hard to let go of this cowboy and the connection between them that had started so many years ago.

Beau seemed to stir himself as if his thoughts had taken the same path as her own. "Yes."

They ate in a tense silence, the fire crackling in the living room, the kitchen warm.

"This is good," she said, even though she hardly

tasted the casserole. She was glad when the meal was over and wished that Beau hadn't insisted on helping her with the dishes.

"I think I'll turn in," she said as soon as they'd finished cleaning up the kitchen.

He looked almost disappointed. "See you in the morning."

She watched him go to the bar and pour himself another bourbon. When she headed up the stairs, he was standing in front of the fireplace, looking into the flames.

Her steps halted, but only for a moment. She *did* understand him. They had a bond that went back all those years. She felt as if she'd always known him. Always…felt something for him.

That thought sent her on up the stairs to her room. But she knew she wouldn't be able to sleep. She felt lost, and she knew that Beau did, too.

She lay in bed, remembering the older woman's voice on the phone. Her grandmother. And hearing the woman crying so hard that she couldn't talk. Was this really a woman who wanted her dead?

BEAU HAD JUST put the coffee on the next morning when he heard DJ coming down the stairs. The phone rang. He'd had a hell of a time getting to sleep knowing that DJ was only yards down the hall. He couldn't help worrying about what the day would bring. A phone call this early in the morning couldn't bode well.

"Beau Tanner," he said.

"It's Marshal Savage, Beau. I've got some news. A man by the name of Jimmy Ryan, a suspected small-time hit man, was found dead on the ranch this morning. Based on the evidence we found in his vehicle, we believe he was the shooter yesterday. He had a high-powered rifle and a photo of DJ with a target drawn on her face."

"You said he's dead?"

"His throat was cut. Earlier last evening, he'd gotten into an altercation with a local man here on the ranch. We suspect the disagreement ended on the road on the way out of the ranch. Jimmy Ryan was found some yards off the road by one of our barns."

He couldn't believe what he was hearing. "So, it's over?" he said and glanced at DJ.

"It certainly appears that way."

"Do we know who hired him?"

"Not yet. We'll continue investigating. I'll let you know if anything new turns up. Dana wanted to make sure that DJ knew. She has her heart set on her cousin staying until after Christmas, and since it is so close…"

"I'll tell DJ and do everything I can to keep her in Montana until after Christmas." He ended the call and found himself grinning in relief. It seemed impossible. The hit man had gotten into an argument with someone and it ended in his death? He wouldn't have believed it if it wasn't for what the marshal had found in the man's vehicle.

"That was the marshal," he said. "They think they have your hit man."

"They caught him?"

Beau didn't want to get into the details this early in the morning, so he merely nodded. "He's dead, but they found evidence in his vehicle that makes it pretty apparent that he was the shooter. I don't know any more than that."

"I heard you ask if they knew who'd hired him."

He shook his head. "I'm sure they'll check his cell phone and bank account. But all that takes time. Hud did say that Dana would be heartbroken if you didn't stay for Christmas. He begged me to get you to stay." He held up his hand as he saw that she was about to argue. "Whatever you decide, I'm sure you don't want to leave until we know more. So…while we're waiting, I have an idea. Have you ever cut your own Christmas tree?"

She looked surprised before she laughed. "I've never even had a real tree."

He waved his arms toward his undecorated living room with Christmas so close. "Never bothered with it myself. But this year, I feel like getting a tree. You up for it?"

DJ HAD A dozen questions, but she could see that they would have to wait. To her surprise, she was more than up for getting a Christmas tree. "After that amazing news, I'd love to go cut a tree."

"Great. Let's get you some warm clothes, and then we are heading into the woods."

She loved his excitement and her own. Clearly they were both relieved. The man who'd shot at her was dead. It was over. She had planned on being gone by Christmas. She still thought that was best. But what would it hurt to help Beau get a Christmas tree?

Dressed as if she was headed for the North Pole, DJ followed Beau through the snow and up into the pine trees thick behind his house. They stopped at one point to look back. She was surprised again at how quaint his place looked in its small valley surrounded by mountains.

"You live in paradise," she said, captured by the moment.

"It is, isn't it?" He seemed to be studying his house as if he hadn't thought of it that way before. "Sometimes I forget how far I've come." He glanced over at her. "How about you?"

She nodded. "We aren't our parents."

He laughed. "Thank goodness." His gaze lit on her.

DJ saw the change in his expression the moment before he dropped the ax, reached out with his gloved hand and, cupping her neck, drew her to him. "I believe you owe me a kiss."

His lips were cold at first and so were hers. The kiss was short and sweet. Their breaths came out in puffs as he drew back.

"You call that a kiss?" she taunted.

His gaze locked with hers. His grin was slow, heat in his look. And then his arms were around her. This kiss was heat and light. It crackled like the fire had last night. She felt a warmth rush through her as he deepened the kiss. She melted against him, wrapped in his arms, the cold day sparkling around them.

When he pulled back this time, his blue eyes shone in the snowy light in the pines. Desire burned like a blowtorch in those eyes. He sounded as breathless as she felt. "If we're going to get a tree…" His voice broke with emotion.

"Yes," she agreed. "A tree." She spotted one. It was hidden behind a much larger tree, its limbs misshapen in its attempt to fight for even a little sunlight in the shadow.

"Dana has this tradition of giving a sad-looking tree the honor of being a Christmas tree." She walked over to the small, nearly hidden tree. "I like this one. It's…"

He laughed. "Ugly?"

"No, it's beautiful because it's had a hard life. It's struggled to survive against all odds and would keep doing that without much hope. But it has a chance to be something special." There were tears in her eyes. "It's like us."

He shook his head as if in wonder as he looked at her, then at the tree.

"Okay, you want this one? We'll give the tree its moment to shine."

"Thank you." She hugged herself as she watched him cut the misshapen pine tree out of the shadow it had been living under.

He studied the tree for a moment before he sheathed his ax. "Come on, tree. Let's take you home."

BIANCA DIDN'T ASK until they were both on the plane and headed for Montana. "You knew about her? My sister? Since the beginning?"

Ester nodded. "Your mother couldn't keep anything from me."

"But you didn't tell Grandmama?"

The housekeeper sighed. "Your mother made me promise, and what good would it have done? I'd hoped that in time… Marietta sent your mother to Italy to stay with an aunt there while she quietly had the marriage annulled. The next time I saw your mother, she was married and pregnant with you."

Bianca shook her head. "How could she have just forgotten about the baby she left behind?"

"She never forgot. When I made that rag doll for you, your mother insisted I make one for your…sister."

"That's why you left my doll and a photograph in her apartment."

"I had a nephew of mine do it. I wanted to tell her everything, but I was afraid."

She turned to look at the older woman. "Afraid my grandmother would find out."

"Afraid it would hurt you. I'd done it on impulse when I realized your grandmother was trying to find DJ."

"DJ? Is that what she calls herself?"

"It was a nickname her father gave her."

"So you saw her occasionally?"

Ester sighed. "Only from afar. Her father insisted. I would tell your mother how she looked, what she was wearing…" Tears filled her eyes. "It was heart-breaking."

"She was well cared for?"

"Well enough, I guess. Her father wouldn't take the money offered him by your grandmother's lawyer at the time the marriage was annulled."

Bianca scoffed. "So maybe he isn't as bad a man as Grandmama makes him out to be."

"Your grandmother had good reason given that he never amounted to anything and is now in prison. But he raised your sister alone and without any help from the family. I admire him for that, even though it was not an…ordinary childhood for DJ. I know he feared that the family would try to take her. I was the only one he let see her—even from a distance."

"I always wanted a sister," Bianca said more to herself than to Ester.

"I know. And I always felt sad when you said that growing up, knowing you *had* a sister. But it wasn't my place to tell you."

"Until now. Why *did* you tell me now?" Bianca asked, turning in her seat to face Ester.

Ester hesitated. Bianca could tell that the housekeeper didn't want to say anything negative about her grandmother.

"Because you were afraid of what my grandmother might do," Bianca said, reading the answer on the woman's face.

"No, I was afraid of what Roger Douglas would do. I knew I couldn't stop him, but you could."

"But did I stop him in time?" Bianca looked out the plane window. *She had a sister.* Her heart beat faster at the thought. How could her grandmother have kept something like this from her? Worse, her own mother?

She'd seen how her grandmother had used money to control Carlotta. She had always told herself that she wouldn't let Marietta do the same thing to her and yet she had taken all the gifts, the Ivy League education, the trips, all of it knowing that she'd better bring the right man home when the time came.

"Do you think she'll be all right by herself?" she asked Ester.

The housekeeper smiled. "Your grandmother is much stronger than any of us give her credit for. But I called my sister while you were getting our tickets. She can handle Marietta."

"Thank you. No matter what she's done, she's my grandmama."

"She is that."

Bianca closed her eyes. She'd lost her father at an

early age, so all she'd had was her mother, grand-mother and, of course, Ester. It was Ester who had kissed her forehead each night, who got her off to school, who doctored the scrapes and lovingly applied the medicine. Her mother had always seemed lost in thought. She assumed that no one noticed how much wine she had at night before she stumbled to her room in the huge house overlooking the ocean.

Now Bianca wondered if giving up her first child had haunted her. When she'd often had that faraway, sad look in her eyes, was it Dee Anna Justice she was thinking about?

If so, she knew she should have been jealous of the hours her mother had been off—if even in her mind—with her other daughter. Had she loved her more? It didn't matter. She felt no jealousy.

Opening her eyes, she looked out the plane window again. They were almost there. She wasn't going to let anything—or anyone—keep her from her sister.

Bianca had always felt as if there was something missing from a life in which she seemed to get anything she wanted.

What she'd really wanted, though, was a sibling. She remembered asking her mother once if she could have more children. She'd wanted a brother or sister so badly.

"Don't be ridiculous," her mother had snapped.

"I know Daddy's dead, but can't you find another man—"

"Stop it, Bianca. Just stop it." She'd sent her to ask Ester about dinner. As Bianca had left the room, she'd looked back to see her mother go to the bar to pour herself a large glass of wine. Her mother had been crying.

She'd never seen her mother cry before, so she'd made a point of keeping her desire for a sibling to herself after that.

Now she understood those tears. Had her mother ached for that other daughter just as Bianca had ached for her?

The captain announced that they would be landing in the Gallatin Valley soon.

"Maybe we should call this ranch," Ester said, but Bianca shook her head.

"I don't want them to know we're coming." When Ester seemed surprised by that, she added, "If you were my sister, would you want to meet us? I can't take the chance she might leave to avoid us, especially if Grandmama has…done something."

Ester nodded.

Bianca reached over and took the housekeeper's hands. "I hope she likes me."

Ester's eyes filled with tears. "She will love you."

STACY WAS IN SHOCK. When she'd told her sister what had happened last night, she hadn't heard yet about Jimmy. "Burt wouldn't kill Jimmy. He wouldn't kill *anyone.*"

"You said yourself that you'd never seen him so angry and that he hit Jimmy twice," Dana argued after she had told Stacy about Jimmy's body being found out by the barn, his throat slit. "Anyway, Hud has only taken Burt in for questioning based on what you told me."

Stacy got up from the kitchen table to pace. She'd lived around her brother-in-law long enough to know how these things worked. Hud would have to go by the evidence. "Burt hit him. Jimmy fought back. Of course there will be some of Burt's DNA on him, but that doesn't mean Burt killed him."

She couldn't believe this was happening. Jimmy was dead. But that wasn't as upsetting as Burt being blamed for it.

"Hud will sort it all out." Her sister eyed her with a mixture of pity and concern. "I thought you weren't interested in Burt."

Stacy hated to admit that she'd felt that way until last night. But she'd seen a different side to him. "He rescued me from Jimmy. He followed us from the restaurant because he was worried about me. And with good reason. I don't know why I agreed to go out with Jimmy. I made excuses for him back in high school when he forcibly took my virginity. He said he was so turned on by me that he couldn't stop himself and it was my fault."

Dana shook her head in obvious disgust. "All while you were saying no?"

She nodded. "I tried to push him off…but I didn't try hard enough back in high school. Last night I would have fought him to my dying breath."

Her sister didn't look pleased to hear that. "I told Hud what you told me, but he will want your side of the story," Dana said, picking up the phone.

Stacy shook her head as her sister started to hand her the phone. She realized that Hud would have questioned her earlier, but she had taken the kids to school. "I'm going down to his office. He's questioning the wrong person."

"I should warn you, he'll want to know where you were last night," her sister said behind her.

She turned slowly. "You can't think *I* killed Jimmy."

"Of course not."

"If I was going to kill him, I would have done it years ago after he raped me. I think until last night, I was still blaming myself for what happened—just as he let me do all these years. Now that I think about it, if Burt hadn't shown up when he did…" She looked up at her sister. "I would have killed him before I let him rape me again."

She went out the door, knowing that she'd made herself look guilty. Better her than Burt.

Chapter Seventeen

Andrei heard the news at breakfast in a small café at Meadow Village. He had tried to go about his day as usual, pretending to be one of the many tourists at the resort for the holidays. No one paid him any mind, since he wasn't limping as badly as he had been.

It wasn't like he could go to Cardwell Ranch. The law was crawling all over the place. Dee Anna Justice wasn't there, anyway. He hadn't seen her or the cowboy since the two had driven away together. But he was convinced she would be back, and the ranch was much easier for his purposes than driving back into the narrow canyon to get to the private investigator/cowboy's house. He assumed the cowboy would take her to his place.

As he ate, he knew that after last night this would be the perfect time for him to just leave, put all of this behind him.

But his pride wasn't going to let that happen.

"The man's throat was cut," a woman whispered to another at the next table. She shuddered and then leaned closer to the other woman. "I heard from my friend at the marshal's office that the dead man was a professional killer."

That caught his interest. His heart began to pound, making it hard to hear what else the woman was saying. So, there had been another contract. He swore under his breath. Things were getting so damned complicated.

"Do they know who did it?" the other woman whispered back.

"Well...you know Burt Olsen?"

"The *mailman*?"

Out of the corner of his eye, he saw her nod. "I heard he's been taken in for questioning. He had gotten into a fight with the man earlier that night."

"Burt Olsen? I just find that hard to believe. That he would...cut a man's throat." She shivered. "Burt always seems so nice."

"You know what they say about deep water."

Poor Burt, he thought. Common sense told him that he'd been given the perfect way out. The cops would think they had their man. Dee Anna Justice would let her guard down. So would her cowboy. He could still finish this job, collect his money and leave the country before his birthday. That's how he had to play this while his luck held.

BEAU STOOD UP the Christmas tree in the living room and stepped back to consider it. "Wow, it looks better than I thought it would. Pushed against the wall like that, it really isn't bad." He turned to see DJ smiling at the tree.

"It's beautiful. It doesn't even need ornaments."

He laughed. "That's good, because I don't own any. I thought we could string some popcorn. I'll pick up some lights when I go to town."

His gaze met hers. That kiss earlier had almost had him making love to her in the snow up on the mountain. He stepped to her now. She moved into his arms as naturally as a sunrise. He held her close, breathing in the fresh-air scent of her.

"DJ," he breathed against her hair.

She pulled back to look up at him. What he saw in her eyes sent a trail of heat racing through his veins. She stood on tiptoes to kiss him. Her lips brushed against his. Her gaze held his as the tip of her tongue touched his lower lip.

He felt a shudder of desire. Taking her hand, he led her over to the fireplace. "Are you sure about this?"

"I've never been more sure of anything in my life."

Golden light flickered over them as they began to undress each other. He could feel her trembling as he brushed his lips across hers.

He trailed kisses from the corner of her mouth down to her round breasts. He found her nipple and teased the hard tip with his tongue, then his teeth. She arched against him as they slowly slid down to the rug in front of the fire. The flames rose. The fire crackled and sighed.

On the rug, the two made love as if neither of them ever had before.

BIANCA AND ESTER landed at Gallatin Field outside Bozeman and rode the shuttle to the car rental agency. While they waited, Bianca looked out at the snow-covered mountains. She'd never driven on snow and ice before. For a moment she questioned her impulsiveness at jumping on a plane and coming here.

Wasn't her grandmother always telling her to slow

down, to think things out before she acted? Just the thought of her grandmother made her more determined to get to Cardwell Ranch—and her sister.

"Here's your key," said the man behind the desk. "Your car is right out there. Do you know where you're going?" he asked, holding up a map.

"Big Sky," she said and watched as he drew arrows on the map and handed it to her.

"Maybe we should call," Ester said as they left. "Just showing up at their door… Maybe we should warn them not only that we're coming but that maybe your grandmother did something she regrets."

Bianca shook her head. "I'd rather take my chances. Anyway, call and say what? We have no idea what is going on. For all we know…" Her voice broke. "I know she did wrong, but I still can't get her into trouble. I keep telling myself that Grandmama wouldn't…hurt her own grandchild."

"In Marietta's eyes, *you* are her only grandchild."

"I'm furious with her, but I can't throw her under the bus," Bianca said, making Ester smile.

"I've wanted to do just that for years, but I understand what you're saying. You don't want her going to prison. I don't, either. It's why I called you and told you what was going on."

"We are only about forty miles away." Bianca shot her a look as she drove, following the man's directions from the rental agency. "Roger was the one who hired someone. Maybe she didn't stop him, but it wasn't her idea, right?"

Ester looked away. "I doubt the law would see it that way. She saw Walter Justice as a problem." She shrugged. "Now she sees his daughter as one."

"But Walter is still alive."

"Last I heard, but he's also in prison."

Bianca shot her a look. "You can't think she had anything to do with that!"

Ester shrugged. "I wouldn't put anything past your grandmother. Let's just hope that phone call she made was…real and that she has stopped all this foolishness."

Bianca stared at the highway into the canyon and the steep mountains on each side. "Look what she did to my mother. Forcing her to keep Dee Anna a secret from me. I'm not sure if I can forgive her if something has happened to my sister."

DJ FELT AS if her life couldn't get any better. It was a strange feeling. After years of holding back, of being afraid really to live, she'd given herself to Beau Tanner completely. Her heart felt so full she thought it might burst.

"It is really over?" she asked him the next morning on the way to Cardwell Ranch. Dana had called and invited them over for brunch, saying the crime scene tape was gone and the ranch was back to normal.

Beau squeezed her hand. "You're safe."

Safe. She realized she'd never felt it before. It was a wonderful feeling, she thought as she looked out on the winter landscape. It had snowed again last night, huge flakes that drifted down in the ranch light outside Beau's home. She'd felt as if she was in a snow globe, one with a cozy little house inside. Wrapped in Beau's arms under the down comforter, she'd found paradise.

Last night she hadn't thought about the future, only the present. But this morning as they neared the turn-off to Cardwell Ranch, she couldn't help but think about her mother's family. What now? If it was true that they'd tried to kill her, fearing she wanted their money... The thought made her heart ache.

Beau reached over and took her hand. "It's going to be all right."

She couldn't help but smile at him. Nor could she help but believe him. With Beau in her corner, she felt she could take on the world.

BIANCA TURNED OFF the highway at Big Sky and stopped a few yards from the Cardwell Ranch sign that hung over the entrance. She glanced at Ester, who quickly took her hand and squeezed it.

"You can do this," Ester said. "She's your sister."

She nodded, smiling in spite of her fear, and drove under the sign and across the bridge spanning the river. She felt as if she'd been waiting for this her whole life. Even with all the lost years, she and DJ still had time to get to know each other. If her sister wanted to.

Bianca felt a stab of fear. What if her grandmother was right and this young woman wanted nothing to do with her family? With her?

A large new barn appeared ahead along with a half-dozen cabins set back in the woods. But it was the rambling old farmhouse that she drove to, with the black Suburban parked in front. She saw a curtain move.

"Tell me I'm not making a mistake," she said to Ester.

"Letting your sister know she's not alone in this can't be a mistake," the older woman said.

Bianca smiled over at her. "I don't know what I

would have done without you all these years." She opened her door, Ester following suit.

The steps seemed to go on forever, and then they were on the porch. Bianca was about to knock when the door opened, startling her.

A dark-haired woman in her thirties looked surprised. Was this DJ? Was this her sister?

"I'm Bianca," she said at the same time the woman said, "I'm sorry, I thought you were…someone else."

The woman looked from Bianca to Ester and back. "Did you say Bianca?"

She nodded. "I'm looking for Dee Anna Justice," Bianca said.

"She's not here right now," the woman said excitedly. "But I'm her cousin Dana."

Feeling a surge of relief at the woman's apparent welcome, she said, "I'm her…sister, Bianca."

Dana smiled. "Yes, her sister. What a surprise."

"I hope not too much of a surprise," she said. "This is Ester, a…a friend of mine. Is my sister here?"

"Please, come in," Dana said and ushered them into the warm living room. "I'll call DJ…Dee Anna, and let her know you're here. Please, have a seat. I was expecting her when you drove up."

Bianca sat in a chair by the fire, glancing around at the Western decor. Until this moment, she hadn't felt like she was in Montana. As Ester took a place on the couch next to her, she spotted the Christmas tree.

Dana turned her back, her cell phone at her ear, and said, "You should come home now," before disconnecting and dialing another number.

When she turned back to them, she saw what they were looking at—and no doubt the expressions on their surprised faces. "That's my orphan Christmas tree," Dana said with a laugh. "It's a long story." She seemed to be waiting for the call to go through, then said, "You aren't going to believe who is sitting in my living room. Your sister! Oh, it's her all right. She looks enough like you that there is no mistake. Okay, I'll tell her." Dana disconnected, smiling. "She's on her way and should be here any minute."

Bianca had never felt so nervous. Ester reached over and patted her hand. "It's going to be fine," the housekeeper whispered.

She nodded, smiling and fighting tears as she heard a vehicle pull up out front. Dana said, "In fact, she's here now."

"ARE YOU SURE you heard right?" Beau asked as he pulled up in front of the house.

Earlier DJ had been sitting cross-legged on the floor in front of the fire, stringing popcorn for their Christmas tree. She had been wearing one of his shirts over a pair of jeans. Her face had been flushed, either from the fire or their lovemaking earlier. She'd looked relaxed, content, maybe even happy. He'd lost another piece of his heart at the sight of her.

Now she looked as if she might jump out of her skin. "My sister. That must be her rental car. Why would she be at the ranch?" she asked, turning to meet his gaze.

"Apparently she wants to see you."

She shook her head, relieved after her call earlier to the hospital that her father was going to make it. "This is crazy. One minute all I have is my father, and now I have cousins and a *sister*?"

"Who might have hired a hit man to take you out." He pulled out his cell phone. "I'm calling Hud."

"No," she said, reaching for her door. "I want to meet her. I don't need the law there. She isn't going to try to kill me."

He hesitated and finally pocketed the phone. "She'll have to go through me first."

"Seriously, I don't think she'd be here now if she was behind this."

"Apparently you haven't dealt with as many criminals as I have."

DJ laughed and leaned over to give him a kiss. "I have a good feeling about this."

He wished he did.

Chapter Eighteen

DJ couldn't believe that she was going to meet her half sister after only recently finding out that she even existed. "How long do you think she's known about me?" she asked Beau as they walked to the porch steps.

He glanced over at her. "I have no idea."

"Sorry, I just have so many questions."

"Ideally she will be able to answer them all for you. Including who hired someone to kill you."

She looked over at him as they reached the door. "I haven't forgotten. But she's here. That makes her look innocent, don't you think?"

"I'd go with less guilty. But you have no idea what this woman wants. Or why she's shown up now. You have to admit, it's suspicious."

"Which is exactly why I don't think she's involved."

She could tell he didn't agree. "Well, you'll be here to protect me," she said as she reached for the doorknob.

"Yes, I will."

But before she could grab the doorknob, the door swung open, and there was Dana, practically jumping up and down in her excitement.

"Easy," he said behind her. "Let's not get carried away until we find out what is going on."

"I'm glad Beau's with you," Dana said as DJ entered the house. "Hud's on his way," she whispered to Beau loud enough that DJ heard it.

"Really, the two of you…" She stepped into the living room and stopped dead. The woman who rose from the chair by the fire looked more like their mother than even DJ did. DJ stared at her half sister. They looked so much alike it was eerie.

"Bianca?" she asked, although there was little doubt this was the half sister she'd been told about.

"Dee Anna. Or is it DJ? Oh, I'm just so glad you're all right," Bianca said, rushing to her to give her a quick hug. "I have wanted a sister my whole life. I can't believe we were kept apart." She stepped back to take in DJ. "We look so much alike. We could be twins." She let out a nervous laugh.

Out of the corner of her eye, DJ had seen Beau start to move. But he stopped short when Bianca merely threw her arms around DJ.

"I am so glad to see you," Bianca said as she stared at DJ. "I was so worried."

"Worried?" Beau asked only feet away.

Her sister hesitated. An older woman, whom DJ had barely noticed, stood then and moved to her. There was kindness in the woman's eyes. "I'm Ester."

"Ester," DJ repeated as Bianca stepped back to let Ester take DJ's hand.

"I made your doll," Ester said. "Your father kept me informed on how you were doing over the years. I wish I could have done more."

Tears welled in DJ's eyes. "Thank you. I named her—"

"Trixie. That's why I sent you Bianca's, so you would know there were two of them. Two of you. I couldn't let you go on believing you had no family or that no one cared other than your father."

DJ looked to her sister. "And my grandmother?"

Both women hesitated. Bianca looked guilty, which sent a sliver of worry burrowing under her skin.

"Grandmama is not well," Bianca said.

Ester let out a snort.

Just then, Marshal Hud Savage arrived. "What's going on?" he asked after Dana introduced him as her husband.

"That's just what I was about to ask," Beau said. "Where does a hit man fit into this happy reunion?"

ROGER DOUGLAS'S CELL PHONE vibrated in his pocket. It surprised him. All the way to the airport it had been buzzing constantly, but it had finally stopped until now. He'd thought, as he'd waited for his flight, that both Marietta and the accountant had given up.

Now he pulled it out, curious which one had decided to give it one more try. He saw who was calling and hurried to a quieter area before answering.

"You didn't tell me about the private investigator who isn't letting her out of his sight," Andrei Ivankov said.

Roger wasn't sure what to say. He'd taken the call only because he'd thought the hit man had finished the job. "I take it you haven't—"

"You take it right."

"It's just as well. The client wants to call off the—"

"I'm sorry, I must have misunderstood you."

"She doesn't want you to finish the job." Roger knew the man was born in Russia or some such place, but his English was better than Roger's own.

"I have been out here freezing my ass off and now she wants me to forget it? I had my doubts about dealing with you. I get paid no matter what, plus extra for my inconvenience, and if I don't get paid, I will track you down and make you wish you'd never—"

"Don't threaten me. There is nothing you can do to me. I really don't give a damn if you kill her or not." He'd raised his voice, and several people had turned to look in his direction. He disconnected the call, then tossed the phone to the floor and stomped it to death. Now a lot of people were staring at him.

Roger felt heat rise up his neck. He'd always prided himself on never losing his temper. But he wasn't that man anymore, he reminded himself. He wasn't the meek lawyer who had to kiss Marietta Pisani's feet.

He'd picked up what he could of the cell phone, tossed it in the trash and started back to his seat when he heard his flight called. Clutching the bag full of Marietta's money, he smiled as he got in line.

It wasn't until he was sitting down in first class, drinking a vodka tonic and dreaming of his new life, the bag shoved under the seat in front of him, that he relaxed. Just a few more minutes.

Glancing out the window, he felt his heart drop like a stone. Two security guards were headed for the plane along with several police officers. He downed his drink, figuring it was the last one he'd get for a while.

"IT WAS A MISUNDERSTANDING," Bianca assured the marshal. They had all gathered in the dining room around the large old oak table. She turned to her sister. She couldn't believe how much they looked alike. They really could have been twins. "You have to forgive Grandmama. It was her attorney, Roger Douglas. When she found out what he'd done…she was beside herself and demanded he put a stop to it."

Hud and Beau exchanged a glance. "I called the power company. They didn't have any men in our area."

"So the man who was seen on the power pole?" Beau asked.

Hud nodded. "It must have been the shooter."

"Shooter?" Bianca asked.

Dana filled them in on what had happened, first someone taking a shot at DJ, then a man found dead near one of the old barns. "He apparently had been hired to kill DJ."

Bianca's eyes welled with tears. "I'm so sorry. I had no idea. My grandmother had no idea. I'm just so thankful that he missed and that he is no longer a problem."

Hud's cell phone rang. He stepped away to take the call. The room went silent. Bianca prayed that it wouldn't be bad news. She was worried about her grandmother and what would happen now.

"That was the police in San Diego," Hud said as he came back to the table. "They've arrested Roger Douglas. Apparently he made a deal and told them everything, including that he had hired a hit man through another man to kill Dee Anna Justice. He was carrying a large sum of money that he admitted had been stolen from your grandmother, Bianca."

Bianca let out a relieved breath. "I never liked Roger."

"Me, either," Ester said. "He certainly pulled the wool over your grandmother's eyes for years."

"Where is your grandmother now?" Hud asked. "The police said they'd tried to reach her…"

Ester saw her alarm and quickly waved it off. "I got a text from my sister a few moments ago. May was looking after Marietta. She said the fool woman packed a bag and took the first flight out, headed this way."

There were surprised looks around the table. Then Dana got to her feet and announced, "I've made brunch. I think we should all have something to eat while we wait for our new arrival."

Hud said, "I'll have someone pick her up at the airport and bring her here. But the police in San Diego will still have a few questions for her."

DJ FELT AS IF she was in shock. She kept wanting to pinch herself. She'd gone from having only her father to having this family that kept getting bigger and bigger.

Dana told Bianca and Ester that they could stay in one of the cabins on the mountain as long as they wanted. "I know you and DJ have a lot to talk about. But first you have to share this brunch I've made."

"Are you sure there is enough?" Bianca asked. "We don't want to intrude."

Dana laughed. "I'm used to cooking for ranch hands. I always make too much. Anyway, you're fam-

ily. There is always room at my table for family." She
motioned DJ into the kitchen. "Are you all right?"

"I don't think I've ever been this all right," DJ said,
smiling. She felt exhausted from everything that had
happened. The Cardwells. Beau. Her near death. And
finally meeting her sister and the woman who'd made
her Trixie and had watched out for her from a distance. It felt as if it was all too much. And yet she'd
never felt happier.

She hugged her cousin. "Thank you so much."

"It's just a little brunch," Dana said with a laugh.

"That and you, this ranch, everything you've done.
Somehow I feel as if it all had to come together here
where it began."

"Have you heard how your father is doing?" Dana
asked.

"He's going to make it. His sentence is about up.
He's getting out of prison soon." DJ wasn't sure how
she felt about that. She could understand now why he'd
been afraid of her mother's family finding out about
her. The fact that he hadn't taken their money made
her almost proud of him. Maybe there was more to
her father than she'd originally thought. Maybe when
he got out they could spend some time together, really
get to know each other.

From the window, DJ could see Beau outside talking to Hud. Both looked worried. "They aren't going
to arrest my grandmother, are they?" DJ asked as Dana
followed her gaze to the two.

"No, I'm sure it is just as your sister said, a mistake,
since that man has confessed to everything."

DJ hoped so. The marshal and Beau turned back
toward the house. DJ stuck her head out the kitchen

door to see Beau and Hud enter the house. Beau caught her eye and smiled reassuringly.

She felt a shaft of heat fall over her like the warm rays of the sun and almost blushed at the memory of their lovemaking. Beau was so tender and yet so strong and virile. Her heart beat a little faster just at the sight of him.

MARIETTA HAD ASSUMED she was being arrested when she landed at the airport and saw the two deputies waiting for her. She was pleasantly surprised to hear that she was being taken to the Cardwell Ranch, where her granddaughters were waiting for her.

On the drive up the canyon, she stared out at the snowy landscape, rough rocky cliffs and glazed-over green river. She'd never seen mountains like these, let alone this much snow, in her life. It kept her mind off what might be waiting for her once she reached the ranch.

Whatever was waiting, she deserved it, she told herself. She'd been a fool. The police had left a message that Roger Douglas had been arrested at the airport carrying a large amount of money on him. Her money. She shook her head. Who knew how much he had squandered? She would deal with that when she got home. If she got home.

Her chest ached. It was as if she could feel her old heart giving out. *Just stay with me a little longer. Let me try to fix this before I die.*

She was relieved when the deputy driving finally turned off the highway, crossed a bridge spanning the iced-over river and pulled down into a ranch yard. She stared at the large two-story house and took a breath.

One of the deputies offered to help her out, but she waved him off.

This was something she had to do herself. It very well might be the last thing she ever did.

Chapter Nineteen

They had just sat down to eat Dana's brunch when they heard a patrol car drive up.

Everyone looked toward the front door expectantly. DJ wasn't sure she was ready to meet her grandmother. This was all happening too fast, and yet she couldn't help being curious. This was the woman who thankfully hadn't put a hit out on her. But she was the woman who'd apparently planned to buy her off.

Standing up, DJ prepared to meet her grandmother. Everyone else rose as well and moved into the living room. Hud went to open the door for the elderly woman who'd just climbed the steps and pounded forcibly on the door. She remembered Bianca saying the woman wasn't well, a bad heart. Now she wondered if that was true or if that was just what her grandmother wanted her to believe.

Like Beau, she hated always being suspicious. Wasn't there a chance that they could change? That love could make them more trusting?

Love? Where had that come from? She glanced over at Beau and felt her heart do that little jump it did when she saw him. She did love him.

The realization surprised her. She'd cared about

some of the men she'd dated, but she'd never felt as if she was in love. Until this moment.

What a moment to realize it, she thought as an elderly woman with salt-and-pepper hair and intense brown eyes stepped into the room.

DJ felt Bianca take her hand. Beau was watching the older woman as if waiting for her to do something that would force him to take her down.

She almost laughed. He was so protective. He shot her a look that said, *You can do this*. She smiled. He had no idea how strange all this was for her. She'd dreamed of family, and now she had all the complications that came with one.

WHEN THE DOOR OPENED, Marietta almost fell in with it. "I want to see my granddaughter before you arrest me!" she said to the man in the marshal's uniform. It was just like them to have someone here to arrest her the moment she arrived at the house. But she wasn't leaving without a fight, she thought as the man stepped back and she barged in, more determined than ever.

What she saw made her stagger to a stop. Bianca standing next to a young woman who could have been her twin. Their resemblance to each other gave her a shock that almost stopped her old heart dead. This was the child Carlotta had given birth to? This beautiful thing?

"What are you doing here?" Ester demanded. The accusation in her housekeeper's tone shocked her. Clearly their relationship had changed.

"You're starting to remind me of your sister," she snapped. "I came to see my granddaughter."

"*Which* granddaughter?" Bianca asked. She was

holding DJ's hand, the two of them looking so formidable, so strong, so defiant. Her heart lodged in her throat as she looked at the two of them. She couldn't have been more proud or filled with shame. If she hadn't been the way she was, these two would have gotten to grow up together.

She could see her daughter in both of the women, but especially in DJ. The woman was more beautiful than even she knew. Marietta thought of that Bible verse about not hiding your light under a bushel basket. DJ was just coming into her own. Marietta wondered what had turned on that light inside her, then noticed the cowboy standing near her, looking just as fierce. Of course it had been a man.

"I came to see *both* granddaughters," she said and had to clear her voice. "But especially you, Dee Anna. I can't tell you how sorry I am that this is the first time we have ever met."

Carlotta was right. All she'd thought about was the family fortune and some ingrate of Walter Justice's trying to steal it. Staring at these two beautiful women, she felt a mountain of regret. She hadn't thought of Dee Anna as anything more than a mistake. She'd simply acted as she'd done all those years ago when she'd had Carlotta's marriage to Walter annulled. Both times she'd listened to Roger.

"DJ," Bianca said. "She goes by DJ."

Marietta smiled at her other granddaughter. She could see that the two women had already bonded. "DJ," she amended, her voice breaking as she held out her wrinkled hands to her granddaughter. "Can you ever forgive me?"

THERE WERE TEARS in her grandmother's eyes as DJ stepped to her and took both her hands in hers. Marietta pulled her into a hug. The older woman felt frail in her arms, and she was truly sorry that she hadn't known her before now.

"We should all sit down and have something to eat," Dana said. "Food and family go together."

"I need to ask Mrs. Pisani some questions," her marshal husband said.

"Not now. We are going to eat this brunch I made," Dana said in a no-nonsense tone as they gathered around the table again. "DJ, sit here by Beau and your grandmother. Ester and Bianca, would you mind sitting across from them? Hud—"

"Yep, I'm sitting down right where you tell me," he said.

A smattering of laughter moved through the room.

"I married a smart man," Dana said and introduced her husband and herself.

DJ didn't think she could eat a bite but was pleasantly surprised to find she could. "This is all so delicious," she told her cousin.

Everyone seemed to relax, commenting on how good the food was. Ester asked for one of the recipes. They talked about Montana, life on the ranch, Christmas and finally how they had come to know about each other. Marietta said little, picking at her food, her gaze on DJ.

Ester informed Marietta that Roger Douglas had been arrested. "He confessed not only to stealing your money but also to being behind hiring a hit man, so it looks like you're off the hook."

Her grandmother shook her head, smiling sadly.

"We both know better than that. So much of this is my fault. Carlotta was right." She teared up again but quickly wiped her eyes. "I'm just so happy that my granddaughters have found each other."

WHEN THE MEAL was over, DJ was sorry to see it end. Dana had offered the cabins on the mountainside to Bianca, Ester and Marietta, but Bianca had declined, saying she was worried about her grandmother.

"She looks too pale," her sister had said confidentially to DJ. "She shouldn't have flown. I think all this might have been too much for her. I want to take her to the hospital to make sure she is all right."

"I'm not sure what good that will do," Ester said, not unkindly. "The doctors have told her there is nothing they can do for her. We've all known she doesn't have much longer."

"I know," Bianca said.

"Do you mind if I come with you to the hospital?" DJ asked.

"No, not at all," her sister said and smiled.

As Hud left to head back to work and they prepared to leave, snow began to fall as another storm came through. The clouds were low. So was the light. "I know you need this time with your family," Beau said as they all headed out onto the porch. "But if you need me…"

That was just it. She needed him too much. He crowded her thoughts and made her ache for the closeness they had shared.

"I'd like to finish helping you decorate the tree," she said.

"I'd like that, too. But we have time. Christmas is still days away."

"Yes," she said. "It's a date, then." She bit her tongue. "You know what I mean."

He nodded. "We kind of skipped that part. Maybe… well, depending on what you have planned after Christmas…"

They left it at that as he started toward his vehicle.

THE CRIME SCENE tape was gone. Everything seemed to be back to normal around Cardwell Ranch, Andrei thought as he watched the goings-on through the crosshairs of his rifle.

There'd been a lot of company today. He'd watched them come and go, the man with Dee Anna Justice giving her a little more space.

Several times he could have taken a shot, but it hadn't been perfect.

Now everyone seemed to be leaving. His birthday was only days away. He had to make his move. His leg was better. Good enough.

He adjusted the high-powered rifle and scope. It didn't take him long to get Dee Anna Justice in the crosshairs. A head shot was the most effective, but at this distance he didn't want to take the chance.

For days he'd been conflicted. But now he felt nothing but calm. His reputation was at stake. He would finish this.

Shooting into a crowd was always risky, but the confusion would give him his chance to make a clean getaway. Now it felt almost too easy. Was this the shot he'd been waiting for?

He aimed for DJ's heart and gently pulled the trigger.

DJ AND HER newfound family stood on the porch, saying their goodbyes to Dana. Her grandmother stood a few feet away. DJ heard Bianca ask her if she was feeling all right.

Beau had stopped near his pickup. She could feel his gaze on her. Something in his expression made her ache to be in this arms. He was dressed in jeans, boots and that red-and-black wool coat. His black Stetson was pulled low, but those blue eyes were on her. Her skin warmed at the thought of his hands on her.

"You're my granddaughter in every sense of the word," Marietta said as she stepped to DJ and took both of her hands again. "If I have any money left—"

"I don't want your money. I never have."

Her grandmother nodded. "I am such a foolish old woman."

DJ shook her head and hugged the woman. Marietta hugged her hard for a woman who looked so frail. As she stepped back, DJ heard Beau let out a curse.

She looked past her grandmother to see him running toward her. He was yelling, "Shooter! Everyone get down!"

DJ couldn't move, the words not making any sense at first. Then she reached for her grandmother. But Marietta pushed away her hand. As she looked up into the older woman's face, she found it filled with love and something else, a plea for forgiveness, in the instant before the woman stepped in front of her as if to shield her.

The next thing she knew, Beau slammed into her, knocking her to the porch floor. "Everyone down!"

In the distance came the roar of an engine. Beau

was pushing her to move toward the door of the house. "Get inside! Hurry! DJ, are you hit?"

She couldn't do more than shake her head. "My grandmother?"

That's when she looked over and saw the woman lying beside her. Blood bloomed from her chest. DJ began to cry as Beau ushered them all inside the house, then carried Marietta in.

"Put her down here," Dana ordered, pointing to the couch near the Christmas tree. She had the phone in her hand. DJ knew she was already calling Hud and an ambulance.

She and her sister rushed to their grandmother's side.

"Stay here! No one leaves until I get back!" With that, Beau was gone.

BEAU DREW HIS own weapon from his shoulder holster. The sound of a vehicle engine turning over filled the icy winter air as he raced to his pickup. He could make out the silhouette of a vehicle roaring down the road toward Highway 191.

He started his engine, fishtailing as he punched the gas and went after it. By the time they reached the highway, he'd gained a little on what appeared to be an SUV.

The driver took off down the icy highway. Beau followed the two red taillights. He quickly got on his cell and called in the direction the man was headed, then tossed his cell aside to put all his attention on driving.

The highway was empty as the driver ahead of him left Big Sky behind and headed deeper into the canyon, going south toward West Yellowstone. But it was also icy. The last thing Beau wanted to do was end up in a ditch—or worse, the river. But he wasn't going to let the man get away.

As he raced after the vehicle, his mind raced, as well. Hud had been so sure that they had the hit man and that a local man had killed him. Was it possible another hit man had been hired when the first failed? Or had there always been two?

THIS WOULD BE how it ended. Andrei could see that now. For so long he'd had trouble envisioning his life after his forty-fifth birthday. Now he knew why.

He'd just killed some old woman. It was worse than he could have imagined. Shame made him burn. He had failed to kill his target and he wasn't going to get away, he thought as he looked back to see the pickup right behind him.

It was that cowboy. What was his story, anyway? The PI had been suspicious and jumpy from the start. Otherwise he wouldn't have spotted him just before he'd fired. The cowboy had probably caught the reflection off the rifle scope. Just Andrei's luck.

Ahead all he could see was snow. He hated snow. He hated cold. He hated this contract. All his instincts had told him to let it go. Stubbornness had made him determined to finish it no matter what. And all because of the coin toss. It had never let him down before. Not that it mattered now.

He felt his tires lose traction on the icy road. He touched his brakes as he felt the back of the car begin to slide and knew immediately that had been a mistake. But it was just another mistake, he thought as he cranked the wheel, trying to get the car to come out of the slide. Instead, it spun the other way. He was going too fast to save himself. He saw the guardrail coming up and closed his eyes.

BEAU'S HEART WAS POUNDING. He still couldn't believe how close DJ had come to being killed. If he hadn't lunged for her. If her grandmother hadn't stepped in front of the bullet. So many *if*s.

The taillights ahead of him grew brighter as he closed the distance. He knew this road. He suspected the would-be assassin did not. He could see that the vehicle was a white SUV. Probably a rental.

The canyon followed the river, winding through the mountains in tighter turns. He pressed harder, getting closer. His headlights shone into the vehicle, silhouetting the driver. A single male.

Just then, he saw that the driver had taken the curve too fast. He'd lost control. Beau watched the SUV go into a slide. He let up off his gas as best he could. He knew better than to hit his brakes. They would both end up in the river.

The SUV began a slow circle in the middle of the road. He could see that the driver was fighting like hell to keep it on the road, no doubt overcorrecting. The front of the SUV hit the guardrail and spun crazily toward the rock wall on the other side, where it crashed into the rocks, then shot back out, ping-ponging from the guardrail to the cliffs on the slick road until it finally came to rest against the rocks.

Beau managed to get stopped a few yards shy of the SUV. He turned on his flashers and jumped out, glad there wasn't any traffic. Drawing his weapon, he moved to the vehicle.

The driver was slumped to one side, his deflated air bag in his lap and blood smeared on what was left of the side window. Beau tried to open the driver's-side door, but it was too badly dented. He could hear sirens in the distance as he reached through the broken glass to put a finger to the man's throat. He was still breathing, but for how long?

"GRANDMAMA," BIANCA CRIED and fell to her knees beside the couch. DJ, taking the towel Dana handed her, pressed it to the bleeding wound in Marietta's chest.

"An ambulance is on the way," Dana assured her, sounding scared. The towel was quickly soaked with blood.

DJ joined her sister, her heart breaking. "You saved my life," she said to her grandmother. "Why would you do that?"

Marietta smiled through her pain. "It still can't make up for what I've done. If I had time…"

"You have time," Bianca said. "You can't leave us now."

Her grandmother patted her hand weakly. "My old heart was going to play out soon, anyway. I didn't want you to know how bad it was or how little time I had." She looked from Bianca to DJ and back. "Seeing the two of you together… I'm happy for you. You have a sister now."

She looked to DJ, reached for her hand and squeezed it. "Forgive me?" she whispered.

"Of course," DJ said, and her grandmother squeezed her fingers. "Take care of each other." Her gaze shifted to Ester. "Take care of my girls."

Ester nodded, tears in her eyes.

Marietta smiled and mouthed "Thank you" as her eyes slowly closed. Her hands went slack in theirs. She smiled then as if seeing someone she recognized on the other side.

Bianca began to cry. DJ put her arm around her, and the two hugged as the sound of sirens grew louder and louder.

Epilogue

Beau looked out his office window, watching the snowstorm and feeling restless. It was over. DJ was safe. The bad guys were either dead or in jail. It hadn't taken Marshal Hud Savage long to put all the pieces together with Beau's help. The man Roger Douglas had hired was arrested and quickly made a deal, naming not one but two hit men. Andrei Ivankov, a professional hit man, died before reaching the hospital in Bozeman. Jimmy Ryan, a thug for hire, was also dead, killed, according to lab results, by Ivankov.

Mailman Burt Olsen was in the clear. According to Dana, Burt and her sister, Stacy, had a date for New Year's. Dana figured they'd be planning a wedding by Valentine's Day. Apparently Stacy hadn't waited for Burt to ask her out. She'd invited him to the movies and they'd hit it off, making Dana say, "I told you so."

Meanwhile, Dana's best friend, Hilde, went into labor Christmas Eve. She had a beautiful eight-pound, nine-ounce baby boy. Dana had called earlier to ask if Beau had heard from DJ. He'd said he'd been busy and now wished he'd asked how DJ was doing, since he was sure Dana had talked to her.

"You going to spend the whole day looking out that window?" demanded a deep female voice behind him.

Beau turned to look guiltily at his assistant, Marge. She stood, hands on hips, giving him one of those looks. "What do you want me to do?"

"You should never have let her leave in the first place."

"She was going to her grandmother's funeral in Palm Desert."

"You could have gone along."

He shook his head. "She needed time."

Marge scoffed at that and shook her head as if disappointed in him. "You mean *you* needed time. Apparently you haven't had enough time in your life."

"I hardly know the woman."

Marge merely mugged a face at him.

"It was too soon," he said, turning back to the window. "She had too much going on right then." He glanced over his shoulder. Marge was gone, but she'd left the door open.

He walked out into the reception area of the office to find her standing at her desk. "What? You aren't going to keep nagging me?"

"Would it do any good?" She sounded sad. Almost as sad as he felt.

NEW YEAR'S DAY, Dana listened to the racket coming from her living room and smiled to herself. There were children laughing and playing, brothers arguing good-naturedly, sister and sisters-in-law talking food and fabrics, cousins discussing barbecue, since they had a batch of ribs going outside on the large grill. The house smelled of pine, fresh-brewed coffee and cocoa, and gingersnap cookies decorated by the children.

She wished her mother were here. How happy Mary Justice Cardwell would have been to see her family all together—finally. It was what Dana had hoped for all her life. It was one reason she would never leave this old house. Her children would grow up here— just as she had. She hoped that someday it would be her grandchildren she would hear playing in the next room.

"Do you need any help?" her cousin DJ asked from the kitchen doorway.

Dana stepped to her and pulled her into a hug. "Having you here means more than you can ever know." She drew back to look at her cousin. She'd seen how much Beau and DJ had loved each other. But for whatever reason, they'd parted. It broke her heart.

She'd had to twist DJ's arm to get her to fly up for the New Year. "You wouldn't consider staying longer, would you?"

"I have to return to California. My editor has a list of assignments she wants me to consider."

"I have to ask about your grandmother's funeral," Dana said.

"It was quite beautiful. As misguided as she was in the past, she saved my life. I'll never forget that. Also, I've been spending time with my sister and my father, actually. He's trying to figure out what he wants to do with the rest of his life. That was nice of you to offer him a place here on the ranch."

"I hope he takes me up on it," Dana said. "After all, this is where he belongs. Zinnia would love to see him again. You know, she's a widow."

DJ laughed. "You just can't help matchmaking, can you?"

"I have no idea what you're talking about," Dana said, smiling. "Bianca is also always welcome here on the ranch. I spoke with her about coming up and spending a few weeks. She wants to learn to ride horses. So you have to come back. There really is no place like Montana in the summer."

"You sound like Beau." DJ seemed to catch herself. "He mentioned how nice it is up here once the snow melts."

"Yes, Beau," Dana said, unable to hold back a grin. "The night I saw the two of you dancing down at The Corral, I knew you were perfect for each other."

DJ shook her head. "I'm afraid you're wrong about that. I haven't heard from him since I left."

Dana laughed. "Trust me. I'm never wrong."

IT WAS ALMOST midnight when there was a knock at the door. The old ranch house on Cardwell Ranch was full of family. Dana had just passed out the noisemakers. DJ had seen her watching the door as if she was expecting more guests, but everyone was already there, including DJ's cousins—Jordan and his wife, Stacy and Burt, and even Clay and his partner.

Dana ran to the door and threw it open. A gust of cold air rushed in. DJ saw her cousin reach out, grab Beau and pull him in. They shared a few words before both looked in her direction.

She groaned, afraid of what Dana had done to get Beau over here tonight. Her cousin was so certain she wasn't wrong making this match. DJ almost felt sorry for her. As much as she and Beau had enjoyed their time together, as much as DJ felt for him, sometimes things just didn't work out, she told herself as he walked toward her.

If anything, he was more handsome than the first time she'd seen him standing in the airport. His blue eyes were on her, and in them she saw what almost looked like pain. Her heart lodged in her throat. Tears burned her eyes.

"We need to talk," he said as he took her hand. She was reminded of the night at The Corral when he'd said the same words. Only that night, he'd dragged her from the dance floor, out into the snowy night.

Tonight he led her into the kitchen and closed the door. When he turned to her, she looked into his handsome face and felt her pulse pound.

"I'm a damned fool," he said. "I should never have let you go. Or at least, I should have gone with you. Since the day you left, I've thought about nothing but you. I would have called, but I was afraid that once you got back to your life…"

"Are you just going to talk, or are you going to kiss me?" DJ managed to say, her heart in her throat.

He pulled her to him. His mouth dropped to hers. He smelled of snow and pine and male. She breathed him in as he deepened the kiss and held her tighter.

"I never want to let you go," he said when he drew back. "If that means leaving Montana—"

"I would never ask you to leave a place you love so much."

He looked into her eyes. "Then what are we going to do? Because I don't want to spend another day without you."

"With my job, I can work anywhere."

He smiled, his blue eyes sparkling. "You'd move to Montana if I were to…ask you?"

"What are you saying, cowboy?"

He looked down at his boots for a moment, then met her gaze again. "I never saw you coming. This was the last thing I expected, but now that you've come into my life… Come back. Come back to me. I know it probably seems like we haven't known each other that long, but…" His hand went into his pocket. He seemed to hesitate as he studied her face for a moment.

DJ held her breath as he pulled his hand from his pocket and opened it. Sitting in the middle of his large palm, something caught the light.

She felt her eyes widen at the sight of the diamond ring lying there.

"It was my mother's. She left it with her sister so my father didn't pawn it."

DJ couldn't help but smile knowingly. She and Beau. Their connection, as odd as it was, ran deep.

"Would you consider marrying me? Not right away. We could have as long an engagement as you need." He seemed to catch himself and dropped to one knee. "I know this should have been more romantic—"

She shook her head. "It's perfect," she said, seeing his discomfort. She held out her left hand. "And yes, I will marry you. And no, I don't need a long engagement. Leaving here, leaving you, was one of the hardest things I've ever done. It was breaking my heart." Her eyes filled with tears. "Montana feels like the home I've never had. Somehow, I've never felt that I deserved to be happy. But with you…"

He slipped the ring on her finger, rose and pulled

her into his arms. "That's exactly how I feel. As if I deserve this if I'm smart enough not to let you get away."

She smiled as he lowered his mouth to hers. "I love you, DJ," he whispered against her lips. In the next room, a cheer arose. It was a new day, a new year.

* * * * *

"Let me go, Rush. Let me go back to France and save Gwen and Jackson."

He crossed the office to sit beside her once more. "I have friends all over the world, Lucy. We can track down where he's holding your sister and the baby. Let me make some calls."

"No! You can't alert anyone or he'll kill them. He gave me a week and it's going by too fast. The man following me might already suspect I caved and told you. It has to be his way."

"We'll find a better option," he promised.

She shook her head, tears blurring her vision again. "I'm not taking you down with me. Destroy the ghost files," she pleaded. "Wipe out all records of Garmeaux. Forget I was here."

"I can't do that." His voice turned hard again. "I won't do that."

She opened her mouth to say more and he smothered the words with a kiss. What might have originated as a kiss of comfort ignited like a match struck, blazing across her senses.

INVESTIGATING CHRISTMAS

BY
DEBRA WEBB
& REGAN BLACK

First Published in Great Britain 2016
By Mills & Boon, an imprint of HarperCollins*Publishers*
1 London Bridge Street, London, SE1 9GF

© 2016 Debra Webb

ISBN: 978-0-263-91924-0

46-1216

Our policy is to use papers that are natural, renewable and recyclable products and made from wood grown in sustainable forests. The logging and manufacturing processes conform to the legal environmental regulations of the country of origin.

Printed and bound in Spain
by CPI, Barcelona

Debra Webb, born in Alabama, wrote her first story at age nine and her first romance at thirteen. It wasn't until after she spent three years working for the military behind the Iron Curtain—and a five-year stint with NASA—that she realized her true calling. Since then the *USA TODAY* bestselling author has penned more than one hundred novels, including her internationally bestselling Colby Agency series.

Regan Black, a *USA TODAY* bestselling author, writes award-winning, action-packed novels featuring kick-butt heroines and the sexy heroes who fall in love with them. Raised in the Midwest and California, she and her family, along with their adopted greyhound, two arrogant cats and a quirky finch, reside in the South Carolina Lowcountry, where the rich blend of legend, romance and history fuels her imagination.

For Debra, the best mentor, writing partner
and friend in the world! It's a joy to be
on this marvelous adventure with you!

Chapter One

France, North of Paris
Tuesday, December 15, 5:40 p.m.

Lucy Gaines swapped her heels for flats for the short walk home from her new job. Her employer's butler watched patiently, opening the door when her heels were tucked into her tote.

"Have a lovely evening, Miss Gaines," he said in precise, formal French.

"Merci," she replied, crossing the threshold. Outside, she paused on the top step and breathed in the crisp evening air as the butler closed the magnificent oak door with a near-silent *whoosh*. Every day she marveled that she worked here, lived *here*.

December in France. It seemed her new reality might never sink in completely. Just over a month ago she'd been staring down the dark emotional tunnel of a melancholy holiday season in Chicago. Her life had once more taken a U-turn and this time she couldn't be happier. Practically skipping down the steps, she tugged at the collar of her wool coat, keeping the dropping temperature at bay although the brisk winter air here was balmy compared to the bite of the Windy City this time of year.

She lived and worked in a dream world. Chantilly and Paris were only a short drive away from this sleepy, rural neighborhood that barely qualified as a town. *Commune*, she corrected herself with the French term. Growing up, she and her sister, Gwen, had dreamed of trekking through Europe after college, immersing themselves in history, culture and new discoveries with each day. They'd made it, though the timing and circuitous route of ups and downs had been grueling for both of them.

Technically, Lucy's MBA from Stanford University made her overqualified for a position as a personal assistant. But Dieter Kathrein was no ordinary entrepreneur. A French billionaire known for his business acumen and reluctance to socialize, he'd promised her an experience and connections that would make even the interview worth her time.

Odd how she'd thought he was overselling it then, only to discover he'd left several perks off the original attractive list. Being able to walk to and from work was merely the start. Mr. Kathrein had shown an unexpected degree of generosity when he added a car and driver along with a rent-free cottage to her benefits package. With those worrisome personal details handled, the scales had tipped in favor of her accepting the position.

Obviously pleased to have her on board, his sharp gaze had turned misty under his bushy white eyebrows as he shared his family's rich history in this pocket of France. Lucy had been sucked in immediately, thoroughly captivated by the sad and brave story of Dieter's parents, killed while assisting the French Resistance against the Nazis. The sole survivor, barely out of his teens, he'd pledged his life to preserving the family legacy and ensuring the security of future Kathrein generations.

He's certainly done that, Lucy thought, soaking up the views and serene environment. Day in and day out, everything she could see belonged to the Kathrein estate. He and his wife must have been delighted to raise their two daughters in such an idyllic area—the perfect balance between the past and present, vibrant cities and quiet countrysides, staggering history and a lovely, hope-filled future.

She marveled that the man whose extreme preference for privacy and solitude had so graciously shared a corner of this sublime region with her and her remaining family. At the time he'd said, in his cultured French accent, "Family is the only reason to do anything in this world." She couldn't agree with him more.

Following her interview, once she'd signed the contracts, Dieter had entrusted her to the estate manager, who'd given her a full tour, culminating with a walk-through of the cottage. Considering the regal elegance of Dieter's sprawling residence she shouldn't have been so stunned by his definition of *cottage*. The four-bedroom manor house had two parlors, a dining room, a renovated kitchen and a sunroom downstairs—all fully furnished. The modern updates throughout the house had been expertly crafted to blend seamlessly with the original, old-world charm. She'd fallen in love with the space immediately, knowing this would be the fresh start she needed.

When she rounded the bend of the lane, the front door of the house came into view and Lucy's shoulders relaxed as the last of the day's challenges fell away. At ninety-six, and firmly set in his ways, her elderly boss could be more than a little difficult at times. Those speed bumps would smooth out in the weeks ahead. This wasn't her first experience with an eccentric boss who expected people and details to fall into place. For her part, she knew it was simply a matter of acclimating to his personality, communication style and priorities. The holiday season, with the influx of family and happy traditions, would help them both bridge that gap.

For now, work was behind her and she'd be home momentarily. *Home* in France! The lovely thought brought a smile to her lips. In a minute or two, she'd be able to see the progress Gwen had made with the Christmas tree today and then she'd tickle a smile out of her nephew, Jackson. Only eight months old and already the little guy was an incurable flirt. On a second wind infused with happiness, she picked up the pace and hurried along the lane.

This wasn't how she'd pictured her life would be at twenty-six, but she thought the three of them were settling into a pleasant and hopeful routine as a family. Despite the headache of the overseas move—no one hated flying more than Lucy—Gwen seemed to smile more often, the grief fading from her eyes with each new day. Lucy celebrated every small, positive change in Gwen after the heartbreaking and unexpected loss of her husband only two months after Jackson's arrival in the world.

Having her sister and nephew around gave Lucy a much-needed anchor as she learned her new job and let go of her own heartbreak. Her loss had been mild in light of Gwen's tragedy, but moving from California to France, embracing a new career and direction in life, had helped them both.

"I'm home," Lucy called out as she walked through the front door. She set down her briefcase and purse to shrug out of her coat, hanging it on the antique hall tree. The house was quiet and she didn't hear any of the typical noises or catch any savory aromas from the kitchen. Maybe Gwen and Jackson were playing in the garden out back.

Lucy dropped off her purse and briefcase in the smaller parlor room at the front of the house they'd repurposed as her home office.

Kathrein had requested she keep flexible hours regardless of where she chose to live, since he had an unpredictable sleep pattern. Lucy had yet to seek out a social life, so it didn't bother her to be available whenever her boss woke with a concern or fresh idea.

"Where's my favorite little man?" Lucy singsonged as she walked down the dim hallway. Her shoe caught in something and she bent for a closer look. One of Jackson's cotton blankets, she noticed, picking it up. How strange. Gwen, older by four years, had always been a bit compulsive about keeping things neat and tidy.

Lucy slid back the pocket door and stepped into the larger parlor they used as a family room. Her mind went blank. She couldn't make any sense of what she was seeing.

It looked as if a tornado had ripped right through the room, overturning furniture and twisting everything in its path. The fresh Christmas tree Dieter had had delivered to the house just days before was toppled over. The pine scent rising from broken branches and crushed green needles weighted the air in the room, making her queasy. The antique glass ornaments they'd inherited from their grandmother were scattered and crushed, strewn along the floor like sparkling, hazardous confetti.

No. *No.* The word echoed through Lucy's mind. This disaster didn't make any sense. Gwen would never make this kind of mess or leave it for someone else to find. *Where are they?* Lucy's heart stalled out in her chest.

"Gwen." What she'd intended as a shout came out as a rasp. She cleared the terror from her throat and tried again. "Gwen!" She raced to the kitchen. The destruction wasn't as bad here, though the chairs were out of place and Jackson's stroller was missing.

Maybe they'd missed the terror. Gwen often took Jackson out for a walk before dinner. Lucy clung to that hope right up until she noticed the cracked wood frame around the back door latch. Fumbling with her phone, she dialed Gwen's cell phone number. No answer. She ended the call before the voice mail greeting finished. Tears threatened to spill over as Lucy raced upstairs, hoping the baby would be in his crib, safe and oblivious to the destruction downstairs. Jackson wasn't there.

Her legs weak and shaking, she returned to the kitchen and leaned against the countertop, struggling to breathe. The signs were all too clear. Something awful had happened to her sister and nephew. She couldn't make her heart accept it. Picking her way through the house again, she searched for a note, missing valuables, anything to put this chaos into context.

She stood there, helpless and scolding herself. Calling 911 wouldn't help, and she didn't know the local equivalent to reach the police.

Who could possibly gain from targeting a widow and infant? Lucy didn't have enemies and very few friends were aware of her overseas move. She and Gwen had decided to save the announcement for the annual Christmas letter, a cheerful high point to counter the sadness of the past year. She dialed Gwen's number again and left a pitiful voice message this time, pleading for a reply.

Devastated, Lucy fell to her knees, the baby blanket she'd found in the hallway clutched to her chest. Her sobs tangled with fear and desperation. Who would do this? Crime in this area was practically nonexistent. Everyone they'd met in this quiet, isolated part of France had been friendly.

Too isolated to be random, a small voice in her head declared. Dieter Kathrein might be a recluse, but he was also a legend. The estate was well-known and he had enough staff to make it obvious when he was in residence. At his age, with his massive business success, he'd racked up a few enemies along the way. The attack could be retaliatory and Gwen and Jackson were taken by mistake.

Her boss could help. He would know who to call and he had nearly limitless resources. He'd help her navigate the system, help her through the next steps. His money and influence would make recovering Gwen and Jackson a priority for the authorities. On a surge of hope, Lucy went into her office, where she wouldn't have to look at the wreckage while she spoke with him.

She jumped a little when her cell phone rang in her hand. Gwen's number showed on the screen and Lucy's body sagged with relief. "Gwen! Where are you? Are you okay?"

"Lucy, we aren't hurt but you need to listen very carefully."

Gwen's voice, normally calm and strong, trembled with fear. The sound dragged Lucy back to that terrible day when her sister had called to say her husband had died. Gwen's sorrowful tears and inconsolable shock on that day still haunted Lucy. "Where are you?" she asked again.

"In—" Her sister's reply ended on a startled gasp.

"Lucille." Dieter Kathrein's curt tone confused and startled her all over again. "This call shall suffice as proof of life."

"Mr. Kathrein?" She'd left his offices less than an hour ago. Had the kidnappers grabbed Gwen and the baby and then attacked his house, as well? Whoever planned this knew how to cull the weak, seizing the elderly, a young mother and a helpless baby. "Are you injured?"

"I am well." He didn't sound the least bit rattled by the circumstances. In fact, this was the tone he used in his business conversations. "We are negotiating new terms."

"Pardon me, sir?"

His English was flawless, though gently rounded by a French accent when he was stressed or tired. Then the accent grew heavier and something else seeped in, drenching the words with a harsh elegance that was tougher to understand.

"Negotiating." He enunciated each syllable and added something at the end that sounded closer to German, which only confounded Lucy. "Your sister and her son are with me. They are safe. They will remain safe as long as you do as I say, young lady."

"You have Gwen and Jackson?" She squeezed her eyes shut and tried to wrap her mind around it but couldn't. Behind her closed eyelids she saw the mangled parlor, the broken bits of the few treasures they'd brought to France. "Why?" *How, when* and *where* all needed answering, as well, but she limited herself to one question at a time.

"They are leverage to ensure your cooperation," he stated, as if it should have been obvious. "You love your family, correct?"

"More than anything," she whispered. He knew how much those two people meant to her. Gwen and Jackson were all she had left. She and Gwen had lost their parents in a plane crash during Lucy's second year of undergrad. Gwen had been the steady, reassuring voice of reason when grief would have derailed Lucy's goals. She swore. "How could you do this?"

"As I thought. Look in your desk drawer. The top one. There is an envelope."

Thoroughly devastated, she did as he directed, withdrawing a plain white envelope. Only the weight of the paper gave away the means and quality of the man behind this treacherous attack.

"Did you find it?" he demanded.

"Yes," she replied, lowering her voice. Countering belligerence with a calm and composed response was a trick she'd learned in her MBA program. In her early days with Kathrein it had been surprisingly effective at defusing him when he grew agitated over something.

"Everything you need is in the envelope. A man seeking to ruin my grandson's political plans went digging through *my* background. My past is irrelevant! Nosy reporters," Kathrein ranted. "It is no more than slanted, ancient history and vicious rumors. My Daniel is a good boy. He will *not* pay for the mistakes of my youth. Family is everything, yes?"

"Yes," she agreed. Apparently one member of his family—his only grandson and heir—was worth her entire remaining family combined. The envelope crinkled as her hands fisted, wishing she could wring his leathery, wrinkled neck. Her pulse hammered behind her temples. She had to think, to find a way around this. What kind of threat, what ancient secrets from his past had pushed the wealthy recluse to these drastic measures?

"The man stored electronic copies of these damaging rumors in a Gray Box," Kathrein said.

Gray Box. Memories that Lucy would rather have

continued to forget emerged, vying for precedence in her troubled thoughts.

"As outlined in your instructions," he went on, "you will retrieve every document and then destroy everything in the cloud, removing all traces of the electronic records."

Break into a secure Gray Box? Kathrein had no idea what he was asking. Rush Grayson, the brilliant creator of that particular secure cloud storage service, had contracts with the United States military and intelligence agencies. His proprietary Gray Box encryption was *that* reliable and impossible to hack. To date, there had never been a successful breach. "What you're asking is impossible, Mr. Kathrein."

"You'd best hope not, Lucille. Since the man I contracted was not successful with the password and such, I presume it will require a more feminine ingenuity," he suggested.

Her mind caught on his words and suddenly his determination to bring her to France, to give her anything and everything she needed to make the transition became clear. She was as much a pawn as her sister and nephew, caught in a life and death game of speed chess. Dieter Kathrein didn't need a personal assistant as much as he'd anticipated a need for her to pry open software. He'd selected Lucy based on *her* past.

Oh, dear God.

"If you contact the police or anyone else I will terminate your family," he said. "If you fail I will terminate your family."

Renewed fear tightened her chest. "Mr.—"

"You have one week."

Her heart stumbled. Seven days to break into a Gray Box? He might give her a year and she wouldn't be able to deliver. No matter what she'd learned during her time with the company founder, she didn't have any confidence she could accomplish the task in the next decade. "Sir, I'm begging you to reconsider."

"Begging does not an ounce of good. Results matter to me. You know this. Retrieve the information or you will never see your family alive again."

If someone on Kathrein's extensive staff had already tried and failed to crack the secure storage site, she couldn't possibly hope to succeed long distance. The inevitable scenarios played like a house of horrors tour in her mind. "Wait! Please, I need more than a week." Lucy floundered for a believable excuse. "I'll have to return to the States." For the first time in years, the plane trip would be the least of her challenges.

"One week, Lucille. Not a single hour more."

"Don't hurt them," she pleaded. Silence was the reply. He'd ended the call. She reflexively redialed Gwen's number. No answer. Tears rolled down her cheeks. How could he threaten Jackson? Just last week, he'd stooped over the stroller and smiled warmly at the baby during one of Gwen's walks around the estate. Kathrein must have lost his mind. Clearly a crazy man held the lives of her sister and nephew in his arthritic hand. *Damn it*. No matter what her insane boss believed, cracking a Gray Box was not possible.

She upended the envelope and poked through the

contents. Along with a substantial amount of cash, presumably to assist with her travel expenses, Kathrein had provided detailed background on investigative journalist Mathieu Garmeaux. How had this one man gathered secrets damaging enough to push Kathrein to such an extreme and irrational response?

Kathrein probably assumed Lucy could magically derive the man's username and password from the background. Not likely. She dashed away her tears with the back of her hand, forcing herself to concentrate on solutions rather than the cold dread sinking into her bones. If Garmeaux would be reasonable, if she could convince him to help her, maybe she could avoid a pointless attack on a secure Gray Box and she could get her family back by morning.

Nothing lost by asking, she decided. She booted up her laptop and did a preliminary search for the man based on the background provided. First she'd send an email and follow that with a phone call. Or not. Her stomach sank at the first search result.

Mathieu Garmeaux, based in Paris, had died two weeks ago, the victim of a traffic accident just a few blocks from his apartment.

Dear God. Lucy dropped her head into her hands and flexed her fingertips hard into her scalp, tugging on her hair as the dates lined up in her mind. She'd been with Mr. Kathrein in Paris at the time. In light of the kidnapping it seemed far more likely that the journalist's motorcycle had lost the fight with a panel truck on purpose. If Kathrein had had Garmeaux killed, what wouldn't he do to gain control of the documents?

A shudder racked her shoulders as she brought up an airline website and booked the next available flight to San Francisco. Gwen and Jackson were counting on her and, like Mr. Kathrein, she would do anything to save her family. Oh, she hated having even that much in common with the wretched old man. Air travel and returning to Rush Grayson's territory were small costs compared to the priceless value of the people who mattered most to her.

Her ticket booked, she tried not to think of anything but the next step and failed miserably. Knowing she'd be facing the man who'd broken her heart last year had her agonizing over every item of clothing as she packed. Circumstances aside, deceiving Rush went against her nature. Though he'd hurt her, she'd never wanted to hurt him. Saving Gwen and Jackson meant damaging the Gray Box reputation, and that left a sour taste in her mouth.

"Can't be helped," she said aloud. Zipping her luggage closed, she called for the car and driver to take her to the airport. As the estate faded into the distance behind the car, Lucy's thoughts bounced from past to present and leapfrogged into the near and distant future.

Starting with a business introduction and a surprising mutual respect, she and Rush had developed a friendship that had become so much more. Chills raced along her skin at the memories she couldn't suppress. She'd been foolish enough to fall in love and he'd been smart enough to adhere to his personal boundaries.

Despite the knowledge that their business interests

and efforts had served them both well, she didn't entertain any illusion that he'd be particularly happy to see her on a personal level. What Kathrein required of her would push the mutual professional respect across a bed of hot coals.

If by some miracle she succeeded in her task, her foolish heart's persistent, feathery hope to someday reconcile with Rush would be blown out of reach forever.

Chapter Two

San Francisco, California
Wednesday, December 16, 11:45 a.m.

Rush Grayson returned to his new company head-quarters in the Financial District absolutely frus-trated. He'd walked out on the morning meeting after more than an hour of zero progress. Time was pre-cious and he refused to waste it. If the prospective client didn't experience an attitude adjustment soon, they could find a different security solution for their data. It wouldn't be as effective as the system he'd designed, but that wasn't his problem.

He'd learned the hard way to walk away and let go. His desire to help others didn't mean they wanted his help. He had to remember Gray Box was no lon-ger at the point where one contract would make or break the company.

He took the express elevator up to the executive office suite and the stress fell away when the doors parted and he entered his domain. His journey to the top hadn't always been pretty, but he'd made sure the gorgeous view he enjoyed now rewarded him every day.

"Good morning, Melva." He paused at the receptionist's desk to pick up his messages. With a little more life experience than Rush or any of the other executives on the floor, the woman had been a godsend, keeping them all grounded with the discreet, calm professionalism he wanted to project to clients and competitors alike.

"How was the meeting?" she asked, peering at him over her bold, red cheaters.

"I lost patience and walked out." He shrugged. "How has the day been treating you?"

"Glorious, thank you." She flicked a hand at the stunning, panoramic views of San Francisco beyond the glass walls surrounding the space. "Your messages." She slid a stack of small paper squares across the marble counter.

Rush grinned. Although everything within Gray Box systems was completely electronic now, she insisted on backing up phone message emails with her old-school habit. He loved it.

"You have a visitor waiting in your office." Melva's practiced smile turned warm, almost affectionate.

The expression stopped Rush short. Melva had used that particular soft smile with only one person and that person was now rusticating in France, working for a musty old man with almost as much money as Rush. He turned slowly toward his office suite, which occupied one full corner of the floor, noticing the brunette seated in the waiting area near his assistant's desk.

"Where is Trisha?"

Melva's lips flatlined with disapproval at the mention of his assistant's name. She'd never warmed to his current girlfriend. It didn't help that since he and Trisha had been involved personally, he had yet to find a more suitable place for her within the company. "It appears she is away from her desk," Melva stated.

His gaze swept over the other glass-walled offices and conference rooms. "I can see that." Just as he could see the long, glossy sweep of his unexpected guest's hair falling straight and sleek well past her shoulders. His pulse kicked, though he knew it couldn't be the woman he most wanted to see. Despite Melva's warmth, he knew that very special brunette was in France. Still, his body moved automatically, propelling him closer as if hope alone would change the stark reality.

He wanted to stride on into his office like a consummate professional, giving his assistant room to do her job and make introductions, but Trisha wasn't anywhere on the floor. He could go back downstairs and catch the private elevator that opened into the hallway behind his posh office. That would create an entrance worthy of the primary developer and top dog at Gray Box.

Or he could stop being ridiculous and get on with his day. Hadn't he been lamenting time wasters a few minutes ago? Irritated with himself, he strode forward to meet his guest.

The familiar vanilla-laced scent stopped him as effectively as a brick wall. His heart slammed against his ribs when she looked up and he saw those big brown eyes full of nerves.

"Lucy?" He had to be hallucinating. She'd left him a year ago, effectively disappearing overnight. One day here—and his—and the next, he been left holding a note that she'd moved to Chicago with no plans to return. He folded his arms over his chest, not giving a damn about defensive posture. She didn't look capable of rendering destruction, but he knew better. "This is…" The multiple ways to finish that sentence became a logjam in his head.

"A surprise, I'm sure," she finished for him, coming to her feet.

He had to back up a step to stay out of her personal space and to keep his hands to himself.

"My apologies for dropping in unannounced, Rush." Her smile flashed and disappeared from one second to the next. "I just got back in town. Can you spare a few minutes?"

Hearing her say his name brought back images and memories best left until later. "For you, always." He caught the subtle twist of her lips and winced. His time and attention had been the one sore spot during their relationship. They were both busy professionals and he couldn't always insist that global markets and prestigious clients wait while he wrapped up a date.

Things were different now, calmer and more predictable since he'd achieved his goal and positioned his company at the forefront of the electronic information security industry. *Calmer, but not nearly done*, he thought, as part of his brain slid back to the wasted morning meeting.

Recognizing the doubt about his availability in Lucy's eyes, he pulled his attention back to the present. Bending over Trisha's keyboard, he sent his secretary a text alert to clear his calendar for the afternoon. "There." He stood tall, smiling at Lucy. "I'm all yours for the rest of the day." The idea of it cascaded over him in a wave of effervescent anticipation. Only Lucy had ever had this effect on him. He held open his office door, encouraging her to enter ahead of him. The soft fabric of the smart evergreen dress she wore swirled at her knees, and he enjoyed the distraction for a moment.

When the door closed behind him, he flipped the switch that turned the clear glass panes of his office opaque, giving them privacy from anyone else on the floor. "What do you need?"

"Oh, my," she breathed. "Your view of the bay is stunning." Lucy turned a slow circle in the middle of his office, a bittersweet smile wobbling on her lips as she took it all in. "The world at your feet, right?"

"I saved the best view for myself," he confessed.

"As you should." Her smile blossomed, a little less wistful. She cleared her throat. "The building, the new offices…it's all amazing, Rush. Congratulations. You deserve it."

"You think so?" Pride swelled up at her praise before he could battle it back. He'd never reconciled the way she'd constantly encouraged him with the fact that she'd walked away without a single word of warning. Never one to leap without looking, her sudden departure from him as well as the city had completely baffled him.

She nodded, interlocking her fingers at her waist. He remembered that little habit showing up whenever her self-control was about to snap. What was going on?

He shrugged out of his sport coat and hooked it on a sleek stainless coat tree near the door. "Why don't we sit down," he suggested briskly. He considered rounding his desk, emphasizing his position and power in the room. Instead, he moved toward the long, elegant leather couch. How many days had he envisioned her right here beside him with a cup of coffee in the morning or a glass of wine after a long day?

Lucy chose a chair on the other side of the art deco glass coffee table and that spark of hope that this might be a personal visit withered.

He catalogued every nuance and change as she settled into the chair. Fit as ever, her sense of style still radiated elegance and class. Yes, her hair had grown longer over the past year. And the warmth in her big brown eyes was tempered with something he couldn't pinpoint. She'd done her eyes with subtle color, framed by those thick, dark lashes, and she'd swept soft gloss over her rosy lips. He didn't care for the tense lines bracketing her lovely mouth. What had happened to her since she'd left him?

He'd kept tabs on her, always in search of a way to bring her back home to California. Not finding the right combination of timing and opportunity, he'd been forced to admit defeat and move on. He hadn't managed to forget her, even after sinking all his energy into a year of aggressive corporate growth and dodging the grasping pursuit of equally aggressive, gold-digging women.

He waited, offered her coffee and water. She graciously refused, but didn't seem willing to explain what had brought her here. "I heard about your brother-in-law," he said, breaking the silence. "I'm sorry for your loss."

"Thank you," she replied, her gaze drifting past him to the view of the bay.

"How is Gwen holding up?"

"Better day by day." Lucy's big brown eyes shimmered with tears until she blinked them away. "I think." White teeth momentarily nipped at her full lower lip. "Moving to France helped all of us."

That caught him off guard. "I didn't realize she went with you."

Lucy nodded. "Her son, Jackson, is eight months old. It's amazing watching him grow."

The worry in her eyes launched an internal battle as his need to shield himself battled against his need to comfort her. "Strong name." As he'd hoped, the words brought out her smile. She'd often lamented her name was a hurdle in the corporate world.

God, he couldn't take his eyes off her, stunned and delighted to have her in his office. Terrified he'd drop his heart into her hands and she'd reject the gift again. His palms itched to touch her, to hold her fine-boned hand in his again. How many nights had he tossed and turned, wishing for one more touch of her lips, gentle as rose petals, against his skin? Her chest lifted on a deep inhale and sent his mind on a sensual, inappropriate detour.

"I know you're busy," she began, "so I'll be brief. I could use a job, Rush. If you can find a place for me."

He knew the perfect place for her, though it had nothing to do with the professional answer she was seeking. Sitting forward, he propped his elbows on his knees. She knew him too well to bother hiding his excitement about bringing her on board. "A job here, with me?"

"With Gray Box." Her lips pursed. "France has been a great experience. Beyond beautiful, but—"

"We have plenty of wine country here," he interrupted. A voice in his head roared at him to shut up. He was an idiot to think she reminisced over their weekend adventures the way he did. He'd heard how quickly she'd replaced him with a new man in Chicago.

Her lips curled into another distant smile and she smoothed her hands over her dress. "California is home," she finished.

"I'm glad to hear you've come to your senses," he teased.

Her serious brown gaze didn't share his humor. "Do you have any openings?"

He glanced past her, had to assume Trisha's desk remained empty on the other side of the privacy-frosted glass. "I could use a personal assistant," he said, making the decision as he spoke.

"You're well aware I have an MBA. Maybe I can be of more use in—"

"Your current post is what, precisely?" Her gaze turned sharp with a hint of temper and he knew he

had her just where he wanted her. Well, profession-
ally anyway.

"Yes, my current title is personal assistant," she
allowed. She crossed her legs at the ankle, distracting
him again with far more intimate memories. "When I
took the post with Dieter Kathrein everyone involved
knew I was overqualified."

"I can assure you as *my* personal assistant you'll
have more challenges."

"I'm sure you're right." Lucy tilted her head toward the desk on the other side of his office. "What
about your current assistant?"

"She's not the dedicated PA I need," he countered.
"Trisha manages my calendar and answers the phone
right now, but it's a stopgap measure. She doesn't have
your business acumen and I don't have time for her
to develop it." The ease of his admission didn't surprise him. He'd always been able to talk with Lucy
about anything.

Her dark eyebrows arched and her lips parted for
a moment, then she clamped her mouth shut. "I see.
Tell me more."

"We've been searching for a better fit for her
within the company," he added. "What were your
duties with Kathrein?"

She shook her head, her gaze dropping to her
hands. "Beyond telling you I managed his calendar,
the rest of my responsibilities are confidential."

"Right. Of course." He waved that off as unimport-
ant and quickly outlined his professional expectations.
A savvy, analytical mind like Lucy's could help him
keep Gray Box at the top and develop new ideas and

market applications. She would be the perfect liaison between him and clients who waffled around wasting his time, too. "What do you think?"

"Salary and benefits?"

"Name it, whatever you need. I'll make sure it's all written into the contract." He twisted, pointed out a building across the street. "You can even have the corporate suite at the hotel until you find a place to live."

"That's very generous. Thank you." Her smile didn't quite reach her eyes as she accepted the ridiculous offer.

"You're worried about *me*, aren't you?" He sat back, stretched his arms across the back of the couch. "About our history?"

"No," she said, her denial a little weak. "I came to you as a colleague and friend. We both have new interests, now. You can reassure Trisha or whomever you're seeing that I won't interfere with your personal life."

He didn't appreciate that promise or the vague reprimand. Lucy had been his only "interest" for over a year. She still was, if he was brutally honest about it. The women who'd followed her had floated through his life without any real substance or impact. Contrary to rumors, he didn't date in the traditional sense of connecting to someone. Trisha was the latest in a line of women willing to spend time as his public companion in exchange for his opening a few professional doors for her.

"I won't lie, Lucy. I've missed you. If you want to reconnect personally, I'm all for it."

Her eyes went wide. "Rush."

He flared his hands, let them fall. "Call it full disclosure. When it comes to you and me, the ball is in your court. If you're here for purely professional reasons, I respect that."

"I am." She swallowed. "Thank you for the job. You won't regret it."

He already did. Lucy Gaines had been everything he'd wanted from a woman in both his personal and professional worlds. Smart and kind, lovely and compassionate, they'd shared interests from wine country to stock market trends to pitching in with local charities.

"Let's get out of here." If they stayed in this office, he'd be tempted to unload every stray business idea he'd wanted to discuss with her over the past year. Not only would that border on employee abuse, it would leave him wide open and vulnerable. He wanted her, he intended to have her, but only when he knew she'd stick around. Standing, he urged her to her feet as well. "I'll show you what's changed since you left." Reflexively he checked his watch.

"Only everything," she said with a short laugh. "Don't wreck your entire day for me. I'm sure Melva can fill me in and give me instructions about the hotel suite."

He picked up on the edge creeping into her voice. How could he convince her he wanted to give her every minute today? "Melva is absolutely capable," he agreed. "We can skip the full tour if you're tired from the trip." He wasn't sure why he was pressing her, only that he wasn't ready to let her out of his sight. She was everything he remembered and more, but he got the feeling she was hiding something about her time with Kathrein. He didn't stand a chance of figuring it out if he left her alone.

"I feel fine, Rush," she said, her smile tight. "We've agreed to terms. You don't have to entertain me."

"Ouch." He laid a hand over his heart, feigning pain. "I'm going to play tour guide anyway. There's no one better than me to bring you back up to speed, on Gray Box specifically and the Bay Area in general."

She shook her head, but not before he noticed the little lift at the corner of her mouth. His arrogance had often amused her. He switched off the privacy glass and caught sight of Trisha at Melva's reception desk. An even better reason to leave the office behind for the afternoon, he decided. While he'd been honest about searching for a better post for Trisha, he hadn't focused on the issue. Now he had an excellent reason to move forward on that adjustment immediately.

"You know," he said, turning his back on the rest of the executive floor, "I should start the tour right here." He gestured toward the door in the opposite wall, tucked behind a floor-to-ceiling display case filled with books and myriad industry awards. "My indispensable PA should know my secret escape route." He led her out of the office and into a narrow service hallway. "Private bathroom," he said, pointing out another door. "There's a bedroom as well."

"A *bedroom*? Good grief, Rush. It's a wonder you haven't been sued for harassment."

Well, that stung. The gossip rags and paparazzi greatly exaggerated his personal exploits whenever he chose to spend time around town with models or actresses. "It's not a space I share," he replied through clenched teeth. When and why had her opinion of him plummeted so drastically? "You know how things go during research or a product launch, or—"

"When you're closing a major deal," she finished for him. "I remember."

He swallowed the urge to point out if he wasn't constantly focused on building up the business, Gray Box wouldn't be such a convenient fallback option for her. Except a woman with Lucy's skills and credentials could name her salary and benefits, and choose from numerous offers. Knowing that, knowing how talented she was, it was tough to accept she'd returned to him without any intent to rekindle their personal relationship. He couldn't decide if his decision to hire her made him an easy mark, sentimental or selfish. Time would tell.

"This is my private elevator." He reached out and punched the button. "Most of the time I use the public one or the express, but occasionally this is necessary."

One side of her mouth curled in a half smile. "You pulled out all the stops here," she said.

If she'd seen his heart on his sleeve as he eagerly shared this with her, she didn't give him any reaction. "The office isn't just about the show of power, though it helps." The doors parted and he ushered her inside. Her fragrance, the dark sensual notes smoothed with a whisper of vanilla, filled the small space. He hoped the scent lingered a while so he could breathe her in at will. He punched the button for three floors down, pulling himself together. That spark they'd once shared seemed to be missing now and it wasn't her problem that he hadn't been able to get over her.

"This must make it easier to avoid distractions," she murmured.

"Exactly." So she remembered how people cornered him in elevators, pitching ideas and résumés.

"As your PA, is it my job to fend them off now?" Her gaze narrowed and she pretended to glare at potential intruders lurking in the corners.

"No." He laughed a little and then reconsidered. Though she stood several inches shorter, even in the heels, she could be formidable. "Well, maybe."

The doors parted and he escorted her to the human resources department. After making introductions, the department manager sat down with both of them, drawing up the details they'd agreed upon for Lucy's employment. Once the legalities were out of the way, Rush insisted on taking her down to the waterfront for a late lunch.

"You don't have to convince me to stay," she repeated when they were seated at a table with a stunning view. "I've signed the contract."

"This is my new favorite place," he said. He'd wanted to bring her here since it opened. "The food is better than the view."

She tilted her head, clearly surprised by his gushing endorsement. When her gaze followed his to the bay, he heard her sigh a little. "I didn't expect to miss it so much."

He was determined to bridge the gap, to earn the trust of the one woman he'd always been able to confide in. "What really brings you back here?"

Her eyes went wide and her chin dropped a little. "I was homesick."

He wasn't accepting that anymore. "A year ago it appeared Chicago was home," he countered. He paused while they gave the waitress their drink order. "Then you moved the family to France." What had happened over there?

She studied him a long moment. "Are you having second thoughts already?"

"No way." He shrugged. "I'm the luckiest CEO in the city. You could write your own ticket anywhere." In the back of his mind, he couldn't make it all add up. Better just to ask. "I'd like to know why me and why now?" He couldn't shake the feeling that she needed him to leap out in front of her and fight off an invisible enemy.

He'd be an idiot if he hadn't already considered and discarded the idea of corporate espionage. Lucy didn't play unethical games. While following her career meant he had a basic knowledge of Kathrein's business interests, the older man hadn't shown any intention of seriously competing with Gray Box.

"Kathrein didn't send me here to spy on you." Her words proved how well they knew each other. "If he had made such a suggestion, I would have refused."

"I know." He recognized the steel in her gaze, respected it. He could take her "homesick" answer at face value or ruin lunch with an argument. Taking the high road, he turned the conversation to other topics. He would wait her out. They were too alike, had been too close, for her to keep any secrets from him for long.

The waitress came by with drinks and he ordered the lunch special for both of them, with Lucy's approval. "When we're done here, we can go on to the suite. It should be big enough for you and your family in the short term."

"Don't worry about that," she interjected. "Gwen and Jackson are staying in France through the holidays. That gives me time to find a place."

"Really?" That set off alarm bells. Unlike him, Lucy had been raised in a close-knit family. She and Gwen had only grown more inseparable when they lost their parents. "Will you go back to be with them over Christmas?"

"I'm not sure yet." She gazed out over the water, apparently captivated by the traffic on the bridge.

"Talk to me, Lucy." Something was way off. He reached across the table and covered her hand with his. "What happened in France?"

She closed her eyes and gave her head a quick shake. "Nothing. Nothing," she repeated. Opening her eyes, she gave him a hard, forced smile. "Gwen and I decorated the most amazing Christmas tree last weekend. Her eye for design is remarkable, despite putting all the fragile ornaments near the top, out of Jackson's reach. He's crawling now, pulling himself up every chance he gets and he's very curious."

"So why wouldn't you go back for Christmas?"

"The flights," she said. "And I wasn't sure how things would go here, if I'd have the time off."

"We'll be closed the entire week." He paused as the waitress delivered two plates piled high with aromatic rice noodles, shrimp, and colorful shredded cabbage and vegetables. While they ate, he steered the conversation toward the charitable effort she'd insisted he dive into before she vacated his life. Using the wealth of brain power at Gray Box, he coordinated tutors for kids in need—those falling behind in school and those eager for a chance to leap ahead.

"Wow. You've made serious progress." This time her smile and eyes showed equal enthusiasm.

She could soak up the views until her homesickness faded while he enjoyed the even lovelier view of her. The deep, soulful eyes, those high cheekbones and that tender mouth were igniting fires in him that only she could tend. "We'll launch a new tech-focused camp next summer. I'll start scouting ideal sites soon." That would be the perfect assignment for Trisha, he realized. She knew the city well, enjoyed being out and being seen, and it would keep her away from the executive floor. Pleased with himself, he apologized to Lucy and sent quick text messages to Trisha and his HR department.

"Forgive me," he said, catching the small frown on Lucy's face. "I just thought of something that would move the process along."

She waved it away. "Don't worry about it."

"Appreciate that." He tucked his phone back into his pocket. Good grief, he'd missed her low-maintenance acceptance of his nature balanced by her high-energy ambition to reach her goals. Why had she walked out on the amazing chemistry they'd shared?

The question was right there on the tip of his tongue and he had to bite it back repeatedly as they left the restaurant for a walk through the marketplace and then on to explore a few other nearby changes in the city. He kept his hands in his pockets, away from her, reminding himself today they were two old friends catching up. Having cleared his calendar for the afternoon, he wanted to make the most of this precious time with her.

She'd helped him push harder toward his goals even as she wrapped up her graduate work. The day she'd presented her thesis, he'd been in the back row of the auditorium, silently cheering her on to victory. They'd celebrated that night and memories of getting creative with the second bottle of champagne in the bedroom still powered his fantasies a year later.

He'd missed her so damn much. Not just the sex, though that had been amazing, but simple conversations, her quiet appreciation of the small things people overlooked as they pushed to get ahead. Lucy had a gift for seeing through the puzzling motivations of people behind the deal and it still annoyed him that he'd taken that gift—among her other talents—for granted.

Regardless of her true reasons for coming home, Rush vowed that this time around he wouldn't let her slip through his fingers.

Chapter Three

As the cable car moved west up California Street, Lucy wished she could escape to her hotel room and hide until morning. She needed time and space to boost her resolve. More, she needed some distance from Rush's warm conversation and familiar gestures and habits before she dumped all her problems into his capable hands. Kathrein's terrible threats, echoing incessantly in her head, kept her silent.

"You okay?" Rush nudged her shoulder. "We can hop off and take a taxi if that's better."

"This is wonderful." The boyish grin on his face was as infectious as it was charming and she grinned back. "San Francisco has such a different scent and pace than rural France."

"Rural?"

"I worked with Kathrein primarily on his estate near Chantilly. Only a few streets made up the nearest town." She didn't trust herself to mention the brief trip to the Paris office. "It surprised me how quickly the cities faded into serene countryside."

"Same thing happens here."

She swallowed the lump in her throat as his words

stirred up lovely memories. The two of them had enjoyed great weekend drives north into wine country and south to hike and sail around the coastline. Though they'd tossed around the idea of traveling abroad, her reluctance to fly and his busy schedule limited their recreational choices. "I suppose you're right."

As they came into the heart of Nob Hill, pretty as a postcard on this clear afternoon, she admired the surrounding architecture and the latest restoration efforts Rush pointed out.

Her heart lurched in her chest, knowing his efforts this afternoon would be the last of their friendly moments. When he learned the truth, he'd be so furious with her and himself that even a professional reconciliation would be impossible. It was highly possible he'd destroy her career.

He'd been too eager to bring her on at Gray Box, letting her dictate all the terms. Eventually he'd demand real answers about why she'd walked away and she appreciated his candor about leaving any potential revival of their personal life up to her. He'd never cleared his calendar for her before and this time— when it should've been the sweetest of gestures—she was using him.

Her ruse, although necessary, made his generous compliments about her skills ring hollow. She hated deceiving him and soon he would hate her for duping him. During the long flights, she'd come to the conclusion that she would never be able to fulfill Kathrein's demands and save her family without getting caught. This wasn't some average company she was trying to infiltrate. This was Rush's design. The man had successfully hacked into sensitive government sites as a middle schooler. With every ongoing minute she despised herself more for this charade. Finding a chink in the Gray Box armor was the only way to save her sister and nephew, and Rush didn't deserve the inevitable fallout of what she had to do.

Rock and a hard place, she thought. There were no good options. Even with more time, she had no chance of finding where Kathrein had hidden Gwen and Jackson on her own. The Kathrein real estate holdings offered the old man too many options on top of his endless resources.

As the cable car neared the last stop on the line, a motorcycle passed by, raising the hair at the back of her neck in a little shiver of fear as she thought of the reporter's accident in Paris. Kathrein had shown her only the wise, occasionally cranky old gentleman when she'd interviewed and subsequently worked for him, effectively masking his ruthless streak.

Rush politely offered his hand as they hopped off the cable car at the stop. "Why don't we head up to the Presidio?"

"We're not tourists," she replied. "And it's a long walk in these shoes."

His gaze slid down over her legs, and her body warmed as if he'd touched her. "I can fix that." He pulled out his phone and started texting.

She suppressed the urge to roll her eyes at him. Of course the hunky billionaire could fix a long walk. Rush loved cars. Just before her move to Chicago, he'd been debating about whether he should invest in an existing car service or purchase a dedicated fleet.

"The driver will meet us on Polk," Rush said, turning down the block. "Did you rent a car?"

It took her a moment to process such a normal question. "No. It was more practical to catch a shuttle from the airport and book a hotel within walking distance of your office."

"Practical and expensive." Rush frowned a little, the expression she remembered as intense concentration.

She knew better than to interrupt whatever puzzle his brilliant mind was sorting out. Her warm affection for him persisted, despite the time and distance. *My burden to bear*, she thought, with some desperation. He might have said the ball was in her court, but rekindling their relationship would make this all worse. She'd left him when she recognized she would never be his first priority. Walking away from him had been the hardest choice of her life up to that point. She'd never expected him to put her ahead of everything in his world—she'd only wanted to know she ranked among his general top five priorities. As much as she respected the building phase of his business, consistently settling for last place wasn't in her nature.

"You really don't have to spend the afternoon with me," she said as they glanced in store windows.

In the past, when they'd walked this route, he might have taken her hand or draped an arm around her shoulders. Today, they were two comfortable friends out in the city. She told herself to enjoy it while it lasted. By this time next week she wouldn't have even that much of him.

"I've missed you," he replied. "I don't want to be anywhere else."

Her heart skipped, wanting to imbue those words with significance and meaning. She reminded herself he missed discussing business or market shares or how to fine-tune client proposals with her. He might miss the sexual attraction, though she knew there was no shortage of women willing to take her place in his bed.

Any dent in her ego over that fact was her own fault. She couldn't blame him for moving on after she'd walked away.

She searched for a neutral topic. "Why were you late to the office this morning?"

"Potential client. You might still be waiting in the office if I hadn't walked out."

"You didn't." She shook her head.

"Don't give me that look." He shrugged, eyeing a display in a florist's window. "They kept talking in circles. A complete waste of time." His eyebrows bobbed above his dark sunglasses. "You can smooth it all over for me tomorrow. That will be fantastic."

Her opinion of his assessment had to wait as the car arrived and Rush gave the driver their destination.

"So what did you decide about the car service?"

"You remember that?"

"Vaguely." She nodded. She'd thrown herself into work and freelancing, using her remaining energy for Gwen, and still her heart and mind had replayed every marvelous and frustrating minute she'd enjoyed with the man beside her. "So which was it?"

"Made the most sense to buy a small fleet and hire drivers for the day-to-day," he said.

She didn't ask about the weekends, knowing all too well how he'd enjoyed taking out his expensive cars for their road trips. On the short drive across town, she returned to the topic of his client, doing her best to remind them both she was his employee and they could conduct business regardless of the setting. He seemed determined to be contrary and leave business at the office today, pointing out new restaurants along with their old favorites.

When the car dropped them near the park, she resolutely turned her back on the yacht harbor and Rush's house on Marina Boulevard, where she'd spent far too much time with him during their last few months together.

They strolled along in a companionable silence and she savored the sunshine and crisp breezes blowing in from the bay. It was good to be home and this could very well be her last chance to enjoy the area. If she succeeded in rescuing her family, Rush would hardly allow her to walk away unscathed. Whether or not he understood her reasons, the only way to save his reputation would be to expose who caused the breach.

A strand of her hair caught in her lip gloss, and as she flipped her head she caught Rush staring at her. "Why are you looking at me that way?"

His lips quirked up at one corner and he raised a hand to her hair before he checked the motion. "You're lovely."

She focused on her breathing while he continued to study her.

"I changed my mind," he announced.

Her knees turned to jelly at those four words. He couldn't mean it. She needed to be on the inside of Gray Box if she had any chance at all of recovering the journalist's documentation for Kathrein and saving her family. "About what?" She forced the question through her stiff lips while she moved to the nearest available bench.

"You should move into the house on Marina," he said, sitting down. "I know I offered the corporate suite, but you've always loved the bay views."

Her stomach bucked at the idea. She couldn't impose on his hospitality, couldn't possibly move in to the guest suite there while he was down the hall with a new girlfriend. The evenings they'd watched the sun set over the bay, glass of wine in hand, swept through her in a tide of nostalgic agony. Not to mention how impossible it would be to meet Kathrein's demands with Rush in the same house.

"That's hardly walking distance to the office." She presented the most logical argument first, praying he didn't counter with a suggestion to carpool. As he'd outlined her responsibilities, she would be with him much of the time, but not enough that they could get away with only one car. Public transit was decent in San Francisco, but she'd rather rely on her own two feet during the brief time she planned to be here.

"So choose a car. You know I have plenty. Or I can assign a driver to you."

Her mouth dropped open. "Rush, that's crazy," she

said. The prickly conversation, so similar to being hired by Kathrein, made her queasy. What was it with billionaires tossing money around?

"Impulsive, maybe," he allowed. "Not crazy." He tapped a finger to the corner of his lips. "Whatever happened in France, the tension is showing on your face. I want to make this transition as easy as possible for you."

His astute observations weren't helping. "That's the stress of travel," she said. "You know how I am. You've done enough by giving me the job."

That unrepentant grin returned with a vengeance. "The job is one more excellent reason to stay in the boathouse," he said, using a drastically understated term for the coveted property.

"Not a good plan. I'd charge you overtime if you knocked on my bedroom door in the middle of the night with a scheduling conflict." Joking with him was her only way through this ridiculous quagmire.

"I can afford it," he assured her with a cocky grin.

"You say that now." She hadn't been fooled by his vague references to Trisha. As a way to prepare for the interview, she'd checked out recent social headlines about Rush. His current secretary-girlfriend would be furious that he'd extended the boathouse offer. She didn't want to wreak havoc in his personal life, too. Once she had what Kathrein needed, she would be gone. She couldn't let Rush burn through any bridges while she was here. "Does Trisha use one of your personal vehicles?"

"She doesn't drive," he replied with a one-shoulder shrug.

Leave it to Rush to miss the bigger point. He was insulting all three of them, and oblivious or not, she couldn't let him get away with it. "The hotel suite is the better choice for me right now."

"Too bad. It's booked. I just remembered."

She gave him a long look. "Really?"

He nodded and the lie was patently transparent in his eyes and his grin.

She had no business being amused by the man. She needed to treat him as her boss. "As your personal assistant, I can verify that easily enough, and I'll add it's no problem for me to stay where I am."

"Starting tomorrow you can verify whatever you want. Right now, as a friend, you'll have to take my word on it." He leaned back on the bench stretching his arms wide, much as he had in his office, providing an outstanding impersonation of a king regarding his domain.

She didn't mind. Humble wasn't his best look. Confidence should go hand in hand with being one of the wealthiest men in the world. The start-ups he'd sold in his twenties had netted him billions, and thanks to the dynamic software powering Gray Box, his net worth increased exponentially year after year. "You didn't pull out the timing argument when we were talking business on the drive over here."

"I was being polite," he said. "Honoring your topic of choice and bringing you up to speed simultaneously."

"I'm not staying at the house on Marina." He needed to accept her choice though she knew he didn't approve of it. "Thanks for the offer."

"Consider it an order instead of an offer," he pressed, lowering his voice.

"Is that supposed to be a threat?" If so, he needed a few lessons from Kathrein.

He arched an eyebrow. "Any hotel is way too public if that scheduling conflict occurs to me in the middle of the night. Think of the rumors when I storm the castle. The company stock could plummet."

She rolled her eyes, grateful once more for the sunglasses. "You won't storm anything. I'm *not* moving in with you. That's demanding too much from a PA." Too late she realized how that sounded. They'd had a similar argument when they'd been dating. He'd wanted her to move in and she'd insisted on maintaining her own apartment, despite the amount of time she spent with him. If there was a way to make this awkward reunion worse, she'd found it.

His body had gone utterly still and the only movement was the breeze ruffling his thick black hair. She hadn't noticed until now that he was overdue for a trim. He probably thought she was here to win him back as much as to secure a high-paying job.

"I don't live there anymore," he said, his voice tight. "I bought a condo down on Fremont Street."

"Oh." She couldn't bring herself to ask when he'd moved out or if it was because of her. Those questions put too much emphasis on her, when Rush's choices and actions should be all about what was best for him and his business. It made her inexplicably sad.

"Closer to the office." He stood up suddenly, shoved his hands deep into his pockets. "Why don't we get you moved in right now?"

"Stop it. I'm not moving into one of your personal properties." A slightly hysterical laugh bubbled out of her. "As the proud owner of one suitcase, I think I can manage it when you relent and give me the corporate suite."

"One suitcase?" He frowned at her. "You moved back home with one suitcase?"

Her pulse skittered over that unwise slip. She scrambled for excuses. "You know I travel light," she reminded him. "And…and everything else is in storage," she fibbed. "Besides, I wasn't sure you'd give me the job."

He pushed his sunglasses up to his hair and his eyes were hard. "Have you forgotten everything about me? Everything about us?"

Unfortunately it seemed as if the specific details of their relationship, both good and bad, would haunt her forever. Although she'd made sure he heard that she met someone else in Chicago, the rumor hadn't been true. The first white lie in what was turning into a lengthy list. Shame rolled through her and she averted her gaze to the magnificent rotunda and the curve of the colonnades behind him.

"Is there someone else?" Rush demanded. "Someone who would be upset or jealous if you accepted my hospitality?"

Resigned, she gave him as much honesty as possible. "Only Trisha," she replied.

"Let me worry about her."

"All right." She certainly didn't want to worry about the woman. "I don't want to cause any more friction than necessary taking this job." She wanted to gain access, recover the documents and hopefully get away before Rush realized what happened.

"And I'm telling you she won't be a problem."

"Okay." Lucy still couldn't look at him.

"Come on," he said abruptly. "Let's get your one suitcase moved into the boathouse." He held up a hand when she started to protest again. "Call it a new perk. The boathouse and job go together as of right now."

"You're being absurd. I'd rather you treated me like a normal employee."

"That's impossible and you know it," he argued. "When you talk your sister into visiting for the holidays, you'll appreciate my decision. Allow me to be considerate."

"Dictatorial is more accurate." She rubbed a hand over her heart, easing the ache at the mention of her family. Counting today, she had six more days to be sure Gwen and Jackson lived to see Christmas.

"Not even close." His lips—lips she'd loved kissing—flattened. "You can always turn the job down."

Oh, how she wished that was true, that her return to San Francisco was a simple case of homesickness. Being on the inside was her only real chance of breaking the Gray Box security within Kathrein's time frame. "Fine. If you say the boathouse goes with the job, so be it."

His mouth curled into a smug, satisfied smile. "Would you rather have a car or a driver at your disposal?"

"Neither." She laughed at the idea of having her own driver.

"It's my terms or no terms, Lucy."

Her heart skipped again at the familiar sound of her name on his lips. "You realize HR thinks all the terms are settled," she said.

"They answer to me." That dark eyebrow arched again, daring her to push him. Rush would happily flex his influence and get his way. He didn't hear the word *no* often enough and he wouldn't hear it from her, either. Not this time.

"I'll accept the generosity of the boathouse and the most efficient car available, on the condition that you'll allow me to move as soon as I'm reestablished here."

He nodded and stuck out his hand. "Deal."

"Thank you."

With another quick text, Rush had the car and driver waiting for them when they reached the south side of the park.

"I think you're more stubborn than ever." She sank into the supple leather upholstery of the backseat.

"Not a chance." He laughed. "I haven't changed a bit. It's a matter of working only with the best, from people to equipment. Having you on board will be a huge asset for the company."

The company, right. The reminder that he was set in his habits settled her more than anything else he might have said. When they'd met, his expensive tastes were obvious early on, but it had been his common sense, creative problem solving and grounded nature that won her over. "Do you ever drive yourself anymore?"

"Sure. This is better for working." As if on cue, his phone rang. "Excuse me, I need to take this."

She caught sight of a sly blonde on the screen and recognized the picture of Trisha, his current "calendar manager." Sitting beside him, Lucy couldn't avoid overhearing Rush's side of the conversation. Trisha didn't sound too happy with the way her day was going.

Rush's answers became increasingly clipped, his tone terse as the conversation continued. Having seen him in action, Lucy knew Trisha's protests about being moved to a different department were only working against her. Rush didn't tolerate simpering, clingy women and having to repeat himself was a particular pet peeve. The woman's time with Rush would be cut short if she didn't respect the hard limits he put on his personal life.

Mentally, Lucy aimed a string of curses at Kathrein. How many lives would be irreparably altered by his demands? She was tempted to interrupt and explain everything to Rush—until the pictures from the reporter's accident flashed through her mind. Veering from Kathrein's instructions would put Gwen and Jackson in more danger.

She slid a glance at Rush from behind her sunglasses and told herself he'd find a way to mitigate the problems she was about to create.

He ended the call, though Trisha's voice rattled on. "My apologies," he said.

Her stomach cramped with anxiety. She'd never enjoyed causing someone trouble. "If hiring me interferes with—"

He cut her off with a sharp look as the driver pulled to a stop in front of her hotel. "She'll get over it." He shrugged. "Or not. Right now, I don't care."

She worked to keep her mouth closed, to smother the truth of her purpose as she got out of the car and withdrew her keycard.

"I'll wait for you here," he said as they entered the lobby.

She was grateful for the reprieve. The past few hours proved she wasn't even close to being over Rush. All the little things she'd loved about him were still there, tempting her to give in to his invitation to revive their relationship. She couldn't let herself fall back down that rabbit hole, not when her return was based on a lie. On top of that, he was with someone else and she refused to be the other woman.

Alone in her room she swore, vowing impossible retribution on Kathrein as she packed up the few items she'd pulled from her suitcase before meeting Rush at his office. She reached for her laptop and saw the corner of a paper caught between the monitor and keyboard. Carefully, she fished it out and her blood turned to an icy sludge in her veins.

"We await news of your interview." The statement captioned a grainy color picture printed on plain copy paper of her and Rush having lunch.

Cold, her hands quaking, Lucy spun around, as if whoever had been here would suddenly appear. Asking how he'd managed this was pointless. She should have expected Kathrein to have someone following her, verifying she didn't involve the authorities. Anger revved up and chased the cold from her skin. The creaky old man better stay far away when she was reunited with Gwen and Jackson because if Lucy ever saw him again she'd rip him apart with her bare hands.

She folded the paper in half and tucked the note deep into a document pocket in her laptop bag. After one last sweep of the room, she headed downstairs with her luggage. At the front desk she discovered Rush had paid the bill.

She wheeled on him, her temper seeking the nearest available target. "That wasn't necessary," she said, biting each word. "Get a refund so I can take care of it properly."

"No."

"Yes." She planted her feet and gripped the handle of her suitcase to keep from lunging at him. "I'm neither helpless nor in need of your charity."

His gaze skimmed over the lobby behind her. "Can we discuss this in the car?"

Of course the most eligible bachelor in the city wouldn't want to make a scene in the middle of a hotel. She forced herself to take a breath, to be rational. A public argument would undermine her determination to impact his life as little as possible. She relented, struggling for composure. "Sorry."

He cautiously reached out and took the luggage from her. With her suitcase and laptop bag stowed in the trunk, she slid into the backseat and he followed, nudging her across. "That wasn't a challenge to your independence," he murmured.

She folded her arms over her chest. "I disagree."

"What is the real issue?" He shifted, one arm

stretched along the seat back, his fingertips close enough to brush her shoulder if he chose. "You weren't prone to tantrums before."

"This isn't a tantrum." She scooted as far from him as the car allowed, her gaze on the city passing by. "This is resistance to you stepping in and just handling things for me. I'm your personal assistant, remember? Not the other way around."

"Starting tomorrow. Today you're my friend."

She could hardly confess that his thoughtfulness made it harder to deceive him. "Friends don't just pay a friend's hotel bill," she pointed out. "I'm not broke, Rush." No, she was only breaking from the emotional pressure.

"Fine." He withdrew to his side of the seat. "I'll have payroll take it out of your first check."

"Thank you." She hid her misery behind a gracious smile. His solution might have made her happy if this new job was as real as he believed it to be. She supposed she could leave a check with Melva when this was over.

They didn't speak again until they reached the boathouse. The driver pulled into the garage and waited as Rush carried her bags upstairs. Inside, the space held an empty, stale chill, confirming he'd moved out. He walked to the sliding glass door overlooking the yacht harbor and stood there, his back to her, tension radiating from his shoulders.

At last he turned around, but he didn't smile. "A grocery delivery is scheduled. It should be here in a few hours."

"You said you didn't live here."

His gaze drifted around the space. "I don't. I made the call while you were packing up."

"I see."

His inscrutable gaze locked on her suddenly. "I wonder about that." He toyed with his sunglasses. "There's a thing tonight I can't change, or we'd have dinner together."

"I'll be fine on my own." The solitude would be a welcome relief after the travel and whirlwind day.

His chest rose and fell on a big sigh. "Did I ever tell you your independence is attractive?"

She snorted, clapping a hand over her mouth too late to smother the sound. "Not once."

"I should have mentioned it." His smile was wide and easy again, putting a spark in his cornflower-blue eyes. "Make yourself at home. I'll have the most efficient car available delivered later." He winked. "If you don't like it, just let me know when you get to the office."

"Great." She was done arguing about his generosity. He'd just given her the one thing she needed, an evening alone to try and break into the deceased Garmeaux's box. "What time should I be in?" she asked as Rush opened the door to leave.

"Melva is always there first," he said with a wry smile. "I asked her to have the office ready for you by eight."

With that settled, Lucy thanked him once more and closed the door. Much as he'd done, she turned her gaze to the boats and the sunlight sparkling along the dark water of the bay. She'd missed this. The view, the ideal address and homey space outfitted with luxuri-

ous finishes, the scent of the water and crisp ocean air
that provided a deep counterpoint to the masculine
scent and energy of Rush that saturated every corner.

Not anymore. The house had obviously been un-
occupied for some time and the only fragrance was
the trace of cleaning products. Telling herself that
was for the best, she carried her suitcase upstairs to
the bedrooms. She stopped short at the doorway to
the master. It looked exactly the same as when she'd
shared it with Rush, with the king-size bed sprawling across dark hardwood floors and the sleek furniture softened by soft white and nautical blue fabrics.

Troubled, she turned down the hall to the guest
suite. If Rush found out and asked about her decision,
she'd lean on his theory of a family visit and claim
the master had more room for her sister and the baby.

She closed her eyes on a wave of guilt. She had to
stay positive, had to believe all three of them would
make it through this. Four, if she counted Rush. After
quickly unpacking to complete the charade in case
there was a visit from a housekeeper in the next few
days, she headed back downstairs.

Feeling like an interloper in a space Rush had created for himself, Lucy set up her laptop on the traditional polished-oak desktop in the sleek home office.
When everything was connected properly, she turned
on the device and soaked up the view of the Golden
Gate Bridge while she waited for her system to boot
up.

Taking a seat in the black leather chair still adjusted to accommodate Rush's taller frame, she
opened her email. The contract from Gray Box was

there, along with the new-employee handbook and other documents she should deal with.

The handbook made her smile. She was proud of everything Rush had accomplished, dragging himself from his stint in juvenile detention to these stunning heights. If there was a silver lining in this dreadful situation Kathrein had created, it was the privilege of seeing Rush content and happy and completely in his element as an industry leader.

An instant message window flashed open on her screen and she frowned at the unfamiliar name. A progress report is required.

Kathrein. As if the note in her hotel room hadn't been bad enough. Lucy hunched her shoulders against the trickle of fear sliding down her spine.

Are your guests safe? She typed into the chat window.

Report first.

She sighed. He had the leverage and they both knew it. I am working on it, she replied.

You are wasting time, his next message warned.

As she was typing in her response, a picture popped into the window. Jackson smiled, perched on Kathrein's knee. It looked as if they were a perfectly innocent grandfather and grandson until Lucy noticed the man standing behind Kathrein, holding a menacing black gun aimed casually at the baby's head.

Her eyes welled with tears and her breath caught in her throat. Her fingers fumbled, but she managed to save the picture for later study, hoping to find a clue to their location. Knowing questions about Gwen wouldn't be answered and pleas for mercy wouldn't sway Kathrein, she told him what he wanted to hear and prayed she could make it happen.

You'll get the files.

Waste no more time. Another picture appeared, this time of her and Rush facing off in the hotel lobby.

She rubbed away the rash of goose bumps that raced over her arms with this additional proof Kathrein's man had been trailing her all day, well within striking distance. She couldn't continue to be so naive and oblivious. How had she not noticed?

The chat window disappeared and Lucy raced for the half bath down the hall, her stomach no match for the stress of his vile threats. When the heaving stopped, she sat back on her heels and let the tears flow.

Standing on wobbly legs, she splashed water on her face and rinsed her mouth, then she went back to the office and set to work to save her family.

Chapter Four

Thursday, December 17, 7:20 a.m.

Rush managed to reach the executive floor ahead of Melva and had the coffee brewing when she walked in. "Good morning," he said as he continued work at Trisha's—Lucy's, he reminded himself—desk.

The older woman stopped short, staring at him through the glass walls. "You're early today," she called out.

"First time for everything," he said. "Couldn't sleep," he admitted as he continued clearing the desk before Lucy's arrival.

Melva walked over, her short silver hair styled as perfectly as her subtle makeup. He'd once tried to find out how old she was and been given a runaround he chose not to unravel. Sharp as a tack, she managed the various personalities of the Gray Box top executives with proficiency and kindness.

She wrinkled her nose at the nameplate. "Did you come to your senses about that one?"

And the occasional sharp, maternal touch, Rush added to his list of Melva's attributes. "Trisha has been moved to marketing. A better fit for her skills." He glanced up when Melva sniffed. "What? I thought you'd be thrilled."

"The girl may have a degree, that doesn't give her skills." Melva glanced around. "Why isn't she here taking care of this?"

A question Rush had deliberately stopped asking himself. The answers were too revealing. "I wanted to do it."

Melva pursed her lips. "Knowing how that one was, I figured I'd better come in early to make sure there wasn't a catfight when Lucy arrived."

"Please," he argued. "You're early every day."

She beamed at him with motherly approval. "Hiring Lucy is just what you need."

"She's overqualified to be my assistant." Going on the offensive was the only way to save face.

"Better that than the underqualified string of spokesmodels you've been running through lately." Melva opened a drawer and showed the contents to Rush before dumping everything into the box of personal items on the floor. "Look at this mascara, man-killer red lipstick and nail polish. The only job she wants is Mrs. CEO."

"She knew my rules going in. So what if she takes care of herself?" Rush said. "I respect that."

"I take care of myself," Melva corrected. "What she does is different. She's cotton candy and you know it. Pretty on the outside and no substance underneath."

It was tough to defend Trisha, or any of his recent

companions, to Melva. "I give her points for sticking it out through the transition."

"Which transition would that be? Out of the executive suite or out of your life?"

Rush ignored this astute comment. Trisha knew he didn't do long term. She'd used him for a career boost and he'd used her as a distraction for the media. It was a functional system and it sounded better than calling her an emotional crutch. It had been mutual and he'd been clear with her about the true nature of their association.

He couldn't even define his time with Trisha as a relationship. That term had been eliminated from his vocabulary when Lucy walked out on him. Or maybe he'd never truly owned the term. Rush clenched his teeth as the familiar ache pulsed through his system. He'd promised Lucy anything personal between them would be at her request. It might have been the dumbest promise of his life.

His persistent attraction to her defied all logic, all common sense. She'd *left* him and he'd never quite been able to hate her for it. He'd been ready to propose, unaware that she'd been ready to move on. His bruised pride had been nothing compared to the overwhelming sense of loss.

Yesterday he should have sent her packing, yet he'd welcomed her into his business. Eagerly, damn it. He was settling for the smallest crumbs she might toss his way, yet he couldn't stop himself, giving her the job, the boathouse and a car. All of it despite the secrets she was keeping. Throughout his dinner obligations last night he couldn't shake it off, couldn't keep his thoughts away from Lucy. She was back and he wanted to keep her right here where he could enjoy her every day.

He wanted to find a way to get her back into his bed, where he could enjoy her every night, as well. To do that, he'd have to make Melva's day and extricate himself from any perceived personal ties to Trisha.

"Trisha will find someone in marketing to latch on to. It will be better all around."

Melva's pewter eyebrows arched, her gaze full of skepticism. She reached into the box and flipped open a notebook. Rush leaned closer, cringing at the looping handwriting and heart-shaped doodles filling the page.

Mrs. Grayson.

Mrs. Rush Grayson.

Mr. and Mrs. Grayson.

Mrs. Trisha Grayson.

Well, she had excellent penmanship. He groaned. "She knew better. I was clear."

"*You* knew better," Melva scolded.

"I never gave her a reason to think long term was an option with me," he said, putting the lid on the box.

"Hmm, I don't need three guesses why," Melva replied. She hefted the box that contained every last remnant of Trisha's time in the assistant's office.

"Let me get that," Rush said.

"It isn't heavy." Melva shook her head and turned. "I'm only stowing it under my desk for now."

He knew better than to argue when she used that tone. With the desk clear, he sat down to deal with the computer, searching out any files or records

Trisha might have added that Lucy wouldn't need. Finding a mocked-up wedding invitation, he sat back in shock. The file had been created yesterday afternoon after he'd messaged Trisha to set up preliminary list of locations for the summer camps.

He should thank Lucy. Her unexpected appearance had helped him dodge a major bullet. Rush scrubbed a hand over his face and deleted the project from the desktop along with several other inappropriate items. Maybe he should just give Lucy a new computer to start fresh. He didn't need to hide his personal life from her. There were always mentions and pictures of him online at gossip sites and in the society pages of the local papers. He hadn't been a monk in her absence, he just hadn't been happy.

The thought jolted him. Of course he was happy. He'd propelled his company to the top and made Gray Box the platinum standard of cloud storage security. His personal life entertained him and served a purpose. He didn't need a serious, meaningful relationship for fulfillment.

So, what was his problem?

He powered down Trisha's system and unplugged everything. Only the monitor would stay. With a text message, he ordered the hardware and software packages Lucy would need and arranged to have them delivered as soon as possible.

He might only have her on a professional level as a personal assistant, but he could be patient and creative about reaching his ultimate goals. What they'd shared was special, even if he hadn't expressed himself well at the time. Their history gave him some excellent ideas about tempting her back into an intimate relationship.

It was five minutes before eight when the elevator doors parted and Lucy appeared. She seemed relaxed as she greeted Melva. Today's dress was a deep sapphire blue. The color reminded him of the water of Wineglass Bay in Australia when he and Gray Box cofounder, Sam Bellemere, had visited several months ago as part of a private consulting gig.

Her hair spilled over her shoulders and her heels clicked softly on the marble floor. As she approached he found himself inadvertently cataloging all the differences between her and Trisha. From the smile to the shoes, the women were night and day. Lucy's smile was confident and open, though at the moment she seemed a little shy, as if he might rescind his offer. Trisha's smile most often appeared with a calculating gleam in her eyes that kept a man on edge. The women were built differently, Trisha tall and slim while Lucy's shorter frame boasted lush curves that had filled his hands. Lucy had a thing for shoes, he knew, but Trisha's spiked heels could have been registered as weapons.

Lucy paused at the door. "Good morning."

Rush shoved his hands into his pockets to keep from grabbing at her and scaring her off. "Welcome to your first day at Gray Box. Has HR been in contact?"

Her smile widened. "I went through as many training units as possible last night. Whoever designed those for you did a thorough job."

"Thanks." Had he ever hired less than the best for any task? His gaze skimmed the desk that was

Lucy's now, an obvious contradiction. Well, he had the best person in his assistant's post now and that's what mattered. "A new computer will be here soon." He stepped back and opened his office door. "Once you're settled, grab a coffee and come see me. We'll use this morning to get you up to speed."

"Sounds good." She stowed her purse and a slim laptop bag in the cabinet behind her desk. "I'm ready."

"You didn't bring anything to personalize the space?" With an effort, he suppressed a flare of anger. Was she marking time with him again? He wouldn't tolerate it.

Her gaze dropped to the clean, spacious surface of the desk. "I, *um*…" She cleared her throat. "Most of my belongings are in storage, as I said. I wasn't exactly sure where you would have space for me," she finished.

Her hesitation and obvious scramble for a valid reason irritated him as much as the lack of personal details. There must be someone else in her life, another man she didn't want him to know about.

"Has your working routine changed?" she asked.

"What do you mean?"

"I remember you being single-minded at the office. I'll keep up with you during office hours and personalize the space on my own time."

He deserved the polite pushback. Maybe it had been too long since he'd had a serious employee in this role. He gave in and pressed his fingers to the tension in his neck. "You're right. That hasn't changed." When he dug into a project, he didn't stop until he could call it done and perfect. With plenty of tasks

here at the office, she didn't need to know he'd la-
beled *her* his next primary mission.

"Shall we?" She tilted her head, her hair swaying
over her shoulder. He wanted to believe she'd left it
down today for him.

"Sure." He led her into his office and switched on
the privacy glass. This time he moved to his desk.
"Would you rather have pen and paper or an electronic tablet?" he asked. He'd anticipated her answer,
torturing himself with another round of the mental
game of how well he knew her.

"Tablet, please."

A point for him, he thought, handing her the device. "It's preloaded for Gray Box employees with
typical apps, and a guest username and password."
He gave her those details. "You can personalize it—"

"On my own time," she finished his sentence with
a bright smile.

Frustration rode him hard that she could so effectively behave as if they'd never been more than
friends. "Did you sleep well last night?"

She did a double take. "Yes, thank you."

"Good." Wrenching his mind away from the last
time he'd seen her in that king-size bed, her dark hair
spilling over the white linens, he started to explain
how he set his calendar when his office door opened.

He stood up, stifling an oath as Trisha sauntered
in, her long legs quickly devouring the distance until
she was pressed against him in a hug far too personal for the office. "The privacy glass is on," he
said, barely keeping his irritation at bay.

She flicked that away with her white-tipped fingernails. "Oh, I know that doesn't apply to me, darling." Her gaze raked over Lucy, that calculating smile in full force.

"Trisha, let me introduce Lucy Gaines. She'll be taking over as my personal assistant."

He shouldn't have been surprised by Lucy's gracious and warm greeting. Trisha, conversely, was clearly put out. He'd been sure they'd settled this privately.

"A pleasure," Trisha replied.

He nudged Trisha back a step, closer to the door. They'd discussed the camp locations and her move to marketing following last night's dinner at the mayor's house. He refused to allow her to throw a fit here after being so accommodating last night. Her goals of becoming a Mrs. CEO aside, she knew he didn't do personal drama.

"I just need a minute with Rush," Trisha said to Lucy in a tone so sweet his teeth ached. "If you'll excuse us."

"Of course," Lucy replied. "HR just sent me a text message," she added, raising the tablet. "I'll be back as soon as you're ready for me."

He watched Lucy depart, exemplifying the discretion of a valuable PA. "The privacy glass was on, Trisha." It was the safest thing he could say.

"I noticed. Moving me to marketing is bad enough," she pouted. "I only came up here to get my *Rush* for the day." Her fingers trailed along his shirt collar as she giggled over her pun.

"Trisha." He sank into his chair and held her back

when she tried to perch on his knee. "You have a communications degree."

She fluttered her eyelashes at him, waiting expectantly for him to continue.

"Marketing is lucky to have you. You knew that desk outside my office wasn't permanent."

The flirty maneuvers ceased instantly. "Who is she, Rush?"

How could he safely answer? "A colleague," he hedged. "She has connections I need to secure some key contracts for us."

"*Us* has a nice ring to it." She tried to capture his hand with hers.

He'd meant it as a company-wide *us*. An unwelcome image of Trisha's "Mrs." doodles flashed through his mind. He resented that he'd have to speak with her about that later, not on company time. "Go have a terrific first day with the marketing team."

"Okay." She bent to kiss him, taking her time so he had a good view of her cleavage. Rush turned and she caught his cheek. Standing tall, she studied him for a long minute before her expression cleared. "Don't work too hard," she said, sashaying out the door.

When the door closed behind her, Rush used a remote at his desk to lock it. He needed a few minutes to get his head on straight. He might have more expertise with technology—and with good reason—but Trisha's possessive signals were inappropriate. Their deal had been for her to be affectionate in public. She'd never pulled a stunt like this at the office. Hearing Melva's warnings in his head, he wished there was a way to convince the older woman to set Trisha straight on his behalf.

He nearly laughed. Melva managing his personal mistakes was less likely than him making any woman a Mrs. Grayson. Between the bad example of his past and his big vision for the future, he wasn't cut out for a conventional marriage and the baggage that came along with it.

He'd packed away the ugliness of his childhood at sixteen, when he'd been busted for hacking, yet those images slid through his mind now. Countless fights over money had ended with slamming doors and his mother's tears, and nothing ever changed. The overtime and weekend shifts, the incessant nagging had divided his parents and pushed Rush deeper into the unfailing logic of computers and code.

People talked about the concept of love as if it was tangible, but he'd never been able to see it. Most people didn't see the programs and code powering their lives, but that was real; it drove operations and made a difference. He sure as hell had never seen love function enough to help anyone. Actions made a difference. *Love* was just another cheap word.

Lucy had been the one woman who'd made him reconsider life as a permanent bachelor. Strong-willed and independent, she'd accepted him as he was. She'd given him space to think and work, and she didn't complain if he interrupted a kiss to jot down an idea. She'd agreed with his assessment that messy emotions ruined a great sexual relationship.

He wanted to reclaim that magic. Surely he could find a way to make her want him again, too. More

than his lust for her body, he valued her partnership,
affection and unconditional understanding. He didn't
believe anyone else could give her the same devotion
and satisfaction.

ARMED WITH HER TABLET, Lucy left the executive floor
and headed downstairs to HR while Rush shared a
private moment with Trisha. The tabloids hadn't done
the woman justice, amping up the glam and minimiz-
ing the shark factor.

In those few seconds, Rush's girlfriend had painted
a clear picture about how they spent time out of the
office. Lucy chided herself for letting that little scene
bother her. Since she still cared for the man and
wanted what was best for him, shouldn't his happiness make her happy, too?

She had no right to feel hurt or cast aside by Rush.
She'd made the decision to leave him *after* he'd kept
her waiting at a restaurant one too many times. A little voice in her head wondered if he was more careful
with personal endeavors now. Based on the evidence
Trisha presented, it seemed so.

Lucy shook off the misplaced jealousy. She
wouldn't be here long—she only had today and four
more to satisfy Kathrein's demands—but she wanted
the office staff to know she had the brains to do the
job right. Being lumped into the same category as his
recent arm-candy assistant would crush her pride.

Keeping a low profile was smarter, yet the more
she knew about the office and staff, the better her
chances of getting the information for Kathrein. Last
night she'd made too many incorrect attempts on the

journalist's Gray Box and the system had locked her out. She'd painted herself into a corner and had to hope she could break in through a weakness on the administration side.

Having checked in with HR, she stopped by the other departments, all except marketing. Lucy asked several questions of the small team dedicated to providing tech support to the office. At the encouragement of the department manager, she took a plate of holiday snacks back upstairs to Melva.

When she returned to the executive floor, Rush's office was still frosted with the privacy glass. All the details he'd implemented or invented to make this building state-of-the-art impressed her. Under different circumstances, working here—in a capacity other than his assistant—might well have been her dream job.

Melva hopped up the minute she saw the covered plate. "Is that from Joey in IT?"

Lucy nodded, smiling through another wave of sadness. Melva would be disappointed in her when the deception was exposed.

"That boy loves me, praise God. Have you had a taste?"

"Not yet."

"Well, bring over a chair and prepare for addiction."

Melva peeled back the plastic wrap covering the plate and they dug into the sweet, colorful holiday treats while Melva walked Lucy through the corporate calendar program and explained how Rush typically scheduled his time. She blotted her lips with a napkin. "I'll introduce you to the others since his highness is still tied up," Melva said.

An unwelcome image of Rush tied up and defenseless against Trisha's blatant sexuality popped into Lucy's mind. Her cheeks heated, remembering the first time they'd played with blindfolds and handcuffs in what had been a phenomenal night of pleasure.

"You don't need to worry that they'll write you off as another useless Trisha," Melva was saying. "They'll see you for who you are."

Just like old times, Melva could read her mind. This time, Lucy hoped the older woman was wrong. She was here to crack open a Gray Box, and if word of that breach got out the company would suffer.

But was there any way of doing what she had to do without the world finding out?

Don't think about the consequences. Do what you have to do.

Melva introduced her to the chief financial officer, Ken Lawrence, as well as Torry Harrison, currently the vice president of research and development. She shook hands with both men, silently commending Rush for acquiring superb talent.

"I know who you are," Torry said, a smile wreathing his face. "Rush used to quote you all the time in meetings."

Lucy blushed for a far more appropriate reason this time. "He mentioned you and your innovative outlook during a lecture when I was in grad school. It's a pleasure to finally put a face to the name." After Gray Box had locked her out last night, she'd spent the rest of her evening reading up on all of the senior staff, telling herself that was what any responsible assistant would do.

"Will you join Rush at the fund-raiser tonight?" Ken asked.

"Oh, I haven't heard about that yet," she replied, glancing at Melva for help.

"Rush adopted the children's hospital expansion as a pet project." Melva fanned her face. "He booked the Palace," she finished with a reverent whisper.

"That sounds lovely," Lucy said. She could imagine the glamour of Trisha and Rush emerging from a limo and strolling through the indulgent grandeur of the restored building.

"The open bar is the real perk," Torry joked. "As his new assistant, you should be there. Everyone else from Gray Box is going. The place is sure to be packed with people who might be assets or allies in the future. You could network and lay some groundwork. My wife and I can pick you up."

She floundered for a polite excuse, knowing she didn't have suitable formal wear with her or the time to shop. On top of that, with someone tailing her for Kathrein, she didn't dare do anything he might interpret as wasting time.

"Stop it, Torry. He's being ornery," Melva interjected. "He just wants to one-up Rush and arrive in style with two beautiful women."

Lucy laughed. "I think I'll have to pass tonight. Maybe next year." If everyone was going, she'd have the office to herself. It was the opening she needed.

"What would be even better," Torry said, "is getting your opinion on our latest ideas."

She caught Melva's encouraging smile. "Why me?" Lucy asked. "I don't even have a full day to my credit yet." She didn't want to like everyone so much. Even Trisha had the singular redeeming quality of marking Rush as off-limits—something Lucy needed to keep at the front of her mind.

"As I said, Rush talked about you a great deal. I think your perspective on this is just what I need to clarify our branding."

Her tablet chimed and she saw a message from Rush that he was ready for her again. "Can I take a rain check? The boss is calling."

"The man has a sixth sense." Torry shrugged, shooting her a wry smile. "Come see me this afternoon if he gives you some breathing space."

"Sure thing." Lucy hurried away and gave Rush a quick wave through the clear glass as she approached.

"I appreciate your patience," Rush said as she resumed her place in one of the chairs in front of his big desk. "Trisha—"

She cut him off. "You don't have to explain a thing." She couldn't handle any details. If Rush claimed nothing was going on between him and Trisha, Lucy's hormones would wreck her concentration, and if he said things were serious between them she'd be heartbroken all over again. "My job is to assist you and that means adjusting my schedule to yours."

"Okay." He pushed up the sleeves of his black sweater. "What did Torry have to say?"

"Oh." She glanced back over her shoulder. "Melva

made introductions," she said. "He mentioned the fund-raiser tonight."

Rush rolled his eyes. "Yeah."

"I noticed it isn't on your calendar."

"I tend to leave off the events I don't want to attend," he admitted. "Especially those scheduled for after hours."

"That kind of habit makes it easy to overbook you." She typed it into the calendar and he groaned when it appeared on his computer monitor. "Melva says this fund-raiser is important to you. A new pet project—her words. Why don't you want to go?"

"I have a new project on my mind, but I do need to be there tonight," he finished. "Now, are we all synced up?"

She reviewed the calendar on her tablet. "I guess we'll find out over the next few days." Despite the fact that he was a recluse, it had taken her almost a week to get all of Kathrein's appointments organized so everyone in the household and office knew what was happening. Although he rarely traveled, people frequently came to his estate or sought meetings by video conference.

Rarely traveled. Her mind stuck on that one point. Kathrein had sent those pictures to torture her, but also to prove he had Jackson. It was a stretch to think he'd separated mother and son. That meant he had to be holding them somewhere close to his house. Or not. Kathrein had three properties she knew of in Europe and she had to assume he had more hideaways scattered around the globe. With his private jet, he could be anywhere and move his hostages at any moment.

"Lucy?"

"Hmm?" She yanked her attention back to the far-more-handsome billionaire in front of her. "Yes, we're synced up. Sorry, my mind wandered."

"Nowhere pleasant," Rush observed. "All that tension is back. Are you sure you're okay?"

She smiled so fast she thought her face might split. "Of course. Yesterday you outlined responsibilities that went beyond calendar management and screening your calls. Can you tell me why the phone at my desk doesn't ring?"

He cleared his throat. "Melva is in the habit of handling the calls."

"She and I can make that change right away. What about the other items?"

He smiled, but there was a weary regret in his eyes. "Tomorrow. Talk with Melva about the calls and go ahead and chat with Torry. He could use your insight."

"All right." She was at the door when he stopped her with one more order.

"And put something personal on your desk by the end of the day."

He'd practically growled the demand and her body reacted with a fervent sizzle. She turned and gave him a cheery smile, hiding the reaction. "You're the boss."

Chapter Five

Rush had better things to do than watch Lucy work through the glass that separated their offices. Unfortunately, he couldn't keep his mind on any of them. More than once he'd reached for the switch to apply the privacy glass and couldn't do it. Having her back, having her right there within view—if not quite within reach—played havoc with his mind.

Only a fool would be distracted with the worry that she'd disappear again if he took his eyes off her, yet he couldn't shake the feeling that her return wasn't permanent.

It was their ugly history, he told himself more than once as the day wore on. His bruised pride over the way she'd left him before. He was competitive and he'd lost her. The failure didn't sit well.

A message window popped up in the corner of his desk monitor. It was a direct message from Sam in the security department asking Rush to trek down to the basement for a meeting.

Irritable, he glanced again toward Lucy's desk. Her computer had been delivered and he knew she was getting up to speed with the company systems. She'd apparently ignored his instruction to personalize her space. Would it be a picture of her sister and nephew or maybe a trinket from France? God help him if she put up a picture of herself with another man.

He stood, took two steps toward Lucy and then abruptly turned on his heel, choosing to use his private access to get downstairs. He had a company to run and yet he'd spent last night searching every possible media outlet for some new detail on Lucy's personal life. The fact that she'd worked with an aging recluse didn't help his cause. He had no problem using his substantial resources to keep tabs on her, but it was aggravating that she'd managed to keep her personal life a secret. He'd never figure out how to win her back if he didn't know who else was on the playing field.

Entering the security offices from the stairwell, he took a moment to just appreciate all they'd accomplished. At one time, he'd been a kid on the other end of a computer connection, breaching firewalls and protective algorithms far weaker than those Gray Box employed now.

As he walked toward Sam's workspace, he couldn't suppress the sense of pride in their accomplishments. He and Sam had met in juvenile detention, both serving time for cyber crimes against government agencies. Now, still friends and equal partners in business, they were entertaining requests from government agencies worldwide for the proprietary and far superior security systems they'd developed.

"What's so sensitive you won't use the company email, Sam?" Rush waited while his friend's fingers flew over the keyboard, his face lit by the glow from the multiple-monitor array.

At last Sam sat back, cracking his knuckles. "It's subtle and I'm still tracking things down, but I think someone out there is taking a shot at us," he replied with a grin.

Attacks were fairly common, considering Gray Box was the pinnacle of cloud-based security. Hackers who resembled Rush and Sam in their youth frequently tried to break the unbreakable Gray Box. The person who succeeded would have bragging rights within the shadow community for life.

Rush studied the screens, though the pattern wasn't clear to him. "Have you picked up a code trail?"

"No." Sam scowled at the center monitor.

"Were they taking a crack at specific boxes? Our big clients aren't exactly confidential."

"That would be near impossible to figure out." Sam eyed him over his square black-framed glasses, his lip curled in disgust. "That kind of thing is beneath my paygrade. We have countless forgotten-password lockouts every day. Hell, every hour of every day."

"Then why haul me down here?" Rush propped a hip on the edge of the desk.

"There was an attempt on the main system through an admin access," Sam replied.

"Doesn't that happen every day, too?"

"Not on old backdoor usernames." Sam's mouse circled code on another screen.

Rush listened attentively to Sam's explanation. Subtle was definitely the right word if this was an attack and not another standard poke at the bear. "We haven't used that goofy name on anything current have we?"

"Of course not. We retired it as an outdated antique."

Rush stood up and rocked back on his heels. As fast as their tech business advanced, a term, an approach, even a username could be rendered useless in less than a year. This particular admin name had been one they'd used as kids when they'd left back doors open for later access. Still, among those with a hacker mindset, especially a young hacker mindset, it wasn't impossible to come up with that character combination.

Sam leaned back in his chair, fingers drumming on the armrests. "Did you fire anyone lately?"

"Not anyone capable of this."

"So the latest assistant didn't have any tech skills?" Sam wiggled his eyebrows. "She had great legs."

"I didn't fire her, I moved her to marketing." Trisha didn't qualify as jilted and she definitely didn't have tech skills. Per their original agreement, he'd set her up with a job that suited her and since they were attending tonight's gala fund-raiser together, they'd still be seen as a couple by the media. "What about you?" He turned the tables on Sam. "Any boastful pillow talk lately?"

"You're kidding, right?" Sam sat up straight, throwing an arm wide to encompass the aisles and aisles of servers behind him. "You're the only one who gets out of the office enough to have a social life."

Rush laughed. It was an old joke. Sam, terminally shy, preferred to keep a computer screen between him and his romantic liaisons. Not even the fortunes they'd amassed and invested seemed to give his friend much confidence in social settings. "Come to the fund-raiser and I'll introduce you to someone."

"No, thanks. I don't need your weepy castoffs," Sam joked. He surged forward and tried another search, sat back disappointed again. "Have you pissed off anyone lately?"

"I piss off people every day," Rush admitted. "No one comes to mind as a possible culprit."

"Fine," Sam said with a resigned sigh. "This bugs me enough that you needed to know. I'll keep working at it and see if anything pops open."

"Thanks. I'll mull it over and let you know if I think of anyone who might use that name."

Sam nodded absently, his fingers already tapping out more commands on the keyboard. They were a pair. Rush might be the face of Gray Box, but Sam was the virtual muscle and together they were the top minds in software and development. If there was a problem on the horizon, they'd root it out and take appropriate action.

Back upstairs in his office, Rush switched gears and reviewed notes from his recent talks at local schools. Had he inadvertently used that backdoor name as a part of his example? If so, it would've been the first time.

While he always gave a quick background explanation of the cocky hacker kid he'd been, and his stint in juvie because of his mistakes, he never dwelled on it or gave up information that could be used as a guide to send a kid down the wrong path. Usually he focused on the creativity, team effort and hard work that had eventually made Gray Box a household name.

When he was satisfied that he hadn't inadvertently planted ideas in the head of an ambitious youngster, he returned to the other items on his agenda. He really wanted the contract with the company he'd walked out on yesterday morning. Considering the sensitive nature of the Family Services offices, the information security package he'd presented should have been a no-brainer.

Yes, the holiday season was a tough time to wrap up that kind of deal. On the flip side, Rush knew they were still in the first quarter of their fiscal year and he wanted a slice of that security upgrade budget. He drafted a snarky email making it clear they could contract his company to do it right or they could contract him later to fix the inevitable mess.

Reading it through he knew his lawyers would have a collective heart attack if he sent it, so he deleted it and started over. The second draft was worse than the first, so he shoved back from his desk. Pacing the width of his spectacular view of San Francisco, he fought to corral his fragmented thoughts.

At the soft rapping on his door, he turned hoping to see Lucy. *Not my day*, he thought, waving Trisha in. Why couldn't the woman stay at her new desk with the marketing team? Behind her, he saw Lucy wasn't at her desk. Was there something about the space that actually repelled his assistants?

"How is your day going?" he asked.

She gave a delicate shrug of one shoulder, setting the silk of her top rippling. "I won't complain." The curt tone and sharp smile set off alarms in his head. "What time will the limo come by tonight?"

"Limo?" Rush spotted Lucy in the conference room with Torry. They appeared to be discussing a presentation spread across the table. Why just the two of them? The hem of her dress rose just a bit as she leaned over the table and Rush's brain flooded with the memory of her warm, ticklish skin just above and behind her knees. Yes, he'd told her to meet with Torry, but she was *his* personal assistant. She wasn't here to help everyone with a random question. He closed his eyes, willing away the childish jealousy.

"The children's hospital fund-raiser." Trisha snapped her fingers at him. "It is *the* social event this week. Don't even think of ducking it."

"Sure." His gaze remained locked on that conference room where Lucy laughed as Torry grinned. Rush willed himself to get a handle on the surge of jealousy before he did something stupid, like toss Torry out on his ass along with his stock options.

"Rush? Rush!"

"Yes?" He gave Trisha his full attention, but he could see from the temper in her eyes, coloring her cheeks, it was far too late.

"Who is she?"

He met her angry outburst with the cool detachment he relied on when personal attachments turned sticky. "I answered that question last night."

"No," she countered immediately. "You dodged that question." With a toss of her hair, she stomped out of his office and into the space that had been hers only twenty-four hours ago, leaving the door open.

"Come back here." The last thing he wanted was to air this out in front of everyone.

"I won't. You could have shown me the courtesy of being discreet." Her voice, breaking on false emotion, carried through the executive space and heads turned to watch. Lucy's included.

"Trisha," he warned. "Let's discuss this like adults." He tipped his head back to his office. "Please," he added.

"Is this a conquest issue? You just need a challenge?"

"Enough." At the moment, he just wanted her to stop shouting. "This is a silly misunderstanding."

"Silly!" she screeched, throwing up her hands. "Hardly." Snatching a picture frame from Lucy's desk, she shook it at him. "You, God's gift, probably think you can convert her."

"What the hell are you talking about?" Why hadn't he installed privacy glass on the assistant spaces as well? Not that it would help much since only the executive offices and conference rooms had actual doors.

"She'll be the first thing you fail at, you idiot!" The picture frame landed with a thud against his chest and he barely caught it before it tumbled to the floor.

"Trisha, stop."

"No! I quit. That lousy marketing job is beneath me." She turned up her nose. "And all your charities and community events are boring as hell. You aren't worth it."

She dashed at her cheeks as if she was crying, but

he was close enough to see her eyes were dry. The elevator doors opened just as she reached them. He had to assume Melva had called up the express car. Trisha flounced off, making a dramatic exit on her spiked heels.

In the ringing silence that followed, he looked at the picture in his hands and smiled with relief. Not a boyfriend. Lucy had personalized her space with a candid shot of Gwen and Jackson cuddled up in front of a Christmas tree. Trisha must have assumed by this that Lucy was gay.

Suppressing a laugh, he replaced the framed picture on Lucy's desk and returned to his office, switching on the privacy glass. If that was the way Trisha needed to save her dignity, he'd manage the inevitable ribbing from his executive team. Having her out of the offices and out of his life was worth the momentary embarrassment.

Everyone up here had started as his friend and they all understood the limits of his personal life. Even Lucy. *Especially Lucy*, he thought with a grimace.

He briefly considered inviting her to attend the fund-raiser with him and decided it was a bit much to extend her first day like that. The dark shadows under her eyes gave away her travel fatigue and he couldn't ask her to come along simply to save his pride.

Besides, with just the one suitcase, he doubted she'd packed anything suitable for a gala. *I travel light.* Somehow those words made him feel worse, although he couldn't pinpoint why.

Usually he worked past six, but not today. He needed

to get out of here and get his head together for tonight and he sent Lucy a note that he was going home.

During the short walk to his condo he had a rare flash of regret. Home used to mean the boathouse and evenings with Lucy. Now it was a cold, modern condo with no soul and dinner for one prepared by his personal chef. Trisha was right about one thing— he was an idiot for letting Lucy get away.

He warmed up the food as directed, seriously debating skipping the fund-raiser. It wouldn't be the first time he'd blown off a charity event at the last minute. The guest list would be littered with locals loaded with money and good intentions along with a few celebrities.

Trisha was right about that, too. He couldn't duck out tonight. Rush needed to set the fund-raising bar high enough to make a difference and get the new expansion off the ground. He and Sam had toured the children's cancer ward just last week, bringing the latest video game consoles into the lounge and taking on all challengers. The kids who couldn't make it were able to watch from their rooms and when nurses approved, they'd been able to duel with a few of those isolated patients on handheld systems.

He ate dinner, not really tasting the food. Reluctantly, he pulled together his tuxedo for the gala and shored up his gloomy mood by calling the building valet for his Tesla Roadster. So what if it was the car Lucy's laughter had filled while he'd navigated the seaside cliffs on a hot summer night? He relegated the memory to the back of his mind, along with all the other mistakes and unfixable problems of his past.

Although he could walk or take the limo, he wanted to make a statement. The magnificent lines of the near-silent car earned admiring and curious looks everywhere he went. When he pulled up at the hotel tonight, he wanted all eyes on his solitary arrival.

Life had taught him early the best way to climb out of any difficult situation was to keep moving forward.

Chapter Six

Outside, darkness had fallen over the city and the lights from surrounding buildings twinkled like stars around the Gray Box office. Everyone had gone home and, in the quiet of the empty executive floor, Lucy could hear the clock ticking. Not a real clock; the interior design was too modern for that. No, she heard that incessant ticking in her head and her heart, knowing Gwen and Jackson were running out of time.

Just after lunch she'd received another picture of Kathrein with her nephew. Both Kathrein and Jackson were wearing different clothing and the old man gripped a calendar page with red Xs marking the days she'd lost. The pictures gave Lucy zero reassurance that her family was safe. The armed bodyguard loomed like a vicious shadow in the background. Her demand for a current picture of Gwen remained unanswered.

He'd given her one way out of this. She had to get inside that Gray Box and get out before anyone discovered her breach. Definitely to save Gwen and Jackson, but to protect Rush, as well. Nothing good would come of her return to his life.

His current girlfriend had dumped him, making a public scene Rush surely hated. No matter his flattering words about her having the background and mindset to assist him, once she succeeded in stealing the documents, he'd never forgive her.

Since Kathrein had kidnapped her family and dumped this outrageous task on her, she'd been racking her brain for all the tips and tricks she'd learned while listening to Rush talk about computer security. It couldn't be impossible. The consequences of failure shivered through like a cold wind as she glanced at the picture of her family.

No, she had to believe. Rush had taught her very few things were unbreakable. Despite the Gray Box motto, she knew there had to be a way in. She'd gone as far as possible with direct attempts on the journalist's box and come up empty. Now her only hope was to find a back door or a weaker administration access. She poked and prodded through the system, getting no closer to the documents she needed.

When she'd taken herself on the tour today, she'd met people from several departments and asked questions about the various roles within the company, under the guise of understanding how things meshed and overlapped. The answers gave her insight she intended to use as entry points, but those replies also confirmed that Kathrein should have blackmailed a real hacker. Someone as good as Rush had been before he'd flipped his focus to protecting data.

She dropped her head into her hands and ordered herself to think. Rush had also taught her the value of tenacity. He lived it every day. The man never gave up on a target.

That's why she'd left without a word and faked a new boyfriend in Chicago. That last evening hadn't been the first time he'd stood her up. Rush had been clear from the start that he never planned to shift his remarkable dedication from business to nurture a personal relationship. He wanted physical intimacy and friendship. In turn, she'd never wanted him to change into something he wasn't. It hadn't been his fault she'd broken the rules and fallen for a man who didn't believe in love. He was too perceptive. She'd had to get out on her own terms before he discovered how deep her emotions ran and forced her out of his life.

Frustrated with that useless train of thought, the tick-tick-tick banging in her head, she rocked back in her chair. Swiveling around, she peeked through the glass wall, half expecting Rush to be sitting at his desk. The office was dark and empty, the lights of the city skyline sparkling from the other side of all that glass. Rush always pushed forward with relentless tunnel vision and this unarguable statement of success was the latest proof.

She still admired him for his dedication to improving himself, his work and the community. One night at the boathouse after she'd cooked dinner, he'd reluctantly shown her a picture of himself and Sam as teenagers. It hadn't been long after their release from detention. At sixteen, he'd been rough around the edges, with shaggy black hair and gritty determination in his bold blue gaze. He'd been down on his luck, but she could see he was already looking for a way back into the game.

That candid picture had shown her everything she needed to know about him. A brilliant man with a creative entrepreneurial spirit, he'd hauled himself up and out of that mess and made his first windfall in his early twenties. Maybe she should tell him the truth. If anyone could understand why she was doing the wrong thing for the right reasons, it would be Rush.

If anyone could devise a better solution, it would be him, as well. When they'd been dating and she'd been sincerely frustrated over struggles and aggravations in academic circles as she'd worked on her MBA, his creative, hypothetical solutions ranged from innocent and ornery to complex and dazzling.

This was different. Any deviation from her instructions would have Kathrein taking horrific action against her sister and nephew. Instinctively, she glanced to the exterior windows, wondering who was watching and if they had eyes on her now.

She turned her attention back to the empty office, weighing one lousy option against the next. If she could get into Rush's system, surely the entire company would be at her fingertips. With what amounted to a Gray Box master key, she could find a way to manipulate the settings and access the files Garmeaux had stored here.

Wiping her damp palms on her skirt, she stood up and took a step toward Rush's sanctuary. In the increasingly small world of technology security, if a breach like this came to light, he would be ruined.

"No choice." Speaking aloud muffled that inces-

sant ticking in her head. Gwen and Jackson were all
the family she had. And really, who would complain?
Rush would be furious but he wouldn't publicize it
if she succeeded. Garmeaux was dead. Stealing the
files wouldn't tarnish his reputation as a journalist.
It wasn't much of a silver lining, but she clung to it.

Lucy's breath shuddered in and out of her lungs as
she crossed Rush's office. The carpet felt too plush;
the air was imbued with lingering traces of his cologne. She stopped at the corner of his desk as a small
voice in her head screamed for her to turn back.

No. When her computer was installed, she'd
learned how Rush segmented the hardware and software to suit each facet of the business. Only Rush
and Sam, as the head of security, had the ability to
delve into any department. She had a much better
chance of figuring out Rush's passwords than those
of his partner.

She sat down at the desk and laid her fingers on
the keyboard. Rush could rebuild a business. During her trek through the offices, she'd seen all sorts
of ideas in development. He could rebound from an
attack on the company, but her sister and nephew
would die if she failed.

With another glance to confirm she was alone on
the executive floor, she brought his desktop computer to life. As she fidgeted in the chair, his scent
surrounded her. Familiar and enticing, it sparked a
new reaction this time—guilt.

Before she'd walked away from Rush as a matter of
self-preservation, the masculine fragrance held only
sensual, happy memories. She used to fall asleep in

that big bed in the boathouse, utterly satisfied and content, wrapped in his strong arms and the enduring deep notes of his favorite cologne warmed by his body. Her muscles went lax as she sat there, her body eager for one more encounter with the man. She'd dared more with him, trusted him in bed and out, more than either of the men she'd been close to before him. And, contrary to the rumors she'd started, she hadn't been with anyone since.

When he discovered her deception, there wouldn't be a second chance with him in her future. Even if Rush eventually understood her reasons, if she cracked Garmeaux's box and someone else in the company learned about the breach his legal team would insist on prosecuting her. Ignoring the tears stinging her eyes, she set to work in the darkened office, carefully thinking through every keystroke, planning and tracking her attempts with pen and paper.

To her shock, she succeeded on her second login attempt and the reporter's files on Kathrein filled the screen. Her momentary sense of victory was quickly muted by what she had to do for Kathrein. By tomorrow morning, she'd be back on a plane to France for a reunion with her family and Rush would be a permanent part of her past.

THE GALA WAS going exactly as Rush anticipated. Bored and unhappy, he beamed at acquaintances while pretending to sip the champagne on offer. It wasn't his favorite beverage, but it was a far better choice than the open bar, especially with so many women in the room who'd noticed his solitary arrival. Despite his best efforts, his thoughts drifted back to his favorite champagne moment with Lucy at the boathouse. God, what an experience. Her body had always intoxicated him more than any liquor and he struggled to suppress an instant erection at thoughts of sipping ice-cold trails of bubbly from her soft, warm skin.

Since the evening he'd walked in to find the boathouse deserted, he'd tried and failed to purge her from his system. Part of him hated having her back. None of his successes mattered when held up against his stellar failure with her. His subsequent failure to get over her eroded his self-confidence, though he didn't let anyone close enough to notice.

The engagement ring he'd purchased remained in the safe at the boathouse. He'd never had the guts to return it to the jeweler. In fact, he'd never gone back, taking the coward's way out and using other jewelers so he wouldn't have to acknowledge his mistakes with Lucy.

With his society-page smile, he did his part for the fund-raising, shaking hands and issuing friendly challenges to those in attendance to dig into their deep pockets for such a worthy cause. He posed for pictures, ignoring humanity's fickle nature and short memory. Sixteen years ago he'd been in police custody. Tonight, no one seemed bothered that his past exploits as a juvenile delinquent had been an integral foundation for a system they used to preserve and protect information online.

As the jazz ensemble took their second break, he

decided he could leave during the next set without raising eyebrows. He scanned the room, wondering about the wisdom of leaving with a beautiful woman on his arm. Though it wouldn't be the first time he sought a one-night stand, tonight it pricked his long-dormant conscience.

He'd rather have Lucy beside him, exchanging knowing looks at the outrageous personal proposi-tions and professional queries he constantly fielded at events like this one. She had a knack for evading pushy people without causing any insult. On top of that she never failed to put him at ease in a crowd whenever he felt that old anxiety of being trapped creep up on him.

As another hospital patron took the stage to elo-quently narrate a heart-wrenching story designed to create a tidal wave of donations, Rush's phone vi-brated in the inner pocket of his tuxedo jacket. He slipped out of the ballroom to check the alert.

He read the text message from Sam asking if he wanted to split a pizza. What the hell? They often did that when pulling all-nighters during the devel-opment stage of a project. Pizza at the office sounded a hell of a lot better than going the distance here at the fund-raiser. He sent a message back, offering to pick up Sam's favorite, black olive and sausage, on his way back.

Back? Thought you were upstairs, came the reply.

Rush started for the valet stand, his stride devour-ing the expansive lobby as he pressed the button to call Sam's cell phone. "Why do you think I'm up-stairs?" he asked when Sam answered.

"Your computer is logged on."

Crap. "Hold on." Rush bounced on his toes as he waited for the valet to bring his car. Sam offered to send security upstairs, but Rush held him off. There was a logical explanation. He tipped the valet and slid into the driver's seat, syncing the phone with the car's stereo speakers. "Is anyone else logged in?" he asked, pulling away from the hotel.

"A few people here and there."

"I mean on the executive floor?" Rush ground his molars until his jaw ached. Silently, the car slid through traffic like quicksilver, pushing the upper edge of the speed limit as well as his luck.

"Oh. Sure. Lucy's system is on," Sam answered after a few seconds.

Rush eased off the accelerator and his pulse slowed as well. "Then no big deal. That's okay."

"How do you figure?"

He didn't know. Off the top of his head, he couldn't think of any reason she would be in his office, much less on his computer. "Just—I don't know—just don't send up security. I'm on the way and I'll talk with her personally."

"If you say so," Sam teased.

"I do." Rush snapped. "Thanks for the heads-up," he added.

"And the pizza?"

Rush laughed. He could always count on Sam to be practical. "Call it in and I'll pick it up." He heard Sam's fingers speeding over his keyboard.

"Order in," Sam said after a few more seconds.

"I'm glad we convinced them to upgrade to online ordering."

"Uh-huh." Rush's thoughts were devoted to Lucy and what she was up to when Sam's swearing interrupted his budding theories. "What now?" Rush drummed his fingers on the steering wheel while he waited for a traffic light to change.

"You want the good news first or the bad?"

Rush sighed. "Informant's choice," he replied.

He didn't want any bad news if it pertained to Lucy, but Sam was focused on the data rather than personal sentiment. With any luck, Lucy was using his corporate account to order some indulgent lingerie. Unfortunately for his vivid fantasy life, she wasn't the type of woman to abuse access that way.

"Looks like your new assistant used an older login and went straight for a particular Gray Box."

Aw, hell. Luck wasn't on his side tonight. "She's not in the research and development or financials?"

"No," Sam stretched out the word. "Are you telling me you hired someone you thought *would* breach those areas?"

"Of course not." Lucy wasn't capable of corporate espionage. He didn't believe her capable of using him or his money at all. He slammed the car to a stop in front of the pizza joint. "Don't confront her. Just keep tabs on what she's doing."

Sam groused and swore, but he agreed to let Rush handle it.

Rush picked up the pizza, hiding the turmoil seething under his skin. What the hell was she up to? He returned to the building and carried the pizza straight to

Sam's office. "Any update?" He cleared clutter from one corner of Sam's desk and stacked the pizza box, napkins and paper plates there.

"No." Sam tilted his chin to the monitor array. "She's still in that box. Almost an hour now."

Rush couldn't believe she'd managed to fool him. The pain in his gut was worse than the beatings he'd survived in juvie, a complete sucker punch. Rush wasn't sure he'd ever trust anyone but Sam again.

"You'll fire her, right?"

"My assistant, my business," Rush said, taking a bite of pizza.

"Per the usual," Sam grumbled, dragging two big slices onto his plate. "I created a ghost of the box. Whatever her intention is, I'm protecting the client's content."

"Good job." With a nod of appreciation, Rush left his half-eaten pizza slice behind and headed to his private elevator. Lucy had one chance to give him the logical explanation.

Chapter Seven

The ticking clock in Lucy's head fell silent as she read and reread the documents Garmeaux had assembled. The reports and research implied Dieter Kathrein was an imposter. Every startling revelation caused an inescapable dread to pool in her belly. She was up against a man capable of anything, a monster who had killed without any sign of remorse.

In the month she'd been with Kathrein, she'd learned his absolute commitment to family, especially his grandson and only heir to his fortune. The information here would definitely end his grandson's political aspirations and possibly destroy anyone close to him.

Tears rolled down her cheeks as she considered the potential fallout of the terrible secrets Kathrein could never allow to come to light. She transferred the Gray Box contents of old records, articles, interviews and images to a thumb drive and deleted the items from the box one by one. She took a screen shot of the empty box and added it to the files on the thumb drive.

Assuming it was all true, she was now the only

other person who knew about Kathrein's awful past. If he honored his deal and spared her sister and nephew, Lucy would be killed. There was no alternative, no other way to keep his grandson safe. Did she have any hope of convincing him she hadn't opened any of it?

How had her ideal job turned into a nightmare?

She heard the chime of the elevator arriving in the private corridor and her heart kicked with a spike of adrenaline. Knowing it had to be Rush didn't bring her any comfort. Yanking the thumb drive from the computer, she hurried to erase her tracks.

She wasn't fast enough.

He hit the office lights, his eyes dark and dangerous as his tall frame filled the doorway. His bow tie was undone, hanging loose, and the top button of the crisp white shirt was open. "Lucy."

Not a query, a statement. He wasn't surprised to find her. She closed her eyes as shame washed over her. Naturally, he'd have some safeguards in place, maybe even hidden cameras to protect his interests. He was the king of modern security, after all.

"I'm sorry," she whispered.

He didn't move or acknowledge her apology.

"It's not what it looks like," she said.

"It looks like you're in my office taking advantage of my absence."

She swallowed back protests and lame excuses. Rush wouldn't tolerate either. She rapidly blinked away more tears, afraid he'd think she was trying to play on his emotions. Emotions he kept locked away as securely as any bit of data in his Gray Boxes. She didn't want to lie to him any more than she already had. "I was working late and I came in here when my own system didn't cooperate." There. She'd given him two truths.

"Lucy." His black eyebrows arrowed up toward his hairline and he leaned against the doorjamb, his arms folded over his wide chest.

She wasn't fool enough to believe the relaxed posture. He was in full predator mode and she was the hapless prey. She shook her head, unable to force out the right lies. "I'll go." She stepped away from his desk.

"You are not dismissed."

His voice was cold, each syllable an icy shard separate from the others. She froze.

"Your previous boss has shown little interest in developing cloud-based security."

Another statement. Lucy willed her feet to move away from his personal space behind the desk. With every second her misery mounted. Rush wasn't a man to easily forgive such an invasion. He smiled for the cameras, knew how to play the game in public to get what and where he wanted, but he valued his privacy. More than once, she'd seen how the publicity took a toll on him. "It's not what it looks like," she repeated.

"Kathrein," he barked. "He put you up to this?"

She glanced toward her desk and the framed photo of her family and straightened her shoulders. "No," she lied.

Eyes narrowed, Rush took a step inside the office. "Then what are you up to?"

Before she could reply, he moved to the desk and snatched up the notepad she had left behind. Damn!

Lucy scurried to the opposite side of his desk as he dropped into his chair and set his hands to the keyboard.

"Who is Mathieu Garmeaux?" Rush demanded.

"He's not important," she answered, sticking with the few honest answers she could give. No chance of escape, but she wanted to protect Rush.

"You broke into his box."

She nodded. "He won't file a complaint." One more weak truth that failed to make her feel better. The knots in her stomach pulled tighter. "Really, Rush. Ignore my stupid mistake. Please. I didn't mean to cause trouble. I just... I just..."

"What?" he roared.

The single word caused her entire body to spasm and her resolve shattered like the Christmas ornaments left behind in the manor house in France. Her knees wobbled; a dark haze crowded her vision. She sagged into the nearest chair before she passed out. "I had to do it," she said, ignoring the tears rolling down her cheeks. "Kathrein is holding Gwen and Jackson hostage." She gulped in air and choked on a sob. "He demanded the documents and information from that box in exchange for their lives."

On a dark oath Rush came around the desk and pulled her up into his arms. He smelled like expensive perfume, spicy tomato sauce and there, underneath it all, the man she loved. She burrowed closer, her hands sliding up his back under his jacket and her tears soaking the fabric of his tuxedo shirt.

"I'm so sorry," she mumbled into his chest. "He

didn't give me an option, but now I know the truth and—" Panicked hiccups cut off her explanation.

"Easy." Rush rubbed a hand up and down her spine. "Breathe."

She relaxed under his soothing touch, sighing as he freed her hair of the clip that had held it up since dinnertime. "Garmeaux is—was a reporter, Rush." She gripped his lapels. "He's dead. Kathrein had him killed. I'm sure of it now that I've seen the files." She struggled to get the words out around the lump of fear lodged in her throat. "Even if he releases Gwen and Jackson, his only choice is to kill me, too."

His muscles went rigid at her words and then relaxed again. "Shh." He cupped her face in his hands and stroked away her tears with his thumbs. "Slow down." His blue eyes were full of tenderness and longing as he studied her face, as if searching for the right place to plant a kiss.

She wasn't worthy of his kisses and she tried to squirm away, more embarrassed than ever by the mess she'd brought into his world. Hiring her had forced his girlfriend out of the picture, and now that Lucy had proved secure boxes could be cracked, she'd put his reputation at risk.

He didn't let her get away, pulling her back to his hard body. "This wasn't a publicity stunt to embarrass me or the company?"

"No," she replied immediately.

"Good." His lips brushed her forehead. "Here's how this will go." He slid an arm around her waist and guided her to the couch. "We're going to sit here while you tell me everything." He removed his jacket and tossed it over the opposite chair. Sitting down, he situated her so she was sheltered by him, her hip pressed to his, his arm over her shoulder. With his free hand he traced the length of her fingers.

She couldn't remember the last time she'd felt so safe. Maybe with all the facts, Rush could find the way to save them all.

"Start at the beginning," he prompted gently.

She took another breath and let it all pour out. "Kathrein didn't hire me because of my skills, he chose me because he needed someone who had a chance of infiltrating Gray Box."

"He wants my company?"

"No," she insisted. "He only wants the contents of Garmeaux's box."

"All right." Rush's fingertips traced lazy circles over her shoulder, much as he used to do when they snuggled in bed at the boathouse.

It was easier to admit all her failings when she could stare at his knee rather than look him in the eye. She told him everything from her first day as Kathrein's assistant right up to the day Gwen and Jackson were kidnapped, the old man's reasons, threats and everything else. The entire time, Rush's fingers kept circling her shoulder, stroking her hand. He didn't interrupt or ask any questions and when she finished, she thought her story sounded too bizarre to be believable.

"Show me the pictures and messages."

Her eyes gritty from crying and her body exhausted from days of unceasing tension, she felt as if she'd been hit by a truck as she retrieved her cell phone. She returned to find Rush standing at the window, legs wide, staring at the city spread out at his feet. With the stark contrast of his black tuxedo slacks and white shirt he reminded her of a pirate searching for new booty.

"Here."

He took her phone and scowled in concentration as he skimmed the text messages and pictures. "It was you trying to use that antiquated admin back door trick?"

She nodded. "Last night. The system locked me out after too many failed direct attempts on Garmeaux's box."

"Sam caught the attempts and accused me of planting bad seeds in young minds." He slid her phone into his pocket. "I should've known. You're the only woman who's ever listened to my stories."

"Maybe you should be more selective about your women." It surprised her that she could tease him in light of the circumstances.

He ignored the jab. "Sam didn't mention the IP address was the boathouse."

At least something had worked properly. "The admin back door wasn't the only thing I learned from our conversations."

His black eyebrows dipped low into another serious scowl. She wasn't sure she wanted to know what he was thinking now. "Are you going to let me go?"

"Hell, no."

Her heart plummeted. Gwen and Jackson were as good as dead if she couldn't convince him to let her take that information to Kathrein. "Rush, please. My sister's life—her son's life—is on the line."

"And they're your only family," he said. "I'm not the callous bastard you seem to take me for, Lucy."

"I've never thought that." She bit back the urge to protest further. She'd never found him callous, only singularly focused on business. A trait she would never ask him to change for the sake of her ego. "The callous bastard is Kathrein. I'm scared. No." She shook her head. "I'm terrified."

He pressed a finger to her lips to stop the brewing rant. Retreating, she curled into the end of the long couch and hugged her knees to her chest. Rush could think for days and it wouldn't change a thing. The first step in rescuing her sister and nephew was turning over the files.

"Sam noticed the problem and ghosted the box contents," Rush said, crouching in front of her.

"Oh, no." Lucy dropped her head to her knees and struggled not to give up. "If Kathrein suspects that, he'll come after you and the company." Every move she made exacerbated the problem.

"Telling you about a ghost box makes you only the third person in the world who knows it's possible," he said. "I think we're safe."

She heard him moving through the office, heard his fingers rapping on his keyboard and knew at the sound of his muttered curses he was reviewing the files on Kathrein.

"Lucy." His tone, more gruff than she'd ever heard it, compelled her to look at him. "Even if you turn this over, he has to kill you."

"Haven't you been listening to me?"

"I'd hoped you were exaggerating, but your logic is sound."

"Gee, thanks." She rubbed her damp cheeks on her sleeve, grateful for the insult that put a little zip of heat into her bloodstream. Maybe the warmth was just the man himself. "No one ever has to know any of this happened—here, tonight."

"No way." He pushed a hand through his black hair.

"Then what?" She flung her arm toward his desk. "You just read it all, right?" At his nod, she barreled on. "Kathrein is old, but I can assure you he's no less ruthless than he was as a Nazi. The documents and pictures Garmeaux uncovered are convincing evidence that Kathrein assumed his dead cousin's identity to escape punishment for his war crimes. He's determined to see his grandson's political dreams come true. This entire mess is proof of how far he's willing to go. If he thinks I told you or involved the authorities, we're all dead."

"I'm not going to let that happen."

She stared into his vivid blue eyes and the resolute line of his jaw set her heart pounding. She wanted to believe his confidence over the stark facts. "Let me go, Rush. Let me go back to France and save Gwen and Jackson."

He crossed the office to sit beside her once more, taking her hand between both of his. "I have friends all over the world, Lucy. With a little time we can track down where he's holding your sister and the baby. Let me make some calls."

"No! You can't alert anyone or he'll kill them. He gave me a *week* and it's going by too fast. The man following me might already suspect I caved and told you. It has to be his way."

"We'll find a better option," he promised.

She shook her head, tears blurring her vision again. Why couldn't she stop crying? "I'm not taking you down with me. Destroy the ghost files," she pleaded. "Wipe out all record of Garmeaux. Forget I was here."

"I can't do that." His voice turned hard again. "I *won't* do that."

She opened her mouth to say more and he smothered the words with a kiss. What might have originated as a kiss of comfort ignited like a lit match, blazing across her senses. His lips moved over hers, hot and firm. She knew his mouth, the velvet stroke of his tongue, and recognized the urgency in his fingers. The familiar excitement sizzled along her nerves and danced through her bloodstream.

As if drawn by some invisible, magnetic force, they moved together until she was under him, caged by his solid, sculpted chest and arms. She flexed her hips, grinding her eager body into his obvious arousal. He kissed her as if they'd never been apart and she responded in kind, releasing a year's worth of desire and yearning.

Sex and passion had never been their problem. Her body was pliant, already aching for the ultimate sensual satisfaction only Rush could give her.

"Lucy," he murmured as his lips skated down the column of her throat. "You don't know how I've missed you."

"I've missed you more than I wanted to admit was possible." She tugged at the studs of his tuxedo shirt until she could slide her hands inside. She moaned his name at the tantalizing combination of heat and strength under her palms.

His hands cupped her bottom, gripped hard as he drew her pelvis tight against his. He hiked up the fabric of her dress and his fingers followed the line of her panties across her backside. Oh, yes. She wanted to rewind the clock, to go back and relive some of their most sinfully mesmerizing nights.

She pushed at his chest until he sat up and she could straddle his hips, tugging his shirt free of his slacks. *He has the most glorious body*, she thought, running kisses across his chest. If this was her last week of life, she wouldn't let this last chance for pleasure slip through her grasp.

"Lucy, wait." He brought her face back to his, kissed her lightly.

"I can't." She nuzzled that sensitive spot just under his jaw. If he stopped her now, she might start crying again. "Please, Rush. I need you. Need you inside me."

In the past those words would bring one of two reactions. Either more delicious, erotic foreplay or a swift and intense coupling that would leave her breathless.

"You've got me." His lips brushed hers again, feather soft. He gripped her waist and moved her to the side, pulling the skirt of her dress down over her legs. "You've got me, Lucy, but this isn't the time or place."

She laid a hand over his heart, buoyed that it beat as wildly as hers. She pulled back as far as his embrace allowed, her dignity a lost cause. "Okay, I get it." She'd walked away from him in a desperate attempt at self-preservation, but her reasons were irrelevant. Her decision, the way she'd executed it, had created a wedge between them, a distance she had to respect.

"How can you understand when I'm not sure I do?" He shook his head. "I'm going to take you home. You need rest. In the morning we'll come up with a plan that satisfies you, me and the bastard who sent you here."

"But—"

He gave her a squeeze. "Hush, sweetheart. You used to trust me."

Sweetheart. The phrase melted over her like warm chocolate as she met his gaze. Although she'd tried to relegate him to the back of her mind, tuck the memory of him behind a wall in her heart, she'd never really stopped trusting or loving this impossible man. "You won't make any calls tonight?"

"I won't if you won't," he replied.

"You have my phone," she pointed out.

He brought her hand to his lips, his breath warm on her skin in that pleasant instant. "I think I'll keep it. Just for tonight."

She thought that might be the best idea she'd heard in a long time.

Chapter Eight

Friday, December 18, 7:45 a.m.

Rush kept his promise to Lucy, but it proved to be one of the most challenging nights of his life. Just walking up to the door of the boathouse with her had made him break out in a cold sweat. He hadn't set foot inside the place since the day she'd left him. No, he'd hired a team to clean it up and maintain it for rental potential, although he couldn't bear the idea of strangers here, either.

Now he stood on the balcony off the living room, watching the fog roll across the span of the Golden Gate Bridge. Dressed for the day in jeans and a black button-down shirt with the Gray Box logo his house-keeper had sent from the condo, he sipped his coffee and waited for Lucy to wake up, as if the past year of personal hell hadn't happened. Only Lucy Gaines could bring him to his knees this way.

Last night in his office, his arms full of her, he couldn't come up with the solutions she needed. All his attention had been diverted to far more primitive and immediate needs. Fearful that spending the night together in the boathouse would make matters worse, she'd apparently come to her senses and quickly disappeared into the guest suite. He'd woken in the master bedroom, alone and frustrated, with a few workable ideas.

Hopefully he'd be able to convince Lucy to give one of his ideas a try. He planned to start by researching every detail about the sneaky bastard holding her family hostage. Sam had ways of doing those searches without raising any suspicion. They needed confirmation of Garmeaux's findings. After that, there were friends he could call, friends with tactical skills, weapons expertise and successful track records with sensitive rescue missions.

Rush turned at the creak of a floorboard on the stairs. The once soothing sound put him on edge, uncertain how the night might have changed Lucy's perception of her situation. He walked inside and pulled the slider closed. Trying to greet her with a smile, he felt the gesture freeze on his face as she came around the corner.

She wore loose cotton boxers and a clingy tank top, her hair tousled from sleep. If not for the faint smudges of weariness under her eyes, he would have scooped her up and taken her back to bed until they were both sated. In the clear light of a new day, he didn't think she'd let him get away with that kind of distraction. It was likely best that they waited until after she was reunited with her sister and nephew.

He filled a mug with coffee, leaving room for cream, and set it on the counter for her. "Did you get any rest?"

"A little." Her mouth twisted side to side, lips pursed. "What about you?"

"A little," he echoed. He pulled the cream out of the refrigerator and passed it to her, along with a spoon and the sugar bowl.

She made a humming sound. "You remember."

He watched her over the rim of his mug while she slid onto the counter stool and doctored her coffee. She'd be shocked by how much he remembered. From every morning habit, to her favorite yoga studio and sushi bar downtown, to the sultry moans of pleasure when he was inside her.

Patience, he thought, keeping his ideas to himself while the caffeine did its work. He'd get her through this and then he'd win her back. He just had to resolve her trouble one step at a time. He'd sensed the fatalistic desperation pushing her last night in his office. He wanted her body, was pretty desperate himself, but not as a grand farewell to life. By some miracle he'd realized the timing would have backfired if he'd followed his body rather than his heart.

His *heart*? He nearly laughed. Lucy would freak out if she could read his mind right now. As close as they'd been, she accepted his theory that he only had a heart for his business and innovations. And she'd stuck by him, encouraging him every day, until the day she hadn't. It was a quirk unique to her that he hadn't been able to replicate with anyone else. No matter how he tried, how clear he was about expectations, women believed they could change him.

She walked around the counter to start rummaging for breakfast and he waited, rewarded when she burst into a happy dance at the sight of the bag of doughnuts from the kiosk across the street. "Oh, you got maple and bacon."

"Only the best."

She took his coffee cup out of his hands and gave him a fast, hard hug. "*You* are the best," she said emphatically as she stepped back. Pulling plates from the cabinet, she carried the bag to the table.

His chest ached at the normalcy of it as he brought the coffees along. He'd leave her phone in his pocket until she finished a doughnut. What he had to say would cast a pall over the morning and he wanted to put it off as long as possible.

"Any new messages from Kathrein on my phone?" she asked, licking frosting from her fingers.

His body reacted to the tempting sight of her lips closing around her fingertips with a predictable surge of arousal. The best defense against his physical needs was to give her the awkward news. He set the phone on the table. "Posturing, mostly," he assured her.

Her eyes went wide and her gaze darted from the device to his face and back again. "Mostly? Are there new pictures?"

"Not from Kathrein. I did take a few pictures of the man who might be his spy."

She blanched. "Do you think he's already…already hurt them?"

"No." Rush hated the fear and hurt in her big brown eyes. He reached out and covered her trembling hand. If he ever got his hands on Kathrein, he wouldn't be responsible for his actions. "He won't give up his leverage too soon."

"Leverage." She bit her lip and gazed out at the view of the bay. "I want to *kill* him for putting Gwen through this. She's been through enough already."

Rush stuffed the last bite of his doughnut into his mouth before he blurted out that he could make that happen. Better to keep *that* secret a bit longer. "I'm thinking there's quite a line ahead of you."

"What do you mean?"

He hesitated. Explaining could expose him. "I've looked into Kathrein before." The week he'd heard she'd been hired by the bastard. "Occasionally, our investment interests cross," he fibbed. "You're aware his lawyers and representatives have a reputation for being nasty?" She nodded and he continued, "My thought is that even without taking over his dead cousin's life, he became a recluse to make himself a smaller target."

"And yet there are plenty of people who benefit from the jobs he creates and the charities he funds."

"True." Rush pulled out another doughnut for each of them. "On the way to the office, I want us to be seen at the coffee shop two blocks up from the office."

"That's a popular place." She cupped her hands around her mug. "Why?"

"Because it *is* a popular place." He thought she'd already guessed his real reasons, but he spelled it out. "I want Kathrein to believe you're working me as a personal asset. It will also give us a chance to determine if the man I saw is, in fact, the spy."

She lifted her coffee mug and eyed him carefully. "Have you warned Trisha?"

"No need. My lawyers had a chat with her yesterday after her tantrum."

"Still playing hardball, I see."

She said it with a wry grin and he mirrored the expression. "Trisha's misguided behavior was effectively a breach of contract."

Lucy's brown eyes danced with amusement. "Is that the dating equivalent of a prenup? Do you require all your dates to sign a noncompete or nondisclosure agreement as well?"

He smiled broadly to hide his discomfort. "Nondisclosure is a must if they spend any time at Gray Box." Her comments struck too close to the bone. The return to the boathouse, the conversation, the very real threat to her were all piling up and making him want to hurry this along so he could capitalize on the moment. Only the awareness that, if he moved too soon, the consequences to her family as well as to his goals could be catastrophic kept him in check. "It is as calculating as it sounds," he confessed. "I like having someone with me at events but I refuse to let a woman think there's a chance for anything more than the terms strictly outlined. The contract protects everyone from unreasonable expectations."

"On the upside, you probably have your pick of spokesmodels for new products well into the next millennium."

He laughed, helpless against her honest, edgy wit. "There might be one or two I'd feel safe to approach for a launch down the road." He leaned in close. "At the moment, *you* are my sole priority."

"Rush."

Her breathy whisper slid under his defenses. Would it be so bad to take her to bed and make her forget the jerk in Chicago she'd used to replace him? "Don't tell me you're surprised."

"No. I always admired your focus." She barreled on before he could enjoy the compliment. "I didn't want to upend your life. You certainly don't owe me any heroic measures. Maybe we should use your publicity idea a little differently."

He braced his elbows on the table, eager to hear this. "I'm all ears."

"I'll take the information to Kathrein and trade it for Gwen and Jackson. He won't kill me if my name and face are in the spotlight, linked with yours."

"Are you forgetting he made the world believe Garmeaux died in an accident, Lucy?"

"Not at all." She grimaced. "You're different. Influential."

"It won't be enough," he stated. "I'm not going to let you martyr yourself."

"That isn't my intention." She pulled a knee to her chest and wrapped her arms around it. "So what's your next step after we play out the scene at the coffee shop?"

"We make some social noise, you send him an email that you're almost in, and then I'll make an announcement that you're a new key player at the Gray Box offices. Then, while the media is chewing on that, I'll apply all my effort, contacts and resources to locating your family."

"You can find them?"

"Yes," he said. With his friends it was absolutely possible. "It's the best plan," he pressed.

"It's an option with huge potential to backfire." Her gaze narrowed as she calculated the risks. "I'm running out of time."

Rush inhaled slowly. "Other than you, when have I failed at anything?"

Her lips parted on a surprised gasp and a jolt of desire shot through his system. If she remembered the effect she had on him, she'd learned to hide it well in the past year. Other than the hug, she hadn't even tried to touch him today. He cursed himself for stopping last night. The physical release could have benefitted them both and he might be able to focus on something other than his persistent state of arousal.

Her gaze lowered to his lips, then slid away to the view outside. She stood and paced to the window, leaning her forehead against the glass. The muted light painted her body and he had to resist the temptation to wrap her up in his arms.

"Have you worked up a program to find them?" she asked.

"In a manner of speaking," he replied. "If we're in agreement, I'll make a call and set things in motion."

She didn't move. "Who do you want to call?"

"I've made several interesting friends through Gray Box clients and contracts. Do you trust me, Lucy?"

"Yes."

Her immediate reply gave his ego a boost. Pushing back his chair, he gathered up the dishes and carried them to the kitchen sink. "I'll let you know more details on the way to the office."

"Okay." She turned, her arms wrapped around her midsection. "About last night…" Her voice trailed off, though her gaze remained steady.

"Can we table that discussion for now?" *Please*, he added silently. "Unless you think you'll have trouble being friendly and affectionate at the coffee shop."

Her smile was shy. "I won't have any trouble with that."

As she went upstairs to shower and dress, he hoped she meant it. However she'd come back into his life, he looked forward to reclaiming the closeness they'd once shared.

While he waited, Rush made several calls. Doubts pestered him as he turned over the various scenarios and outcomes and what they needed to do to rescue her family. He was the worst kind of hypocrite for being jealous and doubting her while resenting her for assuming the worst of his contract with Trisha. He'd told her the personal stuff had to wait, yet when she came back downstairs, he returned to the issue, inexplicably worried there was more she was hiding. "No one in your life will be upset seeing you with me?"

"Answer is still no." Her lips twisted to the side. "Gwen, should she catch the news, will be thrilled. She always liked you."

He tried not to let the compliment go to his head. Call him a jerk for making her repeat it, but he felt better having a definitive answer. Lucy's only secret had been her kidnapped family. She never would have kissed him if she was involved with someone else. After all, she'd left Chicago to work in France.

"May I have my phone back?" she asked, slipping into black heels. She looped her computer bag over her shoulder and picked up her purse. "Rush?"

The woman mesmerized him and he couldn't stop staring, couldn't stop thinking of all the places on her body that he wanted to touch and kiss. She'd also chosen jeans today, but she turned casual to elegant with a snug white shirt topped with a colorful, long, open sweater. Silver drops at her ears were echoed in the silver necklace sparkling against the white fabric. And then there were those sexy black heels.

"Your phone." He held it out. "I may need to play with it later, depending on how the next few hours go."

They left the roadster in the garage and let the service do the driving. When the driver pulled to the curb at the coffee shop, Rush noticed his calls had been effective. The people from the right papers and blogs were there to see Lucy get out of the car with him. She played it perfectly, immediately reaching for his hand, leaning into his touch and smiling up at him.

He thought his face might crack under the pressure of holding back when he wanted so desperately to make the role they were playing real. She didn't know the shock and despair she'd created when she left him. No one did. Although he'd buried the surprising sense of loss and grief in work and made the expected social moves to keep up his image, he'd never given up on winning back Lucy. Psychologists and gossip rags would have a field day with that admission, he thought as he gazed into her warm brown eyes.

On the executive floor, Melva greeted them with such obvious delight he felt guilty. His office manager had always loved Lucy's effect on him, claiming she gave his life balance and stability. Of course, Melva often chided him for working harder than ten men just for the bragging rights.

He purposely left the privacy glass off as they drafted a press release about Lucy joining the Gray Box team. After another protest about the effect this would have on him and the company when she left, she agreed to let him send it.

"It won't be a problem," Rush assured her again, shoving his hands into his pockets. "Hell, with your reputation the stock is likely to go up." Here at the office he wanted to keep the affectionate displays to a minimum, if only so he didn't set himself up for her rejection. He was starting to think last night's kisses were the sum of stress, exhaustion and inhibitions reduced by darkness. "Now, let's get to the real problem. He gave you a week?"

"Yes. If I don't hand over the information by Monday, he'll kill them," she said, her voice tight. "Did you see the spy at the coffee shop?"

Rush nodded. "He tailed us from the boathouse. Kathrein will probably be in touch any minute."

Setting her phone on his desk as if it might explode, she pressed a hand to her stomach. "I can't stand this. My imagination is going crazy with how they're suffering."

Now he did turn on the privacy glass. "Sit or pace,

but start talking. Tell me everything you know about Kathrein."

"I did that last night."

"I don't mean about the kidnapping or the reasons behind it. I want to know about the man. You were his personal assistant." He knew how quickly Lucy picked up facts and concepts. Her brain fascinated him as much as her beauty.

"Only for a month." She laced her fingers and rocked her hands back and forth while he stared her down. "Okay, okay." She sucked in a breath. "I know what you're getting at."

At his desk, he listened, making notes about Kathrein's living habits, ethics, the briberies she suspected, his staff and his most recent connections. Rush did this all while his mind and body indulged in a deep appreciation of her inherent grace as she paced the length of the windows.

When the company had moved into this building, he'd drafted dozens of emails with pictures, as excited as a kid at Christmas to share the success with her. He hadn't sent any of them and eventually had cleared them off his computer. An email reply, if she'd bothered to send one, wouldn't have satisfied him. He'd wanted her here, in person, so he could enjoy the thrill of her smile as she took in the expansive, inspiring views. He'd wanted to press her back against the glass and feel her legs lock around his hips as he drove himself into the tight heat of her body.

Before they'd made the leap from friends to lovers, he'd once overheard her protesting to a girlfriend that she wasn't his type. In an instant he was back at that moment, realizing how much better Lucy was than the glossy, empty women he typically dated to keep up appearances. He nearly laughed. It seemed Melva had a valid point.

Unique and beautiful, Lucy had enchanted him from the first question she'd asked during his guest lecture for her graduate program. He'd wanted to hire her on the spot but waited until they had more privacy over coffee after the class. She'd blown off him and his outrageous offer with her merry laughter.

That might have been the moment his obsession started, though he'd hidden his immediate needs. He eventually won her over with several casual dates, even working dinners, followed by extravagant surprises until finally landing in a bed during a weekend cruise on his yacht. There they'd discovered another mutual interest in creative, bold sexual play and passion.

God, she'd been a wonder, his ideal companion in every sense.

"Are you listening?" She'd stopped pacing and perched on the edge of one of the chairs in front of his desk, studying him with a narrowed gaze.

"Just thinking," he replied, quickly typing up the last thing he'd heard her say. "I'm going to forward this file to one of my contacts."

"I'm still not sure it's worth the risk."

He wiggled his eyebrows, trying to lighten her mood. "I know a few things about encrypting files."

"It's not that. If Kathrein could hack your system he wouldn't have sent me." She let out a frustrated oath. "He has a spy out there, proving he has a long reach and plenty of contacts, too. If you're suddenly taking meetings with tactical security experts, he'll assume I've told you what's going on. He's old, not stupid."

"I believe you. Now that my team isn't following you, looks like we've got an ID on the spy tailing you," Rush said as he skimmed an incoming email. He immediately returned his attention to the task of framing his more urgent request for help to locate and rescue Lucy's family. "We have several clients, from government agencies to private companies, who deal in security and tactical operations. Leaping to conclusions could wreck Kathrein's plan and though he might get suspicious, he'll have to bide his time. The man I've asked to help us could easily be explained as a client disconnected from our real problem. But don't worry, he won't come anywhere near us or the building." *Yet*.

"Back up a second."

Hearing temper simmering in her voice, he glanced up. "Yes?"

"*Your* team identified Kathrein's spy?"

"Just now, yes." He watched, wary as her cheeks and ears turned red. She rarely blushed unless she was angry. With a few strokes of the keyboard, he put the man's picture on a monitor mounted on the wall and added candid shots they'd collected over the past twenty-four hours. "Do you recognize him?"

She shook her head, her lips clamped shut.

"What makes this a problem?" he asked.

"You said you had me followed," she replied, her eyes hot.

"Would you believe it's standard procedure for new hires?"

"I would not." Lacing her fingers in her lap, her silence demanded his explanation.

"Well, it is. In certain cases." He came around the desk, ready to apply liberal amounts of charm to smooth over his careless handling of this detail. "I dug a little deeper. Kathrein has invested in two cyber security developers during the past six months," he said leaning against the desk. "Based on our current dilemma, now I understand why. Knowing you came to me directly from his employ, I had you followed. It wasn't personal," he fibbed. "Anyone coming from a similar situation would have been followed."

Her tension ebbed from her hands and mouth, but he could see she wasn't entirely convinced.

No matter how angry or offended she was, he would be grateful for the decision. His caution had resulted in an inadvertent and additional measure of protection for her that made the ensuing steps easier.

"You've changed." Lucy held his gaze, her outrage over his invasion of her privacy fizzling. She should have expected it and, yes, in his place she would have done the same thing.

"Changed?" He stared at her and the blue depths of his gaze tempted her just as it always had. "No. Not on the things that matter most," he replied after a thoughtful pause. "You don't seem quite as angry."

"I have bigger problems." The way he'd been using "us" and "we" and "our" made her heart melt, but at the end of the day this problem was between her and Kathrein. If she could spare Rush the grief and trouble, she would. "What can I do about the man following me?"

He shifted, obviously thinking it over. Folding his arms over his chest, he stretched out his long legs and crossed his ankles. Did he have to be so irresistibly sexy all the time? She hadn't been with anyone since Rush, and right now she regretted every missed opportunity. She'd dated in Chicago, mostly to appease her sister, but the enigmatic chemistry she shared with Rush had been missing. Wouldn't he crow with satisfaction if he knew?

It was too late for them. Rush wasn't the sort to forgive the way she'd left and he had no interest in addressing the needs of her heart. *Only my body*, she thought as another little spark of anticipation zipped through her.

From head to toe, her body was certain sex with Rush would be enough. Her greedy hormones urged her to reach out and take what she wanted from the man. Surely last night's sizzling kisses and embraces verified he'd be open to one last fling for the sake of closure. Her mouth went dry and her palms damp as her body warmed to the idea. Maybe, she thought, just maybe she would proposition Rush once Gwen and Jackson were safe. For closure.

He still hadn't answered her and she couldn't hide in his office forever. "Come on, Rush. What do you propose?" His eyes went wide and she immediately regretted her choice of words. Love, marriage and romance were foul words in his vocabulary. "Do we use the spy or ignore him?" she asked quickly. "Or should I call Kathrein right now to make the trade?"

"None of the above." Rush returned to his side of the desk. "I want you to go through the motions here at the office while I do some more research on this. We need to make it look like you're scrambling to meet the demands."

"Why doesn't he call?" She glared at her phone again. The constantly evolving knots in her stomach were making it difficult to breathe.

"We'll get through this," Rush said. "I'm fast and creative. We're only making it look like you're still working alone. I'm going to let Sam leak news about an attempted hack. That should convince Kathrein you're trying."

"All right." She stood up, determined to exemplify the courage and trust he was requesting. "You won't forget the deadline?"

"Not a chance."

"And you won't take any action without telling me *before* you do it?"

"Want it in writing?"

She held up her hands in surrender. "No, thank you." He'd gone above and beyond when he could've reported her to the police. Rather than wrestling this out of her control and dropping her behind an army of guards while he solved her problem, he was keeping her close, keeping her involved. "I wish he'd confirm something about Gwen."

"Jackson looks content in every picture," Rush reminded her. "Can you believe he'd be that happy with only the care of Kathrein or his guards?"

When he put it in that context, a fraction of the tension lifted from her shoulders. "You're right."

"Almost always," he said with a cocky grin, until his eyes landed on his monitor and his thinking scowl returned. "I'll give you an hour at your desk, then we're taking a tour of the R & D floor."

"Yes, boss." She wondered what kind of software he had in Research and Development that could save her family. Her distraction didn't last long. While she was updating Rush's calendar and commitments, she received an email from the charitable foundation managed by Kathrein's daughters.

Reading it, Lucy swore under her breath. The innocuous message was an invitation to a holiday fundraiser on Tuesday, the day after her deadline. It had been addressed to the Gray Box email address HR had assigned to her yesterday.

Between the sexy, audacious man in the glass-walled office behind her and the nasty bastard playing grandpa with her nephew, she decided there were too many clever and resourceful billionaires in her life. When she fell in love again—assuming she could forget Rush long enough to give another man a chance—she would make sure to fall for a thoughtful, unassuming man with a net worth closer to the half-million mark.

Her light duties as an assistant left her mind free to wander down that diverting path. She and this currently featureless man of average means would get married and say "I love you" every day and leave the city for a typical suburban neighborhood in an excellent school district. They'd invest in a cozy house with a wide porch overlooking a bright green lawn all wrapped up with a white picket fence. There would be children and coffee-klatch friends and even a dog that enjoyed morning jogs with the anonymous man of her dreams.

Melva walked up and burst the bubble, presenting her with a paper plate of something that might have started as cereal before it had been turned into a bright green Christmas wreath the size of a bear claw. "Help me eat this," she said, breaking it in two.

Lucy eyed it cautiously. "You take the first bite."

"The green looks off-putting, I know, but it will be your new favorite," Melva said. "We can all be thankful Ken's wife only sends it in once a year."

"I think I need more information," Lucy said.

"Just hurry up and taste it," Melva insisted, pinching off another bite for herself. "You can't let me eat it all."

Lucy obeyed and the burst of sweetness on her tongue surprised her. "Holy cow. That's *good*."

"Exactly." Melva's smug expression made Lucy chuckle.

"You're crazy to share."

"A shared treat has fewer calories. Scientific fact. We can't all be as young and fit as you," Melva said. "You and Rush looked happy at the coffee shop this morning."

Lucy had to smile, to pretend their reunion was real. "It's nice to be back in town," she said, taking another bite to prevent any verbal slipups.

"You're just what he needs," Melva said with a wink before she walked back to her desk.

Lucy devoured the rest of the treat and licked the sticky bits and pieces from her fingers. She was mid-sigh, her lips clinging to the finger in her mouth, when Rush walked out of his office.

His gaze locked onto her mouth, his eyes full of an unmistakable lust. Going hot, her body leaned toward him, pure instinct and desire. Desperate, she swiveled the chair around and took a moment to pull herself together.

"Time for that tour. Bring the Gray Box tablet along," he suggested. "Leave your phone here," he added under his breath.

She did as he asked and followed him to the elevators. He pressed the button for the express, and when the doors parted he encouraged her to enter first. She felt his eyes on her backside and quickly turned around to face him.

That made matters worse. The doors had barely closed when he pulled her in for a kiss. Nothing sweet or easy as he'd done at the coffee shop; this was a thorough possession, his tongue twining with hers in hot, velvet strokes. She gripped his sleeve with her free hand to keep her balance.

He made a little humming sound in his throat. "You taste like Christmas."

"You can't kiss me here." She protested, trying to establish an appropriate distance though it was far too late.

His fingers flexed on her hips and he kissed her again. "Seems like I can." The car stopped and he reached over and smacked at the panel. His hands slid under her sweater, up her spine, setting her nerves on fire through her shirt. "No cameras in here. Don't worry."

A year ago that might have made her feel better. Right now she could only imagine the other women he'd kissed in here since the building had opened. The thought that she was bookending his flings turned her voice sharp. "Are we going to R & D at all or was it a ploy to get me in here for an elevator quickie?"

He stepped back, looking a little hurt. "Tempting as you make that sound, we are down here for a reason."

"I'm sorry," she began.

"No." He cut her off. "I should apologize." He hooked his thumbs in his back pockets with a heavy sigh. "Kissing you last night opened the floodgates for me. I don't want to stop."

She bit back the admission that would only urge him on, searching for a way to be honest without giving him the wrong idea. "I understand," she said. It sounded lame to her ears. "Better if I could kiss you without the distraction of your reputation and Kathrein's leverage hanging over my head." That was a far more honest and complete answer.

He grinned. "You're worried about my reputation?"

She rolled her eyes at him. "Yes. You have a company with global interests to protect. A different woman every week can make investors worry about your stability."

"Oh, bull. You don't believe that garbage any more than I do. Gray Box is the best program of its kind. My investors appreciate the returns and our clients appreciate the security we offer. Why are you really pushing me away?"

She couldn't admit she was trying *again* to mitigate the risk to her heart. Steamy kisses and blazing sexual chemistry hadn't been enough for her a year ago. By his own admission, the romantic happy-ever-after didn't suit Rush. She didn't want him to resent her for having feelings he couldn't reciprocate.

"Kathrein will surely retaliate if he discovers you've helped me," she said, seizing on the most logical argument. "You've worked hard, Rush. I don't want to put all of your effort and success in jeopardy."

"I can deal with any corporate attack," he said. "What else?"

"We're at the office." She clutched the tablet to her chest like a shield. "You said we'd table talking about us. Why do you keep bringing it up?"

"Now is later enough for me," he said with a shrug. "What did last night mean to you?"

To her chagrin, she felt a wave of tears brimming. If there had been an escape hatch, she would have leaped through it rather than face him at this low point in her life. "You listened with compassion." She could stick with the truth and still protect herself. "Rather than turn me over to the authorities, you offered to help me. I appreciate that more than words can say." His gaze narrowed and a chill slid down her spine, bumping along over each vertebra.

"You ripped open my shirt and crawled all over me as a show of appreciation?"

"You started that part," she snapped. Her jaw was cramping, her teeth were clenched so tightly. "Stop making it bigger, more important than the flash of lust between old lovers." Desperate for a way out of this elevator as well as the unbearable conversation, she reached for the control panel and pushed the Open Door button, but the doors didn't budge. "Come on, Rush. Nothing really happened."

"Huh. I'm not feeling much appreciation for my extraordinary restraint and courtesy," he said.

"Why are you picking a fight?"

"I want to know where the boundaries are."

The man made her want to scream. She calmed herself with a quick visual of pounding some sense into his thick skull. "It's not as if we ever had many of those."

His grin flashed across his face and disappeared so quickly she thought she imagined it. "If it wasn't solely a matter of appreciation, what prompted you to rip open my shirt?"

"Stop saying that!" She clapped a hand over her mouth at the outburst. "You're impossible!"

"Is that why you walked out on us?"

She'd walked out because she needed him too much and he never thought twice about leaving her stranded, consistently less valuable than his growing business. "This is not the time or place," she said, using his words from last night.

"I'm not opening the doors until you give me an answer."

"To which question?"

He shrugged. "Lady's choice."

"Fine. You win." Her free hand fisted at her side. "Last night I wanted to take every ounce of comfort any way I could get it," she said, keeping her voice low. "Last night I wanted to forget the terrible moments of recent days and sink into the memories of how good we were together." His chest swelled with pride at her words. "Last night I was grateful for your common sense as well as your kindness and thoughtfulness. You were a perfect gentleman. But right this second?"

"Yes?" he urged.

"I'm working to remember that you're going above and beyond to help me. Right this second, if I had a better option to save my family, I'd give in to the urge and give you a kick rather than let you steal another kiss."

"You're mad at me?"

Her shoulders sagged. "That sums it up, yes."

"Then we're even."

"Pardon?"

He caught her chin and held her gently, forcing her to meet his gaze. "Here are a few answers to questions I wish you would ask me. I was furious when you moved to Chicago. Livid when you replaced me with another man. I promised myself if you ever stepped foot in San Francisco again, I'd find a way to infuriate you in kind."

"Payback?" When he nodded she barely kept from giving him that kick. His tirade, his anger over something personal was so out of character she could hardly process the words. She opened her mouth to admit she'd lied about the new boyfriend and caught herself in the nick of time. She couldn't leave herself that vulnerable. "You do know how obnoxious that sounds?"

"Yes." His smile of pure satisfaction made her pulse skip. "I don't plan to stop, although I'm done being mad about it." His lips feathered across hers once more and then he reached for the elevator panel.

She caught his arm, stalling him. "You realize I was mad at you when I moved to Chicago? You being mad at me made us even last year."

"How could I have known?" He tugged free of her grasp and pressed the button to release the doors. "You didn't stick around long enough for us to kiss and make up."

The doors parted to reveal a small crowd of people who scrambled back in a comic tangle, pretending they hadn't been eavesdropping on the private conversation.

Finally his behavior and the bizarre argument made more sense to Lucy. Like the coffee shop earlier, he'd staged a scene that would underscore her role here, in case Kathrein's spy managed to get someone inside Gray Box to talk.

In spite of the sudden, lonely ache in her chest and the sting of tears behind her eyes, she had to give him points for the performance.

Chapter Nine

While his blood pounded from the combination of impossible arousal and heated argument, Rush introduced Lucy to everyone and gave her an extensive tour of the R & D floor. He ignored the smirks and speculative glances along the way. He should've thought about the potential gossip, especially on the heels of Trisha's tantrum, and kept himself in check.

No one would dwell on it long. Most of his employees assumed the worst about his social life anyway. "Spoiled billionaire" and "incorrigible player" had become more common descriptors for him than the previous references to his brilliant ideas and business savvy. He endured it by imagining the utter shock on their faces if they knew how completely his relationship with Lucy had altered him.

She made him think and feel on a completely different level. Though it was more than lust, he knew it wasn't love. He needed her and he valued her. He'd thought those feelings had been mutual.

Watching her, guilt nagged at him for picking a fight. When Lucy was close, conflicting priorities went to war inside him. He wanted to confide his latest concepts and keep her at arm's length. He wanted to charge into battle beside her and whisk her off to an island where Kathrein would never find her. He wanted to show her the facets of his personality only being with her had revealed.

More shocking was the urge to admit he hadn't slept with anyone since she'd walked away, but the confession battered against his pride every time he thought about her replacing him. The public displays of affection with his various dates had been nothing but smoke and mirrors. Now that she was here, the self-inflicted abstinence was starting to take a toll. The next time a kiss turned that hot, he wouldn't let either of them off the hook. That was one good reason to start applying some of his notorious self-control.

She made notes as they moved along and he explained the potential of several projects. Her astute questions reinforced his opinion that they were a smart match in any industry. Her mind was as gorgeous as the rest of her.

When they reached the far end of the lab, he aimed a hard look at the closest team and the trio quickly moved out of earshot.

"I had more questions," she said.

"So ask. I'll give you the answers." He picked up a plastic ring, examining the piece that made up part of a drone propeller so he wouldn't be mesmerized by her eyes.

"Uh-huh," she murmured. "I had no idea you were working on so many hardware applications."

"I don't intend to bring all of these ideas to the

general market. We're integrating cutting-edge software for a few specific applications."

"For a few contracted clients, you mean."

"Yes." He ran his finger over the seamless plastic repeatedly. If he looked at her, he'd be hard-pressed to maintain that self-control he'd just promised to apply. "We might take a few of these out for a field test in a day or two," he added. They had only three full days left to find her family.

He took her quiet gasp for understanding. Several of the cameras, drones and surveillance programs being developed down here could help them find and capture Kathrein without Lucy caving in to his demands. It would never be official and he'd never be able to brag about it, but if any of these devices worked, the right people would be more confident and inclined to sign his development teams for additional projects.

"Which item is closest to completion?"

He met her gaze. "For general market?"

"Sure." She held her stylus over the tablet, ready to make notes.

"The drone cameras have the greatest consumer potential. They're completely operational now. We're just tweaking the software to make it more user-friendly and we're beefing up the optics quality to meet expectations."

"That's exciting."

She sounded more pensive than excited. "And?" he prompted.

"You still face the issues of who can fly drones and where," she said. "The market seems limited."

"Don't you believe a small market is worth my time and attention?" He walked around the end of the worktable, hoping she understood they were discussing far more than his position leading the field of cutting-edge technology.

What he focused on, he brought to life. He didn't give up on technology or people.

He scowled at the plastic ring and carefully set it down. He'd never given up on having her in his life again. Telling himself he was giving her space, honoring her wishes, he'd never moved on with someone new. He refused to squander this chance to win her back, no matter what stood in his way.

An enormous pressure weighed on his shoulders. There was far more at stake than his happiness or his ability to make Lucy happy. Even with his skills and connections, there were no guarantees. Kathrein held the lives of her family in his hands. An overwhelming desperation washed over Rush. He would do anything to reunite Lucy with her family and spare her any more grief and loss. That mattered above all else. She evaded him, keeping the worktable between them. "How would you like me to proceed as your assistant? I can draft press releases or contact trade magazines about interviews or events."

"We're not at that stage yet, although the teams are eager for that step."

"So how does the stunt in the elevator and this little tour affect a certain French hostage taker?"

"He's not French."

"Not the point." She rolled her eyes. "Do you think someone down here is working for Kathrein?"

"Absolutely not. We're keeping up appearances. I wanted you to see I have the tools to assist the particular situation. If you'll trust me." He supposed if he wanted her trust he should stop irritating her at every turn.

"Got it." Her gaze slid toward the other end of the room and then she peered at him from under her thick, dark lashes. "Thank you." She cleared her throat. "You have two appointments this afternoon and the first is scheduled in fifteen minutes."

They returned to the executive floor in silence, each of them lost in thought. Rush valued the quiet as much as the fact that his first appointment was early.

If Lucy recognized Parker Lawton's name as he ushered his friend into his office, she didn't show it. Calling in this favor was a big risk. Despite what he'd told her, if the man Kathrein sent to keep an eye on Lucy caught wind of this, Rush might have blown the element of surprise.

Kathrein had given Lucy an impossibly tight timeline to crack the strongest cyber security company in the world. While Rush assumed it was to bring the matter to an end swiftly, he wanted to be sure they weren't missing a critical piece of the puzzle.

Lawton, formerly with military intelligence, now consulted and conducted investigations for private clients, like Rush. He knew how to track down real-world intel almost as fast as Sam could unravel a trail online.

Flipping the switch for the privacy glass, Rush asked, "What did you find?"

"Not as much as I could get with even one more

day," Lawton replied. "Paris officials did rule the journalist Garmeaux's death an accident, but you were right to be suspicious." He held up a hand to waylay Rush's question. "I don't have anything conclusive. His boss said he was on the story of a lifetime, but he hadn't turned anything in. All the normal substance screens were clear but the witness reports don't add up and the bike disappeared from police custody."

"Not good." Rush resisted the urge to get up and pace.

"Nope," Lawton agreed. "As for the other issue, Dieter Kathrein is definitely a paranoid recluse. The public persona is managed by his daughters and his grandson who is poised to make a big political splash."

"What about his real estate? Did you find him?"

Lawton slid a report across the desk. "This is every property I could tie to him in Europe." He sat back. "That email attachment you sent me is pretty inflammatory."

Rush had only sent Lawton two pages of documentation connecting Kathrein to the Nazi regime. "Is it true?" A silly question considering the bastard was holding Lucy's family hostage to keep a lid on the information.

Lawton nodded. "While I'd appreciate more time to verify any loose ends and conduct my own interviews, my answer is yes, Kathrein assumed his dead cousin's identity. On top of that, my contacts were able to verify Garmeaux had been reaching out for interviews and diving deep into Kathrein's past. If he brought this report to your attention, be confident he was exercising due diligence, not throwing out wild accusations."

Rush let out a low whistle. "If this gets out, the consequences will destroy his grandson's political dreams. There's no way to spin a family fortune built on lies and war crimes."

"It's unfortunate," Lawton said. "The grandson could be an asset in French government. He's smart as a whip and well-respected. I'm currently checking to see if he shares his grandfather's old ideals, or if he is as ignorant of the truth as the rest of the world seems to be. No charge for that, it's my own curiosity."

"Any idea if the journalist had a safety valve on the story in case he died?"

"If he did, it fell through. The man's been dead for weeks and so far there's not so much as a whisper anywhere in Europe about this story."

Meaning Kathrein had every reason to believe controlling the content of the Gray Box would clear up everything. "All right."

Lawton bounced his fist on his knee. "My guess is the hard evidence connecting Dieter Kathrein to the Nazis by his real name is still buried in war tribunal records. Using the French Kathrein family tree I did a fast track through the German branch and called in a favor, as well." He cleared his throat. "To be fair, there were several men on that side of the family who joined the Nazi party. In particular, a young officer never returned from his assignment in Mauthausen and was presumed killed by Allied forces when the Austrian extermination camp was liberated. It would have taken time, but it's entirely possible for a young man to trek through the mountains and escape into France. If you want him prosecuted, I can track down his service record."

Rush scrubbed at his jaw, two days' worth of stubble rough against his fingers. "Not today, but I definitely intend to see him prosecuted." There was no statute of limitations on the crimes Kathrein committed.

Lucy would be furious when he explained Lawton's visit. He respected her concern about more people becoming targets, but asking the right questions was the only way to understand their enemy. They needed solid intel before they attempted a rescue. As she'd said last night, Kathrein would believe the only way to guarantee his family continuing generations of peace would be to eliminate Lucy. Not a stretch considering Kathrein's cruel and merciless past and present. Rush would not allow the old man's plots to end in tragedy for any of them.

"Thanks for your time and discretion," Rush said, coming around the desk to shake Lawton's hand.

His friend hesitated on his way to the door. "Can I ask how you came across this?"

"Only if I don't have to answer," Rush replied.

"I know you and your assistant, Grayson. She worked for Kathrein. Speaking hypothetically, if you take action on this, it won't be long before someone tags her as your source."

"It wouldn't be true," Rush stated.

"We both know truth doesn't always prevail."

He wasn't worried about Lucy's standing in the media. His priority was keeping her and her family alive. "We're also both well aware that having more money than God and dozens of lawyers on retainer can do a great deal to scrub away any mud."

"Billionaire against billionaire." Lawton cocked one eyebrow. "The press would make that interesting."

"Hypothetically speaking, what you're suggesting won't make the news," Rush replied. "When I move on Kathrein, it won't be public."

Lawton rocked back on his heels. "Good. My speedy verification isn't enough to take those documents public. I'd like more time."

Time was the only commodity Rush couldn't afford. Impatience snapped like a whip across his shoulders. "It's a delicate negotiation," he added, with a calm he didn't feel. "Things go better when I know the nature of the person calling the shots."

"Better you than me." Lawton rolled his shoulders. "I feel nasty just from the research. Why aren't you reporting him and walking away?" Lawton stared him down. "What are you and Lucy really up to?"

Rush swore. Lawton always saw too much. "I didn't give you all of it," he admitted. "The dead journalist stumbled on this story when he discovered a money trail from a Kathrein charity to a defense fund for a recently found war criminal, Alfred Portner. He went looking for an explanation."

"Holy crap."

Rush could see the wheels turning as Lawton made connections. "That's putting it mildly, my friend."

"You need more than a PI if you want to pin him for murder."

"Yes, I will, and soon." He'd intended to raise the topic with Lawton after he and Sam narrowed down a location, but a head start would only help. "What are you prepared to offer?"

"Anything you need."

"Sit down." Rush filled him in on the kidnapping and together he and Lawton reviewed the information he'd gathered on the European estates and assets. When they had a basic plan in place, Lawton agreed to go down and spend time with Sam.

Rush ushered Lawton past Lucy's desk and straight to the elevators. "Thanks for your time," he said.

"Be careful, Rush," Lawton said under his breath as he stepped into the elevator.

"You, too." He clapped his old friend on the shoulder. If everything went well, they'd see each other soon.

Returning to his office, he paused at Lucy's desk. "Cancel the next meeting. We need to talk."

"All right." She took care of it and stood, gracing him with a cool, professional smile. "I'm all yours."

With those three words, he was immediately aroused. Closing his office door behind them, he switched on the privacy glass and pulled her into his arms for a deep, lingering kiss.

"Stop it." She made a small effort to pull away. "We're at the office."

"I'm aware." He stepped back and tucked his hands into his pockets. "Thank you for coming to me, for trusting me." His pulse raced at the looming danger, though she was right here, safe and whole. He be-

lieved her sister and nephew were still alive and yet
his entire being wanted to give in to panic.

"I came to your *company* to break into your system."

Semantics. "And you did." That she'd succeeded
made him far happier than it should. "We knew about
the breach, but you actually did it."

She gawked at him. "What is *wrong* with you?"

"Nothing." He moved toward his desk, drawing the
file on Kathrein's properties out of her reach. "Never
mind. That meeting just made me think."

"Uh-huh." She folded her arms over her chest and
stared him down. "That was Parker Lawton."

"You remember him?"

"I remember you're good friends. I remember how
he'd dig up the background on people you planned
to deal with."

He sank into his chair. "That still holds." She was
perfect for him. He should have taken better care with
her the first time around. If there was any constancy
in his life, it was his refusal to repeat his mistakes.
Once this crisis was resolved, he would convince her
they belonged together. Not for a night or a few more
weeks, but for a lifetime. She might not realize it, but
they were the ideal team. Love had nothing to do with
it, he reminded himself.

She planted her hands on her hips and glared at
him. "You asked him to investigate Kathrein."

He swallowed, sensing this was the defining moment. This was the time to start a new habit of complete honesty with the only woman he'd ever trusted
with his true self. Twenty, hell, fifty years from now

he'd look back and realize this was the moment his life changed. "I did."

"Rush!" Fiery temper blazed in her eyes. "What if—"

"Hear me out."

"Then talk fast. When did you even reach out to him?"

"I checked his availability before you woke up this morning."

"So much for teamwork," she said with a sexy little snarl.

"I called him before we discussed teamwork." He sobered. "Are you going to listen?"

She mimed locking her lips and tossing away the key.

"Great. It bothered me that Kathrein chose this particular week to send you on mission impossible."

"As you pointed out, not so impossible."

"Noted," he agreed with a wink. "Still, why now? So far, his money has kept his past buried." He held up a finger when she started to answer him. "It's more than the grandson's political bid. Look, I asked Lawton to verify two pages of documentation I claimed I'd received on Kathrein. I didn't tell him where it came from."

"He recognized me and assumed."

"You know, he worried you'd get blamed if I released any of the nasty skeletons in Kathrein's closet."

"How thoughtful."

"Just logic," Rush corrected. He'd prefer it if she didn't aim warm compliments at other men when she'd been kissing him as recently as two minutes ago.

"Sit down, Lucy." He waited for her to take the nearest chair. "You saw the files. Kathrein gave money to support the defense of one of his old Nazi buddies. Garmeaux followed the money. While there's no real proof, we agree with you that Kathrein silenced him."

She pressed her fingers to her lips. "What if the spy tells Kathrein a man with Parker's history met with you today?"

"Lawton can take care of himself," Rush said. "This company has enough things going on locally and globally that Kathrein can't be sure I had him here to help you."

Her gaze dropped to her lap. "I hope you're right."

"I am." He was betting everything on his being right. Despite the disturbing news about the timing and increasing threat to Lucy, he would beat Kathrein at his own game.

She sat back farther in the chair and crossed her legs at the knee. "What other steps have you taken in your role as team captain?"

He eyed her cautiously. "Are you mad at me again?"

"No," she said, resigned. "But I'm not happy. You promised me we'd handle this together."

"We are. We will. Did you expect my part to be sitting back and holding your hand while he tormented you? Should I just watch quietly from the corner while you throw yourself on his nonexistent mercy?"

"Stop it. Neither of us can afford to be mad. It gives him the advantage." Lucy knew her reactions were unreasonable. Rush cared for her. Whether as an old friend or as a new friend with benefits, the result was the same. "I'm overwhelmed. Yes, I need to *stay* in the loop, but it all feels insurmountable. He could have my family stashed anywhere." She didn't give voice to her worst fear—that he'd staged the pictures and already disposed of Gwen and Jackson. Her heart twisted painfully.

Rush looked to the ceiling and tapped his fingertips lightly on the desktop. His hands, so strong, so capable of creating blinding pleasure, had always captivated her.

"Everything I have is yours, Lucy. Every contact and favor owed me, every dollar and resource will be allocated to save all three of you from Kathrein. He'll put up a fight. It's what survivors do."

"Please..." Her voice trailed off as her heart fluttered in her chest. Words failed her that he would make such a complete pledge. "Enough." She swiped a hand through the air as if the grim images of the looming fight could be erased. "Just tell me how we can beat him. There are only three days left," she finished, though neither of them needed the reminder.

"Background always helps me, right?" It was a rhetorical question. "I've been thinking Kathrein made a mistake taking hostages. For seventy years he's escaped discovery, hiding behind his fortune and support network. His habit of arrogance will be our advantage."

"I hadn't thought of it that way," she mused. "In France, everyone is loyal to him."

"Everyone he let you meet, anyway."

"Oh, I'm an idiot." She twisted her hands in her

lap. "Yes, the man's been a recluse because he's afraid to be identified. During my short tenure, the minimal staff wasn't simply about his preferences, but about who he trusted to keep his deepest secrets."

Rush nodded, encouraging her as she reviewed her time with Kathrein and his staff through this new lens. "I don't think he's taken your family out of France." He reached for a file folder. "We'll pack up some gear from R & D and take my plane. Once we pinpoint where he's holding your family," he added, "we can devise a rescue."

"That sounds fabulous, until you remember he'll kill Gwen and Jackson if he discovers I roped you into helping me."

"Roped me into it?" Rush stopped himself, staring at her with something that might have been pain in another man's eyes. "We'll clear that up later. As for Kathrein, you can count on me." He tapped his chest, showing a great deal of his own brand of arrogance. "I've been a master of diversion and illusion since my first hack as a kid."

She trusted him with puzzles and solutions. She trusted his mysterious resources—having seen an aging billionaire, she could only imagine the protection a man with Rush's modern, technical savvy would have in place. Oh, she trusted him, with everything…except her heart.

Emotions were the one life lesson Rush hadn't bothered learning. He knew how to get along, when to be tough, how to play fair or fight dirty, and he could woo women and clients with almost equal expertise. She knew enough about his childhood to understand his reluctance to let people get close enough to hurt him. Compound that with the fact that in order to maintain his place as a leader in the industry he had to shelter his feelings the way his company protected data.

She'd often wondered if he realized how well he cared for the people who depended on him. Not only Gray Box clients with the product, but the employees who loved working for him. Melva had been the first to give Rush and Sam legitimacy as they turned an idea into a thriving enterprise.

As the king of data and analysis, he had to know how rare lasting partnerships were. In study after study during her grad school days, partners split over big and small disputes. Rush and Sam, both ambitious geniuses, continued to beat the odds.

"Lucy?"

She was startled to discover he'd pulled a chair close to hers and was holding her hand between his larger palms. "My mind wandered."

"I noticed. What's the last thing you heard?"

She squinted, thinking. "You're a master of diversion."

He grinned with approval and gave her fingers a squeeze. "Well, while you were lost in thought, Sam sent a text message. He's on his way up with news."

"Great." What a relief she hadn't missed the entire rescue plan while her mind catalogued Rush's admirable qualities. Why did she love the one man who didn't ever want to be in anything more than lust?

He'd told her more than once that her acceptance of his priorities was as much a turn-on as her adventurous sensual curiosity. She'd been careful not to expect or hope for him to change, just as she'd been very aware of the generous spirit he hid behind layers and layers of personal defenses and alternate vocabulary. He was capable of loving; his actions proved it repeatedly though he'd kick her to the curb if she phrased it that way.

And she'd fallen in love with him anyway. She still loved him, despite his autocratic tendencies and his conviction that love wasn't a viable option for his life. Why? Probably those bone-melting kisses.

He'd shown tremendous affection and care when they were dating. If last night was any indicator, the chemistry between them remained, as did the mutual respect. Maybe closure sex wasn't a good idea, after all.

He got up and crossed to a cabinet on the far wall that turned out to hold a small refrigerator. He returned with a bottle of water. "Here, drink up."

She did as he asked, the cold liquid clearing the last of the cobwebs from her mind as Sam walked in. Of course Sam had something. The man could find a needle in any remote haystack of the internet without disturbing the haystack.

Sam gave her a warm, rocking hug and then held her at arm's length and studied her with concern from behind his black-framed glasses. "How are you holding up?"

She glanced past Sam to Rush. "It's good to have friends helping me." Helping her family. "Thank you." She sidestepped, forcing her lips into a smile. "Rush said you have news."

"I've found all kinds of dirt on the wealthiest recluse in France." Using the tablet in his hand, he entered a command and a panel slid back, revealing the bank of monitors on the far wall. "Did you have any idea you were working for such a tough old bastard?" he asked while pictures and data filled the screens.

"I knew the old part," Lucy said. "Tough was implied based on his business accomplishments and holdings. As for bastard, he was kind to me. At first."

Sam gave a dismissive grunt, a trait she remembered from the days when he and Rush would tackle one idea from two different angles.

"I worked the timeline backward from your arrival. Your sister and nephew must still be in France. In fact, I don't think they can be far from the estate near Chantilly."

She stepped closer, examining the list of properties owned by the extended Kathrein family. There were estates scattered around Europe. "He only had a few hours," she murmured. "With planes and helicopters, that doesn't narrow it down much."

"This will." Sam changed the displays to a sky view of France. Small squares of various colors had been added to mark Kathrein's personal properties. There was a red square around the estate where she'd worked and lived, and another farther east near Strasbourg. Everything else had a different color.

"This winery." Sam zoomed in on the second red square. "It's one of the oldest properties in the deck. Production ended decades ago. When the Kathrein girls were young, the family vacationed there regu-

larly. The views must be amazing," he said on a wistful sigh.

"Sam," Rush interjected.

"Right." Sam cleared his throat. "The family last
visited more than five years ago and yet power was
turned on last week. The family, aside from Mr. Recluse, of course, has been accounted for, going about
their business in other parts of the country."

Pictures of Kathrein's daughters and their families
filled the far third of the display.

"What about homes in urban areas he might be
using?" Rush asked.

"Doubtful," Lucy said. "He really despises crowded
areas."

"Sure that's not an act?" Rush asked. "He's lived
another man's life all this time."

"Necessity or nature, at this point it hardly matters," Lucy said. "If his goal is to protect his grandson's reputation and plans, he's not going to take a
chance of being caught with hostages in an urban
area."

"I agree." Rush folded his arms over his chest
while he reviewed the pictures. "We can run a cursory check on the city properties," he added. "But
you and I will head for the winery." He reached for
his cell phone.

Lucy turned to him. "We're going now?"

He nodded to her while he gave instructions to
whomever was on the other end of the call, presumably someone at an airfield.

She bit her lip and it felt like an eternity before
Rush was off the phone. "When he learns I've left

with you," she warned, "that you're helping me, he'll ruin you. After he kills them." She couldn't live with that on her conscience—assuming she lived at all. Her stomach threatened to rebel again.

"Take it easy, Lucy. I can cover for you here," Sam said. "We have ways to make it look like you're both still working on this problem right here in the city."

She didn't bother asking how. Sam and Rush had amazing computer skills. She turned to Rush. "What about the spy he has tailing me?"

"The private cars and a lookalike team should keep him busy."

She pressed her fingers to her mouth, wanting to believe. He wandered around like a normal guy most of the time and then called in his extensive resources and connections when the situation justified it. "And how are the two of us going to save my sister and her son? He has armed guards and I'm certainly not current on combat rescue training." She'd wait until she and Rush were alone to make her argument that if they were wrong and Kathrein was using the winery as a decoy, storming the place would tip him off.

She could already hear him telling her to think positively and start envisioning scenarios with better endings.

"Do your part as planned," Rush said to Sam, with a tip of his chin to Lucy. "I'll handle this."

Lucy waited until Sam was safely on his way back downstairs. "Now I'm a 'this' to be handled."

"Yes," he answered without the first sign of remorse. "Can't you see how much I want to handle you?"

"Not funny." His words sent some enticing scenarios through her mind, all with very satisfying endings.

"A man can dream," he quipped. "Lucy, I'll be honest, I'd rather you stayed out of harm's way and let my friends handle the rescue."

"Are *you* staying behind?"

"No. Someone who knows the tech gear we have in mind has to be on site."

She really should ask what that meant. Standing there, his expression so earnest, she almost felt guilty for walking away from him a year ago. If she'd stayed in San Francisco, Kathrein would never have been able to use her this way. But if she'd stayed with Rush she would have settled for loving a man who didn't want to love her back. It wouldn't have been awful, but it wouldn't have been right. "You found someone to double for me, too?"

"Yes." He tucked his hands into his pockets, watching her. "I know you and your mannerisms. I know you'd rather be right there with me rather than somewhere safe, wringing your hands and worrying."

The words sent a shiver down her spine and her heart did a silly flop in her chest. "Did you pack for me, too?"

He did a double take and then he laughed. "No. I hired that done. To an outsider, it looks like I moved back into the boathouse with you. In all the commotion, a packed suitcase wound up in the car that will soon take us to the airport."

"You didn't give me much to do besides hold a thumb drive we won't deliver."

"On the contrary." He held out his hand. "You can hold on to me. We wouldn't have made it this far without your insight and composure."

His comments surprised her. "Then I guess I'll be grateful you've thought of everything."

"Smart lady." He smoothed a stray lock of hair behind her ear.

Lucy managed not to shiver at the touch. While he called for the car, she wallowed in the compliment that chased away the dread that had been twisting in her gut since Sam's presentation.

After today, they only had two days to either cooperate or outwit Kathrein. She felt a ray of hope that, with Rush's resources and gear, they all might survive the coming finale.

Chapter Ten

Rush kept a close eye on Lucy as they left the office under cover and slipped into the backseat of a generic sedan with heavily tinted windows. She'd only said a few words since he'd set the plan in motion. The two of them would arrive first in France and would oversee the reconnaissance while Lawton pulled together a rescue squad.

Although Rush wanted to draw Lucy into conversation, he couldn't bring himself to push her too hard. Knowing her as he did, he gave her time to process the swell of information and the space to mentally prepare for the flight.

She wouldn't falter. Once Lucy made up her mind she didn't waste time second-guessing. It was one of her finest traits, even though it had worked against him a year ago. He'd been startled and confused when she'd walked out. After the shock had worn off, the anger and hurt had settled in and stayed. It had taken him months to look past her hurried departure and realize, being Lucy, she would have given the decision plenty of thought.

He wondered if she wished they could talk about

it as much as he did. Their past wasn't the right discussion when she was so obviously frantic about her
sister and nephew. Neither was it the right time to
discuss their future, though he intended to clear the
air on both topics soon.

She sat on the couch across from him in his jet, her
face turned slightly to the window, but he knew she
didn't see anything. Heading east at this late hour at
high altitude, there wasn't much to see except clouds
and the occasional patch of the Atlantic Ocean far
below them. They had a few hours left and he'd encouraged her to lie down in the bedroom, but she'd
been too restless.

In the silence, Rush's mind churned through pos-
sibilities as updates came in from Sam and Lawton.
During the refuel in New York, Lucy had reminded
him that Kathrein maintained the loyalty of plenty of
police and officials. It was an obstacle he had to take
into consideration. They had surprise on their side,
but Kathrein had a home-field advantage.

Rush had insisted she leave her phone at the office so Sam could use it as part of the game plan, for-
warding any messages from Kathrein to a clean cell
phone. The tactic also sheltered Lucy from any un-
necessary angst from the old bastard. The pictures of
Jackson had ceased and the messages had gone from
aggressive to all-out menacing after the pictures of
Lucy and Rush having coffee had been distributed
over the internet.

His phone vibrated on the table and Lucy jerked
upright. "An update from Sam," he explained as he

read the message. "Kathrein checked in again. Sam implied you're making progress."

"Did he back off or send a picture?" She came over to sit across from him at the table.

Rush swallowed a surge of fear as the rest of the exchange came through, including a series of pictures of Gwen. Her clothes were in shambles and she had a nasty black eye on her tear-stained face. He enlarged each picture, searching for a clue in the surroundings to no avail. Thankfully, Sam would break down each shot pixel by pixel.

"Rush." She reached out and rubbed his hand. "You look ready to kill. What happened?"

He deleted the pictures so she wouldn't see them. Brutalizing Gwen made no sense. Had she tried to escape or had one of the guards turned abusive?

Turning his hand, he laced his fingers through hers. "He's the worst kind of bully," he said. "I can't help being furious." During his time in juvie, he'd run up against boys who did terrible things to maintain their place at the top of the heap.

"I should have known the offer was too good to be true."

"Stop." He held tight when she tried to tug her hand free. "You can't take on any blame for Kathrein. He's cornered and has been, one way or another, for seventy years." And he was leading Lucy into the monster's territory. "This is all on him, Lucy."

"He's trying to protect his family," she countered.

"Now you're playing devil's advocate?"

"I've been wondering…"

He waited.

"How far will we go to rescue my family?"

"As far as necessary."

"How does that make us any different from him?"

"Lucy." He set the phone aside and stood up, rounding the table and tugging her with him to relax on the couch. "First, he started it by terrifying you and your family in order to use you. Finishing a fight, sending a Nazi to prison for present and past crimes puts us a world apart from him."

"That's logic and decency, I know." She pulled her knees to her chest and curled herself into a tight ball of misery. "You have connections capable of lethal action?"

"Absolutely." One perk of working with private security programs. "Does that bother you?"

"It should." She bit her lip. "I don't want to stoop to his level," she whispered. "Promise me your connections won't blindly attack the people following his orders."

Leave it to Lucy to ask for something he couldn't give. "We'll have to agree to disagree on that." He gently uncurled her body, and brought her to rest against him. With his legs framing hers, he stroked her silky hair while she stared out the window. "My goal is to get you and your family out of this alive. If—when—this becomes a tactical rescue, it's better for everyone if we handle it swiftly and quietly." As a friend, Lawton would go above and beyond to help, and Rush wouldn't taint that effort by letting them land in political hot water. "The tactical team knows how to be discreet. A pile of bodies doesn't meet that definition."

"Okay."

"I want him to pay for the hell he's caused you, your family and who knows how many others," he continued. "I'll pass on the documentation from Garmeaux to the proper authorities about his real name. Believe me, if I thought we had the time I'd do that first."

"Good." Her cheek rubbed his chest as she nodded.

He wanted to pick her up and tuck her into bed. They had two more hours before landing and she needed the rest. If invited, he'd happily use that time to make her forget everything but the beautiful passion they'd shared.

In the year since she left he'd often tried to pinpoint the moment she became the woman he didn't want to live without. Not the first kiss, though it had been electric. Nor was it the first time they'd made love. Both stand-out moments fueled his erotic fantasies, but neither was *the* moment.

He studied her profile as she studied the dark sky beyond the window. Her high cheekbones and stubborn jaw tempted him. He remembered how she melted when he kissed the smooth skin of her throat, now hidden from his view by her hair. Though he longed to kiss her again, he held back.

The moment abruptly popped to the front of his mind. It was the evening they'd invited Sam and Melva to dinner at the boathouse to celebrate an important contract. Everything clicked into place. Lucy completed the family he'd carefully chosen and trusted implicitly. She'd surpassed his calculated list of pros and cons that focused on business and sex.

He'd bought the ring a few days later and come up with the ideal proposal, but he'd put off asking her until it suddenly became too late. The belated self-awareness didn't resolve anything if he didn't understand her side of the story. "Lucy?" He kept stroking her hair, listening to her soft breath.

"Mmm?"

"Why did you leave me?"

"Oh, Rush." She tilted her head back, her brown eyes full of regret. "This should wait."

"Please, just say it."

"I had to go." Her smile was sad as she traced his lips with her fingertips. She lifted her gaze to him again and spoke clearly. "I'd committed the cardinal sin."

He caught her chin, held her gaze. "You cheated?"

Humor lit her eyes and her lips twisted. "Of course not. I fell in love with you."

"You left because you loved me?" Just using the L word backed up the air in his lungs. "You left—"

"The rules were always clear between us. I respect your boundaries." She sat up a little. "I couldn't hold back my feelings anymore and I refused to put that pressure on you."

"What about the new guy in Chicago?"

"There was no new guy. I lied to drive you away." Her cheeks turned pink while she traced the Gray Box logo on his shirt. "If we're being honest, there hasn't been anyone for me since you."

He could hardly process her admission. "You're serious." She nodded. "God, you're clever." He cupped her head and brought her lips to his for a kiss designed to make up for lost time. Her hair sifted over his skin and his body clamored for more thorough action than he could hope for on this couch. Although the bedroom was a few paces away, he held himself in check. *Again.*

Slowly, he steered their deep, passionate kisses to a sweeter place.

"If you're angry, remember you asked," she said.

He caught her as she tried to get up. "I'm not angry." Not even close. He cleared his throat and cuddled her close to his chest. "You should rest while we have the chance." He rubbed her back, threading his fingers through her hair until her muscles relaxed again. Finally, her long, sooty eyelashes brushed her cheeks as sleep claimed her. Rush carefully extricated himself from under her and tucked a blanket over her so she wouldn't wake up chilled.

She'd left because she *loved* him. Did she still? Did he want her, too? Hell, yes.

He pushed a hand through his hair and tried to breathe. Pouring a drink, he indulged in a vision of life surrounded with Lucy's *love*. Days filled with her acceptance, laughter and intelligence had been pure bliss. How much better could it be if he gave her space to express her heart, as well? Unbidden, he saw himself walking to the park near the boathouse with a dark-haired little girl who had Lucy's big brown eyes.

The image didn't put panic in his chest, only a warm, easy joy. He waited for the noisy, wounding echoes from his broken childhood to erupt, and instead he heard Lucy's voice showering him with *I love you*s.

Wow. How had he missed her feelings? How had he ever been so foolish as to let her get away?

They would get through this and then he'd give her everything he should have given her a year ago. They'd have a heartfelt talk about their future, together. Whatever she wanted, whatever she needed, he knew now he could be that man for her.

France, near Strasbourg
Saturday, December 19, 6:30 a.m.

JUST OVER TWO hours later the plane touched down on a private airstrip in northeastern France. Watching Lucy come awake always stirred him. Today was no different. As she stretched her luscious body, his responded instantly. *Later*, he promised himself.

"We're here?"

"Yes. We'll be at the villa I rented within the hour and should have our first views of the winery shortly thereafter."

"Good." She folded the blanket and slipped on her shoes. "How can I help?"

He grinned at her and held out his hand. "Just stick with me." He managed to shut his mouth before he could modify that request to encompass the future. They left the plane and moved quickly to the waiting car. Although he'd given instructions for the gear and luggage, out of habit, he oversaw the transfer of the tech gear before joining Lucy in the back of the sedan.

"Do you have people standing by regional airfields all over the world?" she asked.

"No," he admitted with a brief laugh. "I just know

who to call to make it look that way." She pulled back and he missed the closeness all the more after talking and holding her on the plane. "My money never bothered you before." She was one of the few people who'd never been cowed by his net worth or treated him like a walking wallet.

"It doesn't bother me now," she said, wiggling a bit in the seat. "You and Kathrein are so different."

"How so?" he asked, giving in to curiosity.

"I've been around many wealthy people," she began. "Kathrein generally uses his money as a weapon and a shield, leaving his daughters to serve as his public presence and run his charities. Do you think they know who he really is?"

"No. If they knew, they would have circled the wagons by now." He wouldn't let her dodge the question. "Other than being younger and far more handsome, how else am I different?"

She smiled bit and her voice was quiet when she spoke. "You've always splurged the most when you're helping others."

He thought of the extravagant diamond ring he'd bought for her. "You're not a charity case, Lucy."

"Hmm." She slanted a dubious glance at him. "Without your resources and assistance, I would have been forced to cooperate with Kathrein to save Gwen and Jackson."

If he dwelled on the likely outcome of that scenario, he'd break out in a cold sweat. Unable to resist, he pulled her close to his side. She leaned in, resting her hand on his thigh as she'd done countless times before.

"I did consider what a breach would do to your business and reputation."

"But not the damage to our friendship if you'd blown in and out of my life again?"

She smoothed her palm over his knee. "I didn't think we had any friendship left."

That made him inexplicably sad. "Do you want to know how I got through?"

"Got through what?"

"Your move to Chicago," he said with more edge than he'd intended.

She looked up at him. "How?"

"I told myself it was temporary, that you were scared. I convinced myself you needed to test your wings, in business and with men, so you could come back and be sure about us." The car swayed along the winding road and her body leaned into his. "I will always be your friend," he promised, pressing a kiss to the top of her head. He'd be her friend until she was ready to say those words again and trust him with her heart.

She didn't reply and they made the rest of the trip in silence, the ramifications of what they needed to do settling over both of them.

The driver turned off the main road, aiming for a sprawling stone villa at the edge of the valley. "When we're unloaded, I'll set up the drones and we'll confirm whether or not Kathrein is keeping your family at the winery."

She leaned forward to peer at the house as they turned into the drive. Then she shot him a grin over her shoulder. "Some rental." She shook her head. "I'd like to meet your travel agent."

He grinned back at her and had to tease. "If we like the place, I'll buy it."

"No need." She unbuckled her seat belt as the car came to a stop. "The flights would be bad enough, but France has lost the glamorous appeal that originally charmed me."

He pushed open his door and brought her across the seat to exit the car on his side. Pausing, he reveled in the play of early morning light shimmering over the house. "Maybe we shouldn't let one bad apple spoil everything."

She opened her mouth to protest and he silenced her with a kiss. "I know," he whispered, pulling back. "I know it seems impossible, but we will rescue Gwen and Jackson."

"I believe you." She stared up at the house. "I believe you," she said with more conviction.

He urged her ahead and Lucy pushed open the big front door. He'd specifically requested no staff on site as a way to manage risk and rumors. He and the driver set the luggage just inside the door, then moved the gear Rush had brought along to the garage. With that task complete, Rush tipped him well for his time and silence.

In the garage he and Lucy set up a workshop area with his computers, and the gadgets and gear for the drones and cameras. As each device was unpacked and checked out, he made some final tweaks to the program. After a quick conversation with Sam back in San Francisco, he was good for the test run.

Lucy worked efficiently and quietly. She didn't ask questions or toss around theories. In the uncomfortable silence, faced with the sadness and worry in her typically bright eyes, he hated Kathrein with a barely leashed violence. It was a good thing Lawton's team would keep the creaky old bastard out of Rush's reach.

He didn't care who Kathrein had paid off along the way. He had two days to find a solution that gave Lucy a happy reunion with her family. If the tight time frame meant he had to take a few chances, so be it. He would never give her cause to regret confiding in him or accepting his help.

UNABLE TO HELP Rush further, Lucy went inside to explore the villa. The driver had gone and it was only she and Rush until his friends on the security detail arrived. Only her, really, as Rush worked methodically on the reconnaissance technology. If this sprawling house had the character or history of the place where she and Gwen had stayed on Kathrein's estate, those details were hidden behind luxurious upgrades now. That was fine with Lucy; she didn't want any reminders of her foolishness.

Hauling the luggage up the wide sweeping staircase that dominated the foyer, she halted in the hallway. Did she take both suitcases into one suite or did she keep her distance and maintain the status quo with separate bedrooms? Her lips tingled as she relived the sensual promise in those kisses on the plane.

She couldn't get a read on him to know if they were working their way back together or if Rush was merely being kind and patient until her crisis was resolved. Better to follow his example and keep her mind on the trouble that brought them here. She rolled his suitcase into one room and hers into the room across the hall before she hurried back down the stairs.

In the kitchen, the cold reality of the thumb drive and cloned phone sitting on the counter depressed her. What if they were wrong and Kathrein wasn't holding her family hostage at the defunct winery just beyond the rolling hills to the west?

This was day five of her allotted seven. There wouldn't be enough time to search again, even with Rush's vast resources. She had to keep biting back the plea to let her make contact and arrange an exchange. Overcome, she dropped onto the bench of the banquette in the breakfast nook and let loose a flood of useless tears. Better to get it out of her system now. Her sister and nephew meant nothing to Kathrein. They were pawns he'd crush without a second thought if she didn't deliver. He might kill them anyway.

The glimmer of hope she'd felt when they left San Francisco had faded the closer they came to the confrontation and she realized how little she could help. She couldn't assist or market her way out of this. She had *nothing* to contribute to a rescue plan. After reading the damaging information, she realized no amount of artful dealing would change Kathrein's mind. He would gladly sacrifice her family to save his.

She dried her cheeks with her sleeve and then went in search of a tissue for her nose. Helplessness had never been her strong suit. Weeping and wringing her hands wouldn't make a difference. She needed a diversion.

Her stomach rumbled and she assumed Rush would be hungry, too. He often forgot to eat when he was in problem-solving mode. Several things about him felt different the last few days, yet the basics hadn't changed. Thank heavens he hadn't asked her outright if she still loved him.

With a self-deprecating snort, she gave herself points for being able to help with sustenance. Poking around the gourmet kitchen, she found the basics on the pantry shelves and the refrigerator stocked with everything from wine and milk to thick steaks and vegetables. A fresh pizza had been prepared and wrapped in plastic ready to pop into the oven. A tent card from the property management company topped a fruit basket and had both phone numbers and website links to order groceries. Even a link to a recipe site was listed.

Lucy wondered if anyone from the rental company or the grocery in the nearest town were still in Kathrein's pocket. Maybe not if it had been several years since the family had been here. They would know soon enough.

Choosing convenience, she pulled out the pizza and set the oven to preheat while she searched the cabinets for a pizza stone. Crouched behind a counter, she jumped to her feet when a door opened with a bang and Rush called her name.

"Kitchen," she answered, raising her voice.

He hurried in, breathless, his presence shrinking the massive space. Excitement rolled off him in waves. Even with the big marble island between them, he smelled of sunshine and rich soil and…the masculine scent she'd burrowed into at night when her world had been perfect. Why the hell had she left him?

"Look!" He held up a tablet and waved her over to his side of the marble island. "We're in the right place."

She tripped over her feet at the news and he caught her, steadied her. "You're sure?" The answer was evident in the bright glow of victory in his gorgeous blue eyes. "Oh, thank God. Show me."

He swiped the screen and she watched the replay of a short video.

"Gwen." She blinked back tears of joy and relief as she watched her sister pushing a stroller along a circular patio behind a stone house, smaller than this one. She kept her head down and Lucy's heart ached. But her sister was alive. Thank God. Thank God. A different angle showed Jackson bouncing his arms, oblivious to the danger they were in. "He let them outside?" she asked, startled Kathrein would take the risk.

"They aren't alone." Rush panned back and pointed out the burly men standing guard at each corner that might offer Gwen an escape. "Unless she bolted into the overgrown vineyard, there's no room to run."

Lucy had to swallow the lump of emotion clogging her throat. "When was this?"

"About an hour ago," Rush replied, beaming. "There's another guard with the car in the front drive. Kathrein must be inside."

"When can we get them out?"

"I've spoken with Lawton and it will require at

least one more flyover, but the team will be here in plenty of time. We just have to keep stringing him along."

The relief was a palpable force coursing through her bloodstream. Gwen and Jackson would survive. "Thank you." She gave in and threw her arms around him. "Thank you!" Her lips found his and she gave him a kiss packed with the rising tide of gratitude.

Distantly, she heard the tablet clatter to the marble countertop as Rush's hands clutched her hips. His palms swept up her back, bringing her body flush to his. Her nipples peaked against the hard planes of his chest. Too fast and yet not nearly fast enough. She threaded her fingers through his hair as her tongue swept into his mouth.

His taste electrified her, simultaneously familiar and new. She'd missed this, missed him. "Rush…" Lucy let her head fall back as his lips and tongue and teeth nibbled the sensitive skin up and down her throat. Her hands fisted in the fabric of his shirt, tugging it free of his jeans. Smoothing her palms along the firm, warm skin underneath, she moaned.

He squeezed her backside, flexing his hips to hers. His arousal was obvious and she wanted him inside her now. Sooner, if possible.

She fumbled with his belt and the button of his fly. He boosted her to the countertop and spread her legs to stand between them, his kisses drifting across her cleavage. She drew his face to hers, needing his lips, the subtle comfort he offered hidden deep in the desire surging between them. "I need you."

The dark spark of desire flared in his blue gaze,

igniting an answering fire in her belly. His kiss, a blatant mating of mouths, sent her pulse into overdrive. She reached for his shirt, flicking open each button until she could push the panels wide, back and over his shoulders. For a moment, his arms were trapped in the fabric.

She reveled in the view of his magnificent chest and her breath caught as she remembered the fun they'd had with far more effective restraints. Gripping his waistband, she dragged him closer and curled her legs around his hips. "Looks like you're mine now," she teased.

"Always have been," he murmured, his kisses tracing her collarbone.

She didn't have time to dwell on any deeper meanings in the words. The sleeve of his shirt tore a bit as he twisted out of it and tossed it aside. His big hands were heavy, sliding up and down her thighs, making her wish she'd worn a skirt instead of jeans.

"Where's the nearest bed?" he asked, his stubble tickling her sensitive skin.

She tightened her grip with her legs. "Please don't make me wait that long."

"Your wish, my command, sweetheart." His thumbs came close to her center, not quite reaching the place where she needed him most. All these layers between them and she was already slick and aching for him. Only him. There was some wild, needy element inside her that only Rush seemed to unlock.

She fused her mouth to his and slid her hands over his chest, sifting through the dark hair, stroking the hard lines of sculpted muscle and following the trail of hair that arrowed under his waistband. He groaned, flexing his erection into her hand as she stroked him. Silk boxers, she realized, smiling inwardly at the wonderful details about him that remained the same.

He dropped his forehead to her shoulder as she teased him, his breath hot and ragged. Suddenly, he bowed her back over one arm and feasted on her breasts. The shift pulled her hand away from her prize, left her clinging to his broad shoulders for balance as he nipped at the puckered tips of her breasts, soothing each sharp sensation with a slow lap of his velvet tongue.

His free hand cupped her through her jeans, promising more sinful pleasure. She gasped his name, ready to beg for a fast release, so close to a climax just from his deft touches through the fabric.

"Now who's trapped?" He traced the curve of her breast. "I could take you right here."

It sounded like a good start. "Please." No point in playing coy when they both clearly wanted each other. She arched closer to the heat radiating from his spectacular body. She could see the strain of holding back simmering through him. "You can take me anywhere you please."

"Lucy." His nostrils flared when she rocked herself against the hand between her legs. "It's been so long."

"Then stop talking." She kissed him, her tongue dueling with his, seeking all the hot pleasure his kisses promised.

He tugged her off the counter, and with her legs wrapped around his lean hips, he carried her into the sitting room, easing her down to the couch. He dropped his jeans and boxers and, nude, reached for her. Though she tried to help and pleaded with him to hurry, he took his time stripping away her clothes and feasting on every exposed inch of her skin as he revealed it.

He brought her to a shattering climax with his fingers, then his mouth, and still she longed for more. She opened for him, body and soul, and he settled over her. Raising her hips, he entered her in one smooth, hard motion.

Yes, this. The beautiful perfection of being reunited soared through her. Her eyes stung with happy tears and she blinked them away. No one knew her the way Rush knew her.

When he started to move, his hips met hers with hard, greedy thrusts. The pleasure rolled through her, building in exquisite waves of passion from the point where their bodies joined and out across every last nerve ending.

Her muscles squeezing his length, she matched his pace and demanded more from both of them. He reached out and captured the tip of her breast between his fingers and she flew apart, clinging to him as another climax swamped her. He reached his peak a moment later, calling her name as his body shuddered over hers. She drifted like a leaf on a gentle river current as her heart rate slowed and Rush's ragged breathing returned to normal.

Shifting so he didn't crush her, he brought her back snug against the warmth and solid security of his chest, his arm a comfortable weight at her waist. As her mind wandered through brambles of true love, contentment and closure, his soft snores became a familiar lullaby behind her.

When she woke a bit later with a start, confused and disoriented, Rush's arm tightened around her reflexively in his sleep and she reached back to smooth a hand over his hip. In the shelter of his body the trouble that had forced her back into his world seemed like a nightmare from someone else's life.

But this wasn't one of those whirlwind getaways Rush had frequently arranged for them. They'd come to France to save her sister and nephew from the crazy old man holding them hostage. Although the sex was unarguably a marvelous distraction, the afterglow had faded, letting her anxiety back in.

Slipping out of his embrace, she found a throw and covered Rush's body, primarily to block the superb temptation. He'd been pushing hard since catching her in his office and she knew he needed some rest, too. Pulling on her jeans and shirt, she gathered up the rest of her clothes. Padding to the kitchen, she put the pizza in the oven and then tiptoed upstairs for a quick shower while it baked.

Her body loose and satiated, she waited for the emotions and regrets to jam things up. Nothing had really changed. She still loved him and though he hadn't pushed her away over the news, he didn't claim to be okay with it. That one-way street hadn't been enough for her before. Could it be enough now, if he could accept her as she accepted him?

She gave herself a blast of cold water before she turned off the taps. Toweling off, she promised herself she wouldn't run away again. She'd talk to him and sort it all out once they rescued her family.

Chapter Eleven

Though he didn't stir, Rush felt Lucy wake up. It wasn't hard to guess what filled her thoughts as she slipped away from him. While her reasons for jumping him hadn't been ideal, he chose to believe that gratitude sex beat fear-of-death sex. He was more concerned about whether or not gratitude sex could be a foundation for winning her back.

He stayed on the couch, weighing the ramifications until the savory scents of the pizza made his stomach growl. Rolling to his back, he scrubbed at his face. With Lucy, he'd experienced that bone-deep affirmation of his best self. She brought out the best in him. In the boardroom, in his brainstorms, and barring this rather frenzied exception to the rule, she usually brought out his best in the bedroom.

He wondered if it was obvious to her that he'd gone a year without sex. He wouldn't mention it, not while she was rightly focused on her family's safe return. It hadn't been intentional and he wasn't looking for praise. By the time he'd recognized the deeper reasons he wasn't clicking with other women, the freeze had gone on too long. His relationship with Lucy had changed something fundamental inside him. Having allowed her to get so close, nothing superficial held as much appeal.

He was desperate to reclaim that connection, yet he wasn't in the habit of showing any vulnerability. This wasn't a business deal and still he couldn't shake the feeling that telling her would backfire and make him sound as if he'd say anything to keep her around. He'd figure it out and turn this unexpected second chance into something that worked for both of them.

No time like the present, he thought. Sitting up, he grabbed his jeans and dragged them on again, not bothering with the rest of his clothes yet.

Although he had people en route for the rescue, he hadn't made any definitive moves to report Kathrein. He didn't want to cause an international incident while her family was trapped, but he didn't want to let the former Nazi off the hook for the current kidnapping or war crimes. Rush wasn't sure he could count on anyone nearby standing up to Kathrein's bribes. Maybe Lucy had an idea. It was high time the two of them got on the same page about that.

Wearing only jeans he strolled into the kitchen, smiling a little to see she'd picked up his shirt from the floor and left it neatly folded on a counter stool. A bit chilled, he put it on but didn't tuck it in.

"Hungry?" she asked, watching with a shy smile as he covered up.

"For you? Always." He walked up and nuzzled his lips to her neck, wrapping his arms around her waist. He wanted to make it clear that once on the couch wasn't enough.

She turned in the circle of his arms, a lovely blush creeping into her cheeks. "I meant for food. The pizza is nearly done." She moved away to check it.

Caring for others was such a Lucy thing to do. Something he'd taken for granted too often. He used the tablet to check for any new data from the drone. Still flying and recording, so that was good news.

"We should talk," he said. Her shoulders stiffened but, with an effort, he kept the conversation on point. "The rescue operation is a go. The team will go in as soon as they arrive."

The timer went off and a spicy aroma filled the kitchen when she opened the oven door. His mouth watered, for the food and the woman.

"But?" she prompted, setting the pizza stone on the stove top to cool.

He tapped his fingers on the counter. "What do you want to do about Kathrein?"

She pursed her lips, her hands fisting in the pot holders. "What I want to do and what we should do are two different things," she said. When she looked up and her gaze met his, he saw the blast of fury in the brown depths. "I wouldn't lose any sleep if he died," she admitted.

"Lucy." He went to her, covering her restless hands with his. Although he hoped, he couldn't be sure it would be that simple. "I absolutely understand the sentiment."

He cut the pizza and served up two slices for each of them. When they were seated at the table, a glass of wine and water for each of them, he gathered his thoughts as he dug into the meal.

"I've been thinking a lot about this bully that ran the detention center," he said at last. "Sam and I must have dreamed up a dozen violent ways to take him down."

Her mouth parted on a soft gasp. "You never told me that."

"There were plenty of things I should have told you," he said, his pulse hammering in his ears. And plenty of things he wanted to tell her now, starting and ending with "I love you." He reminded himself there would be time to tell her that, and more, for the rest of his life. He would make sure of it. "You've seen the pictures. Sam and I were skinny nerds. We didn't have the ability to take him down. It was just the two of us against him and the friends who watched his back."

Silently, she watched him over her wineglass.

He didn't like to dwell on those days when he'd been so utterly inadequate to meet the challenges. "Being incarcerated motivated me in several areas," he said.

She smiled, still waiting.

"My point is, we had to make a plan to work together," he continued. "Not just to avoid the physical assault but to carve our way through it. We'd agree how to proceed and then the idiot would divide us. He knew how to push our buttons."

"He was doing the divide and conquer routine?"

"It's effective," he admitted. "We let him get away with it too long and it's a lesson that stuck with me."

She prodded the pizza crust, breaking off a small piece and chewing slowly. "I'm angry and scared and I believe he plans to kill my family." She stopped, rubbing her hands on her jeans. "He has too much to lose. Are you afraid we aren't in agreement about Kathrein?"

"I just want us to go in united. His actions and history prove the ruthless, deadly nature of the man hiding behind the recluse facade."

"Believe me I understand he's dangerous. What are you suggesting?"

"If we arrange a meet and you give him the files you found—"

"You let me find," she interjected.

"Semantics." He grinned at her. "He gets the files and he wins. Most likely that ends with him killing all three of you to be sure those reports never surface. Unless you convince him you arranged for the documents to be released if something happens to any of you."

She shivered. "Option two?"

"Do you have any idea if he tried to breach Gray Box on his own?"

"I don't know who he hired, but he said the man failed. He manipulated me because he thought I could sweet-talk you or something." She shook her head. "He completely underestimated you."

How was it she couldn't see how tightly he was wound around her little finger? He'd do anything for her, including throw over his company. What was money except a tool to rebuild something better?

"Rush?"

He shook off the thought, drained his glass of water and set it back on the table. "Option two is to contact Kathrein and let him know you failed and can't break into the box."

She bit her lip. "How does that help?"

He appreciated her trust. "He would need to re-group or come after me."

"Stop it." She pressed her hands to her eyes. "In that case Gwen and Jackson die and I'd be next on the hit list."

He felt terrible for taking this approach. "Lucy, look at me." He waited until she did. "I am *not* going to let that happen."

She held his gaze. "I know you don't want to let that happen," she replied, softly. "I can see the in-vestment you've made here for me and my family, but we both know Kathrein has all the leverage," she finished, fighting back tears.

"He doesn't, not anymore. I'm pushing your but-tons now so we can be stronger, united when we face him," he insisted. "He wants you to feel inferior. He'll play on your fear to get his way. We have to be pre-pared or those fears will undermine our ability to outsmart him."

She took a deep breath, held it. "You're right." She fanned her face. "Keep going."

Her courage would forever dazzle him. "We have the element of surprise. He thinks we're still in the States, not around the corner. We're a team," he added, emphatically. "Kathrein can't risk bringing his family into this. On top of all of that, we have eyes on *him*."

She eyed the countertop behind him and the tablet

monitoring the drone. "How long is your drone able to stay out there?"

"It's programmed to fly a random pattern for several hours before returning."

"What if someone on his team spots it and follows it here?"

"The altitude and random route should keep them from noticing anything out of the ordinary," he assured her. "If you'll come with me, I'll show you some other features that might give you a little peace while we wait to make the rescue."

LUCY FORGOT THE dishes and followed Rush to the garage to see the other features he believed leveled the field. Thanks to him, her renewed confidence blotted out the fear that had crept up on her. Somehow she and Rush, along with his team, would prevent Kathrein's escape and she was eager to get on with the rescue.

At the workstation Rush cued up the live footage from the drone's camera. "Let's see if we can find a weak spot." He pulled up an extra stool for her.

"I didn't realize we could have been monitoring this in real time," she said, awed by the clarity of the live feed. Instead, they'd had stunning sex and a great meal while her sister and nephew remained prisoners. Guilt nipped her conscience and she pressed her hands between her knees to keep from chewing on her fingernails.

He leaned over and kissed her temple. "Real time would have simultaneously frustrated you and bored you to tears. The flight path spends significant time well away from the target."

It was little comfort but she realized he was absolutely correct as she watched him work. Various searches and commands appeared on one screen while images flashed by in a rapid slide show on the other. "Give me something to do," she said, restless. "Should I check in with Sam?"

"He'll call us." Rush squinted at something on the monitor. "Use my laptop and bring up the history on this place."

She opened up his personal laptop, momentarily stymied by the password field. "Shall I guess or will you tell me the password?"

"What? Oh." He glanced over and she swore he blushed. "You know it, unless you've forgotten."

She typed in the password she remembered from a year ago, stunned and inexplicably flattered he hadn't changed it. Clicking the folder on the main screen, she saw Sam had added a great deal to the property file over the past fifteen hours. "This winery has always been in the family. Kathrein didn't buy it, he inherited. Or rather, he stole his cousin's inheritance."

"Brace yourself, I might stand up and cheer."

Lucy was distracted by the video segments he was reviewing. "My goodness, that camera is amazing."

"Isn't it?" he agreed absently. "Remind me to give everyone in R & D a raise when we get back." He zoomed in, changing the color filter on the video.

She didn't have a reply for his assumption that she'd return with him to San Francisco. It wasn't as if she had a better option just now, but she didn't want to give either of them a reason to believe she'd used him.

"I'll be damned."

"What is it?"

"Tunnels." He aimed a finger over a recorded feed that was recycling.

She set the laptop aside and stepped up behind him. "Show me."

He slid his arm around her waist and her heart did a quick, happy pirouette in her chest at the easy intimacy. She rested her hand on his shoulder, unable to fight her affection for him even though she knew she was setting herself up for another long, lonely recovery when they parted ways.

He used the mouse to illustrate what he'd found. "This topographical application is a feature we're developing for a potential client. I think we've nailed it."

"Impressive." He'd all but admitted he was inventing for military applications. That was his way, always looking to help someone. "How do we use it?" Without a more familiar map or reference point, she couldn't make sense of the bright colors.

"In this location, the family must have been part of the French resistance." Rush muttered a curse. "Ironic a Nazi cousin stole their rightful heritage." He scowled at the monitors, leaning forward and bracing his elbows on the table. "What are the odds Kathrein doesn't know about the tunnels?" he murmured to himself. "This could be a huge advantage for Lawton's team."

She sat down and dug back into the property file on his laptop. "He assumed his cousin's identity," she reminded him. "Wouldn't he have access to everything?"

"Did he bother looking is a better question. He was a young soldier with a superiority complex, alone and on the run. Would he really care about anything other than establishing himself as his cousin?"

"Can we go check the tunnels first?" she asked.

His fingers flew over the keyboard, but she knew he'd heard her. "He doesn't have guards anywhere near the tunnels."

"They might have collapsed or been sealed," she said.

"Collapsed would show on the image. Sealed up at the house is possible."

Her adrenaline spiked at the opportunity to *do* something. "He took his family there for vacations. Any normal child would have found every nook and cranny."

"His children aren't there." Rush stood up, pacing back and forth. "He planned this kidnapping quickly, but he's a stickler for detail. If the tunnels were a concern, he'd have men standing guard."

She laughed, a bitter sound that broke Rush's thoughtful concentration. "Sorry." She clapped a hand over her mouth. "I can't help it. The idea that Kathrein has had possession of a Resistance house all this time and been too self-absorbed to learn the real secrets is bizarre."

Rush gave her a long study. "What are you willing to risk to find out?" He caught both her hands in his. "The way the winery and cellar are situated, I worked up two ideal attack options for Lawton's consideration. We could take a walk and see about giving them a third choice."

A walk through the French countryside at twilight sounded daring. And possibly romantic under different circumstances. "If we're spotted we blow our element of surprise."

"We're two random lovers out for a stroll." He ran his palms up to her shoulders and back down. "No guards around this end of the tunnel." He grinned at her. "And Kathrein has no idea we aren't in San Francisco."

Lovers. The word derailed her thoughts for a moment. If only that could be true again. If only so much more could be true in the future. Unlikely as that outcome was, her mind reached for more practical concerns. "If the tunnels are open, maybe we can get them out tonight."

Hope swelled through her.

"Let's start with a walk and go from there."

She nodded stepping away from him, missing his touch immediately. "Let me change clothes."

"Choose something dark. I'll shower and do the same," he added, falling in behind her.

In less than half an hour they were back in the garage, debating whether or not to go for a drive through the area first when the replacement cell phone rang. The caller ID showed Kathrein's personal number.

"Pick it up," Rush urged. "It will show you're in California. Put it on speaker."

"Got it," she whispered and accepted the call. "Hello?" Her voice fractured as she answered.

"Lucy?"

Lucy's knees turned to jelly at the sound of her sister's voice. "Gwen!" She reached for Rush's hand. "Are you okay?"

"He took Jackson." The rest of her words were lost in a series of sobs.

"What? How'd you get the phone?"

Gwen sniffled. "He gave it to me." Her voice gained some strength. "Told me to call you."

"Tell her!"

Lucy and Rush exchanged a look at the sound of Kathrein barking the order in the background.

"Whatever he wants, Lucy," Gwen gasped. "Do the right thing. Do *not* give it to him. I love you. Jack's waiting for both of us," she finished, shouting the last words amid an audible scuffle.

Lucy jerked at a feminine cry of pain.

Kathrein's rasping voice came on the line. "Do you hear?" Another agonized wail soared through the garage. "Stop flirting about with your lover and bring me what I need. Time is running out for your family, Ms. Gaines."

The call ended and Lucy stared at the device in horror, as if it were a bomb ready to level the villa. Her hands trembled and the shivers moved up her arms until her entire body shook uncontrollably. "He's hurting her," she said in a ragged whisper. "Who knows what he did to the baby."

Rush wrapped his arms around her, bringing her head to his chest and smoothing her hair, stroking a hand up and down her spine, over and over. "We'll get them back, Lucy."

"She's been through so much," Lucy said into the

soft cotton of his black sweater. "The baby's arrival…
They were so happy. Then Jack died and…and…" She
just couldn't finish it. Gwen had been broken and lost
and there had been a few weeks when Lucy wasn't
sure the baby would be enough of an anchor for her
sister's heart. She poured it all out for Rush as he held
her. Leaning on his strength now as she'd wanted to
do so often then. "Gwen is smart. She might not know
why Kathrein started this, but she clearly knows how
it is meant to end."

"There's a way to stop him," Rush insisted. "No
one is invincible."

"Just like no system is impenetrable?"

He tipped up her chin and she had to look into his
eyes. "You got into my system." He feathered a kiss
over her forehead.

"Only because I remembered the things you talked
about with such passion." She made herself step back,
testing her resolve. "I don't want to cave to his demands or damage your Gray Box reputation, but I
can't allow my family to die for the preservation of
his."

"Let's take that walk," Rush suggested. "The fresh
air will clear your head."

She supposed it wasn't too strange that he'd remember that detail about her. His mind was a steel
trap of facts and trivia. Bundling into the dark coat
and gloves Rush provided, she felt like a spy in cash-
mere, though the warm garments didn't erase the vicious chill of the circumstances.

Rush sent details of the call to Sam and Lawton.
He took her hand and they set off toward the hills in

the west, leaving the villa behind them as they followed the road toward the winery.

"What if someone in town saw the drone?"

"Altitude," he replied. His shoulder brushed hers as he shrugged. "Even if it was spotted, we won't be here long enough to get found."

"Not what I'm worried about."

"He can't have spies everywhere, Lucy."

"Okay." She knew paranoia had seized her, but her sister's plea to let them die kept ricocheting through Lucy's head. "He'll kill them whether I cooperate or not."

"We've known that for some time."

She'd known it on some level since this nightmare began. "I didn't know it soon enough to say no to his job offer."

His hand squeezed hers as they walked along. "Why is it you could tell me no easily enough when I wanted to hire you with your sparkling new MBA degree?"

She slid a glance his way, but it was impossible to read his expression in the deepening shadows. "You didn't need me. Me working for you would have only propelled us faster to the inevitable breakup."

"You were that sure we wouldn't make it?"

The sorrow in his voice startled her. "I wanted us to make it." She still regretted that she'd handled it so poorly. "You were a great boyfriend." She squeezed his hand. "When I showed up in Chicago, Gwen called me an idiot for walking out. Well, she used the term 'running away.'"

"Did you ever consider my average daily bank balance as a reason to stay?"

"No." The words stung. One minute he seemed to know her so well and then he'd lump her in with the other women he'd known. "You actually thought I was that shallow?"

"No. But you're the only one I've found who isn't."

"For the record, I recently decided my ideal man has a net worth of only half a million."

"Shh." He tugged her away from the road, down the slope of grass and up another small hill. He stretched out on his stomach and crept up the rise. "That's the Kathrein winery."

She mirrored him, flattening to her belly on the cold ground. "Where is the closest tunnel access?"

He pointed out to the right. "Near the creek. Let's watch for a few minutes and see how far out he sends the patrol."

His deep voice rumbled through the dark, stirring her. He rubbed her arm, then her back, creating all sorts of inappropriate fires within her. She let Rush worry about time, and she used the necessary silence to watch and pray for her family. Other than the guard who strolled back and forth behind the two buildings, the area seemed totally deserted.

"He must have at least one additional man for every guard we see," he whispered. "There's one in front and one floater according to the drone images."

She had to accept his tally as she only saw the one man. "Can Lawton's team handle six men?"

"And more." Rush agreed. "In the pictures, it

seems as if it's the same guard all the time beside Kathrein."

"That must be David. I don't recall a time, day or night, when he wasn't close by."

"You did a lot of night work for a ninety-six-year-old man?"

"No." She elbowed him. "There were a few overseas calls those first two weeks. He was adjusting some investments." The guard seemed to turn their way. "Can we go now?" she murmured.

"To the winery tunnels or back to the villa?"

Gwen's screams were fresh in her mind. "The tunnels." She'd do anything to sneak Jackson and Gwen out of Kathrein's clutches tonight.

"Good answer." Rush rooted through his pocket and pulled out a new gadget she didn't recognize. "Let me do one more test, then we'll go."

Rush aimed a gadget at the guard and waited. After another adjustment, he tried again and this time, the guard tapped at his ear, then called for a test of his communications device. "It works," Rush said. "Great range, too."

"Won't that tip them off?"

Rush's teeth gleamed white in the dark when he smiled. "No way. Technology glitches are a fact of life."

Praying hard, Lucy scooted back down the slope after him and they jogged toward the creek to follow it to the tunnel door.

Please, God, keep them safe.

Chapter Twelve

Rush appreciated Lucy's willingness to check out the tunnels. This could very well be the best way in and out for Lawton's rescue team. Knowing it was smarter to sit back and wait, he told himself the information would empower the team. The problem was after that call from Gwen, Rush knew Lucy's family didn't have much time left.

He checked the map with an app on his phone, confirming his location when they reached the right point on the bank of the creek. He pressed through a stand of scrubby trees and found a low opening. No door, but he checked the area for any alarms or wiring for explosives. Finding none, he continued deeper into what felt like a narrow, natural cave. He turned on a flashlight and, taking Lucy's hand, led them deeper, hoping for the best.

When they encountered the first signs of supports, old timbers in an arch, he breathed a sigh of relief. "This could be a wild goose chase," he warned. "We can turn back and report it to the team."

Lucy's stared at him with ironclad determination. "We go on."

He knew she was hoping to get Gwen and Jackson out safely tonight. Unfortunately, the odds of that were low. Sneaking in was just the first problem. They had to avoid armed guards and find mother and son, supposedly in separate locations. Although Sam was tracking Rush and Lucy, they didn't carry weapons. Rush forced himself to slow down and take it one step at a time.

Information for Lawton. Rescue if possible. When they were safely away, they could find an official willing to charge Kathrein for his crimes. He had to know someone who knew someone in the State Department who would haul Kathrein in for kidnapping two Americans.

"If we're spotted, promise me you'll run like hell for the villa and call Sam. He will know what to do."

"Sure," she agreed, a little too quickly to be convincing.

He supposed that made them even, though he would have preferred otherwise. Nothing they encountered would force him to leave her behind, either. "No sign anyone's been here in years," Rush pointed out.

"That's good, right?"

"Yes." Every few yards, he paused to check for surveillance gear, relieved they weren't finding any.

"We have to be close," she whispered when he stopped once more.

"Wait here while I look ahead."

"No." She gripped his hand hard. "Forward or back, we stick together."

He nodded, signaling for silence as they inched

along the dusty tunnel. Focusing on each footfall, pausing to listen, didn't keep him from replaying her earlier words. What had she meant by "inevitable breakup"?

How had they been completely at odds over where they were headed as a couple? Through hindsight, he could see why she believed he'd resist any emotional declaration. Back then they could talk candidly about anything except her feelings. He hated that he'd let her down and yet his hope for winning her back gave him something to look forward to when they were out of this mess.

The tunnel widened abruptly and the path was partially blocked by barrels and the thick fragrance of rich wine and dry earth. Seeing the winery logo branded on the barrels, he turned off the flashlight. In the absolute darkness, he listened for any sound, hearing only his pounding heart and Lucy's soft breath beside him.

He wanted to send her back and knew she'd never go. Just as he started to suggest they both turn back and wait for the experts, a baby's cry sliced through the silence.

Lucy jerked forward instinctively and he caught her around the waist. Although he admired her courage in all things, he couldn't let her blow their cover or barge through the door first.

"Careful," he whispered at her ear. He felt her nod once, her cheek brushing his, even as her hands pushed at his hold. "Let me lead."

She dug in her heels, tugging on his arm until he stopped. Pulling his face close to hers she kissed him with an intensity that reached straight into his chest and shook out the cobwebs in his heart. "If you get hurt I will kill you," she murmured against his lips.

He wound his arms around her waist, hugging her so his heart wouldn't drop to the dirt floor and get trampled. "You know how I feel about equality in a deal."

He felt her lips curve into a smile until the baby cried again. They moved stealthily around the barrels and down the cleared space to a door. The old latch creaked as he raised it and the hinges popped and groaned. So much for surprise, he thought, grateful there hadn't been any visible alarm.

They were at the end of a long narrow cellar, under the secondary building. Racks, long empty, stretched along one side, some big enough for barrels, others for bottles. The only light drifted from a bulb at the far end of the cellar, farthest from the tunnel access and closest to the sounds of the distressed infant.

"Where is Gwen?" she asked, mouthing the words.

It would be more efficient to split up and search, but he didn't want to risk it. If they caught her, he knew he'd give up anything for her safety.

Considering Kathrein's impatience to resolve the situation, Rush had to believe he'd set aside one room for his hostages. Easier to control and manage with a mere skeleton crew of his most loyal guards that way.

Keeping Lucy behind him, he moved toward that one lonely bulb. As they approached, he could see three doors set into the walls, two on one side and a third opposite the first. An archway gave way to stairs leading to the upper level. Fully aware that a patrolling guard could come by at any moment, he peered through the small window in the nearest door. The room was dark and he raised his flashlight. But it was empty except for tumbled racks that must have held a prestigious reserve when the winery had been in business.

He moved to the next door with Lucy's hand locked around his. He repeated the process. This time his flashlight found Jackson, wriggling and fussing in a crib that looked as old as Kathrein, only far less sturdy with the spindles and cutouts.

Suddenly Lucy gasped and yanked at Rush's arm, pulling him back just as a heavy fist swung past his face.

The blow glanced off his shoulder with enough power to turn him sideways. Rush let the spin carry him into the fight, drawing the guard back and away from Jackson's cell. With any luck, Lucy would be able to get the baby out of there.

He traded punches with the bigger man, losing his breath when a ham-sized fist connected with his ribs. Another thing he'd learned in juvie was how to fight dirty. He pulled a Taser from his back pocket and when the guy came barreling at him, he zapped him, sending him to the floor in a jerking, quivery heap.

"Lucy?" He sucked in air as quietly as possible, using the wall for support as he made his way back to Jackson's cell.

"He fooled us." Temper whipped through her voice as she held out a doll.

"What the—" He never finished the question, silenced by a hard strike against the back of his head.

LUCY WATCHED, HORRIFIED as they dragged Rush up the stairs ahead of her. The man holding the gun to her back wasn't necessary, she had no intention of leaving without Rush or her family.

Obviously, Kathrein had known about the tunnels and left them unguarded outside, the ace up his sleeve. She wanted to claw his eyes out for winning this battle, but the war wasn't over yet. Rush was strong and healthy enough to recover from that fight and she was ready to negotiate with the monster if that's what it took to get them all out of this.

On the upper level, the guards pushed open the wide doors of a cavernous room and chained Rush to a thick, support pillar. The guards searched them both for devices and weapons, confiscating everything and powering down the tech gear. Without Sam keeping tabs on them, they'd be alone now. Her impatience had backfired.

She was secured with zip ties to the steel pipes on the end of the old wine bottling line.

"Where is my family?" She made her demand in French, then English. Neither query resulted in a flicker of recognition from the closest guard. "Jean-Pierre!" she snapped, letting him know she recognized *him*. "Tell me where they are."

The guard turned his hard gaze on her. "He keeps them close, treats them as if they are family."

If that was meant to be a comfort, it failed.

"Are they okay?"

With a nearly imperceptible shrug, he moved away, taking up a post near the stairs, his back to the cellar below.

"Rush?"

He groaned an affirmative response and lifted his head as he came around.

She didn't have time to offer him any encouragement or even pretend to come up with an escape plan as another of Kathrein's men walked straight up to Rush and started pummeling his midsection, using him like the heavy bag in a gym.

In shock, Lucy begged him to stop. "Wait, please." She swiveled around. "Jean-Pierre!" she shouted. "Tell Kathrein I have what he wants on a thumb drive."

"No such item was on your person," Jean-Pierre replied.

"I have it, I swear. I came to hand it over."

The guard beating Rush landed another rapid series of jabs and he groaned. She prayed his injuries wouldn't be life threatening.

"You do not have what he wants or you would have come to the door like a civilized person," Jean-Pierre said from his post.

"Don't you dare act as if any of this is civilized," she roared. "I will hand it all over if my family and Rush are released without further harm."

The brute plowed fists into Rush's belly.

"Please, please," she wailed. "You'll get nothing if you kill him."

"I'll get whatever I like, young lady," Kathrein's voice carried through the space, drawing her full attention. "I don't appreciate being roused in the middle of the night," he added, leaning on his guard, David, as he managed the last steps. He flicked out a hand and the big-fisted lout pounded Rush again.

She could practically hear Kathrein's joints grinding as he approached her. He stooped close, his beady eyes cold and mean. "If you have the information, give it to me."

"Allow my family and Rush to leave without further harm and it's yours."

"Don't," Rush said, getting a heavy backhand across his jaw for the effort.

"It was always mine," Kathrein sneered at her. "My secrets should have remained buried. When I verify you are speaking the truth, I will release your sister and nephew." He clapped his arthritic hands and David handed him a tablet. "Release her hands so she can prove she is an honest girl."

Jean-Pierre released her right hand, leaving her left secured to the pipes.

Lucy typed in the access code as Sam had taught her and showed Kathrein the reporter's empty Gray Box. "I downloaded the files to a thumb drive before I deleted them from the cloud, as you instructed."

"Where is this thumb drive?"

"Lucy, don't do it," Rush said. "You know he'll renege."

"Let them go first," she said.

"A compromise." Kathrein signaled David and a large door across the room rolled open. Lucy sagged with relief to see Gwen and Jackson alive. "You honor them with this," Kathrein said almost wistfully. "Family is important."

"We were never a threat to *your* family."

"No, but your man is." Kathrein's black eyes turned mean. On his order, the door closed on Gwen and Jackson.

"No! We had a deal."

"You changed that deal, bringing him here."

"Are you kidding?" Inside, Lucy cringed as she delivered the lie. "I seduced him to get what you wanted. Do the right thing and let them go."

"You've left me only one option for how to proceed."

Despite the shoulders hunched from age and the wispy white hair, Kathrein's mind remained sharp and devious. She knew he had zero incentive to honor his agreement with her. In her impatience, she'd walked Rush into a trap. Panic set her blood pounding through her veins as she sought the words that would save her family and the man she loved. "Release them now or you'll have no options."

"You're hardly in a position to make demands," he snarled.

She smothered a scream, glaring at him and searching for a way to turn the tables. She'd shown enough fear and cowering respect. Rush had prepared her for this. She needed another tactic. "Let us all go or my failsafe will kick in."

Kathrein leveled his full attention on her once more. "Failsafe? You would never be so foolish."

Lucy figured she could milk this approach long enough to buy time for Rush's security team to show up. Sam would have leaped into high gear as soon as their tech had been powered off. "Quit while you're ahead, Kathrein. Your past isn't the only problem now. You've kidnapped four American citizens. You'll have your choice of charges to fight when the press hears about this. What will happen to your grandson's political aspirations then?"

He leaned close to her, his garlic-laced breath moist against her skin. "Word will not get out. None of you will get out. Your failsafe is useless against me."

"We backed up the reporter's research with a Gray Box ghost," Rush mumbled. "I will make sure your secrets go public."

"He's lying," Lucy cried, praying he'd shut up before they hurt him again. "Let them go and I will stop the failsafe."

Kathrein swatted her across the cheek with his cane. The painful thwack of hard wood against her cheekbone startled her into silence.

"Prepare her," Kathrein said. "We will see who is lying."

"Mr. Kathrein, this is your last chance." The cane whipped across her knees this time, bringing tears to her eyes. "Let them go."

Jean-Pierre cut away the zip tie and hauled her to a chair bolted into the floor closer to Rush. Obviously this wasn't the first time they'd used the old winery for an ugly, violent purpose.

Her pleas for logic and common sense went unanswered, ignored by the man she'd misjudged so terribly. As her wrists and legs were secured to the chair, Kathrein spoke in low tones to Rush, who paled under the swelling, cuts and blood marring his handsome face.

"There's no such thing as a ghost box," she said, desperate to find another way.

"What do you need, Kathrein?" Rush asked. His words were slurred by pain and his swollen lip. "What will convince you to let them go?"

"Nothing." He stared up at Rush. "I did not survive this long, build up a family from ashes to have it ruined by rumor."

"What rumor? As a Nazi you committed horrible atrocities," she said.

"War is ugly," he replied, his attention locked onto Rush. "What are they worth to you?"

"Name your price and I'll meet it," Rush said.

"Bah!" Kathrein turned away. "I have enough money for the next three generations to live in luxury."

"Care to share your investment strategy?" Rush quipped.

"What I must have is a sterling reputation." Kathrein poked his cane hard into Rush's gut. "How do I stop your pitiful tricks?" he asked Lucy.

"You let us go," she answered. Where was the rescue team? "It's all automated. If I don't give the code at the right interval, your secrets go to the press."

"Nonsense." Kathrein's mouth thinned. Despite the toll of age, it wasn't difficult to picture him terrorizing prisoners. The man showed no remorse over his past and right now she was sure he intended to relive it with gusto. He popped her with the cane again. "There must be a master switch or all sorts of garbage would litter the news."

"Master code is a myth," Lucy groaned, her gaze

on Rush. Behind Kathrein's back he mouthed one word, "Me," and she struggled with the implication. She would not aim the madman at Rush. Where was Lawton with the rescue team?

"Let her go." Rush thrashed against his restraints. "When she and her family are safe, I will give you the code."

"Ah!" Kathrein's mean eyes danced between them. "Now we have progress." The elderly man looked giddy with a burst of anticipation. Behind the cell door, she heard a whimper out of Jackson.

Lucy prayed they hadn't just made a tactical error that would get them all killed.

RUSH SAW THE electric cattle prod in David's hand and knew immediately what they intended. They would shock him and make her watch. Classic divide and conquer approach, hoping to make her talk by hurting him. He'd been trying to get Lucy to aim Kathrein at him, but she wouldn't cooperate.

Didn't the old geezer understand Rush, not Lucy, had control of the system he sought to infiltrate? Either the bastard didn't comprehend how the cloud worked or he didn't care.

"Close your eyes, Lucy." Rush hated what she was about to see and he hoped like hell the team would get here before Kathrein's torture fried his brain beyond usefulness. At least if Rush died Sam would be able to carry on, and since he'd updated his will last night with a call to his attorney, Sam and Lucy as partners would keep Gray Box going strong. He took a breath, willing his body to relax as that cattle prod got closer.

But the beady-eyed bastard surprised him, signaling his man toward Lucy. "No!" Rush strained against the bindings. "No! She doesn't know anything."

"She knows more than you think. She is too quick for her own good. Isn't that right, Ms. Gaines?"

"Let us go now and we won't press charges," she said, unaware of the device behind her.

Kathrein cackled. "You do not dictate terms to me!"

Rush fought the chains, instinctively trying to spare her. "Stop. She can't help you."

Kathrein ignored him. "Garmeaux," he shouted. "Who did you talk to about him?"

"No one," she said.

"You're lying. My daughter took a call late yesterday about him."

The guard sent a jolt of electricity through Lucy's body. Her head fell back and her limbs jerked in a macabre dance.

Rush roared, helpless to protect her. Damn it, this was his fault. He'd set Sam loose with the Kathrein family tree and told him to skip the subtlety.

"Stop!" he shouted again.

Kathrein turned, his black eyes gleaming with obvious delight over Lucy's pain. "She betrayed me."

"You've got no reason to cry foul." Rush mustered as much disdain as possible now that he had the old man's attention. "You used her."

"And I will continue."

Rush discarded the idea of playing to the man as a father. Any capacity for sympathy was erased by the sick joy he gained from hurting others. "I can help you. I am the only person in this room who can make your troubles disappear."

Kathrein ignored him. "Lucy, give me the master code."

"I forgot it."

She got zapped again and Rush swore. "Tell him!"

"I used his old password. Erased it afterward."

"Give it to me," Kathrein demanded.

"No."

They pumped more juice into her and Rush forced himself to keep his eyes open, a source of encouragement and strength if she would only look at him.

"Tell him, Lucy," Rush pleaded. Why was Lucy resisting? She had to know Sam would be on the other side of the connection, scrambling to protect the information.

But Kathrein didn't ask again. This time he asked her how the ghost box worked. When she didn't know, the cattle prod zapped her again.

Where the hell was Lawton? Lucy couldn't take much more of this and Rush would never be able to live if Kathrein killed her.

When the room quieted, Rush blurted out the master code.

"No," Lucy protested. "Don't give in."

Kathrein turned and stared at him. "Again!"

Rush repeated it, symbol by symbol while another man typed it into the waiting laptop.

"Well?" Kathrein asked his man. "Does it work?"

Rush caught the wary expressions on the faces of the guards Kathrein employed. Rush knew then that if his team didn't arrive, they would all be dead.

Kathrein wasn't after access or secrets anymore. He'd gone off the rails, sliding into a gruesome past he'd enjoyed too much.

"Take what you want," Rush said. "Have a damn field day." Every minute Kathrein was distracted with him or the computer was a minute Lucy could use to recover and another minute for the rescue team to leap into action.

"I feel as if you need some compensation for this generosity," Kathrein said.

"All I want is for you to let them go."

"No." Kathrein cackled, the sound rising into the rafters. "I am not done with any of you."

Lucy wanted to believe she was trapped in a terrible nightmare. Her blood felt as if it had been replaced with fizzy candy. Breathing made her lungs prickle and every nerve ending sizzled independently of the others. She'd give just about anything for that to never happen again.

In a blissful lull, her ears stopped ringing and she heard Rush spell out a code. Kathrein's giddy reply a moment later told her he'd unlocked something special.

Except Rush couldn't have done the unthinkable. There was no scenario where Rush relinquished control of his proprietary system to a madman. But... had he? Why? Had he really opened up all of Gray Box for Kathrein?

Based on the gleeful expression on Kathrein's face, he'd hit the motherlode of information.

Tears slid down her cheeks. Rush was ruined. No amount of money or careful media spin would set this right. "Rush," she whispered, trying to decide which of the three visions of him wavering in front of her eyes was the real one. "No, please, not this." He'd worked every day since his release from juvie to reach financial and creative independence. It had been his sole mission, to make a name for himself and use his skills in a way that helped people and gained respect from the world.

Now, the one time he put something ahead of his business, it would cost him everything. It was too much. "I'm sorry," she said, squeezing the words through her dry throat. Her gaze sought his, held it. "Why?"

His lips moved and she knew she must be hallucinating. The Rush she loved didn't use the L word. Another jolt from the cattle prod seared through her and wiped the thought from her mind as she slid into a blissful blank space.

Rush watched Lucy pass out and howled, fighting the cuffs that kept his arms over his head. "I will kill you!" he shouted at Kathrein.

The guard brought that damned cattle prod closer, aiming it at him. Finally. Rush tossed out all sorts of threats and dire promises, desperate to divert the focus from Lucy. Shouting and flailing, he didn't hear the first explosion. When the floor trembled and dust rained from the ceiling, hope coursed through him. Lawton and the rescue team were here, at last.

Kathrein's men sprang into action, protecting their boss, but they were no match for the tactical expertise of the rescue squad. Only six men, they seemed to be everywhere, surging up the steps and closing in from all sides.

The battle was brief, typical of a Lawton strike. When the sound of bullets ceased, Kathrein and the surviving guards were secured. Released from his restraints, Rush went straight to Lucy, who remained unconscious. Although his arms felt as if he'd been stretched on a rack and his shoulders screamed, he lifted her against his chest. He carried her outside, where floodlights cast a pale glow over the scene.

"Come on, Lucy." He pleaded with her, momentarily relieved when her lashes fluttered as she came to. Without a word, she slipped away again.

Lawton called for a medic while Rush tried to rouse her again.

"Sister and baby are already out," Lawton stated. "We didn't want them anywhere near a firefight. That was the delay. Are you all right?"

Rush nodded, his only concern was Lucy.

"Any chance of broken bones?"

"Maybe cracked ribs." Nothing to do for that but rest. Rush jerked his chin toward the battery and cables. "I don't think anything's broken for her. She took too many hits from the cattle prod and he nailed her a few times with that damned cane."

Several minutes later, the medic declared her bones intact and waved smelling salts under her nose, getting increasingly alert reactions. She came around, mumbling Rush's name.

"I'm here, sweetheart." He gripped her hand, brought it to his lips.

"You're okay." Her mouth curved into a weak smile. "Thank God."

"My sentiments exactly." He forced his way between her and the medic. "How do you feel?"

"Like I danced in a lightning storm. Where are Gwen and Jackson?" she asked, trying to sit up.

"They're already en route to the airfield," he explained. "You'll see them soon."

"Good." She sagged back against him. "I'm sorry you had to give up everything to get us out of there."

"The company, the money, the reputation," he promised, "none of it matters if I lost you."

The surprise in her eyes at those words shamed him. He never should've left room for her to doubt how much she meant to him. When she was feeling better he'd tell her the whole story about creating not just a failsafe or ghost box, but a ghost company to trap Kathrein. Right now, she needed time to recover.

"What about Kathrein?"

"Sam's been working on that. He has a friend in the State Department I didn't even know about."

Lucy sat up a bit more. "Thank you for saving my family." She wrapped her arms around him, burying her face in his shirt. "For saving us."

He felt the tears through the fabric and held her close, letting her get it all out.

Leaving Lawton at the winery to coordinate the cleanup with Sam's friend, Rush went straight to the airfield so Lucy could be reunited with her sister and nephew. Once they were all on the plane, he gave the order to get the hell out of France. He couldn't wait one more hour to take her home and keep her safe with him behind American borders and his wall of lawyers.

Chapter Thirteen

Christmas morning dawned clear and bright, and Rush had the best gift curled beside him in the king-size bed, her hand resting over his heart. Most of their bruises were healed and he traced her fingers, wondering if she had any idea how precious she was. To her family, to him, to the world at large.

Her courage and bravery astounded him whether they were in the French countryside or in a development meeting. "I love you, Lucy Gaines," he murmured into her hair.

She didn't so much as twitch. Probably better that he had another practice run at that powerful statement. He'd be more convincing if he was used to hearing himself say the words.

He woke her with gentle kisses, having his way with her in the shower before they went downstairs to exchange presents and mimosas with her sister and nephew. It wasn't the most extravagant Christmas on record, that could wait, but it was definitely the sweetest and most significant of his life. It sure beat skiing at a mountain resort with only Sam and a few women they wouldn't remember by St. Patrick's Day.

The three adults traded off between dinner prep and caring for Jackson until at last they sat down to a feast of ham and all the trimmings. Happy as he was to be here with Lucy and her family, Rush wasn't entirely content. He served himself another piece of cherry pie, to the ribbing of both women, and tried to firm up what he needed to say to Lucy and how he was going to say it.

Gwen cleaned up Jackson's hands and face, and carried him to the rocking chair, shooting a look at Rush behind her sister's back.

It is time, that look said.

He knew it. Past time, really. The small velvet box would burn a hole in his pocket at this rate. He'd thought of taking her to dinner or out on the boat with a sunset glowing on the bay. He was sure she needed more space to forget their ordeal. He should—

His thoughts evaporated as she slipped her arm around his waist. "Thank you for a lovely and very merry Christmas, Rush," she said. "This is exactly what we needed."

"Exactly?"

"You've been so gracious to welcome us to the boathouse. This quiet and peace has helped Gwen immensely."

"What about you?"

"I'm happy to be here with you." She smiled up at him, her brown eyes reflecting all the words he couldn't seem to get out of either of them. She'd loved him once and never said it. In the past few days he wondered if her feelings were still as strong and he had a fresh appreciation for how hard it was to keep love trapped inside a heart—even a damaged one— the words unspoken.

"The boathouse has always felt like home when you're here." He led her out to the balcony and let the breeze tease her hair as she leaned into the rail. Impatient, Rush pulled her around to face him, gliding his hands up and down her arms, his eyes locked with hers. "I love you, Lucy Gaines."

There. It was out. What would she do with the news?

"I know. It shows in your every action, big or small." She pressed up on her toes and kissed him and then looped her arms around his waist. "Even when you didn't want to see it, when I didn't trust how you defined it, love was there."

Enchanting as he found her analysis and kisses, he thought he might lose it if she didn't say the words. If he'd missed his chance with her...

"I love you, too, Rush Grayson. I always have."

His heart kicked back into a normal rhythm, flooding him with energy and hope. "We should give your sister the condo on Fremont Street," he blurted out.

She stepped away, frowning a little before she turned to stare out at the choppy water of the bay. "You moved out of here when I left, didn't you?"

"Yes. It hurt to be here alone."

Her shoulders rose and fell. "But it won't hurt you to be here alone now?"

Was he moving too fast for her to trust the words? He couldn't dwell on possible failure and he shook off the doubts. He had to follow through. "Lucy." He dropped to one knee behind her. "I don't intend to be here or anywhere else without you."

She turned and the frown on her face lifted. Her big brown eyes swept over him and then locked on the glittering diamond ring framed in the black velvet box he held open. "Lucy Gaines, will you allow me the honor of being your husband?"

"Rush." She covered her mouth with both hands, her eyes sparkling with happy tears. "When? How?" She fanned her face and then her gaze slammed back to him. "We've been glued at the hip since…since we've been back. When did you have time to buy a ring?"

"Last year," he admitted, wishing like hell she'd give him an answer to the biggest proposal of his life. "It's been waiting for you—*I've* been waiting for you every day since."

Her hands dropped to her sides. "You're serious."

"Lucy," he said, battling the rising exasperation. "Can you give me an answer?"

She grinned, crossing her arms. "What if I want to negotiate the terms?"

No woman was as perfect for him as this one. "Come down here and give it a try."

She sank to her knees and he immediately worried about the lingering aches from their trouble in France. "Yes, Rush, I'll marry you." She cupped his jaw with her hands. "I only have one condition."

He pulled the ring out of the box and slipped it over the tip of her finger. "Granted."

She stopped his progress. "You haven't heard it yet," she said on a bubble of laughter.

"Don't need to. You've given me everything, Lucy. Acceptance, support, affection and your heart full of belief and understanding. There's nothing you can ask of me that I wouldn't gladly give you."

"You haven't heard it." She pursed her lips. "Maybe I should have my people call your people."

"You are the only people who matters to me, sweetheart. Don't you see that yet?"

"I do, Rush." She let him push the ring all the way into place. "I only wanted to stipulate a weekly date night, no electronics allowed."

"Done." He stood up and pulled her close, kissing her with everything he'd kept bottled up for too long. His heart soared as she matched his affection and passion. "Can we start tonight?"

"Of course." She tipped back her head and laughed as he spun her in a circle. "I'm all yours, for always."

Just inside the door Gwen and Jackson cheered. Following Lucy inside, as his fiancée and his future sister-in-law admired the engagement ring, Rush thought the gift of a loving and exuberant family was the best holiday miracle a man could ask for.

This was the most wonderful Christmas of his life.

* * * * *

MILLS & BOON®

INTRIGUE
Romantic Suspense

A SEDUCTIVE COMBINATION OF DANGER AND DESIRE